The
Clever
Mill Horse

JODI LEW-SMITH

CASPIAN PRESS
HARDWICK, VERMONT

www.caspianpressvt.com

First printing April 2014

Publishers Cataloguing-in-Publication Data

Lew-Smith, Jodi.
  The clever mill horse / Jodi Lew-Smith.
    pages cm
  LCCN 2014931296
  ISBN 978-0-9913412-0-7
  ISBN 978-0-9913412-1-4 (ebook)
  1. Women inventors—United States—Fiction. 2. Textile industry—United States--History--Fiction. 3. United States—History—1809-1817—Fiction. 4. United States—History—War of 1812—Fiction. 5. Historical fiction. I. Title.
  PS3612.E952C54 2014 813'.6

QBI14-600010

Interior design and composition by John Reinhardt

Published in the United States of America
by Caspian Press, Vermont.

For my beloved husband Michael, without whom

I'd be much less than half of the whole.

And for Dame Dorothy Dunnett, a dangerous mentor

whose gifts dispense with the humility required of the rest of us.

HISTORICAL NOTE ABOUT FLAX

FLAX IS ONE of the oldest fiber crops on earth and was widely cultivated in ancient China and Egypt. It thrives in all the cooler regions of the world, including Canada and the northern United States, and was the primary plant-based fiber for cloth until the early nineteenth century, when cotton, which grows in warmer regions, abruptly replaced it.

Taken from inside the stem of the plant, flax fibers are two to three times stronger than cotton fibers. Which means that linen fabric is much sturdier and longer-lasting than cotton. So why did cotton overtake and nearly extinguish linen?

With the invention of the cotton gin, patented in 1794, it became easy and fast to remove the seeds from the cotton boll to make usable fiber. In contrast, flax fiber requires four separate time-consuming steps to first soften the outer stem of the plant and then strip the shards of hard stem from the silky inner core to produce the useable fiber—a process known as "dressing flax."

In the early nineteenth century there were several inventions for dressing flax that received U.S. patents. Unfortunately none of them ever worked anywhere near as well as the cotton gin, which many people credit with the rise of cotton production that led to a concomitant rise in slavery and, eventually, the U.S. Civil War.

To this day dressing flax fiber remains a long and labor-intensive process, such that linen fabric remains expensive and comparatively rare. In this story, though, the contest between southern cotton and northern linen was still anyone's game.

PRELUDE

April 1804

AN INVENTION can become a member of the family. Someone you must attend to even when you're tired to death of it. A pint of your blood.

Fifteen-year-old Ella Kenyon strode the muddy path to the door of her grandfather's blacksmith shop and paused. She wasn't ready to go inside. The twilight air of April was too sweet, too layered with melting snow and fresh black soil. A soft misting rain had begun, raising fog and frosting everything with a veil of tiny drops. Turning from the door she slipped around the building, ducking beneath the small window opening so her grandfather wouldn't see her, and scrambled over scrub and stone to the river flowing behind the shops and mills of Deborahville. Her grandfather's shop was the last on Main Street and his stable, a hundred feet farther downstream, across the stable yard from his shop, was the last building within the village.

She peered across the Bache River to the plowed fields on the other side, where the placid acres of melting snow had become a ghostland of fog, swirling with wraiths of mist. The air out here was alive and fragrant, full of taunting possibility. The river, powered by spring rains, rang with heroic noise and splash beneath puffs of fog. The shop behind her would be stuffy and stale and she desperately didn't want to go in.

A few years ago she wouldn't have been standing here, delaying. Back then she had savored having a role in the business her grandfather's invention would spawn. He persuaded anyone who would listen that his invention for stripping raw flax into fiber to weave linen would bear wondrous gifts to the town and, indeed, the whole new country. It would change the face of the northern states from golden wheat to blue-flowered flax. Who wouldn't feel honored for a role in such a venture?

And only Grandfather Tunnicliff, blithely ignoring the widespread disapproval, had the stature to get away with naming her his apprentice when her aptitude for engineering had come to light. To him, with his own way of seeing things, it was a perfectly reasonable plan. She would help design the invention and then take on the family business of both running a flax mill and licensing new machines to other mill owners. Once working, the flax engine would quickly lift the family fortunes—by which means she and grandfather both understood he meant to get her mother, his daughter, some buffer from the man she had married. Amherst Kenyon, Ella's father. The man from whom they all wished some distance.

But over the last three years she had gone from enjoying the work with her grandfather's invention to slowly coming to begrudge it, for it took her from what she loved better. She'd always preferred being outdoors, but over the past year the woods had pulled her with increasing strength. For she'd begun to see what Pete could see. Neither she nor Zeke recalled asking Indian Pete to show them to read sign, and the former Oneida scout, who now earned his meager living as a smith with her grandfather, certainly never acknowledged his role as their teacher. He only kept an eye on them and deigned to set them tests, in which he occasionally indicated where they might look next. Sometimes they found a clue where he pointed, more often not.

When he deemed it appropriate he spoke to them, in measured words that inevitably said less in the moment than when she thought of them later. Yet his example of how one might move silently through the woods, absorbing intricate detail of the world of plants and animals, served to task her harder than anything else ever had. She was driven by the thought she was missing out—that this beautiful secret world would be seen by select few and she needed to be one of them. For itself, but also because slipping into this world gave her blessed escape from all she could not fix. Slowly the woods were becoming more home to her than anywhere else.

When she'd first begun to spend every spare moment studying sign, it had seemed she'd never get any better. None of it came easy—not like the engineering. Then slowly, in tiny steps, she had begun to make progress. And now, at last, Pete had begun to teach her to throw a knife and the very beginnings of hunting, which would require all the skills she had barely mastered and a host of others as well.

It was always difficult to go indoors, but usually she was all right once it came time to get back to engineering work. Today, though, entering the shop also meant she could no longer avoid the niggling thought that had snapped at the heels of her mind with increasing fervor. The thought that her grandfather's latest idea for feeding the flax straw into the machine was never going to work. They'd labored at it every evening for over a fortnight and her doubts had only continued to grow. It was her duty to tell him but how could she say as much? He'd been so pleased for this newest attempt, in his own gruff way, and he was so rarely pleased these days.

She patted the knife in her boot. Then felt once more for the gold watch in the pocket of the odd short dress she wore over boyish breeches. The gold watch was her other niggling problem. It didn't belong in her pocket, but her father had stumbled upon her hiding place and she'd only managed to whisk it away before he snatched it to trade for rum. Now she'd been carrying it for several days with no idea where to put it. Until, coming to her grandfather's shop this evening, it occurred to her the smith was the one place safe from her father, for Amherst Kenyon gave his father-in-law a wide berth. *Soon,* she thought, patting her knife again, *soon he'll learn to give me the same wide berth.*

With resignation she turned away from the river and, reaching the door of the shop once more, took a last deep draught of the sweet April air before plunging through the low doorway into the smoky thickness inside. A wall of dry heat surged from the broad bed of coals in the forge at the center of the room. The coals glowed deep red except where the blasts of the bellows fired them to white. Her grandfather stood at his anvil, across the forge from the mill horse who worked the bellows. He paused his hammer and said in his rumbling voice, "You're late. Did something happen?"

When she shook her head she could tell he didn't believe her. He squinted as if he suspected she'd begun to lie. And he was right. She lied because his interference no longer helped as it once had. Because her father had become skilled at simmering down for the moment and then boiling back up later. Which was always worse.

She'd tried to explain this to Grandpa Tunnicliff but that murderous look had come into his eyes and she knew it was no good. He wished to save them but what could he do, short of bludgeoning her father to death with his hammer. Instead she'd asked Pete to teach her to throw a knife so she could fight back in the moment, now that she was fifteen years and as tall as her father. It had to be someone there in the thick of it and she was the eldest. It had to be her. Just as it had to be her to work with her grandfather on the invention even if she didn't want it any longer. She had the knack and there was no one else, so what was the sense in complaining.

She paused to let her eyes adjust to the dim light of the forge. Curls of her black hair had come loose from her long braid and tangled into a mat around her head—and were frosted with a mist of tiny drops from outside that now glowed in the light of the coals. Most striking were her eyes, a greenish light grey at odds with her olive skin and black hair. She crossed the dirt floor to the broad scarred table that held the scale model of the flax machine. The machine that would turn worthless rough flax straw into valuable fiber for weaving linen. If only it would work. She stared at the model and then up at the soot-blackened ceiling, wishing for a vision of how to make it work. All the pieces were there, weren't they? Had they missed something altogether?

At the forge her grandfather bent a glowing piece of iron to form a handle for a lantern. How many years, she wondered, had he worked all day at bending and pounding iron and then all evening at his inventions? How did he keep going on this one when it still didn't work? She felt certain she wouldn't have had the tenacity to persist that long. He laid the lantern handle on the anvil and quickly tapped it flat with his peening hammer. Though his hands were huge, half again as large as those of most men, his touch with the hammer was light and sure. Soon he'd put away his workday tools and begin casting another set of pieces for the model. He'd have that same faint look of hope that had begun to make a knot in her stomach.

She made her way around the coals to see Edgar the mill horse as he plodded onward, working the treadle in his unhurried way. "Good evening, Edgar." She reached for a handful of oats to hold under his freckled lips, rubbing his neck with her other hand. "How's my old friend? Still the strongest horse in the whole shop, are you not?" She wrapped her fingers around the girth of his harness saddle and gave it a slight tug. "A little tight I see. Yessir I know how that feels. I bet you're itching to get this off."

Continuing to speak to the horse in a voice loud enough to carry, she slipped a hand under his harness pad and felt around until she found the hidden pocket in the underside. She'd discovered it years ago and recollected it today when she'd searched her mind for a new place to hide the gold watch.

Quickly she slid the watch out of her own pocket and into the dusty pocket on the felted wool pad, fastening the button to keep it inside. *There. That should keep his horrible hands off Aunt Lucille's watch.*

She returned to the flax model and assisted her grandfather in measuring for the newest piece he intended to cast, all the while trying to keep her mind from thinking it was a futile waste of time. An hour later Pete slipped inside the door and was already standing behind her when she became aware of his presence. She would never understand how a man built like an ox could move like a panther—especially when she knew from considerable effort how hard it was to emulate. She turned and nodded at him with a faint smile, already feeling better because he was there. He nodded back, his face still but his eyes alive with pleasure as he gazed into her face. He had a way of looking at her that stripped her cares for the moment and made it seem everything would be all right. Tonight his broad chest stretched the seams of the homespun draw-neck shirt he wore above stained deerskin trousers. A single turkey feather adorned his long black braid and his silver earrings twinkled in the light of the coals.

Grandpa Tunnicliff glanced up from his work. "What's making the horses so tetchy, Pete? Could you see anything?"

Pete shook his head, then moved away to light a lantern and returned to stand beside Ella. They watched the blacksmith as he moved to the other end of the forge—where the bellows were directed—and used a set of massive tongs to remove a crucible of molten metal. He turned it slightly to test the flow, then called to the horse, "Good boy, Edgar." Edgar gave a mild whinny. Tunnicliff took the crucible to a sand mold set in a jig and carefully poured the metal into the mold. He watched it for a moment. "What do you think, Pete, will this be the one?"

Pete shrugged. "Perhaps."

"That's encouraging," her grandfather said in his gravelly voice. "What about you, Ella, you think this is it?"

She grimaced, not liking the question. "I hope not. I've only just begun to work on it with you. How will I claim my share of the grand rewards if you solve it right off?"

"Well," he said, going back to the other end of the forge, "it's clear you have the priorities straight." From the coals he took a piece of iron to shape for a crank arm.

Ella moved nearer to help steady the jig. "Tell me again what that man said about patents—something about pirates?"

Her grandfather snorted. "Bah. *That man's* name is Oliver Evans, and he's a genius of an engineer. What he said was: 'They're going to pirate it anyhow so you best get your name on the patent as soon as you have something that will suffice.'" After a moment he added, "I begin to suspect I should have listened to him and patented my other small contraptions instead of pursuing this one grand achievement above all other."

"How do you mean?"

"Just that at this rate I may die before I ever make that trip to the patent office. It's taken me this long already. Who's to say it won't take another twenty-five years?"

"Don't speak nonsense, Grandpa. You'll build it. If not this idea than the next one."

"You don't think this one will work?" His voice was low and wary.

"I didn't say that," she said sharply, thinking fast. "Only that this one is good and the next one will be even better."

He cocked a suspicious eye at her again. "You're telling me what I want to hear, are you not?"

Suddenly she felt weary of all of it. She stared straight into his eyes. "I have to do that, don't I? It's the only way to have any peace."

He glared at her. Then after a long silence he dropped his eyes back to his work. "Certainly keeping the peace is a worthwhile talent. One we might all do well to cultivate." He looked up and his bushy grey brows came together in a scowl once more. "But take caution it doesn't make a shameless no-account liar and coward of you. You must be prepared to speak truth when the occasion warrants. Isn't that so, Pete?"

Pete looked at them but he hadn't seemed to hear the question. Which was odd. Not like Pete. She raised one brow and stared at him until he dragged himself back from wherever his thoughts had been and, somehow recalling what he'd been asked, nodded slowly.

Her grandfather studied him. "Look here, Pete, if it does come about that I don't manage to build it, you'll see that she keeps working on it, won't you?" When Pete eyed him sharply the older man went on, his voice a low grumble. "Something makes me morbid tonight, but we both know she has as much of a way with engineering as I do—probably more if she'd ever gain any real patience with it. But it will mean keeping the smith open so she has a place to work on it. You'll do that, won't you?"

Pete nodded, his eyes firm on the other man's. Slowly he said, "Yes, Captain Tunnicliff."

Her grandfather turned to her. "You'll work on it, won't you? If anything should happen to me?"

Ella frowned, which made her look old beyond her years. "Yes, of course. But nothing will happen to you."

"Do you give your word?"

"Yes, all right, I give my word. Just stop talking like that, won't you? It's horrid."

"It's necessary to say it because it's in your blood. You're the one to take it up."

It was something he'd said often, but tonight, for the first time, Pete snapped, "Whose blood?" He stared at her grandfather with a strange sort of defiance.

They were both acting so odd tonight. She shook her head at the two of them and moved back to the model of the flax machine. She stared at it, trying to let it speak to her. "It's pulling in the straw, isn't it, that makes it all so tricky? If only we could sort out— " She stopped as a horse whinnied shrilly from the stable, then another.

Her grandfather and Pete looked at one another. In a low voice her grandfather said, "Stay inside, Ella." He and Pete each grabbed something heavy and slipped out the door.

She went to the door to watch, but all she could see was black. She doused the lantern and unhitched the mill horse so he'd stop fanning the coals, then returned to the crack in the door. As her eyes adjusted to the dark she could just make out the stable yard outside. The misting rain had ceased but the moon remained a dim glow behind the clouds.

She heard a shout from the stable itself, on the other side of the yard, and strained to see what was happening. It was a moment before she spotted them, her grandfather and Pete, their backs to the wall of the stable as they crept toward the door, preparing a surprise attack against whomever was inside. She watched as they both seemed to sense something; they stopped and swiveled their heads.

Just then the clouds thinned and broke in front of the half moon rising behind the stable. Against the streaming light she saw something terrible: it was the silhouette of a man, a bandy-legged man, on the roof of the stables, directly above her grandfather and Pete. Bandy-legs stood for a moment, listening. Then he bent and scampered toward them across the roof like a squirrel. When he reached the edge, he dropped to his knees, peered below for just a brief moment, and then, to Ella's horror, propelled himself down onto her grandfather's head. The two of them collapsed in a heap.

Another man lunged around the corner and barreled into Pete. The collision sent them sprawling toward her, out into the stable yard. Pete's weapon flew from his hand and the other man fell briefly to one knee. They regained their balance and began circling one another, coming closer to the doorway from which Ella watched. As they turned, she could see the look of wary intensity on the stranger's face. Pete, though, was grinning. They locked together once again, wrestling for advantage. The man was taller than Pete, and solid, but Pete was quick as a fish, broad and muscled, and she knew a good fight was something he loved best.

Once they hit the ground it was very little time before Pete was on top, sitting on the man's back with one forearm tight against the back of his neck and the other hand twisting the man's left arm up and backward at an unnatural angle.

Ella was just beginning to relax, thinking Pete had this won, when another man emerged from the stable. He was a small man, actually more a boy, with a nervous kind of shimmying walk. She glanced at him and would have looked away, except that he raised a musket and pointed it at Pete's back. He was steeling up his nerve to fire and some sense told her he'd do it.

She didn't really think about it. Her hunting knife was out of the sheath and in her hand, and then she took aim and threw it. Just as Pete had taught her. Just as she'd practiced for so many hours. It flew straight and true, hit him in the throat, and dropped him in an instant.

Pete heard the musket clatter to the ground and swung his head to look. The man below him felt his attention lapse and, seeing his opportunity, twisted his body and swung a vicious blow to just above Pete's ear. Pete slumped to the ground and the man squirmed out from under him, rising to his feet. He was a big man, almost as tall as her grandfather, with long sideburns that curved across to a mustache.

He strode to the body of his young companion and peered down. Cursing, he pulled the knife from the boy's throat. He looked at it and then around the yard before throwing the knife to the ground. Ella, shaking with what she'd just done, melted back into the liquid darkness behind the door, making certain the door didn't move and give her away. She crouched low and put her eye to the crack between the wall and the hinged side of the door. The man kept scanning the yard for the source of the knife. Then he gave a great start as the bandy-legged man slipped to his side.

"What the hell, Willard—stop sneaking around," Sideburns said to Bandy-legs. His voice was surprisingly high for such a large man.

Willard stared at the dead boy. "Who threw that knife, Dennison?"

Dennison shrugged. "Didn't see it." He twisted toward the stable. "Old man, I suppose? Where is he?"

"Don't know." It was Willard's turn to shrug. "He ran off. He was bleeding pretty good, but he could of come round and throwed it, I suppose."

"Bleeding? What from?"

"Knifed him. Didn't mean to, but it was the only way to get him off me. He's an angry bull, that one. Strong for being so old."

Dennison gestured to Pete and said, "That damned Injun was no easy pickings neither. Your brother might have warned us about 'em."

Willard hitched up one shoulder and nodded. "Suppose we should get them horses ready, then."

Dennison made a disparaging gesture. "Nah, not me. I don't care about no horses with a fellow aiming knives at us. He could be taking aim again this minute. Or waiting in the stable to cut our throats. Let's just load up the kid here and go."

Willard was quiet a moment. Then he said, "You ain't been around long. You ain't seen my brother lose his temper yet. I mean, *really* lose his temper. Have you?"

"Nah," Dennison sneered, "but fighting George Loomis or any of the other boys can't be much worse than what we had to fight here tonight. That knife come from far away and hit the kid square."

Willard shook his head in disgust. Then he glanced at Pete, who had rolled to his side with a moan. "We got time to take one or two of them horses and we best do it if we know what's good for us. You take the kid and I'll get the horses and meet you out by the crossroad."

The girl saw the sideburned one called Dennison hoist up the dead boy and carry him out of the yard. Then, with surprisingly little noise, Bandy-legs led two of her grandfather's best horses out of the stable and down the road into the darkness.

Pete groaned and Ella didn't know whether to go to him first or go find her bleeding grandfather. She averted her eyes from the puddle of smeared blood that marked the place where she'd just killed a man. She couldn't think about that now.

Had she really begun the night fretting over that *ridiculous machine*?

PART ONE

June 1810

ONE

ELLA KENYON crouched low by the creek and tilted her head to decipher the curve of the coyote print in the packed wet soil of the deer trail. She traced the print lightly with one fingertip and her face slowly lit with understanding. *Mmmm*, she thought, *Old One-Ear stopped here to listen for me. He hoped his tricks might have put me off the trail. Not that easy, old boy.*

She stood and scanned the area carefully until at last her eye caught the depression of a print in the humus on the far bank, across the racing stream. Focusing on the print and keeping her mind with Old One-Ear, she tucked her knife into the base of her braid, a place it would stay dry, and then waded into the creek, thigh deep with late snow melt. Spring had been slow this year and early summer was still cool. The icy water stabbed her skin through her breeches and by the time she reached the other side she could no longer feel her feet.

She knelt in the shallows to inspect the track and saw it was only one print. One single light impression. No others either uphill or to either side. Her mouth pressed in disbelief and she scanned for the continuing track. There had to be more track.

But there was none. She began to rise to wade back, but by some instinct she turned her head to catch the faint shadow that at last let her see the telltale brush of the outside claw—leaving the faintest scrape in the tangle of soil and half-rotted leaves. She stared down at the single print and the scrape behind it, trying to make sense of what she saw. Pete's long adage to let the track speak for itself afforded no other explanation; Old One-Ear must have reached out from the creek to make a single print and then pulled his paw back.

She absorbed what this meant and had a moment of the same fear from when she was first learning to read sign, that she'd missed an important clue. *Why would he do such a pointless thing?* But then, when she considered it further, her greyish-green eyes began to crinkle and the corners of her mouth began to lift. *It's another trick. But no, it's more of a message. He's calling a truce.* She closely scanned the stream banks upstream and down and still found no other sign. He had left her the one print and then swum down the creek.

Her grin widened and she raised her eyes to look into the treetops as she inhaled the deep metal scent of the water. *This is what Pete means by gifts*, she thought. *The many gifts for those who listen with many ears.* She'd received her share of such gifts over the past years, but they were tiny compared to a print made expressly to tell her something, to speak to her. How often do the animals of the forest bother signing to a two-legged one?

The urge to whoop and holler came on her but she squelched it as quickly as it came, for those of the forest never made noise except where necessary. *But such a large gift. For me?*

She made her way back down into the valley on silent feet that floated an extra foot in the air. She didn't touch the ground with her mind until the elation began to wear off and she remembered what she'd been refusing to think about today. The fact that Pete was back from his travels and that meant she could no longer avoid doing anything more with the machine. It was supposed to be exciting that she'd at last solved the remaining piece of the design, but instead it felt like the noose had tightened. Like her days in the woods were more numbered than ever now that the machine was about to demand her full attention.

For the thousandth time she wished she could live as Pete did, alone in his lodge with only himself to please. A pointless wish in her case, for her father had made such a mess of things she was now the nearest hope her family had to salvation. At least until her brother Jimson grew older. *Pretty sorry state of things.*

She pulled to a dead stop as she sensed movement in the clearing ahead of her. She drew her hunting knife from its sheath at her waist and slipped into the shadows behind a large chestnut. As she was down wind of the clearing, she sampled the breeze to learn who made the movement. Suddenly she made a wry face, sheathed her knife, crouched, and skirted to the trees at the edge of the clearing. Across from her on the far side a young man was kneeling in the matted old grass, intent on setting a snare. He was slender with shaggy black hair above pale skin and only the faintest touch of stubble on his cheeks. Keeping to the rear of his right shoulder, she glided across the clearing and slid to her knees on Zeke's right side. He jumped when he noticed her and the snare snapped taut around his index finger. Howling, he rose and began hopping from foot to foot as he struggled to release the bark twine from his finger.

Ella, laughing, had her knife out to cut the twine but couldn't get him to stand still long enough before a voice behind them both said, "Stay still."

It was a voice they were long accustomed to obeying. Zeke stopped hopping and turned to hold out his finger to Pete, who deftly released the knot that had turned Zeke's finger bright purple.

After rubbing his finger a moment, Zeke said, "That didn't count. I was yelling too loud to have any chance of hearing your approach. No score for that."

Pete shrugged and didn't argue for his point in their long-standing game, but Ella read in his gesture that for him there was no room for excuses. That to be careless in facing a true enemy would mean death. And if Zeke hadn't learned this by now than it was pointless to repeat it. She herself had absorbed these lessons long ago, but of course she had an enemy to face every day—in her own house—where Zeke had little sense of what that was like. For him it had always been, and remained, a game. And thank heaven for that. His innocent good humor was sometimes all she had to make it bearable.

Now, wishing to see him cheerful once more, she pulled both Pete and Zeke to the ground until they sat knee to knee with their legs crossed and embarked on the tale of Old One-Ear and the single print. She drew it out to be as entertaining as possible and was pleased when Zeke began to smile and Pete's eyes began to spark with amusement.

When she had finished Pete said, "Old One-Ear he is born many times. Each time he tell more jokes." Then, with a completely blank expression, he added, "He almost as tricky as me."

When they both smiled he relaxed his face into his odd silent chuckle that was often as amusing as whatever joke he had made. Then, just as characteristic, he threw them off balance with a sharp veer in topic. "Tell me of machine," he said to Ella. "I hear talk as soon as I walk into town that there is new idea."

Ella shrugged, never especially eager to speak of the machine, but the idea was sound and she would require Pete's assistance.

"It was just a few weeks ago, as we were building from a paper plan one of those new mechanical grain threshers from Scotland. We'd assembled nearly half of it when it occurred to me that a similar configuration to the drum and belts used to pull in the grain stalks on the thresher might be adapted to pull in flax straw." When Pete nodded, she added, "We're building a model and Jenny's already begun a set of sketches."

Pete thought a few moments. "This is good news. Your grandfather smiles in his grave. You come to smith later and tell me more of how it can work. But now, I wish a rabbit for my long-empty cooking pot. Let us hunt together once more." He reached a hand to each of them and they rose in unison. He said, "It is good to be here with you."

THEY HAD A MODESTLY successful hunt of two rabbits, a partridge, and a squirrel, at least by the standards of these hills that had been over-hunted by thirty years of settlement in the valley below. Ella and Zeke were cleaning the game in the small clearing next to the brook at the base of the trail when Zeke looked up from the partridge he was skinning. "I should come with you, don't you think? When you leave to go for the patent?"

"Why?" She glanced at him but didn't meet his gaze.

A lock of his dark hair fell down across his eyes and he pushed it away with the back of a blood-smeared hand, leaving a streak similar in color to his red lips, which always appeared painted. He gave a slight shrug. "It just seems a good idea not to travel alone. I'm certain I'd be useful somehow. And I'd like to see the city."

"I don't need a traveling companion. I want to do it alone." Then, less sharply, she added, "Your mother likely can't spare you, in any case. Who'd run deliveries for the store?"

"We'd sort it out. Father's been feeling better."

Ella bit her lip and silently berated herself for mentioning the sore topic of Zeke's place at the store. She and Zeke had been friends since they were babies, his mother minding her at the dry-goods store while her own mother attended at births and sickbeds across the valley. When she was young she'd thought Zeke had the perfect life: living behind a store full of food with a mother who made jokes of everything. Only years later had she come to see how Zeke's life wasn't as it once seemed. That his mother told jokes to cover the strain of trying to run a store by herself while her husband's illness kept him bedridden much of the time, with bills coming steadily from the fancy doctor in Albany. Zeke helped when he grew old enough but he couldn't help hating the store—for he disliked to be indoors as much as she did.

"You should consider it," he went on. "Taking me with you, I mean. You could run into any kind of trouble. It'd be helpful to have a man along."

"Where? What man?"

"Very amusing," he said pleasantly, accustomed to the ribbing that came with looking much younger than his twenty years. "You could use me, though. You'll have to catch game along the way and you know I'm the better tracker."

She rolled her eyes in annoyance. He was goading her for being overly fond of the fact she was the better tracker, and she took ribbing with considerably less grace than he did. "No," she said, "You can't come."

"You'll think about it, then?"

She flicked a piece of bloody fur at him. "Yes, all right. I'll think about it," she said mostly to silence him. She had no intention of taking any companions along. She had never been away from Deborahville on her own and the one piece of this whole wretched patent business that she actually looked forward to was riding away all by herself. She'd still have the machine to fret over, but for once there wouldn't be her father to simultaneously watch and avoid. No mother and siblings to care for and worry over. Thank you kindly, but no. She needed no one else to take along and thus to please. Dapper Dan the horse was all the company she needed. He and her knife.

Zeke rose and began to string the game on a line of twisted fibers as Ella went to the stream to rinse their knives. Zeke said, "Let's take these into town and then get up a card game in the stable loft. The Johnson boys said they could play and I want to win back what you took last night."

Ella shook her head. "No, not today. I told Mother I'd be home for supper and I told Pete I'd come see him later. But I'll walk to the store with you."

A BABBLE OF VOICES greeted them as they entered the front door of Winebottom Dry-Goods. A group of men played back-gammon in the corner, several customers milled about, and, across the store at the counter running the width of the back wall, Ella's Aunt Lucille stood across from Janet Winebottom. Behind them the shelves from floor to ceiling were crammed tight with everything from fire irons to canary cages. The two women were eyeing a bolt of muslin unrolled on the counter and Lucille Tunnicliff, with her gloves removed, was running her hand across the fabric. "I can't make it work, Janet. The weave isn't fine enough. Cannot they bring you any better?"

"Only if you take the whole roll, Lucille. No one else is as persnickety as you—and who else would pay the price for it?"

Lucille waved her hand in dismissal. She was a tall woman wearing an elaborate feathered turban above an elegant, well-cut blue empire gown and a silk Spencer jacket. "Oh bother, Janet. You're so decidedly provincial. What shall I do with you?"

"Leave me be and buy your cloth in Albany, that's what." Zeke's mother rolled her eyes and waggled her thick eyebrows, but she was clearly enjoying herself. "I tell you the same every time you come in to complain about the cloth I keep. Who needs it?"

"You do. Aren't you in the business of selling things, my dear?" Lucille began to draw on her gloves to leave.

"Only to people who aren't a royal pain in my rear end."

"Ah, mon dieu, you *are* a witch."

"That's right. And don't you forget it." Janet looked up and noticed the two young people watching from the middle of the floor. Her face broke into a wide smile, displaying a broad expanse of crooked teeth beneath a prominent and rather bumpy nose. "Ah, son, there you are. I'll be finished here in a trice."

Janet began to roll up the muslin as Lucille turned to make her way out of the store, wending her way between the many goods that cluttered the floor. Reaching Ella and Zeke, Lucille stopped to give an appraising glance at their begrimed hunting clothes, then at the string of fur and feathers they held. She tipped her chin in the slightest of cool nods. "Hello, Ella. Zeke."

Ella nodded as slightly in return. "Hello, Aunt Lucille."

Lucille tilted her turban and moved past them, leaving a trace of French perfume behind her. Ella shrugged at Zeke, who broke off what he was about to say when his mother lifted the flap in the counter to waddle out to greet them. She too wended her way amidst the barrels and bins of many sizes filled with flour, salt, sugar, coffee, dried pork, and numerous other sundries. Joining them in the middle of room, she eyed the dangling game and said, "Oh, isn't that nice. You brought me something pretty."

The men loitering around the backgammon board in the corner gave an appreciative snort. She turned to them. "What? You lot are still here? Your wives are going to skin me if you don't get home for supper time. Now shoo." She flapped her hands as if herding chickens. The vigorous movements caused yet more of her grizzled grey and brown hair to protrude from beneath the Holland cap which framed her narrow face, well scattered with freckles. She said in a loud whisper, "They can't help themselves, they're bewitched by my beauty."

One of the men, still looking down at the backgammon board, drawled, "Oh yes, it's terrible. I can't sleep at night."

Another said, "It's that pickle juice she uses for scent. It's irresistible."

"Now, now," Janet put one hand on her hip. "That's enough of your terribly witty banter. Go home and come back tomorrow." She waggled an eyebrow again. "*If* you can drag yourself out of bed after another sleepless night."

When the men had shuffled out, calling last jibs at Janet, she looked down at the string of game and said, "Oh goodness, you *have* brought quite a nice catch, but I'm afraid there's no one here to cook it today. I've got a delivery to unload and then accounts to do," She pointed a finger at her own ample chest and said, "And then again it's no secret I'd only make leather of that fine meat—you know I can't cook worth a damn. Do me a good turn, Ella, and bring these home to your mother and Jenny, won't you? They're fine cooks and it saves me the trouble of trying to make something of them."

Ella was about to argue, for Mrs. Winebottom was forever pressing food on her as if her family was starving. Not that the food wasn't welcome—with her father having sold off most of the livestock from the farm and drinking most of what he made from the mill—but it had become plain humiliating. She couldn't count how many times she'd sworn she wouldn't accept any more of it. But Janet was implacable in her own sweet way, and now here she was again, smiling up at her so hopefully that she found herself shaking her head as always and saying, "As you like, Mrs. Winebottom."

"And don't you forget to tell your mother the news of the barn-raising at the Purdy farm. First Saturday of August. Tell her I want some of those baked beans she makes better than anyone else—and I'll bring her the sugar as soon as I next get out to your place."

Ella nodded but couldn't find the words to say something appropriately grateful before Janet had wrapped her in a warm, bosomy embrace that made it impossible to speak. Zeke, who was making his way to the door at the back of the store that led to their private rooms, turned to call out, "Best not smother her, Mother. Or you'll have to cook that game yourself."

ELLA'S FATHER NEVER APPEARED at supper, but her mother cooked the heavy-flavored meat into a fine stew they ate with rye bread and summer greens. After farm chores, Ella walked back into town in the long June twilight to see Pete at the blacksmith shop where he often worked evenings. When he was in town that was, which lately had been rare.

The spring peepers were trilling wildly as she reached the swampy area at the bottom of the hill and the air was suffused with the iron scent of marshy water. She realized she should have ridden Dapper Dan, the horse her grandfather had willed her—to get him out—but as usual she'd preferred to walk. The jarring motion of the horse kept her from thinking clearly. And on horseback the only smell was horse.

She passed the small cemetery on the right and then the cluster of houses that marked the edge of the village proper. When she reached the road that merged into Main Street, the bell on the tall white church spire in front of her began to toll the eight o'clock hour. Pastor Whitmarsh loved to ring that bell.

It was quiet in town at this hour, as lamps and candles began to be lit. She could see the faint glow of lights behind the windows as she made her way down the main road. Families had begun to settle in by their hearths with stitching or tack to mend, a bible, or something else to read aloud. Past the houses she came to the heart of town, to the row of mills harnessed to the curve of the river, interspersed with shops and offices. Most all the mills and shops were dark by this hour, but she knew each of them well, had known most of them all her life. The tannery, the dry-goods store, the two sawmills, the tavern, the one remaining fulling mill, the two gristmills, and then her grandfather's blacksmith shop at the far end of the road. She hardly registered the familiar biting reek of the tannery, nor the stink of dye vats in the fulling mill.

The only business that hadn't been here most of her life was Henry Emerston's new gristmill. Never a miller, Emerston had made his early money as a banker and then studied law to set up as a solicitor. Then the old fulling mill had burned and Emerston, from nowhere, had bought the mill site and built a new modern mill, fitted to make the best use of the flour milling inventions patented by the famous Oliver Evans.

Her own father's gristmill sat farther downstream on a much better mill site for water power, but Emerston had installed a newer overshot waterwheel that made more efficient use of what water he had. He had paid eighty dollars to license the full set of labor-saving devices from Oliver Evans and his new mill now ran faster, and with only a fraction the men, than her father's traditional operation. Thus, while her father was busy regaling his friends at the tavern with laughs at Emerston's expense, Emerston had been busy at milling, siphoning the major share of Amherst Kenyon's business within the first year.

Walking by it, Ella thought how she'd heard little but talk of the new gristmill for much of the past year—mostly because there was so little else to talk about. The people of the town felt their own importance, but Ella knew Deborahville was just another button on the same coat all along the river that meandered the long valley. Every small town had the same mills, the same dry-goods store, the same church with the same steeple.

The only other person who had been able to see this was her grandfather, and he'd been determined to change it. He'd held such big dreams for this small town. He was certain his flax invention would transform the place, put it on the map, cause it to triple in size. He was certain it would draw so many people to come have their flax milled that they'd have to build new roads to hold the traffic. Then, over time, when the flax engine made it possible to weave linen—a superior fabric— as cheaply as cotton, and all the fields throughout the north took to growing flax to feed the hungry demand from the linen mills, and the southern cotton plantations began to wither as the prices for cotton plummeted, then, at last, Deborahville would slowly grow famous as the home of the world-renowned flax engine. A place people came to visit just to see where the inventor had lived.

She'd never questioned this talk. When her grandfather spoke people had listened, for he had that way about him. He was outside plain old life somehow and his words rang sound and true. People *wanted* to believe him. It was only now, with the work of completing the flax engine and bringing it to fruition growing closer that it suddenly occurred to her that perhaps the plan might not work as he described. Or at least not as effortlessly. She'd thought nothing of these matters when she'd sworn an oath to him that night in the forge—the night he died—for only much later did she see the promise to finish the engine was also the promise to realize his dreams for the town. Which was a whole other set of efforts for which she was utterly ill-suited. That kind of work—the sparking people's dreams and making things happen— belonged to her grandfather alone. And he wasn't here to do it. Oh why had she ever sworn that foolish oath to finish his work? Because, she told herself yet again, she'd been too young to know better and hadn't imagined her grandfather could die—at least not so suddenly. He'd left a great gaping hole, damn him. He'd left her to miss him and curse him all at once.

As she approached the blacksmith shop she thought of Pete, watching her as she'd tried to keep her promise in the years after her grandfather was gone. He'd seen her at the smith night after night, tinkering with the parts, working at the same elusive puzzle that had eluded her grandfather. He'd seen how she hated her failure and he had never said a word when, after so many ideas and so many failed attempts, she at last stopped coming to the smith to work at it because she'd simply run out of ideas.

Her failure had galled her every day of the two years since she last tinkered with the model. The broken promise dogged her steps like a mangy hound who keeps to the shadows but can't be ignored. Only now, with a new idea at last, did she feel a slight spark of anticipation at lessening the burden of her unfulfilled oath. She felt certain this newest idea was a sound one, but at the same time she had sharp stabs of fear in her chest. *What if I'm fooling myself? What if I'm wasting yet more time and coming not a hair closer to solving it?* But what choice did she have?

But how had he known to make her swear? She'd pondered this question as many times as she'd wondered about the mill horse who'd disappeared the night her grandfather had died—taking with it Aunt Lucille's gold watch she'd hidden in his tack. *How* could her grandfather have known what would happen that night? His horses had been nervous, yes, but horses are often nervous. Why was this time different? And even if he'd known the horse thieves were nearby, what gave him the thought he might die? Horse thieves don't typically murder people.

Horse thieves. She'd learned later they were of that wild Loomis gang from up in Sangerfield. Their leader was George Washington Loomis, the one the men had talked about that night. She thought she'd seen him once, not long after the night her grandfather was killed. He had that glossy black hair and black beard and something about the way he swaggered through their little town, as if it all belonged to him, made her think, *That's him.*

There was never any trial after her grandfather's death. No justice for him. Just a quiet funeral with little time for anyone to put together a just tribute for such a great man. Nor was there talk of the boy she'd killed with her knife. It was almost as if it hadn't happened. Except at night in her dreams. For years she'd woken with her heart racing, waiting for the posse of thieves to cease chasing her, or the jail cell to dissipate. Or the face of the boy's mother to fade.

She'd tried to glean information from her own mother, but if Catherine knew anything she wouldn't speak of it. All her father had said was, "'Tain't none of your business, so leave it be." He'd reached out to strike her when she'd pressed him further, before he recalled her knife and thought better of it.

Her knife, the same one guilty of killing that boy, had afforded them several years of comparative peace from Amherst. But lately he'd become more testy, ever since the new gristmill had come in and he'd had to borrow money against his own mill. He worried about making his payments and tended more often to lash out with the back of his hand, though it was nothing compared to years ago. He'd mellowed some. It was hard to imagine the worst days would return and for that, at least, she could be grateful.

Walking by the tavern where her father would be at this hour, she thought, *I hope he drinks himself to death soon.* She couldn't see how her mother continued to pity him, or how her sister Jenny made excuses for him.

She paused her steps, jerking herself out of her thoughts. She'd sensed something behind her, although she'd heard nothing. She continued walking but turned her head slightly to scan behind her, not wishing anyone following to know she'd become aware of them. She took another few steps and now she could feel the presence of the hidden assailant like a dog senses fear. Sharp and strong. She felt exposed in the middle of the road and had to tell herself that if she chose to make noise she could call out half the town to her aid. Not that she could ever bring herself to call for help.

She walked a little farther and then took another surreptitious look behind her by turning her head slightly to the right. As she did so, someone slipped from the shadows to her left and had a knife in her kidney and a hand over her mouth before she could make any sound. She went completely rigid for a moment. Then, willing herself, she relaxed just as fully, slumping in the man's grip. As he loosened his hold to regain his grasp, she spun suddenly away from the knife, simultaneously aiming a foot upward at the hand that held it. Her foot struck the hand with a good sharp blow and the knife flew to the ground several yards away. But her assailant was quick and was already spinning away from her when she rushed at him. She grabbed him roughly by the sleeve to jerk his upper body toward her, pulling him off balance as she pincered his left leg between her own legs and flung him down to the ground, landing neatly on top of him.

She pinned his left arm down hard, but he was so much stronger that he had his right arm free before she got it fully pinned.

From beneath her he said, "You still slow. Getting a little faster. But you must get both arms down quick."

She panted to catch her breath. "We worked on it this week. You're much faster than Zeke, though. I had him pinned every time."

"Good," Pete said. "Not many faster than me."

"Nor more likely to boast of it."

He nodded as he rose, chuckling silently, and brushed off the road dust. "Come in the smith. Has been too long since we talk."

They walked together the few steps to the smith and she ducked her head to go through the low door of the small, smoky shop. She could remember when she was small enough not to need to duck, but it had been a while now. She wasn't as tall as her grandfather had been, but she was at least the height of Pete and Zeke.

She walked across the dark smith, lit only by the red glow of the forge. She pulled the lantern off the wall and used a scrap of wood to light the wick from the glowing coals. As the room lightened, she gazed at the empty treadle in the corner. Old Edgar's treadle, just where he'd left it. Pete had never replaced him because he could borrow a mill horse on the rare occasions when he needed the higher temperatures the horse-powered bellows could provide.

Pete interrupted her thoughts. "So. Tell me of machine."

She took a deep breath, gathered her thoughts, and told him of her new idea for the flax gin. He listened quietly, then asked a few insightful questions that got at the heart of the idea, testing it for soundness. She knew it had passed the test when he began to ask about parts they'd need to cast in iron for the model.

When he was satisfied, she said, "I keep hearing Grandpa's voice, how he always said that once you solved the design you had to get a patent before anyone else saw it, or they'd pirate it right off and you'd never be able to prove you invented it. I'd like to go down to the patent office straight away, but I'm also worried I'll make a mistake with the papers—you know I'm no good with all that."

Pete considered this. "I know nothing of patents. Your Aunt Lucille is who to ask. She is smart lady. Good with papers. She will know what to do."

Ella was quiet, then she said, "You know I can't do that, Pete. She doesn't like me, and even if she somehow consented to help she'd make me pay in blood. I'd rather figure it out myself."

"Do not say no," Pete said with a firm certainty. "Think on it more. There is no shame in asking help from family."

"She doesn't behave as family," Ella said sharply. "She's my aunt by marriage, that's all. Not even a real aunt to me. She may play aunt to Jenny and Jimson, but she has little use for me."

"She think of you as family. She will help you if she can."

Ella made a dismissive shrug. "Perhaps." After a pause she went on, "On the topic of assistance, I received a note out of nowhere from Henry Emerston, saying he heard a rumor I'd solved the design and wants me to come see him to discuss it. He thinks he can help me."

Pete raised a brow in appreciation of this news. "Emerston is important business man. He knows banking and law and milling. He knows many people."

"Yes, but what good is that? I need to get the patent and do it quickly. Besides, my grandfather always said not to trust anyone outside of the family, and even then to be careful."

Pete gave her a long, measured look. "Captain Tunnicliff he was smart man," he said slowly. "He know of many things. But sometimes he act too quickly. It take patience and also thinking to have success. How you could hunt deer with no waiting?"

Ella gave a grimace of annoyance and paced a few steps across the smith. "That's different, Pete. That's hunting. You know I can wait a lifetime when I'm hunting. It's just this damned machine I can't seem to find any patience for. I promised I'd finish it and now that it's close, it seems something I have to complete before I can think about doing anything else. Grandpa put such store by it."

Pete considered this. "You do it for him?"

"Yes, of course. What do you mean?"

"It is not for you as well?"

Ella stopped pacing. She looked up at the ceiling of the smith. "For me?" She shook her head. "No, not for me. Certainly I like the engineering of it, and of course I hope the machine proves a means to build a business that will ease Mother's way,

33

for she's had a difficult time of it. If there's travel I'm glad of it, for I'm eager to see more of the world. But I dread this patenting affair and trying to realize Grandpa's grand plans. I do it only because it was his whole life's work and I swore I'd see it through. And certainly it's too important to ignore. Or fail at."

"That is so. But what work is yours, then?" Pete pressed her. "You already old for marriage."

"Yes, thank you for the reminder. I may have overlooked that fact if you and every old lady in town didn't think to remark on it. Nearly every day."

"You must decide what is for you. That is all I say. Very simple."

"Simple—is that so?" Ella said sharply. "Easy enough for you to say. You leave when you like. Travel as long as you wish. Come back when you care to. Hunt when you like. Go hungry if you like. Yes, that's certainly very simple. I'd give anything for a life that simple." She glared at him.

Pete studied her face as she took several deep breaths. Softly he asked, "You think I choose this life for myself?"

"Didn't you? You could have married if you'd wished. Fathered a longhouse of children."

Pete held her eyes, his face hard but his eyes suddenly soft. "No. You are wrong. Wife, children, a place at the council fire. These are all I ever wish for my life."

After a pause she whispered, "What happened?"

He shut his eyes a moment and his mouth twisted. "Mostly George Washington War happens. Everything it is different after that."

He'd almost never spoken of the war before—much as she'd pressed him. She held her breath, her own concerns evaporating in light of this sudden revelation. She squatted in front of Pete, looked up at him, and asked softly, "Why did you break from your people?"

Pete, still leaning against the anvil, looked up at the ceiling and shook his head. Then he looked down at her for a long while. He seemed to decide something and turned to carefully place his hammer on the anvil behind him. He turned back, crossed his arms, and met Ella's gaze. "You are grown now. Have troubles of your own. It is time I tell you of mine." He stopped to gather his words and then began slowly, "My people, the Oneida, once were one of Five Nations, the Iroquois, the People of the Great Peace. Then the war come between American and British and the Great Peace it is broken. All Nations go with British except the Oneida. Only my own people, the Oneida people, we fight on the side of Americans."

He paused again and Ella, in a soft voice, asked the question she'd asked many times, but had yet to have answered. "What part did you take in the war, Pete?"

He allowed a spasm of grief to twist his face. "Mostly I am scout for army, but also I fight."

"With General Washington?"

"Yes. I stay at his camp and I fight with his army."

It seemed he would say no more. Ella bit back the many questions she longed to ask, for he'd already said more than he ever had. Resigned, she stood and prepared to take her leave. But then he surprised her.

"There is more," he said through tight lips, as if forcing himself to speak. He drew a long breath. "My people, the Oneida, they take Jesus with Reverend Kirkland and they are Christian. But it is not for me. In my travels I hear the Prophet speak. He is Seneca; he speak at Seneca villages. When I hear the Prophet's words, I know I hear truth. After this I cannot take Jesus with Oneida people."

"What did he say?"

"He speak the Code of Handsome Lake. For three days he tell us what we must do and what we must not do. He say how we must be to children. How we must treat brother and stranger. He show us how to live a good and strong life. An Indian life."

Ella absorbed this, and then the obvious question arose. "But this land here is...or was...Oneida land. Didn't your people all leave here? Why did you come back?"

"Yes, this valley is once Oneida land. But the Oneida follow Jesus and they lose the land. Or they sell it, if you believe that. For pennies. My people leave here, but me, I come back. The Seneca they are my brothers. They ask me to stay. But I am not Seneca. I do not belong with their land. I come back here, to where I hunted as a boy. To my own land. Which white people now say is their land. To stay here I make peace with these white people."

Ella's eyes snapped to his with a sharp look of hurt and Pete added, "This is many years ago. Now white people are my brothers too."

Ella nodded, understanding what he implied. "So that's where you go, then, when you travel? To visit the Seneca?"

But Pete was finished answering questions. He reached around to pick up his peening hammer and turned back to see that Ella was still staring at him. He walked over to put a sinewy hand on her shoulder, giving it a firm squeeze and then turning her toward the door. "Sleep tonight in peace," he said softly. "Travel many dreams."

T W O

WITHOUT RELEASING HER GRIP on either the mortar or the well-worn pestle, Jenny Kenyon rolled a shoulder to push back the thick braid that had swung into the dried herb she was grinding. Bunches and piles of dried herbs and roots lay around her on the long oak trestle table in the main room of the farmhouse. Besides the soft hiss of the water kettle on the Franklin stove behind her, the rustle and squeak of the pestle was interrupted only by the occasional whistle of a snipe outside in the wet meadow across the fence line. As the long June day came at last to an end, the sky began to streak violet and pink. Jenny stopped her work to watch through the window until the colors faded and then turned back to her grinding. The silence in the house was welcome and embracing. She loved quiet work in a quiet house, but no one, except perhaps her father, could ever be truly at ease in this house. Long ago she'd made a peace of sorts with how it was now, but she'd resolved it would be different some day. At least tonight they had eaten well and the June sun had at last begun to grow warm. It was well to take note of the good days.

She startled when the front door clanged open and her mother came in. "Jenny, dear, I can't seem to find Jimson. I've looked in all the usual places and he's nowhere to be found." Catherine Kenyon appeared tired as she pushed a strand of sweaty half-grey hair back up under her mop cap. She moved to the stove to check the kettle. "I see you've got his bath water almost hot."

Jenny smiled. "He must have heard the word 'bath'—he's likely hiding from you."

Her mother wiped her hands on her apron and then put them on her hips. "He hasn't had a bath in over a month now. What am I going to do with that boy? I can hardly take him to church as he is."

Jenny smiled again and gazed back into her mortar. At sixteen, her cheeks yet held an awkward curve of childhood and her skin had not cleared, leaving her plain despite her quick brown eyes and glossy brown hair. She said, "If you were to ask him, I'm certain he'd tell you he'd prefer to be a heathen."

"Jenny! You mustn't say such things. He's just a young boy." Catherine wiped her brow, which had beaded with sweat in the hot room. Her large round eyes dominated her face, giving a childish aspect to what was otherwise haggard and lined. "It's begun to get dark and we'll never find him after that. Come now, dear, won't you help me look for him?"

Her daughter put aside her work and rose, smoothing her skirt. She said, "I'm certain he's in the barn somewhere. He always finds places to hide in there."

They'd combed the hayloft and the empty stalls and were peering into the corners of the tack room and the threshing room in the half light of evening when Jenny heard a small rustle. She gave a gentle tug to her mother's sleeve and put a finger to her lips. Pointing to Dapper Dan's stall, about fifteen feet away, she said, in a slightly raised voice, "You know, Mother, I was just thinking, if Ella ever does get this patent for her machine, I think she might set up shop in New Orleans. I hear it's a great city, on the river called...."

Catherine looked puzzled but then, when Jenny tilted her head once more toward Dapper Dan's stall and gave her an expectant look, her face cleared and she said, "Oh...the Ohio, I believe."

"Oh yes, that's right," Jenny agreed, "the Ohio River. I hear it's a great river, I should like to see it someday." She paused to listen to more rustling from the horse stall. "If ever I should have money enough, I intend to buy a boat you know, to sail all the way down the Ohio River, through New Orleans, and then right out onto the ocean at the Gulf of...? Oh bother, what's it called?"

"Florida, I believe," Catherine said firmly. "Yes, I'm certain it's called the Gulf of Florida."

"No, no, no, no, no," a boy's angry voice rang out. "That's the *Mississippi* River that flows into New Orleans, and it empties into the Gulf of *Mexico*. Don't either of you know *anything* of geography?" Jimson's head appeared over the top of the wall of Dapper Dan's stall. A wide tuft of his hair stood straight up in the air, and all of it was laced with bits of hay.

"Hmm, it appears we don't," Jenny said. "Good thing you were here." She winked at him. "I wonder, would you show me in your atlas from Aunt Lucille where I might find the city of New Orleans?"

Jimson nodded and clambered over the wall. He was already streaking toward the house by the time Jenny and Catherine had shut the door of the barn behind themselves. "That was quick-thinking of you," Catherine told Jenny as they walked the path back to the house. "We didn't have to drag him in."

"Just wait until he notices the bath water."

Later, after wrestling Jimson through his bath and into bed, they turned back to preparing their medicines. They'd spent the spring collecting roots and leaves in the woods and fields. Now, with the herbs drying in the warmth of summer, their work turned to late evenings of grinding and storing. They worked as quickly as they could, for Catherine believed the plants grew stale and lost their medicine if left out too long.

Jenny was just mounting a chair to reach more of the herbs they'd hung from the ceiling when Catherine joined her and said, "Here, let me assist you." She reached up to take the bunches of arbutus, balm, and barberry her daughter handed down. "Ella's out late, is she not?" Catherine asked.

"Yes, I think she went into town to see Pete, now that he's back. They hunted today, but I don't think they're allowed to speak while they're about it."

Catherine smiled gently. "That's just as well, as they brought back a fine catch. I was glad of the meat at supper."

Next Catherine handed bowls up to Jenny, who filled them with spiky handfuls of dried marsh mallow and angelica root from a suspended drying rack. They brought the bowls to the big table, where they each took one and set to their grinding.

When they'd worked in companionable silence a quarter hour, Jenny held aloft a twisted piece of dusty brown angelica root to show her mother. "This is an odd duck. Doesn't it recall one of those symbols Ella used to draw when she was young?"

Catherine nodded. Then, thinking further, she wrinkled one side of her nose and said, "Let's not speak of that time, dear. I came to dread every session of lessons at the rectory."

"Because Ella had such trouble?"

Catherine nodded and let out an exasperated breath. "Had trouble and caused trouble. It seemed interminable."

Jenny looked puzzled. "Ella? I hardly think it was her fault the schoolmaster beat her nearly every day of the school session."

"Jenny dear, she refused to speak during lessons for nearly a month. That's hardly a lack of provocation."

"That was only because he took up a page of her symbols and insisted she explain the translation. You know very well how she felt about giving her private language to that terrible man. It was everything to her."

"That may be, but she also refused absolutely to recite her lessons, which led him to the obvious conclusion she never learned them."

"As if she didn't know them by heart," Jenny said with force. "She refused to answer him because he spoke so rudely."

"And what difference should that have made? Children have no say in such things. I swear she was the most stubborn child I ever knew. And he wasn't the only one she came into difficulties with. She was forever getting into fights in the schoolyard. I was doctoring her daily at one point."

Jenny's face took on a pained look. Perhaps, she thought, bringing up the memory of those days was a mistake all around. Certainly those times had changed how she viewed her sister, who had gone from invincible to beleaguered overnight. But also, when she thought on it further, had given her a new kind of respect for Ella, as she herself could never have borne the universal scorn her sister had faced every day. For her boyish clothes and unkempt hair, for the way she raced and played games and ran wild in the woods. Ella had never needed to please everyone the way she herself always had. Ella didn't care what they said or did or thought, not until they blocked her way. Jenny wished she had more of her sister's certainty.

She debated how much to tell Catherine and finally decided it was time her mother heard the truth of it. "The fighting began because something of the master's dislike for Ella breached a dam of cruelty among the rest. Every day in the schoolyard the boys began to tease her mercilessly for all the ways she was unlike the other girls. Until she had no recourse except to fight back as they began to shove and punch at her, until she'd fought every one of them, some more than once—and sometimes two or three at a time. And then the girls kept at it long after, since she couldn't fight them into silence." Jenny paused, blinked a few times, and looked down into the herbs in front of her. "It didn't really stop until she began slipping away to the woods rather than attend lessons."

Catherine gazed at Jenny, her large eyes troubled. At last she said, "I had no idea it was as bad as that. She never complained of it, and you never said a word of it either."

"She made me swear I wouldn't."

Catherine's brow creased in puzzlement.

"She didn't wish to add to your difficulties," Jenny continued. "She thought it would be easier for you to think she was just getting into childish scrapes. All for fun."

Catherine stared at Jenny before crying, "Oh that foolish child. As if I didn't hear of the fights from various busybodies in town, all of whom blamed her for inciting them. But of course they would say that, wouldn't they, seeing as they were unlikely to tell of the cruelty that provoked it. What was she thinking not to tell me?"

"She thought you had enough to worry over. And after a while she had it mastered, at least enough to mostly ignore."

Catherine shook her head. Jenny glanced up at her mother, afraid that she'd now done just what Ella had sought to prevent. "There's no need to fret on it now, Mother, for it turned out well enough in the end. She eventually gained their regard, especially once she took up the engineering with Grandpa. She has friendly relations with most all of them, even the ones who were so mean I can't bring myself to fully forgive them myself. But she doesn't seem to remember or care. Or if she does she doesn't let on of it."

They returned to their work with only an occasional word between them, each absorbed in her own thoughts. When they had filled all the bowls and mortars, they scooped the powders into jars or small muslin bags that Catherine placed into clay pots for storage.

They were putting away the last of the powdered herb when they heard the singing, the unmistakable singing that meant Amherst was returning from a long evening at the tavern. They hadn't heard it in recent years, as the threat of Ella's knife had sent him somewhere else to sleep it off. But here it was, back again. They froze and looked at one another. Catherine's voice was tight when she said, "You go on up to bed, dear. I'll take care of things down here."

"No, Mother. I'm not leaving you alone down here. With Ella out I'll stay right here."

Catherine took a breath to argue, then, looking at her daughter's face, gave a resigned sigh. "Perhaps he'll go to the barn."

They were both sitting in rockers with their stitching on their laps when Amherst came in a few minutes later. As usual he was coated in a fine dust of flour from the gristmill, which lent a ghostly appearance to his otherwise solid frame. He was of middle height, but seemed shorter because of his unusually thick shoulders—derived from years of hefting flour sacks. Unlike his powerful shoulders, his face, which must have once been handsome in a rugged way, had sagged here and puffed there, until he had come to wear an old man's face on a vigorous body.

He had stopped singing, which wasn't good either. When he saw them he said to Jenny, "Go on upstairs now, girl."

"No, Father, I won't," Jenny said, lowering her voice to keep it from quavering.

"Here, Amherst," Catherine said in a soft tone, rising and smoothing her skirts. "I'll fetch you a cool drink from the well. You look worn out. Sit down, won't you?"

"Don't go anywhere," he said flatly. But then he reconsidered and said, "Fine, then, a cool drink. But be quick with it." He settled into his well-worn stuffed chair.

When she'd scurried out the door, there was a silence and then Jenny said gently, "You're troubled, Father. Might I be of assistance?"

He stared at her. His eyes were bloodshot and bleary, and she could see how his nose, shot through with veins, was starting to turn a similar shade of scarlet. His eyes, which had been dark with fury a moment earlier, suddenly looked nothing more than exhausted and she felt the room grow lighter. He shook his head at her offer but said nothing. Catherine returned with a pewter cup, wiping the bottom with her apron as she handed it to Amherst.

He reached for the cup and as he did so Catherine's hand shook and it tipped, spilling icy water into his lap. Her large eyes flashed horror and she took a quick step back, but not fast enough to avoid the heavy backhand across her cheek as he sprang to his feet. "Stupid woman."

Catherine spun away with her hand against her face and Jenny rose and went to her, pulling away the hand to inspect the welt on her face. She didn't know what she expected to see when she looked in her mother's eyes, but it wasn't the plain relief she saw there. The hope that perhaps he'd spent his fury.

And perhaps he may have, except that one of Jenny's rare fits of temper came on and she turned to her father and said, "You should be ashamed of yourself."

For a moment he did look ashamed, but then Catherine said pleadingly, "Jenny, please go on up to bed. It's all right now.

Something in her tone seemed to incense him, for he glared at Catherine through narrowed eyes and took a step in her direction. Jenny said, "No!" But with a startling speed he lunged forward and grabbed her mother by the arm, yanking her around in a semicircle like a half-stuffed rag doll. Catherine found her feet and struggled for a brief moment, but then she seemed to give up and go limp as he took her by the waist and began to drag her toward the front door. Toward the dark night outside.

Before they reached the door, a clattering disturbance made them all look toward the base of the staircase, where a small figure in a long nightshirt was getting to his feet and rubbing his eyes. Jimson blinked a few times and peered around the room. His eyes widened when he saw his mother and father, and then he did something no one expected. Without a pause he took a running leap at his father and managed to propel himself onto Amherst's back, his hands clutching and pulling at Amherst's face and neck as he strove to cleave him from Catherine.

Amherst didn't react at first, then he shoved Catherine to the floor, reached up, and in a single movement grasped Jimson's nightshirt and flung the boy over his shoulder like a tiny sack of flour. The boy flew several feet through the air and landed on the far side of the carpet, where he crashed into the edge of a rocking chair runner with a revolting crack.

Catherine crawled over to Jimson and tried to shield his body with her own. As she cowered there, Amherst began to kick at her head and back and legs with his heavy-toed boots, landing sickening blows that only seemed to increase his furor. He was in full motion now and seemed not to notice or care that his wife had lost consciousness several blows earlier. Amidst her screaming, Jenny suddenly realized her mother could die if she didn't do something to stop him. She broke her paralysis and flung herself at Amherst, trying to push him away. He took a step back and then swung the back of his hand squarely against her jaw, throwing her across the room.

She hit the side of the oak trestle table so hard that the breath left her. As she struggled to regain her breathing, Amherst turned to kick Catherine again and Jenny shoved herself upwards again, croaking "No!" She reached for a heavy mortar and threw it at him. He batted it away. She found another and made ready to throw it. Seeing what she was about to do, he advanced and raised a heavy arm to strike her down. She squeezed her eyes shut and instinctively covered her face.

A flat voice said, "Don't do that."

Jenny's eyes popped open and Amherst spun to see Ella standing with a knife raised, ready to throw. It was aimed at his neck, but Jenny knew that at the last minute her sister would redirect it to somewhere that hurt terribly but would neither kill, maim, nor disfigure him. At least not permanently. Jenny felt a wash of relief. But when she tried to swallow, the bile caught in her throat.

Amherst lowered his arm slowly, glaring at Ella. "Stay out of this, girl. It's between me and them." When Ella didn't move he said, "Put the knife down and be on your way—or it'll be worse for them later."

"Then it will be worse for you later. Much worse." Ella lowered the knife to point at his left knee. "In fact you won't be a danger to anyone you can't catch by crawling."

Amherst's face filled with disgust and he glared at Ella before sending a thick wad of spittle nearly to her feet. He made a last, half-hearted kick toward Catherine as he shambled to the stairs.

THREE

"**T**HERE'S NO POINT in avoiding Aunt Lucille. She's offered assistance and you must take it. Now go." Jenny trundled her sister out the door and pointed her to the back pasture. Ella did as she was told and kept her feet on the path through the trees that connected the back of their pasture with Aunt Lucille's back field. Though it wasn't easy.

Catherine was healing under Jenny's care over the past three days and the swelling on Jimson's head had subsided quickly. A contrite Amherst had slunk off the next morning and remained scarce ever since. By tacit agreement they'd said nothing of the events of that night, but they all seemed to understand that Ella's plans had changed. She didn't speak of it, but a single refrain had begun to play in her mind: *I'm harnessed to this family and this town and I'm going nowhere. Exactly nowhere.*

In her uncanny way Aunt Lucille had seemed to sense something amiss, for she appeared at their house the very next day, while Catherine still looked her worst, and wasted no time in pulling up a chair to her sister-in-law's bedside. They could hear her through the floor as she urged Catherine to bring the children and come stay with her, at least for a few days. They couldn't hear their mother's quiet reply, but they knew very well what she'd be saying. That it was her duty to remain in place, as she always had and always would. For the sake of her children.

After further useless efforts to sway Catherine, Lucille stalked back downstairs to don her Spencer jacket and feathered hat. Attired to leave, she'd given Ella a piercing look and said, "You're going to require assistance to pursue this patent business. Call on me as soon as you're able and we'll discuss the matter."

Ella had nodded but then managed to delay another two days, until this morning when Jenny had refused to countenance her excuses. Her feet lugged her down the familiar path. It may have seemed a short way for her Uncle John when he'd moved from her farmhouse to Aunt Lucille's after their marriage, but to her as a child it had always seemed a long way. Still she'd walked it nearly every day when she was five and six years old, to see Aunt Lucille and Uncle John, and then Baby Gabriel when he was born. For a short blissful time she'd spent every afternoon with Aunt Lucille and the beautiful laughing baby they both adored. Until the terrible day when a Seneca raiding party had lifted the baby from his cradle and taken him away and Aunt Lucille had grown wild in searching for him. Ella had ceased visiting, and when at last Aunt Lucille had returned to herself, or someone more like herself, a coolness had come up between them that Ella could never explain.

The coolness had been breached only once, when she was fifteen. On her fifteenth birthday Aunt Lucille had inexplicably entrusted to her care the gold watch that she herself had previously kept upon her person at all times. For a time there had been more warmth between them, Lucille smiling in pleasure every time she saw Ella with the watch. But then Amherst had nearly taken it and Ella had arrived at the brilliant solution of hiding it in the secret pocket in old Edgar's harness pad. Where minutes after she'd placed the watch, her grandfather was abruptly murdered and Edgar, when she'd at last thought to check on him a few days later, had vanished as if he never existed. Gone...but where? She'd asked herself this question hundreds of times. Edgar hadn't been stolen, for he was of no value and she'd seen the thieves leave without him. But she could find no trace of where he went. He hadn't even been listed among her grandfather's possessions when his will was read.

She should have told Aunt Lucille right away that the watch was gone. But somehow she kept thinking she'd find Edgar and not have to make the confession. She delayed too long, until at last, after elaborate excuses over many months, she'd confessed to having misplaced the watch and her aunt's sharp blue eyes quickly snapped with anger. Lucille had withdrawn and become even more stony cold than she'd been before, such that they'd hardly spoken for most of the past five years.

Only now, Ella thought. *Only now that the invention is solved has Lucille deigned to take an interest in my affairs. I've at last earned her notice.* She shrugged off her thoughts as she neared Lucille's house and felt the urge to slow her feet, to turn around. Instead she kept her back straight as she stepped up and knocked at the door. She'd hardly finished knocking when the door opened and she was looking directly into Lucille's bright blue eyes. She noticed there were new lines on her aunt's face and her hair was turning silver at the temples. Which made her, if anything, more commanding. She wore a well-cut green morning dress with a high neck of sheer lawn, dangling pearl earrings, and an elegant shawl. She looked, as always, as if she belonged in the sitting room of a country estate instead of a simple country cottage.

"Hello, Ella," she said in her regal manner. "Do come in."

Ella followed her into the parlor and took the seat that Lucille indicated. The furniture was tastefully upholstered in pale blue silk with sprigs of creamy white foliage, and the walls were papered with stripes in the same hues. The colors of the room resonated with Lucille's own blue eyes and silvering hair, as if she herself were an element of the fashionable tableau. As usual Ella felt gangly and awkward in Lucille's presence, abruptly aware of her own rough clothes and dirty hair. She wondered if she'd soil the upholstery in sitting on it.

Then, coming here after so long, it occurred to Ella to wonder for the first time how her aunt afforded this elegance. Her husband, Ella's Uncle John, hadn't left her much when he'd died. She'd since become a sought-after seamstress for local gentry. *But what can she make from that?* Ella wondered. She must trade for things and rework them with her clever hands. But still, the furniture looked expensive and so did the fabrics. Circling the room, Ella's eyes came back to rest on Lucille's, which were fixed on her with an intensity of purpose, together with a glint of disapproval.

"What do you have in place for this patent application?"

So much for the niceties of preamble. Ella pushed her shoulders back and lowered her chin. "I have a good set of drawings, together with a description and argument for its novelty—as best I could write it. I had intended to complete the rest in person, at the office in Washington City. Now that my . . . plans have changed, I must apply by means of the post. What more do you know of the process?"

Lucille studied her, and Ella braced herself for the caustic remark that would preface anything useful Lucille might have to say about patents. But when her aunt spoke at last it was to ask an unexpected question. "Are you certain the machine will work on the basis of just the scale model and a set of drawings?"

Ella sat up even straighter in her cushioned chair. Lucille had asked the exact question that had been haunting her own thoughts. Hearing it from someone else felt like salt on a sore, but was also, in an odd way, a relief. At last it had been said.

She shook her head slowly. "No, I'm not certain it will work. I'd rather take more time over it. It's just that . . . well, Grandfather Tunnicliff always said not to dawdle about a patent if you're certain you have a good idea. That you risk it being stolen." She paused. "But of course he also said just as often that you must get it right before you patent, or others will pirate it and then improve upon it." She reached up and squeezed the back of her neck as she looked at the ceiling of the room for a moment. Then she turned back to Lucille and said, "I think I don't know which course of action to follow."

Lucille's piercing eyes pinned her to the fine upholstery of her chair. Ella tried to keep her face clear and strong as, inside, she kicked herself for admitting so much. She braced for the biting wit that would cut the soft underbelly she'd exposed, but instead she heard, "How much time would you require to build a working model of the machine?"

Quickly recovering, she considered the question. "I think it could be done within a month, perhaps even closer to a fortnight if the iron pieces were cast correctly the first time or so."

"Could Pete cast the pieces for you?"

Ella nodded.

"Where might you build it?"

Ella shrugged. "In our barn, I suppose."

"Your barn has little extra room. Wouldn't it be preferable to have it in town, in a place where people might bring flax straw to use in testing the machine?"

"Yes, of course, but that's much too public. I must keep the design to myself until I secure the patent."

"Ah, c'est absurde," Lucille lapsed into the French of her childhood in New Orleans whenever she spoke most quickly. "Your grandfather and his paranoia about patents has you making foolish decisions. Things have changed since his day, and I'm certain Henry Emerston will have no trouble at all in writing you an affidavit that affirms you to be the original inventor.

51

Something very legal-sounding that no one will dare question. Perhaps we might even send that to the patent office in advance of the actual application."

Ella, ignoring Lucille's use of 'we,' said, "I've never heard of such a document. Are you certain it will be uncontestable? Are you certain Mr. Emerston can write one?"

"Yes," Lucille gave a sharp little nod, "in fact he suggested it to me himself. He's my own solicitor, you know. I was asking him what your options might be." Her eyes grew brighter. "I have another idea as well. You could build the machine in his new gristmill. He's built it larger than he needs at present—in fact he has whole rooms he's not using—and it would be ideal for those who are bringing in grain to also bring flax straw for use in testing the machine. Once you have the documents all signed and sealed, of course."

Ella absorbed this news of a legal document that might solve much of her troubles over having the patent stolen. Then she imagined her machine in that bright new mill. A room full of light, the machine humming quietly as it whisked loads of straw into one end and fiber out the other. She could see Jenny sitting in one corner, refining her drawings of the machine with the full-scale model to help her. With a machine that worked well, a strong description, and a good set of drawings, she might send off the application with confidence; it would no longer require that she be there in person to make corrections or explanations.

Lucille said, "Here's what we'll do. You go off and think on what we've discussed. I'll visit Henry Emerston and get more detail on the legal aspects of securing your invention on paper. I can also ask him about using a room in the mill. If he doesn't like the idea, he'll have no qualms in refusing me—I've known him since we were young. You stop in later this evening to see what I've learned. If his offer is attractive, you can go tomorrow to see Emerston yourself and initiate the papers."

ELLA VISITED HER AUNT again that evening to hear what she had learned from Henry Emerston. Then she walked the forest trails for several hours in silent internal debate. She was still undecided on whether she should allow Emerston's involvement when she went to bed, but after a restless night she rose in the morning resigned to at least hear what he had to say.

She took the steps up to Emerston's office on Main Street in one hop, for she was determined not to be timid. He might own half the town now, but her grandfather and his father had been the closest friends and the Emerstons hadn't always lived in the mansion on the hill. The big house and the small army of servants had only come recently, via the success of the man she was on her way to visit.

She opened the door without knocking and found herself face to face with a young clerk at a high table in an ample reception room. He peered at her from above a wide brown cravat. She said, "I've come to see Mr. Emerston. He asked me here."

The clerk blotted his quill and set it in the stand. "Just a moment, if you please." He slid off his stool and disappeared through the door at the back of the room. After a minute he returned and ushered her into the inner office, shutting the door behind her.

The room she entered was like no room she had ever seen; it made Aunt Lucille's parlor look like a tawdry imitation of elegance. She'd had no idea there was such a room in her town. The carpets were deep and luxurious, in all the rich colors of Persia. The walls were hung with fine portraits, interspersed with elaborate bronze sconces. She recognized Emerston's father, Archibald Emerston, in one of the portraits. He'd never appeared so serious and formal when he'd been in conversation with her grandfather. At last she pulled her eyes from the walls and turned toward the man she'd come to see. Henry Emerston sat behind a massive, elaborately carved walnut desk and, despite the magnificence of the room, she could not help but notice that he looked rather small behind that huge desk.

He finished what he was writing, blotted it, and then rose to greet her. "How good of you to come, Miss Kenyon. Please have a seat, won't you?" He ushered her to a red velvet high-backed chair in front of his desk. She sat in it gingerly, again wondering briefly, as she had in her aunt's parlor, whether her clothes would soil it.

They looked at one another, assessing, having never exchanged more than a polite acknowledgement since she'd come into adulthood. Knowing of his many achievements, Ella had prepared for him to be intimidating within a business setting. Instead she found his expression frank and pleasant. His clothing and demeanor all spoke of a neat competence that suited his small stature, dark hair and eyes, and lithe movements. He was, she thought, someone you could trust to accomplish a task in good time.

"I understand from your Aunt Lucille that you'd like to secure your invention by means of an affidavit affirming your primacy as inventor."

"Yes," Ella said quietly, "Lucille said you've assured her it would sway a court if anyone were to try to steal my design. Is that so?"

"Most assuredly," he nodded with confidence. "As long as the document is properly signed and notarized."

"So..." Ella paused to frame her question as clearly as she could. "If I were to have this paper properly signed and notarized, I could build and demonstrate my machine without concern that the patent could be stolen?"

"Yes, as long as you proceed to secure the patent within a reasonable time forthwith." He gestured to a row of bookshelves along one wall. "I followed a case several years ago that tested just this theory, and the court upheld the affidavit as proof of primacy over a competitor who submitted the patent application ahead of the actual inventor. I believe the case was Stevens v. Meikle, tried in the city of Baltimore."

Ella considered this news, then asked, "What would be the cost for such a document?"

Emerston smiled and waved a dismissive hand. "Your money is no good here. My father and your grandfather traded many favors, and this is simply one more in that series. If and when your great invention takes hold, you can repay me then. Or, even better, you will have repaid me many times over if you make Deborahville a source of talk throughout the states. That cannot help but improve business."

Ella found herself smiling back at him. She felt a burden lift from her shoulders and she said, "All right, then. Let's do that." She began to rise, but then thought of something else and sat back down.

Before she could speak, Emerston said, "It's part of the same arrangement. You may use a room in the mill to build and test the machine. I have the space and no use for it as of yet. The only cost is that you send my own pile of flax straw through that contraption of yours, once you have it operating."

"Done," Ella said. "But that wasn't what I was going to ask you."

"Oh? You have another request?"

"Yes I do. I'd like to know what you know of Mr. Oliver Evans, from whom you licensed all your milling machines. My grandfather spoke of him often, and recently I've been wishing to ask many questions of him. He holds patents on all those milling inventions and I understand he now works on steam engines."

"Is that so? I hadn't known that. I'm afraid I don't know much of him beyond the correspondence we conducted regarding the licensing of his machines. I have his correspondence address, though, if you'd like it. Or," he paused, "better yet, if you'd like, I could write to introduce you and your invention prior to your contacting him. He's something of a cantankerous old fellow, I'm afraid."

"Could you?" Ella said, trying not to sound too eager. She had heard the same description of Evans from her grandfather and had been reticent to contact him with no introduction.

"It would be my great pleasure," Emerston said, rising as she did. "I trust this design of yours will be a boon to us all, once you have it working as well as it might. I am only sorry your grandfather didn't live to see it."

"Yes, he would greatly have liked to see it. Thank you, Mr. Emerston, for all..."

"No, no, none of that. My thanks will be to see that machine working. Come back in a few days and I'll have that affidavit written for us to sign, as I am also the town's sole notary public. In the meantime, begin work on the machine at the mill whenever you like. The chief miller will direct you to where to set up."

"All right then." Ella raised a hand in farewell and Emerston came around the desk to usher her out of the office, closing the door behind her.

But before she could exit the outer reception room, the door opened and a tall young man entered and nearly swept into her as he called backward to someone on the street behind him. Emerston's son Lucas turned and said, "Oh, pardon me, Miss Kenyon. I had no idea there would be someone here." He made a small bow and then gave her a blindingly white smile. He was all gold and white and honey brown, with glinting yellow hair and sun-browned skin. He wasn't perfect in feature, but there was something about him that arrested attention, that made it hard to look away.

As always in his presence, Ella felt her mouth go dry and strange sensations begin in her midsection. Fortunately she had long ago grown adept at ignoring her unbidden and embarrassing reaction so as to treat him with relative indifference. For while Lucas Emerston might make eyelashes bat furiously all over town, she was hardly about to join the fracas.

"Good morning, Mr. Emerston," she said in a neutral tone, making to pass by him to reach the door.

She had her hand on the knob when he said, "Wait! Miss Kenyon, wait—I'd like to ask you something."

She turned and lifted a brow slightly. Lucas seemed about to say something but then, to her surprise, he lowered his eyes and a spot of red flushed either cheek. He said, "Oh, it's nothing. You must be on your way. I hear you've got an idea for that machine of yours."

"What were you going to ask me?" Ella asked in a flat voice with a hint of hardness to it. She refused to be shy with him.

Lucas raised one shoulder in dismissal and then held up the wide black book he had in his hand. "It's just my sketching. I'm attempting to learn portraiture and I'm in search of interesting faces to try and, well...you have an interesting face. I've always thought so." He looked straight at her with a faint smile that expected to be pleasing.

Ella bit back the sharp retort that sprang to her lips, for describing her face as "interesting" was no kind of a compliment. But there was nothing to be gained by insulting him in return. Instead she said, "Here, let me see that," and she made a swift grab for the book. Before he could protest, she had squatted to the floor and was turning pages, studying each sketch. She said, "These are nothing like my sister Jenny's. You have a much bolder style."

He squatted across from her, looking at the book upside down. "By that I take it you mean I have little of her skill?"

"Yes, that might be true," Ella agreed, "or rather, you have a very different skill. Jenny takes many more lines to accomplish what you do with a few strokes. When you get it right, that is. I can see here," she pointed to a sketch of a hand, smudged over and redrawn several times, "that this isn't what you intended."

Lucas laughed, a hearty laugh of real amusement. "No, that is hardly what I meant to do." He rose to his feet. "I would give much for your sister's natural skill with ink, but despite my limitations, I do keep trying to get better. My mother always drew, you know, when I was younger."

Ella, rising also and handing back the book, shook her head. "No, I hadn't known that."

"Not anymore of course, now that she has a larger household to run." Then he gestured toward the door of his father's office. "My father would prefer that I too cease with drawing, spend my time at studying law or something else more worthwhile."

Ella drew in a breath at the intimacy of this last remark, but could think of nothing suitable to reply. There was an awkward silence, and then she gestured toward the black sketchbook. "Your father has offered me the use of his new mill for building the model of my machine, so you might find me there if you are yet in need of faces for your book."

He gave her that blinding smile once more and she, fighting down an urge to run, gave him her best roguish wink in return.

FOUR

ELLA WAS HARD ON HERSELF as she walked home from town. What *ever* had possessed her to wink at him like that? And to invite him to sketch her as she worked at his father's mill? What a truly stupid thing to offer. It couldn't help but be a distraction, for even if he never came to sketch her she'd be half waiting for him, wondering if and when he might appear. She'd succeeded so well at putting that young man out of her mind, and now, in the briefest of exchanges, she'd undermined all that resolve. *Next thing you know I'll be following him around and giggling. I deserve whatever my stupidity will incur.* But beneath her anger, she knew she had reasons beyond the usual to react to this young man, who was once a boy with silky gold hair who liked to sleep out in his family's hayloft.

She had hardly noticed him before the night when she was eight and Amherst had come home singing. In those days it happened every few months or so, and rest of the time they pretended it never happened at all. She was the eldest and, other than Catherine, the only one he ever came after. She'd been carefully warned that she must never ever breathe a word to anyone of her father's "poor spells." But her mother would push her out the back door when they heard him coming, telling her to go find somewhere else to sleep. Which usually meant someone else's barn, if it was winter, or in the woods if it was warm.

In the morning she'd come home and sometimes Catherine would have a bruise on her face, sometimes not, but she'd always be mildly cheerful, as if relieved somehow. Amherst always slept until mid-morning at the earliest. When he woke he was all jokes and smiles, sidling up to Catherine when he thought no one was looking.

That night it had been terribly cold and Ella had just kept walking, not sure where to go. She wished she could go to her grandfather at the smith, where it was warm, but her mother forbade it, knowing Grandpa Tunnicliff would come storming over to the house. No, it was best to let her father get it out and be done with it.

So Ella avoided the smith and wandered aimlessly, until at last she found herself at the Emerston farm, where she had been only a few times before. The moon was just a day or two past full and she could see by its light the nice sturdy barn. She climbed up the hayloft ladder and was settling herself into a pile when her elbow knocked against something hard in the hay. She turned and saw the face of a boy peering over at her. He'd been sound asleep and she'd woken him with her elbow.

"What the...? What are you doing here?"

"What are *you* doing here?" she'd asked.

"It's my barn, or my pa's at least. I can sleep here, can't I? What about you?"

"I, I...I like to wander sometimes, at night."

He peered at her with a quizzical look. "Won't your pa get angry if you're not there in the morning, to do chores and such?"

"I'll be there, I wake early." She could have left it at that; it would have been easy. He was already half asleep and would readily have gone back the other half. But something she never understood came over her, and she found herself telling him the truth, the actual truth.

She'd been hiding it for so long she didn't even know she *could* say it, but there it was, spilling out of her mouth all at once. She'd wondered about it many times since. What made her do it? Was it the hour and the unreality of the scene? Like it was a dream and dreams aren't real, so they must be safe. Or the fact that he was so removed from the rest of her life, a stranger, really, for all purposes? Or was it something about his face that night? She never knew. Only she started telling, and once she started she couldn't stop.

Until the tears came, and then she couldn't speak any more for crying so hard. She did all the weeping she'd never done before. Or ever since. She cried her guts straight out of her nose and wiped them on the sleeve of her dress. He just stared at her, then made a futile effort to wipe her face with hay. Then he gave her shoulder an awkward pat and left her to keep weeping as he rolled over to go back to sleep. She cried until she was a used up, worn out piece of old rag. Until she fell over sideways with a splitting headache and hiccoughed every once in a while as she fell asleep.

When she opened her eyes before dawn the next morning, he was asleep next to her with his arm over her waist. She had lifted it as softly as she could, before slipping off to go home. Over the next fortnight she worried continually that he'd tell of what she'd told him and someone would come asking questions. But nothing happened. She managed to steer clear of him at school, where he was a few years older and kept to his own friends, and if they happened to look at one another they quickly turned away. As far as she knew he had never spoken of all she'd revealed. Yet she'd occasionally catch him looking at her from a distance with a faintly puzzled expression that told her he remembered that night.

She shook herself out of her memories. *I must quit thinking of that young man and focus on the work at hand. The work is much more interesting.* She directed her thoughts into the building of the machine, the parts that would form the frame, the pieces that would need to be carved from wood, and those that must be cast in iron. At last, after too much time in distraction, the wood and the iron began to take shape in her mind as she walked, until she itched to feel her hands on the pieces as she wove them together. Wove them into something that would do the work of many hands.

TRUE TO HIS WORD, Henry Emerston had the officious-looking affidavit written when she returned to his office. After reading it carefully, she signed with him as notary witness and watched as he placed the document in an iron strongbox and turned the key. "You may sleep more soundly now," he told her with a slightly smug nod.

Over the next fortnight the pile of parts for the machine grew piece by piece. Ella, with Zeke's help, sawed and planed boards for the frame, turned rollers, and cut miter edges for the pieces of the drum below which they would feed the unbroken straw. The drum would gently work off the outer wrapper of the straw, while the rollers pulled the inner fibers through to the other end of the machine, depositing them onto a platform from which they'd be bundled and removed, ready to be spun into linen.

The design was in many ways reminiscent of the grain thresher from which she had derived her essential idea. As with the thresher, the drum would turn by means of a set of gears attached to a crank arm, much of which required casting in iron because the parts would undergo constant interaction and must not wear down. It was an utterly different design than the one her grandfather had envisioned and worked on so many years, but from the moment she'd first seen it in her mind she'd known it could work.

Pete worked at casting the parts of the crank and gears while Ella and Zeke began to assemble the frame, drum, and rollers. There had been no sign of Lucas Emerston since she'd seen him at his father's office over three weeks ago and she'd finally broken the habit of looking up whenever the main door to the mill opened. When at last the iron parts were all cast and they had the wooden sections assembled separately, it was time to put together the sections and ask the final question: will it work?

As Ella made the last few adjustments to the assembled contraption, Zeke drove his family's ox-cart to nearby farms to ask for donations of retted flax straw to test the machine. As this year's crop was still in the field, he was seeking remnants of last year's harvest and had to visit a number of farms to find it. By this means he did a fine job spreading the word of the machine's readiness for work and the farmers and their families wasted no time in following him back to the mill to watch. Soon there was a crowd squeezing into the doorway of the small back room in which the machine stood.

Ella looked up at the familiar faces all staring at the machine, wondering how it would operate. She felt her throat tighten, making her swallow hard to keep from choking. She knew the crowd would like her to speak, to extol the wonders of the machine as her grandfather would certainly have done. But she could hardly breathe, never mind speak. She swallowed once more to clear her throat, and then, taking a deep breath to steady the thumping in her chest, lifted a swath of flax straw and gestured to Zeke to commence turning the crank. As the drum began to turn, she fit the dark-stained straw into the narrow slot beneath the drum and felt the rollers catch and begin to pull it through. She fit in another handful and then walked around to the other end of the machine to catch a handful as it fell to the platform. What had begun as rough straw, stained with rot, was now bright gold fiber, silky and soft. But it wasn't perfect; there were yet dark patches among the silk. She hardly heard the watching people murmur to one another as she went back to the drum, lifted a tool, and made an adjustment to tilt the drum slightly and also reduce the width of the slot. Then she fit in two more handfuls of straw and watched them work their way under the drum. When she reached the other end of the machine, bright gold flax fiber was once more landing on the platform with the slightest soft sigh.

She inspected it once more, then again returned to adjust the drum. She repeated the pattern several times more, fine-tuning her adjustments, until at last, when she held up a handful to inspect, there were no dark spots; it was only pure gold. She studied it closely, expecting to find something amiss with it, but it was perfect. *Yes*, she thought with quiet pleasure. *Yes*. Then she noticed the people watching nearby and went over to show them. The fiber was silky and clean, as if it had been hatchelled and combed for hours. The people closest took it in their hands and felt it, rubbing it back and forth over their gnarled knuckles to assess its readiness, just as they would when combing it by hand. Then they smiled to one another and passed it to those behind them.

As it moved through the crowd, the buzz of voices rose and Ella heard her name several times. She lifted her eyes and saw Lucas at the back of the crowd, smiling straight at her. Her heart began to race and she felt herself begin to smile in return, but then Zeke called to her and she turned to be lifted in his gleeful embrace, laughing as he nearly pulled her over. "It works, it works. We've done it. *You've* done it." He hugged her one more time and then announced, "I'm going home to get my fiddle. This is worth celebrating."

Others began to crowd in to shake her hand and she smiled and smiled until her cheeks ached and her hand was sore from so much squeezing. Lucas wasn't among them and when she looked for him he was nowhere to be seen. Zeke returned with his fiddle and people cleared the main floor of the mill for dancing. He struck up "Bridget's Waltz" to start and then played on and on as more and more townspeople heard the news and came in to talk of the machine. People went home and returned with food as an impromptu party took shape around her. Everyone wished to know how she'd solved it and she told the story of the grain thresher over and over until she could only stand to give one or two sentences of it.

They would have liked to see the machine operate longer but the supply of retted flax was soon exhausted, though many promised to ret some and bring it for her. It was well into the early morning before she said goodnight to the last of them and straggled home to bed.

LUCAS EMERSTON HADN'T STAYED long the night before, but he was there at the mill the next afternoon. She was startled to find him there, his sketchbook open on his knee when she came in after visiting his father's office. Her mind had been elsewhere as she'd walked in, on what she and the elder Emerston had discussed of the patent application papers he was helping her to draft. She had also been fretting that as of yet there was no reply from Mr. Oliver Evans in Philadelphia, despite a second letter from Mr. Emerston. She greatly wished to question the inventor before submitting her own application.

Recovering herself, she said, "I've just come from your father's office."

Lucas greeted her with a smile, rose, and made a slight bow, before saying, "Yes, I know. I saw you go in. I thought I'd come over and wait for you here." She cocked an eyebrow at this but he seemed undisturbed. "I apologize for not visiting here sooner," he continued as he sat once more and returned his gaze to his sketchbook. "I intended to, but I had several portraits to complete before I was ready to begin another, and then there was a second cut of hay to take and matters on the farm consumed my attention for several days." He tilted his head to one side as he made an adjustment to a sketch in his book, then he looked up at her. "I am intended to be preparing for my entrance to legal studies, but the farm is always more interesting and our steward is glad of the assistance."

Ella did not see that this statement required a response. She felt herself about to be rude as he sat there so confident of himself, so certain she would be pleased by the attention he paid with this visit. Despite this, her innards betrayed her yet again as her heart thumped hard and her stomach began to pitch. To distract herself she looked around the small room until she located the straw broom and then attacked the piles of chaff lining the sides of the machine.

He stood and put down his book. 'Oh, pardon me, I should have thought to do that myself." He went out into the main room of the mill and fetched a bucket and dustbin and returned to assist her.

When they'd straightened the room and she'd dusted and righted the machine, he said, "Well, then, would it be too much trouble for me to do a quick sketch of you?"

"No, I'd rather you didn't," Ella said without taking much time to think about it. "I'd like to get back to work on adjusting the machine and my sister Jenny will be here soon to begin a new series of sketches herself. I don't care to be indisposed with posing at the moment."

"Oh, there's no worry with that," Lucas assured her, giving another easy smile. "I work so quickly that I move from sketch to sketch just to get ideas. There's no need for you to remain still for any length of time. Here," he said when he saw she was about to refuse once again, "let me show you." He turned his book so she could see her own face, come to life with a few sharp strokes of his charcoal. She was flattered then quickly ashamed of herself for it. Abruptly she wished he'd go away.

He seemed to read her expression. "Please, Ella. I mean, Miss Kenyon. I mean no lack of respect. I simply have a wish to sketch you." He hesitated before adding, "I realize I might have offended when I called your appearance 'interesting,' but I assure you that conventional beauty holds no fascination for me. I am much more…intrigued…by the unusual. Please, take it as the compliment I mean it to be, despite my inability to articulate as much." He stopped and she saw he was flushed again, wearing a distinct look of discomfort. She found it difficult to believe he could have any interest in one such as her, yet he appeared sincere. She felt her resolve ebb.

At last she shrugged. "Fine then, but only until Jenny arrives. I hardly need two of you in here sketching at the same time."

He nodded and settled back to work as she, with more will than she could muster for sending him away, determined to ignore him and focused on cleaning and adjusting the machine after yesterday's labors. Thinking of the evening before and how pleased everyone had been with the machine, she caught herself about to hum before she remembered her visitor and remained quiet.

She would have continued to smile as she worked except she noticed something that made her frown: on the newly cast iron gear turned by the crank arm she saw tell-tale signs of wear that should not have been there after a mere hour of use. Perhaps it happened before the machine was adjusted and would occur no further, but it bothered her nonetheless for it signified poor engineering.

She had nearly finished greasing the crank and gears when Jenny rushed in, apologizing for being late. She pulled up with a puzzled look when she noticed Lucas, who closed his sketchbook and stood. "Good morning, Miss Kenyon," he said to Jenny with a slight bow. To Ella he said, "I am grateful for the time you've given me. I hope not to have to bother you again. But . . ." he paused and then smiled widely, "you may need to indulge me one further time as I develop the portrait."

Ella fixed him with something approaching a glare. "I have little need to indulge you even as much as I have already."

Jenny gave her a questioning look when he was gone, but she only shook her head brusquely and said, "You best get to work."

FIVE

"FIVE, TEN, FIFTEEN, twenty, twenty-five, thirty, forty, fifty, sixty..." Lucille Tunnicliff looked up at the sound of footsteps. She stopped counting and stuffed the money under the pillow, then quickly turned and sat on the bed just as the boy's flushed face appeared in the doorway. "What were you counting, Aunt Lucille?" Before she could answer he'd asked, "Can I have a molasses cake? I saw them on the table when I came through the kitchen."

"Have you had your dinner yet? And did you run all the way over here? Why are you so red in the face?"

"I'm on my way back from the mill. Ma said to get back and help with the garden. I'm a little late, though."

"And soaking wet too. Have you been in the river, Jimson?"

He looked down at himself. "Oh no, I'm gonna catch it."

Lucille was already standing and striding across the bedroom. She pulled a shirt from a drawer and handed it to him. "Here's the one I mended after you ripped it in the city. Put it on quickly. I can't do much about the trousers, but if you leave the shirt out it may not get noticed. I'll comb your hair before you go, it's sticking straight up again. Most disagreeable."

Jimson grinned. "Thanks, Aunt Lucille. You're the best auntie ever. Can I have that cake now?"

"I suppose so."

"Can I have two?" He gave her his best winning grin and she rolled her eyes in return. She could rarely say no to him. She was still combing his hair when he wriggled away and made his way to the kitchen for the plate of cakes. She followed and saw him take a bite of a cake and then, oddly, put it back on the plate. He shuffled his feet a moment and then sat down in a chair, looking rather miserable.

"What's the trouble Jimson? Did I neglect the salt in the cakes?" She took a seat opposite him.

The boy shook his head. "No, it's not them that's the trouble."

Lucille waited, but the boy continued to squirm in his chair and say nothing. "Speak, then, boy. Get out whatever ails you."

He lifted troubled eyes and she realized it was up to her to draw him out. "Do you have a pain somewhere?" He shook his head. She took a deep breath and asked, "Is it your father? What's he done now?"

The boy looked, if possible, even more miserable, and she knew she'd arrived at the problem. She opened her mouth to ask the next terrible question when the boy, with a determined wrinkle forming in his brow, interrupted to say, "It's not what he's done, it's what I done. I told him too much."

Lucille, with the curling edges of dread circling behind her, asked in a voice that sounded as if she was working hard to keep from raising it, "Told him too much of what, Jimson?"

The wrinkle in the boy's brow deepened and he hung his head and stared at the floor. At last he said in a tiny voice, "I told him too much…of the money."

She drew in a deep breath and he shrunk down into himself, as if he expected her to strike him. Seeing this, she reached out a hand to cover one of his with her own cool fingers. She forced herself to say, "Never mind, then, Jimson. It'll all be all right. Just tell me what you told him. Was it about our last trip to Albany together?"

He nodded. Then he told her that Amherst surprised him with a trick question that had him replying yes, they did indeed pay for things in Albany with brand new bank notes. "I knew as soon as I said it that I'd gone and made a bad mistake. He looked so pleased all at once."

Lucille considered what he'd told her, her face creased in a frown. Then she looked up and saw his anxious face. "Now, now, no need for you to worry on it any further. I'll take care of it."

"You're not angry, then? You'll still take me with you to Albany? I know you told me I'm not to speak of the bank notes ever. I know I done wrong to tell my pa."

He gave her a look of such pleading, and the tuft of hair standing up from his head made him look so young and help-less, that despite the hard core of anger in her stomach she said, "No, I'm not angry. It was good that you were brave enough to tell me, Jimson. I know it wasn't easy."

He jumped up and threw his arms out to hug her and she felt the core of anger shift and loosen. She must have been mad to trust a boy with a secret, but that was her own fault, not his. He was just a boy, after all. But still, as many times as she had reminded him . . .

Jimson finished hugging her, then turned and grabbed two cakes with a grubby fist as he darted out the back door.

Through the window she watched him sprint across her back field at his usual flat run, eating a cake as he made for the well-worn path through the woods connecting their houses. When he fumbled a piece of cake and dropped to his hands and knees to look for it, she snorted an unladylike laugh which she was grateful no one was present to witness. He apparently found the cake, as he hopped up and bounded off again. As usual she had a moment of imagining her own baby, Gabriel, at Jimson's age. Of course he would be closer to Jenny's age by now, if indeed he were still alive. But she couldn't even imagine him that far grown; Jimson's age was as far as she ever got.

THAT EVENING SHE FINISHED her small supper and tidied the dishes. Then she changed into a walking gown and short jacket, but for once left her head bare. She crossed the length of the field behind her house and found the path at the far end, leading the opposite way from the one Jimson had taken. The path twisted and turned around larger trees, and she was glad the spring mud of the low spots had finally dried solid by this time in July. She inhaled the sharp spice of pine needles and the milder scents of earth and rotting leaves. The smells she never knew as a child raised in New Orleans, but had come to relish in her many years as a transplanted northerner.

Soon the path emptied into a little clearing at the back edge of her property. The clearing was lush emerald green with ferns, interspersed with occasional moss-covered stones rising up from beneath the ground. At the far side of the clearing sat a small building of saplings bent to make a rounded roof, then covered with a thick layer of bark that shed water. It was an Oneida longhouse, except that it was more round than long— for it sheltered only one person. Her breath caught when she saw the flicker of firelight in the doorway of the house, meaning Pete was home.

How silly she was, after all these years, to feel nervous to see him. He'd been returned from his travels for several weeks now, but until tonight she'd resisted an evening visit. She hardly knew herself if she was trying to wean herself of him, or punish him, or she'd only been too afraid, hiding from some nameless fear. Somehow she had been able to resist and then, tonight, after Jimson's confession, no longer.

He'd heard her approaching long before she reached the house, probably long before she reached the clearing itself. She'd never surprised him. Not once. She stepped to the doorway and looked in to meet his eyes. After a moment she said, "May I come in?"

He'd already begun boiling water, for she loved the Labrador tea that he brought back from his rambles to the northlands. He kept a cache of dried leaves just for her.

She sat on one of the rough wooden benches he kept for use by company, as he himself always sat cross-legged on a blanket on the ground. They didn't speak until he'd handed her the cup of tea. Then he sat back on his blanket, picked up his knife and the piece of wood he was carving, and said, "So. You come to see me. It is good. You visit Albany while I was gone?"

She gestured yes and proceeded to tell him of her most recent trip to the fabric merchants in Albany, where she purchased the fine goods to make the gowns, gloves, and jackets she sold to wealthy ladies throughout the region.

"The boy, he did well?"

"Oh yes," she smiled. "He's a delightful traveling companion. He always manages to point out something I've never noticed before. And you should have seen him at the theater. Watching his face was as entertaining as watching the performance." She closed her eyes a moment, remembering the evening in the sparkling theater, the silks and satins and pearls. The high turbans with every color feather. She was so absorbed in the memory that when she opened her eyes she was startled to find herself in the close, smoky lodge, sitting on a rough wooden seat. She looked down at her own oldest boots. Then she looked up into the twinkling eyes of the man who was watching her closely, apparently amused by something. The harsh planes of his broad face gleamed reddish in the light of the small cook fire in the center of his lodge.

He said nothing of what amused him, but continued carving wood and asking more polite questions of her trip, her health, her business. She answered him with equal pleasantness, knowing he would take his time arriving at wherever he meant to go. She told him nothing of Jimson's confession, for the comfort she sought was not to be found there. She attempted to ask him of his own trip, but as usual he gave only the briefest of answers, and as usual she ceased trying after a short effort.

Finally he asked, "You meet a handsome stranger in Albany?"

She looked at him steadily. "Hardly. Especially as I traveled with a nine-year-old boy whom everyone assumed to be my son."

"Hmph. No mind." His eyes twinkled again. "No one handsome like me."

"Nor as modest. No matter how long and hard I might search," she retorted, the joke well-worn but still of use.

He looked at her in his piercing way. Then he surprised her. Very very gently he said, "Been long time, Lucy."

He hadn't called her that in years. Her eyes prickled and threatened to fill. To avoid it she snapped at him, "You've been away much more than I have. Rambling north and south and wherever else it is you go. Hunting some, I suppose, but visiting more often I would bet. I don't ask you of the women you visit."

After a pause he said softly, "I always come back." Then he beckoned to her. "Come." She hesitated only a moment before she rose and went to sit by him. He reached over and stroked her cheek with a rough finger. His black eyes met her bright blue ones, and he said, "You still sunrise to me."

Her eyes pricked again. She peered hard into his black eyes, unveiled for the first time in a long, long while. Suddenly she could feel her heart thumping and she looked away from him. "Well, you still smell like a billy goat to me. It's a good thing you're so ... handsome."

He laughed his silent laugh, a great rumbling eruption that came up from his belly and went on for a long time. She smiled, ignoring the flush that was burning her cheeks and making its way down her body. She could not explain what it was about him that made her burn as she did. That made her hands itch to touch him. She only knew it as a chord ancient and deep, over which she had little to say.

When his laughter died down, he smiled at her with those large teeth, so striking against his dark skin. "Billy goats know to make lady goats happy."

She felt the heat begin to pulse within her. "Well it's no wonder you smell like that, then."

SIX

ELLA RAISED HER HAND to squeeze her neck again. She took a few deep breaths and then once again turned her attention to the machine. She *had* to discover where the problem lay, why that gear continued to wear and the machine clogged and ceased to work. Pete had re-cast the pieces twice already, but the problem was not with poor casting, but rather with poor design. There *must* be a way to position the sections that would reduce the friction. She studied the crank arm and gears, then she had an idea and began to take the pieces apart. Several steady hours of work later, it was back together with a slightly different configuration.

Wiping her hands on a rag to remove the grease with which she'd lubricated the gears, she happened to look down and notice that her green homespun shirt was nearly as dirty as the rag. Without thinking much about it, she pulled her arms in from the sleeves and spun the shirt around, for it had a simple neck and could be worn either way. Below it she wore an old pair of dark grey linsey trousers that she'd swiped from her father and cinched at the waist. Her mother was horrified that she went about town in such clothing, but she simply couldn't abide skirts that made it impossible to do all she needed to do. At least the trousers were dark enough not to show the grease on them.

The remainder of the mill was utterly quiet today, as everyone from up and down the valley was attending the barn raising at the Purdy farm. She'd seen them all traipse through in the morning, wearing their Sunday finery, but now, in the middle of the afternoon, the silence in town had become almost eerie. But she was glad of the quiet as she prepared to try the machine once more, for she hardly needed an audience for her troubles.

She took a deep breath and faced the machine once more. Then she picked up several handfuls of dark retted straw and fed it into the machine as she began to turn the crank. All at once the crank arm seized up and refused to turn. She jiggled it, and it loosened up and turned one more rotation before catching on something and seizing even more tightly, so she could not even move it. She flipped up the panel to reveal the gears and, to her disgust, saw that several teeth were mangled and the crank arm shaft looked bent.

She smashed a fist down on the panel and then spun away. She pointed her face to the ceiling and reached up to squeeze her neck so hard that she made vicious red marks. *I'm out of ideas. I've gotten this close and I might as well be right back where I goddamn started. I've failed at it, Grandpa. If you were here you'd think of how to fix it because you were always better with these kinds of problems. But you left me to do it alone and I have no more ideas.*

Without thinking about it, she let her feet take her out of the mill and down the road that led most quickly out of town. She tried keeping her mind blank, but images of the machine kept appearing unbidden—including visions of the mangled teeth and bent shaft that made her flinch. She walked at a furious pace for several miles. It wasn't until she finally slowed down and ceased breathing in great huffing breaths that her thoughts cleared. She'd let herself get too angry, too unbalanced. The difficulties with the machine were not unsolvable; she must come at the trouble from another angle and a solution would present itself. She'd already solved the piece that was harder by far. *In comparison this is nothing,* she told herself. But when she probed at the puzzle in her mind, her thoughts twisted and gnarled like the mangled gears and bent shaft. *It will take some time,* she told herself at last. *I require a fresh idea, and those never come when I seek them too hard.*

From over the hill to her right, on the road leading back to town, she could hear voices. She paused, for it sounded like cheering. She realized she'd come upon the barn raising and one of the games of sport that attended such events. *I could use a match to clear my mind,* she thought as she turned to take great loping strides up the hill.

The sport proved to be not a ball game but a race of sorts, across the aging rope bridge that connected the Purdy farm fields on either side of this wide, shallow section of the river. Long replaced by a sturdier bridge upstream, this one had fallen into disrepair and was used only by an occasional child or hired hand with a need to reach a distant field.

Ella, approaching from downstream such that she could see the span of the bridge, noted it was fraying and broken in several places. Anyone crossing it must be not only able, but willing, to swim. She studied the crowd of boys and young men, with a few daring young women among them. She saw that several of the young men were dripping wet.

As she watched, two young men lined up to begin a race and she felt that aggravating flutter inside at the sight of Lucas Emerston's tall, bright head. Opposing him was a young man unfamiliar to her, likely from a neighboring town.

The bridge was suited to this kind of race in being unusually wide, both in width and also in length, but not especially high above the river. There was room to pass one's opponent, but not without the opponent reaching out to introduce impediment. Lucas and his opponent matched stride for stride for a few yards, but then his opponent lost his balance and grabbed at the rope railing to right himself. He made a few more yards before his foot slipped and he found himself dangling from the bottom of the bridge, laughing as he dropped into the slow-moving water below him. Lucas, meanwhile, loped across in graceful strides and was greeted by cheers and back slaps amidst the crowd on the other side. She saw one young man gesture to another to pay up on his lost bet.

Ella moved closer and found a comfortable seat against a tree above the river, from which she had a fine view of the bridge. The day was bright but not too hot, with a sweet breeze wafting here and there. She was grateful to be here outside, amongst happy voices, away from the dusty mill and godforsaken machine. She watched several more uneven matches, including one that Zeke won easily, and then she smiled as Zeke and Lucas lined up to race. *This should be a better match.*

They took off fast, each focusing on keeping his feet moving between the swinging sections of crisscrossed rope that formed the floor of the bridge. Lucas was half a head taller and perhaps the more graceful, but Zeke was wiry and fast and had rock solid balance. They were abreast of one another at the midway point, and even beyond, but then they reached the point at which the bridge had decayed nearly to threads and only small pieces of newer rope held it together. At this point the race inevitably got more interesting if both opponents remained in the contest. They jockeyed for position, each trying to reach the dicey section first so as to get the better footing. Ella could see Zeke was stepping hard to make the bridge swing harder, hoping to send his opponent off balance. Lucas did bobble and Zeke pulled ahead, managing to cross the threadbare section first. It looked like he would win without much trouble, but then Lucas did a risky thing: he began to sprint the remaining length of the bridge without looking down, trusting his instincts to find his footing. He reached Zeke and they tussled briefly as he made to pass him, but then his greater weight and momentum carried him past and he leapt the last few feet, reaching the end first.

Ella, having stood to get a better look, was now striding toward the bridge. She hadn't thought about who she favored in the race, but found herself upset to see Zeke beaten. There was a shout nearby and her brother Jimson appeared in front of her, his hair wild as usual. He grabbed her hand with an iron grip and pulled her quickly toward the bridge.

"Look who I found," he announced as he located Zeke on the far side of the crowd.

Zeke smiled, looking all red, white, and blue with his curving red lips, flushed fair skin, and dark blue eyes. "Good work," he said to Jimson.

"I know," Jimson nodded, grinning widely. "You collect the wagers while I talk up the race."

Ella frowned. She couldn't see being their racehorse to take on Lucas. But then again, she'd watched his technique so she had the advantage. And she liked nothing more than a race. But not in front of all these people. She'd only ever raced in the back pastures with Jimson and Zeke and Pete and the few other boys they'd corralled from neighboring farms. Which meant no one else knew what she could do.

"I get half," she said firmly. Jimson argued briefly, but found he had little leverage over her refusal to race otherwise. He at first had trouble pitching the race, everyone laughing when he proposed that a girl race next. It was only when he convinced them there was easy money to be made by betting on Emerston against the girl that they began to lay their wagers.

Jimson persisted in selling the race until he'd created a whirl of anticipation that traveled all the way back to the main host of the barn raising. When Ella at last found herself standing next to Lucas at one end of the bridge, the crowd had swelled to nearly twice what it had been. Ella felt the usual disarray in her insides when Lucas was near but for once she wasn't sure if it was his proximity or her sudden nerves about this race. Perhaps he had the greater advantage in having run it several times already. She wouldn't know until it was already too late.

A breeze arose as she stood next to Lucas, waiting for the signal to start. Zeke yelled, "Give me five more minutes," as boys and men continued to press in to lay wagers, the word going around that there was easy money to make. Her body tingled from fingers to toes with a mix of nerves and pent-up energy from earlier in the day, from the urge to dispel her frustration with action. And standing next to Lucas so long was beginning to make her perspire; she wanted to be off.

At last there was a countdown and a shout of "Go!" She bobbled right off as she got a feel for the swaying ropes, and he pulled ahead. Soon she had more control and began moving faster, springing from rope to rope. She gained on him and thought to overtake him, but then realized he was likely to try that reckless sprint again, which would mean a dead heat to the finish—and he'd be faster with his greater height. No, she must use surprise to her advantage; she'd have to time her surge for that perfect instant when he'd have no time left to react. Which meant she must bide her time, let him think she was working hard to keep up.

She saw him glance back once, and grimaced in evidence of the effort she was making. She saw him slow slightly and thought, *Oh no, don't do that, I don't want to win like that.* She sped up, swinging the bridge to make him aware of her approach, give him a warning. He sped up as well and she began to think it would be close but she'd just make it work. When they'd passed the halfway mark, she pulled closer to be ready for her surge. Until she could smell him, and could have easily reached out and grabbed his shirt. She was just about to make her move as they came upon the rotted stretch, when there was a sudden snapping sound and his foot broke a rope and went through the bottom of the bridge.

His body twisted down through the strands, and he only just caught a hold of a solid section of railing to keep from plunging straight into the river. Ella had time only to twist away so she didn't pummel straight over his falling body. As she swiveled, her own foot broke the last strands of rope in a poor spot and she too was now dangling from a fragile piece of rope, reaching out with her other hand to find something to keep her from falling. Her hand found Lucas Emerston. As she spun toward him, she saw his face register surprise as she groped a handhold on what she reached first, which happened to be a central section of his trousers. She let go, but it hardly mattered because at that moment the entire bridge severed in two and she and Lucas were thrown together in a thick web of rope that plunged into the river.

Pulled under the water, she kicked against the rope that snarled her legs, struggling to make her way up to breathe. When she surfaced, Lucas was nearby, sputtering, and then, when he saw her, laughing. He swam toward her. "Are you all right?" She nodded, her ears ringing from her awkward impact with the water. He grasped her arm to pull her to shore. Many hands reached for them as they made their tangled way to the shore. When she had shaken the water from her ears she heard the din of voices arguing over the wagers that were made. Jimson's shrill voice was maintaining that Ella was about to pull ahead and win and thus the contest was hers, while others maintained that Lucas was ahead and thus the contest was his, and yet others were calling all bets off and insisting their money be returned. The din grew louder and Lucas stepped toward Ella. "Here, you've got pieces of rope in your hair." In their sudden intimacy he picked them out, one by one. Then he said, "This will seem odd, but I'd like to walk you home. May I?"

She opened her mouth to refuse, but then a stronger instinct seized control of her tongue and she heard herself saying, "Yes, there's about to be a fight. Good time to go."

"Let me just get my things," he said, sprinting toward a cluster of trees a few hundred yards away.

"I WOULD HAVE WON, you know," she said, walking next to him with a light, springy step as they made away from the rising roar behind them.

"Is that so?"

"I was about to pull ahead," she assured him. Then, seeing he still looked skeptical, added, "You would have had no time to catch me. I had it all timed out."

He looked at her as if about to say something politely indulgent, but then he peered a little more closely into her face. "You're quite serious, aren't you? You meant to win." Then, after a pause, "I had no idea...that..."

"I was such a fine racer," she finished for him, smiling to show she joked. He smiled back, his eyes lit with...what? *Can he really be admiring me?* She took another few light steps, as if she bounced more than walked. She glanced upward into the vivid deep blue sky, unbroken by clouds. Until...way across the sky, she saw a wisp of one. She pointed to it. "There, see that? That's my favorite cloud." She turned to him with snapping eyes, daring him to ask why.

He smiled his blinding white smile, his eyes warm on hers. "And why would that be?"

She looked at the little cloud again. "Because it's the only cloud in the world. It's perfectly unique. The only one of its kind." Then, after a pause, she added more soberly, "And it's all alone up there."

She felt Lucas look sharply at her profile as she continued to look at the cloud. Then he said quietly, "You won't always be alone."

She turned to him and met his eyes. "Yes, I will." Then, her grey eyes softening, "But perhaps not this minute."

They turned away, the air between them full of life and light, and walked a bit in joy of it. At last he asked, "How is the machine performing, now that you've run it more? Are you satisfied with it?"

She nodded, and then she shook her head. "The truth is...no, I'm not pleased with it—it doesn't work as it should. There's too much friction in one of the joints. I must determine how to reduce it, but now...actually, I don't care to think of it any more just now."

She took a light skipping step and glanced up at him. He grinned at her and then they looked away from one another again. After a few more steps he reached over and took her hand. The sensation was unexpected, his hand feeling warm and rough, and her own beginning to tingle. She felt suddenly shy and didn't know what to do next. After a minute she twisted out of his grip and playfully grabbed his sketchbook from under his other arm. She danced out of his reach as he made to grab it back, heading for a boulder beside the road. In one bound she leapt up onto the boulder and sat to open the book.

She recognized his sister and his mother, his cousin, another local girl, and then, there she was, her own face. Sketch after sketch of herself, some a few lines, others more detailed. Some better than others. Then, in the midst of the portraits, her eyes were jarred by a sketch of something completely different. There were squares and circles, a frame and a drum and a set of rollers. It was the machine.

She froze, staring at it with little comprehension. Then she held up the book to show him, her eyes posing the question. Why?

85

His eyes flickered something that made her stomach wrench. Could it be fear? Why would he be afraid? Her mind whirled. Then, like a design for a machine, the pieces clicked into place. He had drawn her machine. Without asking. In secret. While he was supposed to be drawing her face. Was the entire sketching-her-face business a pretense for sketching the machine?

"It's not what you're thinking, Ella. It wasn't like that. It was just a whim. All those beautiful lines and circles there, waiting to be put on my paper. I couldn't help myself."

"Why didn't you ask me?"

He shrugged, looking faintly ashamed. "I knew you'd say no."

"You're right. I would have." Her voice was cold.

He raised his hands and then dropped them again, his eyes taking on a faint hint of pleading. "Ella, you must understand. It wasn't intentional. I found my hand making the sketch with hardly a thought—the lines were so enticing. I couldn't stop myself."

"Did you show this to your father?"

"What? No, of course not. Why would I do that?"

Ella stared at him, evaluating. Then she said, "Can I have this, then?"

"Have it? Yes, of course, take it out of there. Rip it to shreds if you like. It's no good anyhow."

"That's not so, I'd say it's quite good. You're much better than you make out to be."

He gave her a piercing look. "You mean that?"

"I don't give false compliments."

She slid off the boulder and landed next to him. She opened the book once more, flipped to the sketch of the machine, and carefully tore it from the book. She studied it. "You know, you've captured an aspect of the design that I don't believe I've described well in the patent application papers. I'd like to amend it while it's fresh in my mind. May I have the key to your father's office?"

SEVEN

ELLA MADE HER WAY silently down the dark streets of the town, keeping to the shadows. She stopped every few minutes to listen, to be certain she remained unobserved.

At last she reached the steps leading up to Emerston's office on Main Street, and, after looking around once more, left the shadows to make her way to the door. From her pocket she took the key she'd wrested from Lucas earlier in the day and slid it into the lock, which turned with a click. Lucas hadn't wished to help her get inside but she'd bullied him into yielding his key as a means of asserting his innocence.

Once inside she stopped and listened carefully. Hearing nothing, she made her way to the door of the inner office, at which she reached up and felt over the door for the spare key she'd heard would reside on top of the door frame. This one also turned with a click and she returned it to where she'd found it.

Inside the dark office she ran her hands over the walls until she reached a wall sconce. From her pocket she pulled out her flint and lit the wicks of the branch of candles. They cast a flickering light. Now she must find the key for the strongbox, which Lucas hadn't been able to help her with. He wasn't even certain his father kept the key in the office, but she had seen Henry Emerston take it out from somewhere when he first unlocked the box to put the affidavit into it.

At the big walnut desk she slid open the top drawer and felt around inside. She tried the other drawers. She looked beneath the items on the desktop, but nothing covered a key. She peered behind the sconces on the wall, behind the books on the shelf, and even under the edges of the carpets. Nothing. She sat in Emerston's massive leather chair and looked around. If she were he, where would she put the key? She looked left, and then right. Then she looked behind her and noticed a pipe stand on the deep windowsill. It was in rather easy reach of the chair. She lifted it, but nothing was below it. Then she brought it closer to peer at it, and sure enough, sitting flat on the base of the stand, in a depression that lay beneath the bowl of a pipe, was a small key.

The strongbox itself was in plain view on a lower bookshelf and she lifted it onto the desk. Slowly she fitted the key, which slid perfectly into the lock. The first pile of papers held nothing of interest to her, so she put them aside. Below them she was startled to find several sheets of bank notes. Brand new ten-dollar notes on the Bank of the United States, still uncut. She took them out and put them aside. Next was a pile tied by a string that quickly caught her attention. There on top was a letter from the Superintendent of the Office of Patents in Washington City, addressed to Mr. Henry Emerston.

Below the letter was a full set of drawings, showing every perspective on the machine. She recognized the hand, as it was the same she'd studied earlier in the day. How could he have done all these perspectives and still had time to draw her? As soon as she asked the question, she felt a perfect fool. He came back of course. Or he'd been there before. It was his father's building; he could come in any time he liked. Draw as many as he cared to. Perhaps his father had sent him. Perhaps he'd been drawing the machine from the moment she began building it. The bigger question was why he'd bothered to draw her at all, as he hardly needed the ruse. Could there have had some other interest in that? *No, I've been enough of a love-addled dupe already. It's high time to cease.*

She put down the drawings and looked back into the strongbox. The next paper in the stack was entitled "Application for United States Patent," followed by a description of an invention identified as "A Machine for the Processing of Flax Straw into Linen Fiber." Below this was a brief description of the machine, and then the name and signature of the applicant. The name was Mr. Henry Emerston, Esq.

There was no sign of the affidavit she had signed and he had notarized. Had he burned it the moment she'd left the office? In fact her own name was nowhere to be seen. Not on the application. Not on the letter to the patent office. Not on the plans. She was removed—wiped clean away.

A buzzing beat of anger began to thrum in the back of her mind like the far-off drumming of a grouse. It grew louder and more distinct as she folded the drawings and the application papers and slipped them into her tunic. *That weasel. That crook. And I trusted him? He's made a perfect fool of me.* She swallowed the bolus of self-disgust that rose in her throat and stared at the pile of brand new, uncut bank notes. *Should I take them too? Why not steal from a thief?* She studied them for what seemed a long time, and then, with a disgusted shake of her head she thrust them back in the box and locked it. She returned the key to the pipe stand. Then, she reconsidered and picked up the key and put it in her pocket. *Make him work to get back into that box.* She blew out the sconce, left the inner office and locked it. Then she exited the building and locked the door behind her. *With any luck*, she thought, *he won't immediately see I've been here.*

She began to walk home, her mind whirling with all she'd learned. Then she had a thought that stopped her in her tracks; she turned and made her way silently back into town. She slipped to the door of Emerston's gristmill and reached to slide open the door, which was never locked for no valuables were kept inside. She slid into the building without a sound. It was a moonless night and very dark in the mill. She heard the scuffle of mouse feet as she navigated by memory around the features of the ground floor. She reached the back room where her machine resided and stopped in the doorway. As her eyes adjusted to the dark, she could begin to make out the shape of the machine. She felt around in a pile of supplies and located a candle stub, then took out her flint to light it. When she had the candle going, she peered around at the piles of chaff and straw littering the room from when she was here earlier in the day, fighting with the machine. It felt like a lifetime ago.

It occurred to her that she could toss the candle in a pile of straw and that would be all it needed. Raze the whole mill. Serve him right. But then she thought of George, the chief miller, and his seven children, and how he'd be out of work, and she tightened her grip on the candle.

She considered her options; then she left the room and headed toward the back of the mill. The back door led to a side yard where George kept a pile of kindling for feeding the Franklin stove in the winter. On a set of hooks under an eave of the building, she located the heavy splitting maul and carried it back into the mill.

It took only a few strokes to bring the machine to the ground, but once she was started, she couldn't make herself stop. Not until the axe was slicing all the way through to the floor because she'd reduced the rest to slivers and twisted bits of iron. She was panting hard, but as she viewed the wreckage a sense of release flowed over her, to be free of the problems of the machine for even a short time.

She looked up at the sound of something and it occurred to her that she'd made an unholy din just now. She listened, and then, hearing the direction of the voices, dropped the maul, slid to the small window across the room, ripped off the oilskin covering, and squirmed her way out. She was down the road in the shadows by the time the first light of the torches could be seen in the windows of the mill.

A LATE CRESCENT MOON rose at last and lit her way as she walked. On and on she walked, her mind racing with a jumble of thoughts. She tried to focus on forming a plan, but her thinking was warped time and again by her shock and fury at what Emerston had tried to do. At what he was capable of doing. It was not that she hadn't thought there was deception in the world, Lord knows she had lived all her life with enough of it at home. But she'd never before known such pure deviousness. Such planning for bad, masked by a face of good. This was new. Of course her grandfather had warned her of it. Time and again he'd told her to trust no one when it came to the machine. She'd tried to follow his advice; she'd done all she could to protect herself with the affidavit. The mistake was leaving it in his possession. That was her undoing.

After hours of walking, she was certain of only one thing: that she owed it to her family to do her best to get the patent and she could no longer stay in Deborahville and pursue it from a distance. She must go to the source and secure it before Emerston devised a new means to steal it from her, despite that he no longer had a set of drawings nor a machine to take them from. It was difficult to see how he might make the application without the drawings—and she didn't see how anyone, even Lucas, could draw that detailed a set from memory alone—but she felt certain he would not give up without more of a fight. Especially as he was no longer hampered by hiding his intentions.

As much as she'd like to travel by herself, she could not leave her mother and Jenny and Jimson behind, so they'd have to come with her. Except she could not imagine her mother agreeing to this, so she'd have to try to convince her. They'd head toward Washington City and she'd pray to solve the remaining design flaw somewhere between here and there. Perhaps travel would open her mind to a new idea.

Well after midnight her feet took her at last to the one place she had always been safe; she walked across the clearing to Pete's cabin. He had heard her coming and greeted her with a nod, gesturing to the kettle of water heating on the coals. "What tea you like?"

"I've woken you. I'm sorry."

"Don't be sorry. I see you have big worries. You need big cup of tea."

Her mouth twisted into a rueful half-smile. "Yes, tea should solve my worries. Do you have any more wintergreen?"

She recounted what had happened, telling him of the problem with the machine, then of the race across the bridge, the discovery in the sketch book and then the strongbox, ending with the conclusion she had reached: that she must leave at once to make for the patent. The only part she omitted was the way she'd behaved with Lucas Emerston, for she couldn't bear to speak of that.

He was silent as he considered her reasoning. Then at last he nodded firmly. "I will come with you. Help protect the children. Get you started on right path. You likely get lost if I not come."

Ignoring the twinkle in his eye that said he was looking for a mock argument, she began to argue in earnest, to list all the reasons he could not leave with them, all the ways they would be fine without his help. He'd already given her so much, she could not ask this of him too. Then she peered into his face and saw that her words moved him not at all, that he'd made a decision and there was no point in arguing. She knew he'd only track her if she tried to leave without him. It was what she herself would do, wasn't it?

She looked at him, knowing she would never begin to repay his many kindnesses. But then she let herself imagine undertaking the trip alone, with Jenny and Jimson and perhaps her mother, and saw how welcome it would be to have his company. He who had traveled every inch of these hills and valleys over many years. But he already knew this, didn't he?

"All right," she told him. "You win. We leave as soon as we can make ready."

PART TWO

August 1810

EIGHT

THEY PASSED THROUGH the next town south as the sun rose above the hills, unfurling beams of gold light onto the walls of the valley. Deborahville receded behind them and Ella felt her spirits rising with the sun. Could it be true that she'd left that hateful house where she'd been trapped all these years? Where that man lumbered home every night?

Then she thought of her mother, still trapped there, and her spirits sagged. They had made a mighty effort to convince her to come with them, but there hadn't been much time and she saw it as her duty to stay. As for Jenny and Jimson, she'd agreed to their leaving once Ella made her see they'd be safer, even out on the wild roads—and that Pete would help protect them.

Once it had been decided, Catherine had remained awake after Amherst snored in his bed to pack up their belongings and whatever food she could find. Then, closer to morning, but while the night was yet black, she had helped Ella usher Jenny and Jimson straight from their beds to the waiting horses. When they were ready she made the briefest of goodbyes, her large eyes hooded and unreadable, and then turned to go back inside.

Ella, thinking of it now, could only marvel at her mother's courage. To turn and go back into that dark house, alone. Knowing that when the sun rose it would be oddly quiet, and it would stay that way. At least until her father noticed their absence. She could not bear to think of what this day would be like for her mother. Or the next, or the one after that. Those big, childlike eyes would be empty and dull with the effort of refusing to cry.

Her body gave an involuntary twist and she willed her mind to go blank, turning her eyes to the green hills as they filled with color in the spreading morning sunlight. She swayed with the steps of Dapper Dan beneath her, then glanced behind to look at Jimson and Pete, riding together on Pete's chestnut roan. Jimson's hair, ruffled from sleep, stood in the air, and he looked to be at most half awake. Behind her own back she felt Jenny stir. When they'd first ridden away in the dark, Jenny had leaned her cheek against Ella's back and gone back to sleep, in part to escape the parting they'd just made. Which Ella had understood perfectly. Now she was stirring awake and Ella knew it would be as difficult a day for her as it would be for Catherine.

They rode a little farther and then, despite herself, it happened again; she felt a bolt of pure joy run through her. She was free. Freedom. Liberty. Those words had meant little in schoolhouse lessons on George Washington and his war, on the struggles with the British. She hadn't *felt* the words. Now, all at once, she knew what the words meant: they were something that happens in your bones when you emerge from underneath something heavy. The urge to leave her father's house had been powerful, but she hadn't actually known what it would *feel* like. That it would have the sense of flight, of a bird pinned to the earth suddenly released to the sky.

She tried to hold on to it, to savor the sense of floating, like a swallow on a breeze, but too soon it was pushed out by thoughts of her mother and also of the tasks ahead of her. As much as she'd dreaded the paperwork of applying for the flax patent, she now longed for the task to be as simple as that of negotiating her way through the unfamiliar terrain of papers and clerks and doing it faster than Emerston. At least that path would be easy to see. She might not care for it, but she could tackle it with energy and direction. Instead, endlessly complicating everything, was the nagging fact that the machine still didn't work, that the design wasn't ready yet. Which, when she boiled it down, left her with the no-win options of either patenting an imperfect machine faster than Emerston or else holding off to improve it and risking that Emerston would beat her to it.

If only she hadn't confessed to Lucas that the design wasn't ready, which was as good as confessing to his father. If only she'd kept that card close to her chest instead of blabbing it in a moment of ridiculous flirtation. In doing so she'd given Emerston the means to hope for the delay he needed, which made her own choice all that much harder. Her disgust with her own poor judgment left the most bitter taste in her mouth, making it all that much harder to think clearly. *I am so supremely unsuited to this task, Grandpa. I fail at every turn. Couldn't you have left me to the woods where my instincts are sound? I don't belong in this role of pursuing the patent. This was supposed to be your work, Grandpa—why aren't you here to make it a shared adventure instead of a chore?*

THEY RODE SOUTH ALL THAT DAY, not setting an overly hasty pace but also not stopping for more than a quarter hour at a time. There was little reason to think anyone from Deborahville would follow them; Emerston could hardly accuse her of theft for taking papers intended to help him steal her patent, and Amherst was a reluctant horseman at best—even if it did occur to him to try to bring them back. Ella also knew Catherine would make him see the futility of trying to follow them. Or, if he was too angry to see reason, she'd slip him something that would make him drowsy before he got very far.

At dusk they made camp in the woods off the road, outside a small village. They were bone-weary after their first full day in the saddle and there was little talk as they prepared a meager meal. Once they'd eaten and were rolling out their blankets near the fire, Jimson grew more animated and claimed he couldn't sleep without a story, as his mother or Jenny always told him one at bedtime. Jenny agreed in a weary voice, but Jimson said, "No, you tell me them all the time, I want to hear one of Pete's. The one about him and his brothers stealing horses from enemy warriors."

Jenny and Ella groaned in unison. Ella said, "Jimson you've heard that story hundreds of times. We all have. Zeke made him tell it nearly every day when we were small."

"But not for a long time," Jimson said firmly. "Pete's been away. And in any case it's the best one."

Pete said, "Why you like that story? You aim to thieve horses?"

"Some day," Jimson agreed.

Pete shrugged, and then with an agile twist he sprang to his feet and hunched to mime a stalking pose, putting a finger to his lips. He reached back his other hand to mime a signal to his brothers, stalking behind him. "We wait at spring above Black Creek, where Algonquin warriors come for drink when on hunt." Pete crouched to indicate waiting, and then, with a terrible battle shriek, sprang forward and gestured to show one brother grabbing the Algonquin horse's halter while another jumped on its back, grasping the rider about the middle and rapidly wrestling him to the ground.

When he'd mimed the full exchange that left the Algonquin on the ground scratching his head as Pete and his brother made off with the horse, he concluded with a hefty silent chuckle, "He has no time to curse our mother before we are gone." Jenny and Ella smiled, but Jimson laughed loudly and continued to chortle well after they'd settled into their blankets.

THEY WERE NEARLY ASLEEP when both Ella and Pete sat upright at once. Hooves had left the road and were coming toward them. Ella's mind raced. Could Amherst have eluded Catherine's efforts and made off after them? Could Emerston have concocted an accusation and called in a marshal? She looked at Jenny and Jimson, sleeping defenselessly. How would she shield them if there was trouble?

As the rider approached the faint circle of light remaining around their damped fire, she and Pete stood back in the shadows, sharp throwing knives in either hand. At first there was nothing but a black shadow coming through the trees, much as a buck emerges from a thicket. They held their knives steady and remained perfectly still, waiting, as the silhouette of the horse and rider came into focus.

Before they could decide whether to throw, the rider said, "Hold the attack—it's only me."

"Zeke!" Ella said in a voice held tight with nerves. "What are you doing here?"

"You didn't think I'd let you have all this adventure alone, did you?" He gave them a tired grin, the creases beside his mouth flashing only a brief moment. "Though I could hardly look forward to riding into here, knowing you'd be standing ready to make holes in me."

"Have you been following us all day? When did you start out?"

"Let boy get down from horse," Pete reproved mildly. He took the reins and helped the tired young man slide to the ground. "He ride faster than us. He is tired."

Jimson and Jenny woke and sat up as Zeke stepped toward the fire. Jimson sprang up to pummel Zeke's chest with the excitement of seeing him so unexpectedly. Zeke, laughing, shoved him off and leaned over to stretch his back. "You know, I didn't know I *had* all the bones that hurt right now." He made a wry grimace.

Ella gave him just enough to time to complete his stretch before she said, "All right, now tell."

"It's nice to see you too, Ella. Yes, my health is excellent, and yes, I had a pleasant journey. So nice of you to inquire."

"Zeke," Ella said severely, "I shall have to beat you if you don't stop that and *tell*."

"Take your time, Zeke," Jenny chimed in. "She's an awful bully."

Ella shot Jenny a look of warning. But then she relaxed, grinned, and said, "She's right, isn't she? I *am* an awful bully." Then, after a short pause, "But do just tell, won't you?"

"Let the boy tell his story," Pete said firmly. "Do not hurry him."

Ella shrugged. She said more quietly. "Go on, Zeke."

Zeke laughed at her. "Clearly I'll have no peace until I do." He put his hands on his hips and leaned back to stretch the other way, then squatted by the fire and looked into the coals. "I had the strangest early morning visit, when was it? Was it really just this morning? It seems weeks ago now. Anyhow, I stepped out the door to feed the stock first thing in the morning and there she was. Your Aunt Lucille, waiting for me."

"Was she?" Jenny asked. "That's not like her. She's not the stand-outside-and-wait type."

"Well, be that as it may, unless I was visited by a ghost, there she was. Standing and waiting."

Jenny took a breath to make another observation when Ella said, "Shhh, Jenny, please. It doesn't matter. Let us hear what she had to say."

Jenny made a face that said, "Fine, see if I mind." But Ella knew her sister was only goading her with interruptions, and that Jenny had a fine sense of when it became dangerous to go on.

Zeke gave Jenny a sympathetic wink, for they shared in the amusement of teasing Ella. Then he looked up, sobered, and said, "Having heard her news, it's not surprising that she waited outside for me, for it was news of a private sort. Not for others to overhear. And... after that I hurried to saddle up and come after you." He paused, seeming uncertain how to go on.

"Zeke...." Ella said harshly.

"I'm not teasing anymore, Ella," he said quickly. "It's not that. It's that I'm afraid it will be quite a shock to you. It was to me."

"Just say it," she warned.

"All right, all right." He ran a hand through his hair and then looked up at Ella. "It's that, well, she told me of that night, six years ago, when your grandfather..." His voice trailed off a moment, then he took a deep breath. "She said... she said Captain Tunnicliff didn't die that night."

Ella took a sharp intake of breath that caused Zeke to pause and look up at her, but she nodded to him to continue and he went on, speaking rapidly. "She said he was wounded but then nursed back to health in a back room of the Emerston mansion. Then, by his own choice, he asked them to stage his death and funeral and let him leave in secret. Which means your grandfather is still alive. Or, at least, he was when he allegedly died."

Ella's mouth twisted in disbelief and she glared at Zeke, before turning abruptly and taking a few paces away from the light of the coals. Zeke glanced at Jenny, who looked after Ella with an anxious expression, then over to Pete, who was looking away with a blank face. In a soft voice, Zeke said, "Pete, Lucille especially asked me to tell you that she was made to promise not to tell you. By Captain Tunnicliff. Because he knew you would track him and almost certainly find him, and he didn't wish to be found. She said it was very hard to keep the secret. And that she only breaks her promise now because it occurred to her he was the only person who could help Ella with the machine—with the part that isn't working right yet. If he's still alive that is, which she doesn't know."

Ella turned back to face them and asked sharply, "She's known all these years and never said a word to Pete or anyone else? I find that hardly possible to believe."

Pete said, "Why? If she was made to promise she would not speak of it."

"Even to you? Even to my mother, her best friend, about my mother's own father?"

"He make her promise."

"And you believe that with no questions asked? You don't think there's any other explanation?"

Pete looked up at Ella, where she stood with her arms crossed glaring down at him. "I always ask questions," he said softly. "Just not always to you."

Ella squeezed her eyes shut as the anger left her face. She took a step closer to the fire and squatted. "I'm sorry, Pete. I didn't mean any of that. It's just such a shock and…and I never know what to think of Aunt Lucille." She shook her head, then another thought occurred to her. "She revealed this because she thinks we should look for Grandpa, but how does Lucille even know of the flaw in the design?"

"I tell her," Pete said quietly.

Ella stared at him, a long, hard stare. "Pete, do you recall she was the one who sent me to see Emerston? Who told me I could trust him? How do we know she's not in league with him to take the machine?"

Pete sat quietly for a time. Then, slowly, he said, "I search inside here." He put his hand on his chest. "Inside here I feel your aunt. I feel she not betray you. It may be she trusts more than is good. But she does not steal from you. This I know."

Ella sat still, looking at Pete and thinking hard. She didn't know what to believe. Her grandfather had once told her that Pete and Lucille loved one another in a way few people could accept, but it was important she try to understand it. She didn't know that she fathomed their attachment or why her grandfather thought it important, but she'd long ago accepted their union. But could Pete really just *feel* Lucille wouldn't betray her?

"And she sends boy to find you with this news," Pete continued, as if reading her thoughts. "Is this not proof she helps you?" Ella shrugged, still not knowing what to think, and Pete said, "Let us sleep now and talk more in morning."

They all settled down once more, but her mind reeled with thoughts and questions about her grandfather and where he might have been all these years. It was hours before she slept and then only lightly. At first light they rose to rekindle the fire and prepare a morning meal. As they ate, Jenny said, "I dreamt of Grandfather and woke feeling anxious to find him. Where do we begin?"

"First we need to decide whether to look for him or go straight for the patent," Ella said in a flat voice. "Which is the same decision I wrestled with all day yesterday. I wish to see Grandfather as much as anything, but we should make a considered decision with respect to the patent. We have two choices. We either assure that we beat Emerston by going straight away, or else we delay to fix the design, taking the measured risk that he gets there first. Looking for Grandpa as a preface to working further on the design will only give Emerston more time to cobble together a new application and set of drawings."

"But if we let him get there first we'll have nothing to work with."

"But if we patent the design and then change it we'll likewise have nothing to work with."

So ensued a long debate that covered much ground but reached little consensus. When at last they fell quiet, Jenny said at last, "Ella, you worked with Grandfather most closely on this machine, what do you think he would do in our place?"

Ella was about to answer when she stopped herself, recalling her grandfather and his careful precise measurements, his attention to the smallest details. "I was about to say that he'd tell us to go fast and get the patent, just as Oliver Evans would say. He would wish to follow that advice. But knowing grandfather and his careful ways, I feel certain he wouldn't be able to bring himself to do it—to patent something before it worked as it should. He'd want to get it right."

"So . . . ?" Zeke pressed her to make a decision.

Ella reached up and squeezed the back of her neck, struggling with how to answer. She wanted to be sure she chose for the sake of the machine and her grandfather, not for her own desperate yearning to see him alive once more. To speak to him. Ask all the questions she'd pent up over six years. She tried to sort her motivations and in the end she came back only to her grandfather's huge hands carefully filing the rough edge from a casting to make it perfectly smooth. He'd loathe the idea of patenting something imperfect. "I think we should find him and enlist his aid to fix the flaw before we patent."

In unison they turned to Pete, who nodded. "Yes. You are right. He would wish to hurry to patent, but in end he would not. He would wait until it is right." After a moment, he said, "If he is alive, we will find him."

In further discussion it was agreed that Jenny would undertake to write to Aunt Lucille as often as possible to enlist her aid in keeping abreast of Emerston's activities and attempting to dissuade him of pursuit of the patent. They would do what they could to hamper him, but Ella was certain he wouldn't give up on it until one or the other of them had it in hand.

Pete had remained quiet during much of this discussion and when it at last subsided, he had already turned his attention to the next set of questions. "I ask myself," he said slowly, "If I am Captain Tunnicliff and I not wish to be found, where I might go? I think I go somewhere my family does not know. I think of people from long time ago, from when he fights in war with British, and I think of Captain Elliott. Captain Tunnicliff knows him long time. He lives south from here, not too far."

"So you've been there? Would you be able to find it again?" Jenny asked, momentarily forgetting Pete's uncanny ability to find most anything.

"Yes, I find that place," Pete said, as if the question were reasonable. "Only one more day ride and part of second day."

"You don't think Grandfather Tunnicliff would still be there, do you?" Jenny asked. "Or even nearby?"

Pete made a noncommittal gesture. "I know only your grandfather. If he travel near Captain Elliott house, he will stop to see his friend."

THEY RODE IN SILENCE for the rest of the day and, after a quiet camp, rose to mount and ride once more. Pete guided them without incident through forest and fields toward the little farm where Captain Elliott, now retired, lived with his son's family.

By late afternoon they came to a wagon track that brought them through an orchard, in which three people were picking small yellow apples into baskets. The apple pickers looked up at their approach. Then they straightened and the older, grey-haired man began to walk toward them with an expression of disbelief plain on his face. He had a thick, barrel chest and the rigid bearing of a military man. He stared at them a moment. Then in a deep voice he said to Pete, "Standing Bridge? Is that you?"

Pete slid down off his horse with Jimson in one arm, deposited the boy on the ground, and stood to face Captain Elliott. "Yes. I am the one you call Standing Bridge. Now I am called Pete." He raised a hand in greeting, but Captain Elliott instead stepped forward and clasped him in a hearty embrace.

"I never thought to see you again, Standing Bridge," Captain Elliott said in his booming voice when he finally released him. "It has been many years."

"Yes. Many years," Pete agreed. He was smiling now and Ella could see he too was pleased at this reunion.

The two men stared at one another, assessing the changes the years had brought, then Captain Elliott seemed to shake himself back to the present. "Let me introduce my son." He reached out an arm toward a younger man, who stepped over to join them, a quizzical look on his face. He wore plain homespun work clothes but he too had a dignified bearing, much like his father. "John, this is Standing Bridge. Standing Bridge, this is my son, the Reverend John Elliott. And this here," he gestured to the young woman beside his son, "is his wife, Mary. Grandmother Elliott is back at the house with the baby. I expect she's exhausted by now. Grandmother, I mean, not the baby. Let us head up there."

They left John and Mary to finish picking the apples while the captain guided them to the house. Along the way he effected his own introductions to the young people of Pete's party, and was clearly delighted to learn they were kin to Captain Tunnicliff.

They found Grandmother Elliott in the house, minding the baby while she stirred a pot of something thick and bubbly which proved to be apple sauce. She greeted them warmly, not the least surprised at their sudden appearance, and then showed herself every bit as adept at giving orders as her husband must once have been. She wasted no time in saying to Zeke, "Here, boy, save the captain's back and take this pot out to the cook fire where you'll find a pot of water boiling. I'm making to can the sauce this afternoon." Then she turned to Jenny. "Here, young lady, mind the baby while I ready the jars for the canning. Though you'll need to look sharp, I warn you—she's a right handful. Has a gift for finding mortal danger, that one."

Jenny needed no asking, for she was already moving toward the child. The baby, of perhaps a year in age, christened Nancy, wore a long white cotton dress and a thick bonnet that might have slowed down another child. Ignoring the strangers, Baby Nancy had used the distraction of their entry to climb a chair and was now standing on the tips of her toes, reaching her chubby fingers toward a shelf on the wall over her head. A shelf on which sat a row of delicately painted porcelain figures. She would have reached the closest of them by now if a cough hadn't wracked her small body and forced her to pause. Jenny was just in time to sweep her from the chair before she grabbed the nearest fragile figure. She sat with the angry baby on her lap and in a few minutes had Nancy's scowl relaxing to a laugh. Soon she asked permission of Grandmother Elliott to take the baby outside, pulling Jimson along to accompany them.

Captain Elliott and Pete had already made their way out, to stroll the farm as they talked, or, rather, as the captain talked. Ella, suddenly left alone with Grandmother Elliott, looked at her as if awaiting an order. Grandmother Elliott, never one to miss an opportunity, said, "Well, what are you waiting on? Take these jars of sauce outside. We'll boil them out there." Grandmother Elliott gave her an appraising look, and then thought to ask, "You do know how to can sauce, don't you, girl?"

Ella considered the question and nodded. She'd helped her mother with canning on occasion, but more often than not she'd begged off from anything that resembled cooking. Grandmother Elliott nodded back, apparently satisfied. "These early apples don't keep for more than a few days before getting soft, so they're best for sauce. I like to put up as many as I can before they turn. I'll make another batch tomorrow." She pointed at a basket of jars and then to the back door. "What are you waiting for, girl? Outside is where you're needed."

Ella grinned and took up the basket of jars to make her way to the outside cook fire, where she found Zeke adding wood to keep the huge kettle of water boiling. She put down the jars and asked him, "Do you know much of canning?"

"Nothing. Can you imagine my mother canning sauce?"

Ella thought of Janet Winebottom, who disliked cooking as much as she did herself. She chuckled. "I'd give much to see her try. I can hardly think of anything more amusing."

Zeke grimaced. "Guess we're about to learn something of the business. The good grandmother seems determined we're to help her."

"That she does," Ella agreed. "And she brooks no argument, eh?" She thought a moment and added, "Hope we don't ruin all her sauce."

"I don't think she'll let us."

THAT EVENING, after a simple supper of salt pork broth and rye-and-Injun bread, accompanied by apple sauce and fresh green beans from the kitchen garden, Jenny reluctantly handed over charge of the baby to her mother to put to bed and went to help with the supper dishes. Grandmother Elliott had Ella washing up while Zeke carried and arranged jars of warm sauce on the shelf at the back of the pantry.

Later, Mary Elliott returned from putting the baby down to sleep, looking near exhausted herself. She sat near Jenny and said, "You're a wonder with the baby, aren't you? You must like them."

"I do," Jenny agreed. "But I especially like her. She's a pure bundle of spirit, and so curious of everything. I like to try and see what she sees." Jenny paused, and then, with some hesitation she said, "I wonder, Mrs. Elliott, would you mind terribly, if . . . Well, I don't wish to interfere, but I do know a remedy for a cough such as she has, and I saw at least one herb I would use just on the far side of the back field." She pointed to the west. "Might I make her a tea to try to ease her cough?"

Mary Elliott looked a bit surprised. "You're welcome to try, but I can't imagine she'd take it."

"Oh, I'll add a bit of molasses if you have some. Or whatever else might be sweet. I've got special tricks for getting the babies to take their medicines." Jenny looked down at the floor then, and Ella, eavesdropping on the exchange, could see she was ashamed of appearing boastful.

But Mary Elliott wasn't the least perturbed. "Are you a healer then? Do you know medicines?"

"My mother is the healer. I only assist her," Jenny said shyly.

"Don't believe that for a moment, Mrs. Elliott," Ella interrupted. "She's as skilled as any healer in our town or those nearby, and then some."

Jenny flashed her a look of dismay, disliking such claims. "It's of no matter," Jenny said, "I only ask permission to try what I may. I make no promises it will work."

Pete, who sat nearby whittling a toy for the baby with his flashing knife, said, "It will work. She is good healer."

Ella looked over at him, a bit surprised. He rarely bothered to offer opinions. His next words told her what he was up to.

"Not like doctors in army. They treat my wound and I grow sick." *Ah*, Ella thought, *he is using the topic to introduce talk of the war, so as to ask after Grandpa.*

Captain Elliott was happy to oblige the topic. "Ah yes, I recall that well. You were wounded at Barren Hill, were you not? Wasn't Captain Tunnicliff in command of that regiment?"

"No. A Frenchman is in charge. Captain Tunnicliff he is only lieutenant then. We hold back British so Americans can cross river. Sachem Sinavis, from my tribe, he die there. I take shot in leg. Lieutenant Tunnicliff he stay and keep firing so British not come finish me. He drag me across river and up hill on other side. The British they not want fight across river, so they go back to Philadelphia. The Lieutenant he is made Captain after that."

"And you were made his aide, then, isn't that right? As I recall, you and Captain Tunnicliff were always together." Then, after a moment, Captain Elliott added, "You stayed on long after the other Oneida had gone home, didn't you?"

"Yes," Pete said, "I am aide. It stay same after war."

Ella felt her head swivel toward Pete, though by long practice she kept her face from showing her confusion. She'd known he'd been at the war, as had her grandfather, and he'd told her a bit of it that night in the smith. But she'd known nothing of this battle, or that he'd been an official aide to her grandfather. So was *that* the reason Pete had come to Deborahville in the first place? Was he still acting as an aide of sorts to her grandfather? She'd always wondered about it, but he'd never answered her questions. Somehow she'd always thought it had more to do with Lucille, for she first remembered him as the man who was called to track Lucille's baby when the Seneca made off with the child.

She pulled herself back from her thoughts as Captain Elliott moved on to another recollection of a particular battle in the long war. Pete had grown quiet and Ella wondered when he would ask of whether they'd seen her grandfather six years ago. But apparently he wasn't ready to ask. She fought down the urge to signal him, to press him to ask the question so they could be on their way. What if her grandfather was nearby somewhere? Just then Pete looked over at her, as if he could sense her impatience, and with the faintest shake of his head he told her to hold back her urgency, to let him work in his own way.

After a time they wished one another a good evening and their little party made its way to the barn, where they would bed in the hayloft. Even from that distance they could hear the baby coughing in the night.

JENNY WAS GONE when they woke and Ella knew she'd gotten up before first light to collect plants for the baby's medicine. She returned with an armful of mullein bigger than the baby herself.

"Are you certain that's enough?" Zeke asked her.

"I hope so," she said with some concern. "I couldn't find any slippery elm or cherry bark, although I was certain I'd passed some wild cherry trees yesterday. But now I'm not sure where that was. And there's no horehound about." Then she glanced down at the great pile of leaves in her arms and realized he'd been teasing. "Oh quiet, you," she said. Zeke grinned at her and she flushed.

She went into the house to brew the medicine tea and Pete mounted his horse and disappeared for a time. He returned with a bag of wild cherry bark and several bunches of hore-hound. Jenny was shredding it into boiling water before he'd finished tethering his horse. She added molasses and some sugar syrup, and when it had cooled she got the baby to take a bit. While Ella and Zeke helped the family with the day's farm work, Jenny and Jimson set to making games to amuse Baby Nancy as Pete finished carving her toy. They gave her more tea at noon and then at supper, and by the evening she coughed up a thick phlegm before falling asleep.

"This is good," Jenny said. "I hope she'll sleep better tonight. And you as well," she added, looking at Mary Elliott. "How long has she been coughing like this?"

"I can't even recall any longer," Mary said in a weary voice. "It seems forever. We have no doctor or healer within a day's ride. I can't tell you how grateful I am that you've arrived here."

"Oh nonsense, she'd have cleared it on her own eventually. They almost always do. It's a bad one, though. As bad as I've seen in a while." Jenny looked at Mary for a moment. Then gently she took her arm and pushed her toward the stairs to the sleeping loft. "Why don't you go sleep while she does. She'll likely wake up later, but you can use all the sleep you can get."

"Oh I couldn't," Mary protested. "I have washing yet to do."

"I'll do it. You go rest. It's no bother at all."

Mary began to argue further, but then her weariness took hold and she gave Jenny a wan smile and let herself be pushed toward the stairs. Jenny went over to take up the washing, keeping an ear to the company nearby as the tales of the war began once again.

Just as with the last night, Pete encouraged the captain to tell more and more tales, but again he let the evening end without asking the question that burned in Ella's mind. Had they seen her grandfather six years ago?

That their hosts hadn't mentioned it on their own by now was in itself something of a statement, she realized. Either he hadn't come here, or else he'd come here and then sworn them to silence about it. Either was possible. If the latter, it meant that when they did finally ask of him, they would be asking the Elliotts to break their vow to a friend. Which would mean they'd likely lie. Which meant that Pete, who would have already thought of this, was taking his time in taking measure of the people so he might better decipher their answer. *Argh,* she thought, *he knows exactly what he's doing, and I've been too slow to see it. I suppose I'd do well to watch him at it, see how he directs them, how he eventually asks the questions.* She sighed. After all these years, she still had so much to learn from him. Would he ever stop being her teacher? And his patience with people—how would she ever learn that? She had it for the woods, and even for machines, but for people, no, next to none.

For the next two days they continued to make themselves useful during the day and then spent their evenings listening to yet more tales of the war. With only the slightest encouragement the captain seemed to have an endless supply. But by the end of what was now the fourth evening of tales, Grandmother Elliott finally piped up to say, "Isn't that enough tales of the war, Ebenezer? We've heard enough to think we've been there and back again. I imagine there are others besides myself who are ready for a change of topic."

There was a dead quiet after this statement, as her guests were too polite to agree, at least not out loud. Ella looked at Pete, giving him the silent message that she wished him to finally ask the question.

He cleared his throat and said slowly, "Captain Elliott, Grandmother Elliott, Reverend Elliott, I have question for you. Very important. Six years ago there is fighting over horses and everyone say Captain Tunnicliff is killed. Even there is funeral. Just now we learn it is not true. That he not die but leave by choice. We have reason to find him and think he might come stay here. Can you tell us?"

The Elliotts all glanced at one another. Even Ella, not nearly as skilled as Pete at reading faces, could see they were preparing a story. Captain Elliott, apparently designated as spokesman, said, "No, of course he didn't come this way. We would have said something of it by now, don't you think?"

"Not if he swore you to secrecy," Ella said. There was quiet for a moment, then she added, "Captain, we wouldn't wish you to break your word to my grandfather, but we have a very good reason to wish to find him." Then she told them of the flax machine and their reasons for needing to locate her grandfather. When she finished she said, "I don't wish you to break your vow by confirming or denying that he was here. All we hope is that if perhaps you...well, if you have any sense of which direction he was heading, you might name for us a place or a person that would send us on our way. I don't believe you have reason to think we wish him harm."

Captain Elliott was quiet, his face clearly showing the conflict in his thoughts. He looked at his son, whose face remained impassive, and then at his wife. Grandmother Elliott stared back at him. Then she said, "Oh you men and all your noble vows and deeds." She turned to Ella. "Try to locate that Seneca man we spoke of the other night. The one who worked as a scout for the French regiment. He will know more," she said with a confident nod.

"I know this man," Pete said, nodding. "His English name is Old Smoke. He live in Seneca village... four, maybe five days ride from here."

"Thank you, Grandmother," Ella added.

WHEN THEY SAID THEIR FAREWELL at dawn, Mary and Grandmother Elliott made a fuss over Jenny, extracting her promise to return to visit them once again. Baby Nancy began to wail when Jenny put her down, and her cries grew steadily louder as Jenny moved away. Watching this, Ella felt a pang of something, could it be envy? Awe? She looked at Jenny, who herself had tears in her eyes at the parting, and chastised herself. Whatever others felt for Jenny, Jenny felt in return, and then some. It was churlish to envy such a trait.

At last they were on their way and Ella, the comforting motion of Dapper Dan beneath her, felt once again that breath of liberty she'd felt upon leaving Deborahville. It was so fine to travel, to be free and moving. She looked around at their little party and saw that the others looked sleepy and resigned, not pleased. All except Pete, whose expression told her quite plainly that he too was pleased to be moving once more. Especially as they headed now to a Seneca village he knew well. To his own people, his own language, his own food.

She had a sudden shiver of apprehension. They were about to enter his world. What if he became a stranger to her when surrounded by his own people? What if her ignorance of his people and his ways, her very whiteness, became displeasing to him? Pete had always been the one person, other than her grandfather, she'd been able to depend upon. But the visit to the Elliotts had already given her a glimpse of all she didn't know about Pete. What more was there?

NINE

LUCILLE TUNNICLIFF'S HOUSE had just filled with the scent of the bread she'd taken out of the stone oven when she heard a pair of large feet stomping up the steps to her back door. Her first thought was Pete, but quickly reminded herself that he was away, and of course he'd never make such a noise. Who else, then, would use the back door? Well, she had a warm loaf of bread to offer a guest, whoever it might be.

She went to open the door just as a loud knocking commenced. Outside stood Amherst Kenyon, with the usual coating of flour dust in his grizzled hair.

Lucille forced herself to keep her voice steady. "Hello, Amherst. This is a surprise. What can I do for you?"

"Just stopped by to set for a spot. May I come in?"

"Ah, of course. Come in. May I offer you a slice of fresh bread?"

He sniffed in appreciation and nodded.

He had chewed solemnly through half a slice without saying anything when Lucille finally said, "May I ask why you're here. I've already told you I know nothing of where your children have gone."

He took his time chewing and swallowing. "I thought it was time we had a little talk, you and me, face to face, like. About the money."

"Money?" she asked, keeping her voice low with some effort.

"You know what money I mean," he said with finality.

She considered her options as she sliced another piece of bread. She could not yield anything to a bully like Amherst, but as he seemed to have learned something of the money from Jimson, it seemed worthwhile to find out what he knew. In a crisp voice she said, "No, Amherst, I don't know what you mean. Of what money do you speak?"

He gazed at her, his sagging face at odds with the shrewd look in his eyes. In his grumbling voice he said, "I know you're spending big notes in Albany, and you know how I know that. Now I could be threatening to report you to the U.S. Marshal, or asking you to buy my silence, but that's not why I'm here. I'm here because I want into the trade. I want you to sell me the notes. What do you pay for them—twenty cents on the dollar?"

Lucille swallowed hard and tried not to gag. *Not in my lifetime*, she thought, but out loud she heard herself say, "Of what are you accusing me, Amherst? I don't know a thing about any false notes. It's true that I brought some larger notes on the trip to Albany, but those were genuine notes, drawn on my own bank. If you've come up with some misplaced ideas in your own suspicious mind, that's no problem of mine."

"This has nothing to do with what the boy told me of your spending in Albany," Amherst said with a pleased look. "That was only the last nail in the coffin. No, I've known of your business for some time now. I watch, you know. I watch you. I've seen where you go, who you meet with. The fancy goods you buy in Albany, or wherever else you go to trade. I see you at the store, with the Winebottom woman. She's in on it too. I can smell it. Now then, I don't ask for much; I only want in too." He paused to assess her reaction. "You don't have to answer this minute. Just think on it. And think on what I might tell if I were to go about naming names. I might call in the marshal, or I might just whisper it all over town, until no one will take your money for anything, and everyone will look at you sideways and move away fast like. Never mind what it would do to the dry goods store, if'n people were to know the money there might be tainted."

She looked up sharply. "Stop that. You're a mad man. Who's to believe a drunk like you?"

"Not everyone. Maybe not even half. But if just a few believe it will make its way around town, and you'll never be free of it. Not ever."

She knew he spoke the truth. It took all her will to bite back the stinging words she wished to hurl at him, and he looked pleased with her distress. "As I said, think on it. You have a week."

When he'd left she began to pace the room. She was angry, almost too angry to think. But then, when the anger began to ebb, there was only a weary sorrow at the sordid state of where her life at taken her. Not for the first time she asked herself, *What has become of the young girl I was, walking through town on a carpet of light, trailing admirers everywhere I went?* It seemed both ages ago and yet only yesterday that she'd had the pick of every young man in town, that every door was open and she need only dance through whichever she liked. *How had all those doors shut so quickly?*

She recalled Amherst Kenyon as a young man, standing amidst her circle of admirers, already heavy built and imposing. She recalled how he would stand at the back of the group and fix her with an intense gaze that never lightened, even when the rest of the group laughed at her witticisms. How he would stare at her gold watch when she used to wear it on a chain. His intensity had been unnerving, but easy enough to ignore when she had other, more handsome beaus to entertain. Such as the dashing Henry Emerston, always foremost among her admirers, and the first of them to work up the courage to propose.

She'd turned them all down, of course. Because they waited too long. They waited until after she'd already met Pete. Which at the time seemed a blessing, that she wasn't already promised to one of them when Pete appeared. But now, so many years later, she'd had more time to consider and blesses and curses were blurring together. She couldn't help wondering how it might have been different. She'd somehow imagined the proposals would just keep raining down and she'd continue to dance among them. She'd been too young to know it might all change so abruptly. And then, after all those proposals, after all her lofty ideas of love, she'd been forced to marry John Tunnicliff, her friend Catherine's brother, a young man for whom she felt nothing more than gratitude. And who had left her with nothing when he'd died a few short years later. What a fool she'd made of herself.

She could still see the rage on Henry Emerston's face when she'd turned him down; it had been the first harbinger of the humiliations to come. She couldn't see how he'd recover from that state. But he had, hadn't he? They'd even forged a friendship of sorts, as business partners and allies. And Amherst, he'd been angry when she'd refused, but then he'd soon asked Catherine, and she'd thought it would all work out for the best. How were any of them to know what Amherst would become? She'd never dared to ask herself what might have been if she'd accepted him, if he'd moved into her house instead of into Catherine's. These were questions she couldn't face. She could only feel responsible to help as she might, do what she could. As little as it had been. And what would it mean for Catherine if she turned down Amherst in this most recent request?

But how could she bring him into the bank note business? She was only a small-time passer herself. She took what she was given and passed it, using the big notes for small purchases and returning home with the change in small authentic notes or coin. She owed thirty cents on the dollar and the rest she could keep. She had only intended to do it once or twice, but then, well…it was so easy. In her elegantly cut gowns and hats, who would think to question her? She'd succeeded in looking like gentry—despite what that had cost her—why not play it for the full value? Literally. And the money was such a blessed relief when it first came. After all those years of counting each teaspoon of sugar to try to make it last the week. Halving each portion of bread and meat to stretch it out. Yet requiring to maintain her wardrobe in order to court clients who could afford her sewing. Taking in whatever stitching work she could get, yet maintaining a pretense of being highly selective. Working at night until her fingers bled, yet pretending it was an idle means to supplement a generous inheritance from relatives in New Orleans. It would have been so much easier to resign herself to taking whatever came her way, but it was just too galling to settle into life as a common, workaday seamstress. What would her mother have said?

No, she had to try to do it better, to live up to her potential. But what a blessed relief when the money from the bank notes began to flow. For the first time she could actually *be* selective, take only those jobs she preferred. Which meant she could snub the occasional wealthy lady who rode from as far as Albany, or the newer settlements at Chenango Point or Ulysses, expecting to be treated like royalty. This had brought her the respect of other wealthy ladies, such that her services became more highly sought, and she could raise her prices. Until the same gown she'd sewn ten years ago was now worth ten times as much.

In fact she hardly needed to pass notes any longer. She could get out altogether, give her share to Amherst, let him take the risks. It was just that it was so very… delicious. To have a secret life. There was a power in it. A spice. It was hard to imagine a life without spice. She stopped pacing and smiled to herself. A life without spice. Hadn't she just summed up everything she feared? What kept her with Pete except that he was spice? What kept her passing notes? But *why*? What made her need so much spice? Others lived without it—or with much less. Why couldn't she?

Her feet took up pacing again and she realized she'd best take herself out of her little sitting room before she wore a hole in the rug. She felt an urge to see Pete, though of course he was far away by now. And for reasons she hardly understood herself—perhaps only an instinct to keep her spice in separate jars—she'd never told him of the bank notes. No, there was only one place to go, of course, only one person she could talk to about this. And she was never difficult to find, for she hardly ever left her dry-goods shop.

Janet Winebottom forgot to keep her voice low when Lucille ushered her into the back room of the store and told her what has transpired. "What!" Then, more quietly, "Oh no, you cannot mean that."

"It's not as if I've promised him anything, Janet dear. I'm only telling you what he proposed. I didn't confess to knowing anything at all about false notes."

Janet shook her head, making her Holland cap tilt to one side over her grizzled hair. "It's time, then, Lucille. You know I've been saying it for a while now. We should get out while we still can. Before it's too late. And if Amherst is sniffing around, that's all the more reason. We've both profited nicely and used it help our other businesses. But we don't need it as we once did. Let us cut the string."

Lucille tilted her head back and looked at the ceiling. "I'm sure you're right," she said at last. "It's only, that...well, I'll miss it."

Janet gave her friend a piercing look. Then she waggled an eyebrow and said, "Then take up some other dangerous pastime. Preferably one I know nothing about. Become a rum-smuggling pirate, or a spy for the navy. Or, better yet, take up with an Indian who comes and goes as he pleases and leaves you all sorry-looking when he's away. Oh wait, that's right. You've already done that."

Before Lucille could react, Janet was already apologizing. "Oh Lucille, I'm so sorry. I didn't mean that as it sounded. It's only that I worry for you. I wish you'd find a way to be happy. To have someone of your own who could keep you better company. It's not that I don't like Pete—you know I do. It's just that you're so... well..." Janet cut herself off as Lucille's steely expression faltered and then her eyes abruptly filled with tears. She leaned into Janet's warm bosom.

After just a short time, Lucille straightened and wiped her eyes. "All right, enough of that. I'll smell like pickles all week if I don't get out of here." She reached into her reticule bag to search for a handkerchief, but Janet was already reaching up with the hem of her apron and wiping at her nose.

"Oh stop that, it's disgusting," Lucille said, swatting away the apron. "I don't know why I associate with you."

"It's because I look so good on your arm when we walk together," Janet said with a sly smirk.

"Oh please." Lucille finished using her handkerchief and put it away. "You know what they say about friends like you, don't they?"

"That we save you the effort of finding enemies? Well, that saying is hardly new, is it dear? You'd think someone as sophisticated as you purport to be could come up with something more witty than that."

"I have no pretense to wit, my dear. You malign me unfairly. I was about to remark that friends like you are the raison d'être. The greatest good there is."

"My arse you were." Janet bustled out the door.

TEN

THE TOWN OF PACHINGTON was the first town of any size they'd come to in the two days since they left the Elliott farm in southern New York. A few miles back Pete had said they must be approaching the border of Pennsylvania, though Ella saw little to distinguish it in such a sparsely settled area.

Pachington was nearly asleep by the time they rode in, with only the tavern and a few houses yet showing light. They'd have to return in the morning to buy the few supplies they wanted, so they headed back out of town to find a suitable camp for the night. As they were about to turn off the main road, two men walking into town hailed them to stop. The taller one had thick black hair and a silky black beard. The shorter one walked slightly behind him, with an odd gait. The black-bearded one said, "I don't suppose you know where we might find a fellow by the name of Gleason?"

"No, sir. Afraid not. We're visitors here ourselves," Zeke answered.

"Well I thank you anyhows," he said. Then he walked over to Ella and Jenny, sitting astride Dapper Dan. He stroked the gelding's neck and flank. "Mighty fine animal you have here. Used to have one like him myself."

Ella nodded to acknowledge the compliment, but her eyes were not on the black-haired man. She was watching the smaller one with the bandy-legged walk. She knew this man. In fact, she would never forget this man. It was Willard Loomis, from that terrible night six years ago, the night she'd last seen her grandfather. *What in heaven was he doing here now? What could it mean?* Then she looked again at the man with the black hair and realized he must be George Loomis.

Her mind raced through the possibilities and quickly came to settle on the certainty that the two men had tracked them here at Emerston's request, to steal back the plans to the flax machine. It was the only idea that made sense. Now here was George Loomis, stroking her horse as pleasant as could be.

She pulled the reins to the right to guide Dapper Dan away from him, then turned the horse full around and, without another word to the two strangers, led her party back to the busy tavern they'd passed in the heart of town. The plans would be safest here in town, she decided, with a shield of strangers to keep them from being molested in the night. Tomorrow she'd figure out what to do next.

Pete had recognized Willard Loomis as well, and together they told the others what they knew of the two men. They agreed to make an early start of it the next morning and keep a sharp eye out, as it seemed unlikely the Loomis brothers' presence was coincidence.

Ella and Jenny shared a bed in a room with several other women travelers. Ella kept the plans where she always had, in an oilskin packet strapped close to her body. But she also slept with an extra knife under her pillow, just in case. She'd seen what these men were capable of, six years before. They'd done damage that night, but she wasn't about to let it happen again.

She lay awake, listening to the breathing of the other women in the room. She strained her ears to hear any sound out of the ordinary, any rustle or scrape that suggested someone was sneaking up the stairs or climbing to her window. From a distance she could hear the occasional bursts of merriment from the rum-sodden men downstairs, or a whinny of horses in the stable, but closer by there was only a deep silence. The silence itself was disturbing and kept her awake. When the first light filtered in between the curtains of the window, she was still clutching the packet and staring at the ceiling.

Jenny woke, blinked a few times, and said within a yawn, "Have you been lying that way all night long?"

Ella turned her head and nodded, then rubbed her gritty eyes. She gave a faint grin at her own expense. "Let's go down to breakfast and devise a plan for making certain they don't ambush us on the way out of town. I've been thinking on it for a good while now."

They joined Pete, Zeke, and Jimson in the tavern dining room. They ate in good cheer, relieved to have kept the plans safe and certain they could now outrun the Loomises with an early start on the road and a close watch for signs of an ambush.

But when they got to the stable, all three horses were gone.

ELLA SCOWLED WITH FURY, mostly at herself for being such a fool as not to think of the horses. Of course any horse thief worth his salt would consider it an obligation to take Dapper Dan, the finest horse in the county, maybe in three counties. The other two, Pete's roan and Zeke's grey mare, weren't worth all that much, but she supposed it was prudent to take all the mounts of the party you are robbing—if you don't care for them to follow you too quickly.

She and Pete studied the ground outside the stable, but there were so many layered sets of prints that it was nearly impossible to distinguish a particular set.

Ella squinted at Pete. "What do you think?"

"I think they live north. We check the roads to north."

But when they scanned the two roads that could possibly lead north from Pachington, there was nothing to suggest their own horses had passed that way. They briefly followed one set of tracks but quickly saw there were too few horses and nothing to suggest their own. At last there was nothing left but to shoulder their baggage and head south, in the direction they meant to travel. They had little hope of picking up a track heading south, so it was almost a shock when, amidst the sparse sign of travel on the small road they followed, the day-old prints of ten horses suddenly emerged from between the trees to the east and turned to head farther south. In attempting to avoid pursuit the party appeared to have stayed off the roads until well south of town.

It was good to be following clear sign at last, but it was slow going without horses. Jimson, who insisted on carrying a load too heavy for his size, soon began to stumble and fall with increasing frequency. Jenny refused to complain, but after six hours of walking her heels blistered and began to bleed, until they were forced to make camp well before sunset.

In the morning they made another few slow miles and stopped for water at a creek that ran close to the road. As they were filling their water sacks, their heads rose in unison at the sound of a horse nickering softly a little way off in the trees. They looked at one another, then Pete motioned to Zeke to stay with Jenny and Jimson as he and Ella prepared to follow the sound. They crept up so softly on the two horses that they could almost touch them when the beasts caught their scent and gave a startled jolt. The horses would have bolted except that Pete quickly said something in Oneida to one of them, and it calmed and came toward him. The other was Zeke's grey mare, Philippa. She too recognized them and came forward for a nuzzle.

The thieves appeared to have grown tired of leading these extra two horses and left them to fend for themselves, assuming they were too far from the town to be of use to those they'd robbed. The horses seemed happy enough to be reunited with their people and the party was more than happy to be astride once more. They began to make better time following the clear trail of Dapper Dan and seven other horses.

By late morning of the next day the track led them to the outskirts of a village somewhere in northern Pennsylvania, where the trail ended in sight of a large red barn. They crouched behind bushy trees to observe the premises.

When it grew dark Pete stayed hidden with Jenny and Jimson and the horses while Zeke and Ella went closer to listen below the window of the worn white clapboard house next to the barn. The night was bright and Ella felt exposed with only the protection of the one scrawny bush beside the house.

The voices inside were all male and Ella soon picked out the nasal tones of Willard Loomis. There was the sound of doors opening and shutting, and then George Loomis' voice boomed out. "What's the count, then, Willard?"

A quill scratched on paper and Willard said, "With the eight we just brung in, that makes seventeen. Seven more should do it for us."

"That many yet to take, eh? I'd hoped not as many. We've near cleared out this here countryside of anything worth selling in Philadelphia."

"There's that stable in Wilkesbarre…" a high-pitched voice offered. The voice was familiar and with a chill Ella realized it could be that sideburned man who'd fought Pete that night—what was his name?

Before she could recall it, George Loomis said, "Risky, that stable. The constable there has seen us one too many times."

"Yes, that's so," Willard Loomis agreed. "And we can't buy any more, not without the remainder of the good notes we were supposed to have from Henry Emerston."

"Don't remind me of that," George Loomis said gruffly. "Telling me his two best passers up and quit on him."

"Especially that dry goods woman. She was right regular," Willard Loomis said with affection. "She could pass the big ones *and* the small ones. Just switch 'em out in the back room, them small ones."

Crouched beneath the window, Ella shifted her position ever so slightly to relieve the tingling pain in her foot. She tried to meet Zeke's eye, but he was avoiding her look. The conversation inside turned back to horses and they listened a while longer before suddenly Ella whispered, "I don't hear George Loomis any more, do you?"

Zeke shook his head no, just as the wide doors of the big red barn behind them sprang open. They crouched lower in the shadow of the house and watched as George Loomis led out a brown and white horse. He tied the horse's reins to a hitching post and went back into the barn.

"That's Dan," Ella said at once of the brown and white horse. Zeke looked at her with a faintly quizzical expression, for the horse looked nothing like Dan. Squinting in the moonlight to get a better look, Zeke peered more closely at the horse. Then he nodded, for Dapper Dan had been transformed. His white markings had all been dyed brown, so skillfully as to match his natural coat with little distinction—at least in the moderate light of the moon. Where there were formerly no markings at all, now there were patches of white, the hair bleached by some agent. He even sported a new white star on his forehead. It was a masterful job of disguise and Ella could see at once that it would be exceedingly hard to prove to any authority that this was her horse.

She made her soft Indian throat sound, a trill so faint as to be nearly indistinguishable from the susurrus of trees in a breeze. But the horse heard it immediately and gave a small whinny in her direction. Any lingering doubt was dispelled.

George Loomis came back out of the barn and strode over to take Dan's reins. There was something in his confident step and air of authority that made her recall the way they'd spoken of him that night six years ago, of how they admired and feared him. Or how Willard had feared him. The other man, the one with the nasally voice she'd thought she'd heard inside just now, had been more defiant. But he'd been new to the gang then; he hadn't sounded defiant tonight.

George Loomis swung into a saddle on Dapper Dan's back and prepared to ride off. Ella didn't recognize the saddle, but the saddlebags looked well-stocked and she realized they would have to act fast if they didn't wish to spend two more nights following this man and waiting for an opening to steal the horse back. She had an idea. She looked at Zeke with a meaningful raised eyebrow and whispered, "Do you think we can do it?"

Zeke shrugged and whispered back, "I've always wanted to try it."

Bending low, they made their way along the house and then skirted behind trees to meet up with Loomis as he arrived at where the long drive came out to the road. He was just turning onto the road when Ella stood straight and called out, "Wait! Mister, wait!"

He pulled up and turned to look at her. She trotted over, trying to appear casual. She said, "Mighty nice horse, that."

He eyed her from head to feet and said, "Aren't you that girl I met in Pachington?" He grinned at her, his teeth gleaming in the moonlight below his glossy black mustache. "Seems I recall you having a mighty fine horse yourself."

"Yes, I do have quite a horse. He's much the same build as this one here, in fact. But his markings are quite different." She tried to look regretful, as if she were wishing she'd find her own horse.

"Something I can do for you?"

"Yes, I was passing this way and…" she thought fast, "…wondered if you might recommend a tavern that serves a good meal?"

"Passing this way?" Loomis frowned, suddenly knowing something wasn't right. He tightened the reins to make off. Before he could move away, Ella darted forward and grabbed the bridle, holding on like a dog to a bear as Loomis began to twist the horse's head to knock her off.

She slowed him long enough for Zeke, who'd approached silently from the rear, to make a dash at the horse at full speed. He timed it exquisitely, pushing off for a wild leap high over the rump of the horse. As he landed on the horse's back he grabbed Loomis around the chest with both arms and, with a hefty grunt, twisted him down off the horse in one fluid move that gave Loomis no time to resist. They landed heavily on the ground, with Zeke managing to cushion much of his fall with Loomis' body.

As they wrestled on the ground, Ella swung herself up onto Dan's back and turned him slightly so that Zeke, untangling himself to stand up, had a clear shot to leap up behind her. Dapper Dan needed no prodding to be off like a shot, galloping for all he was worth, even with the combined weight on his back. Ella looked back once at Loomis, who had managed to sit up and was rubbing his head. It seemed, oddly enough, that he had begun to laugh.

PETE MUST HAVE BEEN WATCHING their antics, for he was waiting for them when they came to the first intersection in the road. He pulled them into a clearing nearby and had them wait while he went to collect Jenny, Jimson, and the other two horses. When he returned, he suggested they make haste to leave the area and led them into the woods, blazing a path by the moon over rough ground, following streams where possible and occasionally doubling back or dividing the party to confuse their track. When there was no sign of pursuit they stopped and rested a few hours.

The next day they came to a different road that also led south and were able to move more quickly, putting distance between themselves and the Loomises. They stopped for the evening beside a marsh and Jenny found a fine stand of Indian potato, which she dug to make a stew together with cattail stems, greens, and wild mushrooms. When she threw in a little cornmeal from their stores, Pete grunted and said, "You, girl, make fine Oneida wife."

Jenny smiled at the rare compliment from Pete, but Ella said, "Watch it there. Don't be giving her any ideas. She's in no rush to start cooking and cleaning for some demanding husband all day long."

Pete just grunted once more and helped himself to more stew.

Later, Zeke and Ella lingered over the coals of the cook fire. Ella abruptly asked, "Did you know about the money?"

Zeke nodded. Then, when Ella didn't pry further, he said, "It didn't take much to notice it. So many of the bank notes are old and ragged. Then, all at once, the money box would have newer bills in it and the ragged ones would be gone. When I finally came on her doing the exchange in the back room, I asked her where they came from. She said it was a service, really, to add new bills to the box. That there were never enough notes and the old ones fall to pieces all the time. I said, 'But where do they come from?' And she said, 'What does it matter? They all work the same. Half the banks that issue notes go out of business. At least these newer ones are drawn on the more reputable ones among them.' So that was all there was to it. She used to wet and wring the bills to make them look used, but you could still see they were new." He was quiet a moment, and then he said, "I never knew they came from Henry Emerston, though. I wonder why she quit."

"Yes, I wonder. And I wonder who the other passer they mentioned might be."

From behind them, Pete's voice said, "No need to wonder. Who else comes back from Albany with new gown every time she go? Who brings Jimson to stop anyone asking questions? She thinks I not notice."

"You mean Aunt Lucille?" Ella asked, incredulous. She started to ask more but stopped, and was quiet a long time. "Pete," she said at last, turning to face him where he lay on his blanket, looking up at the moon, "this is clear evidence that she's in business with Emerston, and that he's into shady dealings. How could you have sent me to ask her advice? Told me to trust her? Or him?"

"I do not tell you to trust him. Only her. Business or no business, she will not sell you to Emerston. This I know is true."

Ella was quiet again. Her mind was racing and she couldn't see anything clearly. She wished she could believe Pete, but she couldn't force herself to it. She could hear her grandfather's voice, cautioning her against trusting anyone when it came to something as valuable as the flax engine. Which reminded her that Loomis and his gang of thieves hadn't said a word about the flax engine or the patent or any of it in all that time they'd listened to them. Could it really be the case that they'd met by coincidence and Loomis simply couldn't help stealing her horse? That seemed impossible. Whatever the truth, she must not relax her guard any time soon.

ELEVEN

ELLA'S SENSES were on highest alert throughout the next several days of travel toward the Seneca village, such that she had difficulty sleeping when it wasn't her turn to keep watch at night. She began to feel a deep exhaustion at maintaining such a state of keen attention. When at last they rode into the village, she had begun to sag in the saddle.

She peered around her as they rode past the first few lodges and then approached the large central fire ring, around which clustered a dense thicket of lodges, the typical Iroquois longhouses of saplings covered by thatch and hides. As she gazed at the faces of the Seneca villagers, who looked back at her with a frank curiosity, she suddenly felt the weight of her anxieties ease. Emerston had always been vocal in his suspicions of Indians, which meant none of these people here were in his employ, or otherwise connected to him. She could ease her guard at last.

She took a deep breath and smelled the village, the pervasive woodsmoke, animal fat, leather, sweat, drying corn. It was a heavy scent, rich and layered, and it was familiar somehow.

They followed Pete as he wound around the huge village fire ring, nodding along the way to many of the people they passed. He headed for the lodges of his own Turtle Clan, grouped to the rear of the village. He had explained to them that by the laws of the Iroquois confederacy, all members of a given clan were legally related, no matter which Iroquois nation they belonged to. This meant the Seneca Turtle Clan were blood relatives of the Oneida Turtle Clan, and thus Pete would be welcomed as family, at least within his clan. The divisions between the nations brought on by George Washington's War had strained these relations nearly to breaking, however Pete had been to this village several times before, both before and after the war, so he knew he would receive a welcome despite that the Oneida and Seneca were no longer one people.

He introduced his companions to the clan elders, who welcomed them with smiles and nods of greeting. In little time the women of the Turtle lodges had directed them to seats around the cook fire and handed them bowls of food. Ella sniffed to determine what might be in her bowl, but finding that unhelpful, took a small taste instead. It was very hot, and as best she could tell it was some kind of corn with some kind of meat, but it tasted good.

As she waited for her food to cool, she noted the many colors and textures of the village. Women came and went, carrying heavy loads of corn in baskets held on their backs by means of a deerskin strap that looped over the forehead, causing the women to lean forward as they walked and turn their toes inward. The deerskin forehead straps were magnificently adorned with colorful beads and dyed quills, as were the women's skirts and tunics.

Jenny gently nudged her to point out the cradleboards, to which the women tied their babies. There were three at their fire, and, beneath all the blankets and straps, all that was visible of the frame of each was the elaborately carved footboard against which the babies' feet rested. Of the babies, there was nothing to be seen except their feet. One of the footboards was inlaid with silver; another had inlays of several different colors of wood. Like the women's clothing, the blankets and straps of the cradleboards were elaborately adorned with beads and quills. Over the children's heads, keeping out the sun, were more elaborately decorated pieces of fabric that appeared to be supported by an arching piece of wood.

A young woman, noticing Jenny's fascination with her cradleboard, pointed to it and said, "Ga-ose-ha, Ga-ose-ha," raising her eyebrows at Jenny to see if she understood. Jenny nodded and tried to repeat the strange word. "Ga-oza?" she said timidly. The woman laughed and shook her head. "Ga-ose-ha" she corrected.

As they finished their bowls of food, Pete, who had been talking to some older men, came to sit by them. "Old Smoke he is dead," he said. "He went last winter. They say Captain Tunnicliff come here six years ago. They remember. But they do not know where he go from here. They say maybe the nephew of Old Smoke will know. He also was here when Captain Tunnicliff was here. His American name is Reuben Doxtater and he speaks good English. He talked to Captain Tunnicliff many nights. He comes for Green Corn Festival. Within a fortnight. Until then they know nothing more."

Ella frowned and sank down into her seat. A fortnight? That seemed an eternity. What would Emerston be doing to snatch the patent for himself while she took eons in finding her grandfather? Had they made the right choice in trying to find him instead of going straight for the patent? She felt certain her grandfather could help her solve the machine's remaining difficulty, but would it be worth it if Emerston got his application in first? She fretted until there was nothing left but to find patience or decide to change their plan, and in the end she knew the decision had already been made and she'd best learn to live with it. For better or worse.

Despite her nagging worries, the life of the village soon drew them all into its rhythms. Jenny, with her endless curiosity for plants and their uses, was quickly adopted by the women of the Turtle Clan as they showed her plants they used for healing, some of which she recognized and others not. She was especially taken with the ways they used all the parts of the corn plant. They boiled, smoked, dried, parched, and otherwise molded the leaves, silks, ears, and kernels into a broad array of foods, medicines, and various other useful products. Even dolls.

A Seneca girl named Deh-he-wa-mis, whom Jenny called Doris, was the daughter of the Turtle Clan chief healing woman and herself in training as a healer. The two girls spent every afternoon on long rambles into the surrounding hills and forests, looking for useful plants and showing each other with gestures what they knew of each one. Jenny collected the ones that were new to her and then later, around the fire in the evenings, sketched detailed drawings and added what she'd learned of each plant's uses. She employed Pete as a translator whenever the language of gestures proved unwieldy.

Jimson likewise was quick to find a place for himself, though his activities required no translation. The boys of the tribe were all in training as hunters and warriors and spent most all their time in the woods. A father or uncle would give an occasional lesson, but mostly the boys learned from winning or losing their many contests. Jimson, who'd never had a brother or cousin close to his age, appeared to think he'd died and was already in heaven. The boys tracked, set snares, swam, fought, and raced, with occasional forays into the village for a bowl of hot food at their clan cook fires. Jimson found it almost too good to be true that food was always cooking at every fire at all times of day, and that he was always handed a bowl. The women took great amusement at his appetite, for he easily ate twice what the other boys did, though a few of the more dour women grumbled at the amount he consumed.

As his admiration for the boys in his band grew, he began to emulate them in this matter as well and began to take a more moderate approach to meals. So too, by the end of the first week he wore a breechcloth and, with his cheeks painted in stripes and his skin browned in the sun, he began to blend into the band. He would have been difficult to distinguish except that his hair was lighter and continued its tendency to stick up in the air, despite his efforts to slick it down with bear grease.

Ella hadn't seen more than a brief glimpse of Jimson in several days when he came running at full speed into the village one afternoon, yelling her name. Ella stood, as did Zeke beside her, and from the corner of her eye she saw Jenny already moving toward them. They reached Jimson at the same time and all stood staring at what he held out to them. It was a piece of old cracked leather that was recognizable as a horse's bridle mostly by the remaining bits of iron on it. Ella took the bridle and turned it over in her hands. Scratched into the surface of an iron ring, in tiny neat letters, was the name "A. Tunnicliff."

Ella stared at the letters. There was something unsettling about this hard evidence that he had been here, that they weren't chasing a phantom. But...what horse could this bridle have belonged to? All his riding horses were stolen or accounted for. Except for...*No, that couldn't be. Edgar wasn't a riding horse. Grandfather couldn't have ridden his old mill horse all the way here. Could he?* She thought about Edgar, that patient old work horse. Yes, Edgar would have done anything her grandfather asked of him. Which meant...*If Edgar was here, what of the gold watch?*

"Jimson, were there more pieces of tack where you found this?"

He nodded. Then he began to look uncomfortable. "I can't take you there. It's a secret place. I'm not allowed to show anyone or tell anyone."

Ella rolled her eyes. "Jimson I don't care one straw for your secret place. I only care for seeing the rest of the tack. It's important. You must take me there straight away."

Jimson gave an importuning look to Jenny, who looked at Zeke, who put a hand on Ella's arm and said, "I think he means he'll be in trouble if he takes you there."

"Trouble? Trouble with who? A bunch of boys?"

"It's more than that to him," Jenny said. "Jimson, can you go get the rest of the tack and bring it back here?"

"No! That will take too long..." Ella began to argue, but Jimson had already turned and sped off, recognizing the lesser evil in the options. Ella watched him leave and then made to follow him, but Jenny grabbed her arm and held her back.

"No, don't do that. The other boys will hurt him, or shun him, or...something," she finished lamely.

"But he could be gone for hours."

"Yes. So? Those bits of old leather have been here for six years at least. What's another few hours?"

Ella reached up and squeezed the back of her neck as she tilted her face to the sky. "I can't just...wait here. What will I do? I need to see that tack. I could be there in half the time if I just track him there."

"No. You can wait. And I don't see what all the hurry is about—it's just a pile of old tack."

Ella was about to refute this when she realized that, even after all this time, she could not bring herself to tell of the gold watch—or how she'd lost it. At last she said, "Fine, what do you propose we do while we wait?"

WHEN JIMSON APPEARED at last carrying an armful of tack and the remains of a ragged blanket, she was up in a flash and rushing toward him. She grabbed the pieces of blanket from his arms and began to knead them with her hands, running her fingers along all the edges to look for the pocket. At last she found it, or what was left of it. The pocket was empty.

She looked up to find a ring of faces gazing at her with curiosity. How could a ragged blanket get this odd girl so excited? She gazed past the faces to see Pete watching her from a hundred feet or more away. He had that maddening twinkle in his eyes that said he was having a good laugh at her expense. As she stared, he raised his arm and held up something that winked in the sun. She looked more closely at the dented circle of tarnished metal and saw it was the gold watch. Pete twirled it around, and even from this distance she could make out the intricate engraving of two overlapping V's on the back.

Later, after she'd had a chance to polish the watch, Pete squatted beside her and explained that a Turtle Clan elder had observed her reaction to the bridle and inferred that she must know of the watch. They had found it hidden in the tack they'd received in trade from her grandfather and they'd been keeping it to return to him whenever he traveled back this way. Seeing as she was blood kin to him and clearly knew of the watch, they were pleased to return it to her.

As their days stretched out in waiting for Reuben Doxtater, Ella and Zeke spent their time roaming farther and farther in their hunting forays. They were warned by Pete against trespassing too heavily on the prime hunting grounds near the village, as this would displease the Seneca braves who hunted daily in small groups. They did incur the wrath of one band, who came upon them silently and made gestures that left no doubt they were being told to move on. The leader of that group was a tall brave with an unusually long braid down his back, who seemed to wear a fixed scowl.

One afternoon, as a lark, Ella picked up four or five corn-cobs that happened to be sitting in a pile and began to toss them in the air, making them spin in a circle. She hadn't juggled for years, not since she was a child and her father had flown into an inexplicable rage when he saw her performing for a circle of other children. So she was surprised at how easily it came back to her hands. And here, so far from Deborahville, the pull of memory was less potent, so she found she was enjoying herself. She hardly noticed when a group of children assembled to watch. But then, when their laughter caught her attention, she found herself putting on a show for them. She pretended to drop one, but then caught it at the last minute. Or she passed one behind her back. A few older Seneca noticed and came over to watch, until at last she became self-conscious at being the center of so many eyes and put down the cobs, laughing off their entreaties to continue.

They didn't quit, but rather continued to coax her to entertain them every evening around the fires, after the meal and before the stories or drums began. She became the opening entertainment. At first she was shy of it, but then, with time, she grew grateful for the chance to entertain these generous hosts of theirs, who clearly enjoyed her shows. In the afternoons she sometimes went off by herself to practice an old trick to show them, or to learn a new one. She wasn't to the proficiency she'd had as child of ten or so—but she was working back up to it. She began having Zeke throw cobs into the circle for her to catch in mid-stream.

ONE DAY DORIS AND JENNY were watching as Zeke and Ella practiced, and Doris nudged Jenny, motioning a question using gestures Jenny had become adept at interpreting. This time the question was unexpected; Doris motioned that Zeke was handsome and she wondered if Jenny was sweet on him. Jenny shook her head firmly and then motioned back that No, he had eyes only for Ella. Doris watched the juggling another minute. Then she asked, "She doesn't know?"

Jenny smiled with a glint of laughter in her eyes. "No, and neither does he. It's better that way."

Doris nodded with sage understanding. "Yes," she motioned. "I can see that."

THE PATTERNS OF WORK and play were interrupted at last by the long-awaited appearance of Reuben Doxtater. He was a friendly, mild fellow of medium height, with a powerful build and rough skin. Pete sat with him for a long talk, after which he reported what he had learned. "He says Captain Tunnicliff was here but he leave after a short time. He hear of work in a glass factory that advertise for smiths and he go there."

"A glass factory?" Ella asked. "Where?"

"He think New Jersey. A town called Glassboro."

"New Jersey?" Ella said, trying to keep her voice from wavering. "How far is that?"

Pete looked at her, his face impassive. "Five, maybe six day ride from here. Not far."

Ella gazed back at him, keeping her face still and steady. She knew Pete wished her to show courage, even patience, but she couldn't believe what she'd heard. Here they were, having to chase her grandfather all over the country. And who was to say that he'd still be there, at this place called Glassboro? She had known it would mean a journey to try and find her grandfather, but all this chasing an old trail, replete with endless delays. Was it really worth it? The only thing they'd accomplished so far was to recover the gold watch. And given its battered appearance, she could hardly delight at the prospect of showing it to Lucille.

Even as the scream of frustration worked its way up her throat, she also knew what her grandfather would say. She could hear his rough voice repeating his favorite adage: "It's not worth doing if it's not worth doing right."

Arrgh, she thought, *why does this have to be so difficult? Why does it involve so much waiting?* Without conscious thought, she stood and her feet took her off into the woods to clear her head. She rubbed the gold watch in her pocket as she walked, and after a time her thoughts meandered to other ideas, old and new. As usual the sounds and scents of the forest calmed her, until eventually her spirit grew lighter.

When she got back to the village she found a large game had begun, apparently in honor of the Green Corn Festival and the visit of Reuben Doxtater. She joined the crowd watching the sport and made her way to stand beside Zeke and Jenny. "What's the game?" she asked.

"Don't know," Zeke said. "It's some kind of a ball game. Pete called it something like "ga' lahs."

"I think the Jesuits called it 'lacrosse,'" Jenny added. "I heard it described once, this game with bats and a ball."

"It's fast," Ella said.

"That's an understatement," Zeke said, "I can barely even follow the ball."

They watched for a while in silence; then Ella felt a tug on her sleeve.

"What?" she asked Jenny, who was frowning.

"You haven't heard a word I've said, have you?"

Ella agreed with a mild nod and returned to her study of the game. The ball was nearly impossible to see as it moved quickly from bat to bat. The bats were merely long, curved sticks with a basket woven between the end of the curve and a point midway down the stick. The small deerskin ball was scooped out of the air with the basket and then carried and flung with quick flicks of the wrist, all while running at full sprint from one end of the field to the other. The players were bare-chested and barefoot, wearing only breechcloths that were soon soaked with sweat, though none of the players slowed; their speed and stamina were a wonder.

Ella began to distinguish the positions and the strategy. On one team the forward player was the tall, scowling brave with the long braid who they'd met in the woods. He was adept at using his height advantage to scoop the ball out of the air from amidst a scrum of players, and then, quick as a flash, sending it down to a teammate waiting near the gate. In this manner they made two scores in quick succession.

The other team was slow to shut down this combination. But then they seemed to cohere their own strategy and they stationed players to intercept the ball when it came flying down the field. A friendly brave named Tawonyas was one of these players, and he was so fleet that he could turn and carry the ball the length of the field by means of outrunning and eluding a host of opposing players. Ella found herself cheering for him. He scored and the ball was given to the other side. Soon, from amidst a tangle of players, the tall brave with the long braid made to grab the ball from the air just as his arm was knocked by a defending player. The ball flew widely toward the sidelines, arcing high over the heads of the watching crowd.

Without thinking, Ella bent slightly and then sprang high in the air and made a wild reach for the ball. She snatched it with her fingertips and then felt her elbow jar someone's head on the way down. She was busy apologizing as the crowd began to talk all at once. Arguments soon broke out between those who admired the remarkable catch and those who were shocked at a woman touching the ball.

Amidst the noise, Ella walked onto the playing field and returned the ball to Tawonyas. Returning to the sidelines, she made her way to Pete and said, "I want to play. Can you find me a place in the game?"

Pete's face took on a grim expression and he said, "No. Ga' lahs is only for men."

Ella glanced at the elders of the Turtle Clan, with whom Pete was standing. They were watching her with varying expressions of curiosity and disapproval. She didn't want to shame Pete, but she couldn't stop herself from asking once again. "Pete, what difference is it from hunting or any other thing I do that's supposed to be just for men?" She paused when his face became, if possible, even more grim. Then she said more softly. "I'd be good at it, Pete. You know I would. Why don't you want me to have a chance?"

"No, ga' lahs is for men. Do not ask me." He turned back to the game and she could see there was no point in further pleading.

Without Pete's assistance she had no chance of getting in the game, so she settled for watching the remainder with intense concentration. She was determined to learn all she could of it, for she was equally determined that some day she would play.

THAT NIGHT SHE SAT with Reuben Doxtater and asked him more about New Jersey. He had arrived at the village wearing the trousers and waistcoat of a respectable man of business, but had since donned the more traditional decorated skins of his people. It struck Ella that he seemed equally comfortable in either attire.

He proved to be well-traveled and very knowledgeable about the country. He described the rich farmlands in southern

New Jersey, full of fruit trees and vegetables and grains. Then he told of the great stretch of sand and pine amidst the fertile lands all around, where little but pine and cedar could grow and the rivers ran brown like wood. He told her these barren areas of pine and sand contained vast bogs that spit up bits of iron, which could be smelted into pure metal using great stone furnaces, around which whole towns had formed within the Pines. He said the endless stretches of trees were used to fuel the furnaces that turned the bog ore into pig iron, and that the wood was used to fuel other business interests as well, including the glass business, for which it melted the sand into glass.

Ella listened in fascinated silence, for it sounded so grand. Soon New Jersey was the one place in the world she most wished to visit, and she was eager to depart. Reuben, with Pete's help, made her a map of their route.

Before saying goodnight to Reuben, she thought to press him for more details of how her grandfather had seemed when he'd been here six years ago.

To her surprise, a look of caution came into Reuben's eyes in response to these questions. "What?" she asked. "Is there something you're not telling me?"

Reuben looked at the ground, lacing his fingers together in thought. At last he said, "I don't have any actual knowledge. I have only an impression, a rather strong impression."

"Yes?"

"I had the impression that Captain Tunnicliff was running from something he'd left back in Deborahville."

"You mean he seemed afraid?"

"No, not that. It's hard to say exactly, but more that he was escaping from something he'd rather forget."

ELLA FELL ASLEEP pondering what her grandfather might wish to forget and why he'd staged his death. She slept badly, disturbed by unsettling dreams. When she went to assemble her party to depart the next morning, she found it had fractured. Jimson flat out refused to leave his band of fellow young warriors, and it seemed that Pete, too, wasn't ready to leave the village.

"I do not see these people for many moons. I must stay longer." Then he added, "Also the Prophet he come in autumn to speak his Code. I must hear him speak."

"You mean Handsome Lake?" she asked. "The one you told me you heard many years ago? He's still alive?"

"Yes, Ganio´dai´io. He is very old now but he come to Harvest Festival."

"What of Jimson then?" Ella asked after a moment. "He wants to stay as well."

"So he stay. I bring him back to Deborahville after festival. Before winter."

Ella thought about this. "He won't be safe if he returns to Amherst's house and I'm not back yet. You'll have to promise that you'll keep him with you, and away from Amherst. Can you promise that?"

"Do not worry. He is old enough. I take him hunting, teach him to smith. He stay with me." Then he added, "Your aunt she will murder me if boy is hurt."

Ella grinned. "Yes, I suppose that's true enough. That will ensure you don't let him out of your sight." She thought again. "He'll be happier, too, to stay with you and be able to hunt and roam. Where we're headed is more civilized—he wouldn't like it. Especially now that he's nearly full Seneca."

Pete rolled his eyes. Then his expression grew serious and he seized Ella's eyes with his own. "All will be well on journey. You have practice now. Follow sun to the east. Cross big river and go south. Ask for this Glassboro after you pass Trenton. Not difficult."

Ella nodded and then took a hard swallow that hurt her throat. "It won't be the same, though. Without you with us, I mean."

"All will be well," he repeated, but Ella could see in the tight press of his lips that he didn't care for the parting any more than she did.

TWELVE

RAVELING WITHOUT PETE AND JIMSON felt lonely and odd. Jenny cried the first night, saying "Jimson didn't even say goodbye to us. He doesn't care one tat that we left. I'll be surprised if he even agrees to leave with Pete in the fall. What kind of a brother is that?"

"Don't worry, Jenny." Ella patted her back in an awkward effort to comfort her. "Pete knows Lucille won't let him come home without Jimson, so he'll kidnap him home if need be."

This made Jenny cry even harder. Ella watched helplessly a moment, then she gave Zeke a look that said, "Do something."

Zeke gave her a helpless shrug, but then he put his mind to it and said, "It's not that he doesn't care about his family, Jenny. It's just that he's a boy and, well, boys forget sometimes. He'll come to his senses soon enough."

Jenny looked up at him. "Really? You think so?"

"Course I do. Especially if he gets sick ... or hurt even. Then he'd remember that he has a ma and a sister who would care for him if they were there."

Jenny nodded, her tears ebbing. "You're right, of course. He would remember then. It's just that he's forgotten us all so completely right now."

"Ah no, not forgotten. Not really. He's just having more fun than he's ever had in his life. The girls have chores to do, but the boys, well, they mainly just play at hunting and fighting all day. It's not like it is for white folks, where boys have lots of hard chores to do. Who can blame him, really?"

Ella and Jenny both looked at him. Then they looked at one another and rolled their eyes. But they were just posturing, for Ella knew they both saw his point perfectly well; Indian boys *did* have it better than most.

ON THE SECOND DAY, heading due east toward the sunrise and slightly south, they emerged at last to get their first look at the Susquehanna River. The river surface danced with bright September sunlight as the water made its thick and quiet way nearly due east. From this point their road ran roughly parallel to the river, snaking in and out of sight of the sparkling water. Out of sight of the river, thick trees walled in the road on either side for mile after mile, broken only by occasional small cleared fields with adjacent cabins and barns. The open vista of the shimmering water was each time a welcome relief from the thick darkness of trees.

Their road hugged the Susquehanna all the way to the Wyoming Valley, where their road stayed east while the river abruptly veered away to the south and west. After all those miles of anticipating glimpses of the river, Ella found herself gloomy in its absence. Normally she loved the deep woods, but here—without the river for relief—they felt too dark, nearly funereal. She was thus unexpectedly pleased to reenter civilization when they rode into Wilkesbarre. The veritable metropolis hummed with saws cutting lumber and carts of black coal drawn by oxen jostling amidst fashionable traps and carriages painted bright yellow or red. Ella found herself grinning at the sight of so much activity and was rewarded when a young man driving a carriage waved a greeting in return. Zeke gave her a bemused look.

Once past the city, the road led uphill out of the valley into the foothills of the Pocono Mountains, which they could now see rising ahead of them. When they reached the mountains they felt sorely tempted to make camp and explore further, as the icy creeks promised trout and there was abundant sign of game. But they resisted the temptation and hunted only as much as they needed, keeping to their trail and heading nearly due east toward the sunrise. They passed only a few travelers in all that time and it again began to feel they were traveling alone in uninhabited country that would never end.

Descending from the mountains into the foothills, the sight of the Delaware River snaking below them came as a welcome change of view. They began to think they were making good time to Trenton, the next big landmark, to which Pete and Reuben had directed them by means of the ferry across the Delaware to New Jersey. Once in New Jersey they'd again head south through Trenton and eventually reach Camden, just across the river from Philadelphia. From Camden, Glassboro was a mere few hours ride. Fortunately Grandfather Tunnicliff's path seemed to be taking them the general direction they would have taken to reach Washington City directly, and thus took them not far out of the way.

But after crossing the Delaware on a ferry and traveling south another day and a half, their confidence faltered. They'd been nearly six days on the road already and had yet to reach Trenton, which was at least a day and a half from Glassboro. Ella began to wonder if Pete had purposely lied about the distance, or whether he remembered it as shorter because he'd rode it much faster during the war years.

When it grew dark and there were yet no signs of Trenton, they made camp in a clearing in the woods, about fifty feet back from the road. The nights had become increasingly cool and began to smell sharply of autumn. They built a fine fire to warm themselves and were just finishing their meal of dried meat and corn porridge when they heard an odd sound from very close by. It might have been a moan, but was more likely branches rubbing. It wasn't the horses, and they looked around and saw nothing but trees, a few shrubs, and several fallen logs. Zeke got up and peered into the trees beyond their circle of light, but there was nothing to be seen.

In the morning the sound came again. Ella looked up from blowing on the coals of the fire and saw a shape tucked into the fallen tree across the clearing suddenly roll over, sit up, and take the form of a man. He was a brown man wearing brown clothes and so thickly coated in mud that he much resembled the bark that had camouflaged him. Only his eyes showed white when he opened them to stare with fright—but also a certain tired resignation. Jenny, standing behind Ella, stifled a shriek.

"Who are you?" Ella asked after a long pause of staring at one another. He made no answer.

After another pause, Ella looked back at Jenny, who swallowed hard and said to the man in an unsteady voice, "Are you ill?"

Just then Zeke returned to the clearing with arms full of firewood, which he promptly dropped. The brown man grunted and reached up to one of the branches of the fallen tree that had sheltered him, grasping it for aid in rising to his feet. When he was upright, he stumbled to another small tree for balance and then into the surrounding woods. They could hear him thrashing through the underbrush for several minutes, and then he was gone.

"I've never seen a man that dark before," Jenny said softly, her voice awed.

Zeke began to collect the firewood from where it had scattered. "It was all the mud, silly."

"No, it wasn't. There was mud, but in the places it flaked off he was even darker. I wonder where he came from?"

"Maybe the south?" Zeke suggested.

"That would be quite a ways," Ella said, rising to examine where the man had lain. On the mud and leaves were specks of blood. When she moved them aside, a patch of deep red liquid had soaked the soil below.

It seemed there was little point in further wondering about him, until they came upon him again just a short time later that morning, shuffling across the road in front of their horses to reach the cover of the woods on the other side. He'd apparently taken a shorter route through the trees to avoid the road and clearly didn't wish to be seen, but he was too injured to move quickly. Jenny slid off her horse to approach him on foot.

"Sir, wait, please. I don't mean to frighten you. I only wish to give you this salve for your cuts. I don't like to see you hurt." The man turned at her words and gave her an appraising look. He was about to turn away when something caught his attention and he peered at Jenny more closely. He paused to wait for her approach and she held out a packet of cloth in which she'd wrapped a vial of salve and some dried meat. Reaching him, she took his hand to put her packet in it. As she did so she asked him, "Where are you headed? Might you like to travel with us for a bit?"

He shook his head. He smacked his lips as if trying to moisten his mouth to speak and then, still peering hard into her face, croaked, "I heading to a place called the Pines. I hear from a nigra back in Maryland that if he ever needed a place to hide, the Pines in Jersey is the best place for many miles around. Can't no one track anyone down in there. You might do well to recall it."

"Well," Jenny said, "thank you for telling us of it. God bless to you. I wish you well."

"To you too, miss." Then he slid into the woods and was gone.

FOR THE REMAINDER of the next two long days on horseback, Ella thought in turns of her grandfather and her impatience to see him again after all these years, of the Seneca and the village they'd left behind, and on occasion of the black man who was heading for a place to hide, a place where no one could be tracked. She doubted this could be true, that no one could track in these pines. But still it was an intriguing idea and she wondered what had inspired the tales. And what caused him to tell them of it.

After finally reaching and crossing Trenton, they followed the road through town after town, most all of them bustling with activity. Whereas she had found each new town fascinating over the first few days of the journey, she now began to think they all looked alike. The journey had taken half again as long as Pete had told her it would and she was anxious for it to end. At Glassboro they'd hopefully find her grandfather, or else find out he was dead and be able to cease chasing him.

At twilight they rode into Camden, a small city of neatly intersecting streets. The first city street they came to was Cooper Street, and then, when they made their way to the bustling port, they were greeted by the sight of more ferries than they'd ever imagined in one place and another street called Cooper Street. A series of taverns lined the waterfront and most of them again were called by the name of Cooper. "A busy family," Ella commented.

Ella felt Jenny tap her shoulder and looked to where she pointed; it was a cheerful-looking tavern. They were all saddle-sore and hungry and in need of a soft bed and a bath before riding into Glassboro the next day. At least if they hoped to persuade anyone they were respectable enough to be given information. Ella turned Dapper Dan's head toward the stable behind the tavern.

Ella was up before the light, impatient to be off with their destination now so close. With good directions from the tavern keeper they expected to reach Glassboro by midday. Their road passed through lovely farmland all around, and even in her haste Ella couldn't help but admire the quality of the land and all that grew on it. So much fruit, so many vegetables and grains, shimmering fields of gold flax.

Their attempts to appear respectable proved useless, if not ludicrous, when they reached the glass factory and Jenny and Ella presented themselves to the young clerk in the business office.

"No one by that name works here, or ever has," the young man said dismissively, not even looking up from his ledger. All they could see of him was his greasy orange hair and the dirty cuffs on his shirt.

"How can you know that?" Ella asked, trying to keep the testy edge from her voice. "You haven't checked the records, and I don't believe you've worked here since the factory opened. The buildings look older than you can possibly be."

He looked up and his freckled face wore a look of smug disdain. "I've worked here long enough to say he's never worked here. Now be off with you."

Ella looked around the office, willing herself to hold her temper. "Is there anyone else I might speak to?" she asked. "Perhaps the owner? Someone who might remember more?"

"The owner?" he sneered. "You mean the Widow Heston? She's away. Probably gone to visit her man at the river again."

He gave a nasty chuckle. "And I can't have you going around and disturbing the workers can I? There are orders to fill. Now, like I said, time for you to be off."

Ella narrowed her eyes and thought briefly of how easy it would be to hold a knife to that freckled throat. She felt Jenny watching her and shook off the thought. Taking Jenny's elbow to steer her out of the room, she said, "We'll have to think of some other way."

They headed back to the tavern next to the green, where they'd hitched the horses and left Zeke to stand watch over the baggage.

They told him of what happened and he said, "Never mind it, Ella. We'll figure out something else. Now let's go in the tavern. That fellow over there told me they have a good beer here."

"Is beer all you can think of, Ezekiel Winebottom?" Jenny asked him.

"No, of course not, how can you say that? I also think about mead."

THE AIR INSIDE THE TAVERN smelled not of beer, but of food, magnificent food. They'd been eating mostly dried meat for the better part of a week, and the rich scents of fresh bread, roasting meat, and frying onions was enough to make Ella's mouth begin to drool.

The girl at the back of the tavern spied them and wasted no time in coming over to shove them into chairs at a scarred table. "Come sit down now, then. Ye'll be wantin' a brew with your meal, will ye not?"

They didn't answer, for they were all three staring at her. She had the most remarkable thick, wavy hair of a bright copper red color, nearly the very color of a copper penny. Nothing like the carroty color of the clerk's greasy tresses. She wore it loose and flowing around her head, which was itself unusual, and she seemed slightly amused by their obvious inability to take their eyes off her hair. She wrinkled her nose, which had a smatter of freckles across it, and said, "Aye, then. I'll bring ye a brew," and she spun to go.

By the time she returned with three mugs of beer, they had recovered their manners. She served them a delicious meal employing deft, quick movements that reminded Ella of a bird; she moved with the same flittering, perfectly balanced but rapid motions of a phoebe building a nest. There was no wasted motion. By the time they had eaten and she removed their plates, Ella was more fascinated by her hands than her hair.

"May I ask you something?" Ella said. "We're looking for a man who came here six years ago, to work as a smith at the glass factory. Were you here then?"

The girl laughed, her big teeth flashing. "Nay, not I. I weren't even in America then, I was a girl back in Dublin."

Appraising her, Ella deemed the girl to be of a similar age to Zeke, maybe twenty years or a bit younger. "His name is Asa Tunnicliff," she persisted. "We asked the clerk in the office of the glass works but he, well... suffice it to say he was no help. You must know most of the people in the town by working here at the tavern. Can you think of anyone who would have known him?"

The girl thought a moment. Then she said, "Nay, I don't know who does what at the glass works, but it'd be in the widow's papers. Do ye have a mind to look at them?"

They looked at one another in disbelief. Then Ella said, "The same widow who owns the glass works? You'd let us see her papers?"

"Oh aye. She owns this tavern as well. She kept the tavern first, and then the glass business came to her when her husband died. She has her office here and she keeps it that way. She moves papers over from the glass factory when the mood strikes her. Most of the older papers are here, seein' as she never parts with a single bloody thing."

They looked at one another again. This seemed too good to be true. "Wouldn't she dislike you letting us in her office? Mightn't you get in trouble?"

"Nay, I don't know nothing about it. If ye was to get in there with the key and look through some old papers, and leave everything just as you found it, what's the harm in it? Ta, not a mouse has to know. Won't harm the widow none. She won't be back for a few more days at the least."

"Do you have the key?"

"Key? Aye, I think so. Let me look." The girl took out a ring, located a key, and said "Come on then, make it quick. But just the one of you, it's a wee little room."

She led Ella up a narrow back staircase and strode to one of three doors across the landing. She tried a key in the lock, struggled with it a moment, and then said, "Nay, it's not the right one." She tried another, which also failed. She looked at Ella for a moment and wrinkled her nose. "All right then, I weren't born in Dublin for nothing, were I?" She peered more closely at the door and then pulled a pin out of her hair and deftly picked the lock. When the door swung open she winked at Ella and said, "Me da was known to pick a lock or two in his time and he made sure his kids all had the skill. He said ye never know when it might be useful like." In a swirl of skirts she was off back down the stairs, with Ella staring after the disappearing copper hair.

Ella turned and gazed into the small room crammed full of crates, furniture, and other jumbled things. She'd never seen so much in such a small space before. The room was dim and felt slightly dank, and she little relished the thought of being kept in such a close space. But she'd had a stroke of luck in being here at all and having the help of that girl with the bright hair. What was the girl's name? She hadn't even thought to ask. She sighed and began her task.

She thought it would take hours, but the widow proved more organized than the appearance of her room would suggest. It took less than an hour to find the crates of payroll ledgers. She began by reading through the records in the most recent crate, knowing it was almost too much to hope that she'd find her grandfather's name. So it proved, for when she'd read it through once, twice, and then again, she was certain his name wasn't on the recent ledger. Which meant he was no longer here. *What did I really expect?*

Next she located the ledgers for 1804, the year he would most likely have arrived, and combed through them week by week until here, finally, here it was: Asa Tunnicliff, smith. *Now what? What does that tell me? He was here, and now he isn't. But wait, those who were here then and knew him might still be here and might know something of where he went. Yes, another smith would know him. Was there another?* She scanned the ledger of the payroll and found two, a Conrad Clinker and a Bernard Dieter, both listed as smiths. Carefully she copied their names onto a scrap she was sure the widow wouldn't miss, then carefully returned every paper to its place in the boxes and put the boxes exactly where she'd found them.

She surveyed the room with her tracker's eye, erasing a few more telltale signs of her presence before making her way back downstairs. Jenny and Zeke were still at the table where she'd left them and they and the girl were having a laugh over something.

She held out the paper with the two names to the girl and said, "These two men would have worked in the smith with him. Do you know either of them?"

The copper-haired girl peered at the names and said, "I never heard of this Bernard Dieter fellow, but Clinker, aye, I know him. He's married to my cousin Bridget. They live just yonder down the way."

"Can you take us there?"

"Course I can, but you'd best wait to morning, as he's an old German and keeps to his time. He'll be to bed at eight o'clock sharp and that's coming quick like. He won't be answering any knocks at this hour."

Ella sighed. Then she remembered herself and said, "I thank you for all you're doing for us. You've been a great assistance. Can you tell me your name?"

The girl raised her chin and said, "Miss Molly McGilligan, at your service." Then she pushed her copper hair back over shoulder and said, "I do believe I spilled a bit of beer just now. I'll go see what I can do about it." She winked at them, gathered up their mugs, and took them back to the tap above the barrel to refill them. Both Ella and Zeke watched her as she went. Then they looked at one another and quickly averted their eyes, both suddenly shy. Jenny watched the exchange between them with a look of mild puzzlement.

THEIR LUCK REMAINED GOOD, as the next day was Saturday and the glass works were closed, such that Conrad Clinker was in his garden when they arrived at his cottage. He looked up at them with pale blue eyes that were cold at first, but warmed when they recognized Molly. His thinning hair showed beneath his brown broadcloth cap and he wore a neat striped waistcoat beneath a close-fitted wool coat.

"Ja," he said when they asked of Asa Tunnicliff, "I knew him. A good smith. He was here. He left two, no, maybe three years ago. When they put out a call for smiths at Martha Furnace. In the Pines, you know."

"Did he say why he left?" Ella asked.

"Ja, he said it was too dull here. Nothing changed from season to season. He said the iron furnace it goes out of blast in winter, so at least that changes the work for a time."

On the walk back to the tavern they asked Molly where Martha Furnace was to be found.

"Oh, it's a might good ways into the Pines. On the other side from here, beyond Batsto and Washington."

They were all quiet for a time, Ella thinking of what the African man had told them of the Jersey Pines as a place to hide. She wondered if her grandfather had been seeking the same obscurity.

She said, "Can you make us a map to get there?"

Molly considered this. "Nay, I wouldn't try it if'n I were you. The Pines is a right place to get good and lost. The sand roads all look the same."

Ella argued, trying to convince her they could find their way, but Molly refused to draw a map. At last she said, "You know then, if ye care to wait until the Widow Heston returns in a few days, I'll take ye myself. I have a mind to see Martha Furnace, seeing as me uncle Michael Mick is the founder there. In fact now, if you're in need of work, he might have a job for ye, he might."

"You have an uncle at Martha Furnace?" Zeke asked her in disbelief. "Is there anyone in New Jersey you're not related to?"

"Oh aye, sure. Though none of them Irish. All the pats are me kin."

They laughed at this. Then Jenny asked, "If we're to be waiting here for Widow Heston for a few days, is there work we might have while we wait? At least to earn our keep?"

Molly considered the question. "Can any of ye throw clay pots? I know they're needing a potter down at the clay shed and they're after me to fill in, seeing as me ma was a potter and learned me in it."

"I thought they made glass here," Jenny said, "not clay pots."

Molly laughed. "It's *for* the glass, ye daft girl. They put the glass in the clay pots when they melt it in the fire. The clay doesn't melt, you see. But they're forever breaking the pots and needing new ones."

"How about you go throw pots and we'll keep the tavern," Ella suggested. "In return for our bed and board."

Molly wrinkled her nose while she thought about this offer. "Can ye cook?" she asked at last. Zeke and Ella both looked at Jenny, who sighed. "I can. Some at least. Not as good as you, but I can manage. I wouldn't let those two anywhere near the kitchen, though."

"What will ye two be good for then?" Molly asked of Zeke and Ella. "Besides forever asking questions."

Ella grinned. Then she gazed around, thinking. At last she said, "We can carpenter. We'll build the widow a new stair to the front door, seeing as that one there is nearly rotted out. Is there anything else that needs fixing?"

Molly gave the room an appraising look. "Aye, I can think of a thing or two, or six or eight." She peered at them, clearly deliberating on whether she could trust them. She seemed to find assurance in what she saw. "All right, ye've got a deal there. I'd be might happy for a change from the tavern." She turned to Jenny, "If ye'll be the one tending to the customers, ye'll have to write down your numbers and let me fill in the ledger. The widow is a right hornet for writing in her ledger." She thought another moment. "One more thing. If ye'll be staying here for a bit, do ye play cards?"

After finishing all the repairs on their list, Ella was becoming restless by the time the Widow Heston at last returned to

Glassboro. Late one afternoon, she and Zeke were seated at one end of the long central table when the widow, wearing heavy dark skirts, appeared in the doorway of the tavern. Ella watched Mrs. Heston glance back at the newly rebuilt step leading up to her newly hung front door. She made no comment, but instead turned to look at Jenny, wearing the apron of a serving girl, then at a group of glassworkers having a drink of mimbo, and then at Ella and Zeke. All she said was, "Where's that Molly McGilligan?"

Jenny had opened her mouth to begin an explanation for Molly's absence when there was a step behind her and Molly appeared at her elbow, saying, "I'm right here, Widow Heston. Just stepped out for a wee moment. This here girl," she gestured at Jenny, "has been helpin' me to serve all them fellows, seein' as we've been busier than a cock in the henhouse." Molly gave the widow a winning smile, her effort only moderately blighted by the streaks of red clay across her cheek and forehead.

Ella looked between Molly and the widow, wondering if Mrs. Heston would believe this obvious tall tale. The widow, however, showed little interest in deciphering the clues to the truth. She stepped to the nearest empty chair and sank her weight gratefully into it, saying, "Bring me a hot tea, will you, Molly?"

"Aye, right away, Mistress. Do ye want it…*spiced* a bit as well?"

"Ah yes, certainly, the usual. You're a good girl, Molly."

Ella stood and made her way to the back in time to see Jenny gape as Molly poured the cup half full with whiskey before filling the remainder with tea. Molly winked at them both and whispered, "Makes a fine sleeping tonic, this does."

The widow closed her eyes in bliss as she tasted Molly's spiced tea. Before long she had hoisted herself off to her sleeping chamber, leaving Molly to arrange for the driver and the horse to have their suppers.

She asked no questions the next morning either, not until Molly informed her she intended to leave Glassboro to visit her kin at Martha Furnace. Then she said, "Who will see to the tavern, then, Molly? You're taking this girl with you too, I suppose?" She gestured at Jenny, whose name she had yet to inquire.

"Aye, I am, Mistress. But not to worry none, my cousin Bridget's girl will come to serve. I saw to her about it and she's well taken with it. I even told her how to make your spiced tea as you like it, Mistress."

"You're a good girl, Molly, you are. I suppose I'll get by without you until you get back." Then, as an afterthought she added, "Don't get caught there by the winter, mind you. You know how they close them roads in the Pines when the snow gets too deep."

"Aye, don't worry on that, Mistress, I'll get back in good time. I don't care to be spendin' a whole winter in a furnace town, that's for certain. They can be bloody rough, those towns."

"Not rougher than you, surely," Ella said mildly, looking up from the knife she was sharpening.

"No, that's the truth, init? None's rougher than me," Molly flashed them a roguish grin, then she said, "We leave tomorrow morn, then. That's time for another round of cards tonight. What do ye say?"

Zeke shook his head. "Play with the locals, Molly. You done cleaned us out already."

Molly gave a pretty pout. "That's none sportin' of ye." After a pause, she said, "All right then, we'll play for chits of some sort. Not for coin—just for sport. What do ye say to that?"

"You've got a game," Ella said firmly. When Molly had left the room she leaned in to Zeke and said, "I swear I'm going to solve it tonight—see how she cheats. No one has luck like she does. I'm certain she comes from a bunch of sharps, back in

Ireland—you should have seen how fast she picked that lock the day we came here."

Zeke nodded, having heard a bit of speculation on this vein before. Then he asked "If you think she's a sharp, can we trust her to travel with?"

Ella was thoughtful for a time. "I do trust her somehow, though why I should I couldn't say. It's as if she knows how to do it and she can't help herself. I expect she would cheerfully give it back if you catch her at it. And I do mean to catch her at it."

THIRTEEN

ELLA'S FOUL MOOD hung heavy on her as they set off from Glassboro the next morning. Despite that she'd only lost chits, she'd been unable to decipher the source of Molly's unaccountably good luck at last night's card game, and remained convinced there was a sleight of hand she'd failed to spot. It wasn't as if she'd never played cards before. Or won more often than not. But against Molly McGilligan, who'd played nearly every day of her life, she felt the gall of being a novice. She was unaccustomed to losing that steadily and didn't care for it, not one jot.

Molly, in contrast, was in a glorious mood, singing the "Lass of Aughrim" at the top of her lungs in a fine alto. She rode an old brown mare she'd borrowed from Conrad Clinker. The mare had a long German name, but Molly quickly discarded it in favor of calling her "Nell," after the pony she'd ridden as a child.

It was a fine early October dawn, with the cool morning mist soon burning off to glaring autumn sun. By noon they'd stripped off their outer wraps and were looking for a place to water the horses. After eating their dinner at the side of a creek, they made their way toward Hammonton, from where it was only about three more miles to Batsto, the closest of the big iron towns in the Pines. Before they reached Hammonton, Molly announced they might wish to stay in Batsto that night.

"In a tavern?" Jenny asked.

"Nay, don't be daft, girl. There be no taverns in these iron towns. The Richardses don't allow none, seeing as not a one of the furnace men would appear sober to work if they did. Nay, I have a cousin who'll give us a place at her table, and there's a mighty fine game that takes up most nights. They're a good sort there."

"Another cousin, how surprising," Ella said drily. Then, ignoring the invitation to yet another card game, she asked, "Who are the Richardses?"

Molly shrugged. "I don't claim to know one from t'other in that lot. There's the da, who just up and retired earlier this year—handed Batsto over to one of the sons—and a then a host of other sons. Together they own most of the furnace towns in the Pines.

"They *own* the furnace towns?" Jenny asked. "How can someone own a town?"

Molly shrugged again. "It's the way it's done, is all. When they own a furnace they get the town what comes with it. It has a store and a mill and a host of cabins for the workers. You'll see when you see it. And for certain you'll see the Richards who owns this one. They're all the time ridin' around on their big horses to see everything what goes on. Like a king or a duke or some such." She chuckled to herself. "King of the world's smallest kingdom."

Indeed, when they rode into Batsto in the later afternoon, the first sight to greet them was the tall figure of Jesse Richards, astride his gelding as he barked orders to his foreman. All around him people swarmed, mostly on foot but a few driving carts loaded with goods. It was a busy anthill of a place. And loud. The Batsto Forge wasn't even *in* the town itself, it was half a mile south, but the ringing of the forge hammers could be heard above and within the clamor of the furnace town itself, which included the hammers of the stamping mill for crushing bog ore and various other hammers in the smith shop. After all those miles of deep, quiet woods, the racket of the furnace town assaulted the senses. Ella had to fight the urge to cover her ears, turn, and run.

"You there, what's the trouble?" Jesse Richards barked at the driver of a paused ore cart. "The flux can't get through and they need it up the hill sooner than they need that ore." He pointed upward, in the direction all the loaded carts were heading.

Ella looked to where he pointed, which was a long sloping hill against which the towering grey stone furnace had been built. The furnace was shaped like a fat man with a delicate head and slender feet. In the center it swelled out to a great curved belly that held the hot molten mass of bog ore. Above and below the great belly it narrowed to an opening on either end: one on top for feeding the raw materials, one on the bottom for removing the purified molten metal.

From where she watched, the furnacemen on the top looked like ants as they pushed their wheeled carts back and forth across the small trestle bridge connecting the piles on the hill with the platform surrounding the great mouth of the furnace. Around and around the ants circled, feeding the mouth with alternating carts of bog ore, charcoal, and flux.

Ella slid off her horse and left her companions to make her way closer. Drawn to the furnace like a moth to a light, she tromped up the hill to the flattened plateau to inspect the huge piles of reddish ore, black charcoal, and grey-white crushed shells, used for flux. With workers milling all around, she threaded her way to the edge of the precipice and peered over the side to view the monstrous bellows below, blasting air into the belly to keep the raging fire red hot. A U-shaped canal looped in from the dam pond beyond, the water of the canal turning the water wheel that powered the bellows. It was an ingenious system for turning something useless—bog ore—into something profoundly useful—pure iron—using the plentiful wood and water of the Pines to power the change.

She trotted down the hill, admiring the glowing belly of the furnace before reaching the molding shed at the base, in which streams of molten metal flowed into molds. She looked up and was surprised to note a second stream of molten material coming out the side of the belly, forming a pile on a ledge of the hill. *That's not the pure iron*, she thought, *so what is it?* She grabbed the arm of the nearest passing man and said, "What's that up there?"

The man looked at her like she was a madwoman, but he paused long enough to tell her, "It's just the slag, Miss. The part that's a mix of coal and half-ore. It's lighter than the pure iron so it floats on top. We'll put it all back through again. Once it cools, that is. There's still plenty of iron in all that."

Ella looked up and frowned. She didn't like the look of all that slag. It looked to be a much greater portion than the iron coming out below. To put all that through the furnace again? There was so much waste in that. How could there be profit in a process that made more waste than product?

But then she stood back farther and looked at the full height of the great glowing tower and the busy men in attendance, and she could not help but feel grateful for getting the chance to see such a sight. Whatever its faults, the furnace was a magnificent beast.

The rest of the town existed solely to serve the beast, and as Molly had intimated, appeared to be ruled in entirety by Jesse Richards, the master and lord. The town was smaller even than Deborahville, and the only house that wasn't a cabin was the master's house, the mansion sitting squarely in the center of the town, where the master could see everything that went on and everyone felt his eye. Around and between the two tall structures—the mansion and the furnace—sprawled a scattering of small buildings, including a store and a gristmill for feeding the workers. It was a remarkable self-contained little unit, all directed to one end, the production of the iron that was sold to feed them all.

Ella was taken with the simplicity of it all, the single-minded focus of all the activity. She envied it. To have one straightforward task and follow it with all one's energy. Her own time was always stretched thin between too many obligations. Never mind how she herself would prefer to spend her time, alone in the forest. That aside, would she be able to focus on a single objective over many years? She'd never tried. *What's the use in wondering,* she thought at last, shaking her head, *seeing how far I am from getting that patent. Seeing as I cannot even find one old man.*

Molly took them to meet her cousin Mary Malone, Mary's husband Henry, and their six children. Ella peered into the tiny, cramped cabin teeming with children and said, "I'll camp at the edge of town."

"Me as well," Zeke agreed.

Jenny looked at the crestfallen face of the eldest girl in the brood and said, "I think I'd rather stay here. I'd like to ask about...uh, that quilt you're working on. It's a remarkable design." The elder girl's face brightened as Jenny stepped over to look at her piecework.

A little later, Ella and Zeke were just leaving the village smithing forge when Jenny flew out of the cabin yelling, "Ella! Ella! Where are you?"

Ella hailed her and Jenny flew across the paths between them until she was in earshot. "Ella! The girl knows him. Or, at least she's met him. At Martha..." Jenny stopped to catch her breath. "The girl, Bridget, Mary's eldest, she used to work as a hired girl at the mansion in Martha. She knows Grandpa Tunnicliff!"

"What did she say of him?" Ella demanded. "Is he alive? Is he well?"

"She doesn't recall much. Only that he was still there this spring, when she last worked in Martha, and as far as she knows he still works at the smith. She remembered him in particular because he was one of the few men the mistress of the mansion would allow in the house. To fix things and such. She didn't trust most of the workers, but she trusted grandfather." Jenny paused, and then, after a moment, added as if it explained something, "The mistress is a Quaker."

Ella felt her heartbeat quicken. Could they really be just a few mere miles away? He was alive last spring and it was now early October—shouldn't he yet be well just a few warm months later? The thoughts she'd been pushing to the back of her mind flooded forward once more and a potent mix of anxiety and excitement made her turn away to begin pacing the paths of Batsto, trying to calm her furious energy. Would they finally have answers to what drove him to this remote place, so far from all he'd built and cared about back in Deborahville? Why did he come here and, even more pressing, why did he stay?

SHE COULD HARDLY KEEP from rushing her companions through the next morning's breakfast. Molly was cheerful as usual, despite a game of cards, well-laced with cider royall, that lasted into the wee hours. Jenny, however, looked exhausted at trying to sleep with a loud game in the same room.

As they were clearing the remains of breakfast, Mary Malone asked Molly, "Ach, what have you heard from that brother of yours, then? Is he still at Martha? I heard Michael Mick gave him the boot at last, for causing such a fuss."

Ella, Zeke, and Jenny all looked at Molly, who'd never mentioned having a brother at Martha. She had the decency to blush. "Aye, my brother Billy McGilligan, he causes a fuss. He's a wee bit of a ladies' man, that one."

Mary Malone said, "Wee bit of a ladies' man? That's like sayin' a horse is a wee bit of a work animal." She gave Molly a reproachful look and then turned to Ella and Jenny. "Watch yourselves, girls. No one in skirts is safe around that fellow. Don't trust a word he says."

Jenny and Zeke looked at Ella, who looked down at her stained tunic over leggings and said, "Thank you for the warning, Mrs. Malone, but fortunately I'm not wearing my skirts at the moment, and I'll resist the temptation to don them."

"What skirts?" Jenny asked, looking at Ella. "I beg your pardon but you don't own any skirts."

"I beg your pardon but I do too," Ella answered with a mocking lift to her chin. "Mother made me pack an old yellow gown of hers in my saddlebag, for when I need to visit the patent office and look respectable."

"You've been carrying a gown in the bottom of your saddlebag all this time? It must be a smelly rag by now."

"Yes, that just about describes it," Ella agreed. "Though I haven't looked at it for quite a while. My whole bag smells of bear grease from the packet the Seneca gave us, so I imagine it must too."

"Bear grease?" Mary Malone said. "That's good and strong—I'd think it should serve the purpose of fending off Billy McGilligan if anything will. You might want to don those skirts fer protecting yourself as soon as you draw close on Martha. You'll hear the stamping mill to give ye plenty o' warning."

"Thank you, Mrs. Malone," Ella said gravely. "I'll take your advice to heart."

"And one more piece of advice for yeh, while I'm at it," Mary went on. "These woods are full of outlaws of all sorts. They is a rough bad lot and ye should be careful to steer clear o' them. 'Twas just last month a girl was, well… I don't need to say. You be careful is all." She turned to Zeke. "You be sure you keep a look out for 'em, hear me?"

"Yes, ma'am," he said dutifully.

SETTING OFF ON THE SAND ROAD between Batsto and Washington, they made good time for the morning. The road was a good one and all around them the pine and oak grew ever thicker, and the sand whiter, as they approached the heart of the Pines. The creeks, where they ran near the road, held the clear tea-colored water that flowed throughout the Pines, water so full of tannins leached from leaves of pines and oaks and cedars that it never went rank, but remained sweet and potable indefinitely. It had, they'd heard, long been favored by sea captains for filling their water barrels.

They turned right at the sign pointing east to Washington, the crossroads in the middle of the Pines. Reaching it, they passed a few small houses and then came to the intersection of five roads. At the midst of the crossroads sat a large and commodious tavern, at which they stopped to take a drink of cider and stretch their legs.

"Which way be you going?" the tavern keeper asked them.

"To Martha, Mr. Sooy," Molly told him.

"You'll not want to be takin' the road to Upper Bank, that's for certain. A coach just brought word that a fire's been sighted that a-way. You'll want to stay north toward Bodine's."

Molly thanked him. Then, turning to her companions, told them, "The road to Bodine's Tavern is a little boggy and we'll have to make a few more turns, but we'll want to stay well clear of fire in these forests. I've never run into one meself, but I've heard many a tale of one. The fires here are right bad."

"Listen well to this young lady," Mr. Sooy warned them. "She's quite right. It's the dry leaves and all that oil in them. They burn fast and hot and the fires move quicker than you can step outta the way. Best advice is to give them a good wide berth."

FOURTEEN

IN DEBORAHVILLE, Lucille Tunnicliff stepped through the door of the Kenyon house and called, "Catherine? Where are you?"

When there was no answer, she checked the yard and saw Catherine's small buckboard wagon was parked in its usual place, which meant Catherine must be here somewhere. She peered in the kitchen, and, seeing no one, stepped through to the sitting room, where Catherine was sound asleep in her favorite rocker.

She heard Lucille and woke with a start, her face relaxing into a smile when she saw who it was. "Oh, it's you. Thank heavens. I was having a terrible dream, but never mind that now." She stood and stretched her back. Lucille thought she looked pale for this time of late summer, when she should be rosy with outside work.

"Are you feeling well?" Lucille asked.

"What? Yes, of course, why wouldn't I be?" Catherine waved a gently dismissive hand. "Here, come in the kitchen and I'll brew some tea. Or would you rather coffee?"

Lucille narrowed her eyes as she watched her friend move into the kitchen. Catherine's movements were slower and less graceful than usual, her long fingers moving from item to item as she struggled to remember what she was about to do.

"Catherine," Lucille's voice was sharper than she'd intended, "you should come stay with me for a few days. Let me care for you. You've worn yourself out with caring for everyone else."

Catherine's gentle smile returned. "Oh Lucille, you're very sweet. But I couldn't do that..." she gestured out the window to the farm, "there's chores and all, and no one would find me if there was an sickbed to attend. And Amherst you know..."

"No, Catherine, I don't know. You've had good excuses all the years you've had children in the house, but Amherst is hardly a child—he can do the chores and feed himself. You need rest."

Lucille stared at Catherine, who sank onto the bench along the oak trestle table and rested her head in her hands. In a muffled voice she said, "I'd like that, Lucille. Believe I speak the truth when I say that. But I can't leave here."

"Why not?"

Catherine lifted her head and her round eyes looked enormous in her pale face, reminding Lucille of how she had looked as a child of ten or twelve. Except then she hadn't looked exhausted and utterly haggard. "Lucille," Catherine said slowly, "after all these years, don't you understand? If I leave here, I'll never come back. I wouldn't be able to make myself and he wouldn't let me return. And where does that leave me? The only pride I have left is in doing my duty, nothing else. If I quit on that, what else is there?"

"What of your duty to others besides Amherst? To all the people you heal with your medicines? To your children when they return? What good will you be if you're a dish rag?"

"What good will I be if I'm a homeless vagabond? Don't you think I've thought of it?"

Lucille was silent a moment, then, knowing it was futile, she said, "You always have a home with me."

Catherine smiled her soft smile. "I know, dear. You've been so good to me. But it's not as bad as you imagine. Some days are bad, but others are mostly all good. I'm fine. Just tired today, that's all. Nothing more."

"All right then, if you say so," Lucille said with obvious doubt. Then, with a brisk wave of her hand she strode over and lifted the kettle. "Here, now, let me make that tea."

Walking home, Lucille could not help wondering if Catherine's exhaustion was due in part to her own continued refusal to help Amherst out of his financial troubles. Or even sanction his belief in the promise of false bank notes. She'd done her best to dissuade Amherst, aided by having left the bank note business herself, but he'd proven more tenacious than she could have imagined. Recently he'd returned to threatening a malicious gossip campaign.

Her feet paused as a thought occurred to her. She stood a moment, then, when she reached her own back pasture, she turned away from the house and made instead for the road to town.

HENRY EMERSTON WELCOMED HER as cordially as always, and as always she was put at ease by the warm colors and scents of his office: the deep brown of the walnut desk, the spicy tang of pipe smoke, the rich reds of the Persian carpet. Something of the room always evoked a faint memory of her father, someone she could recall only in unexpected glimpses. She suspected he must have smoked a pipe, for the scent of the tobacco always brought on a longing for New Orleans, the home of her childhood.

Today there was no time to dwell on long-lost memories; she came straight to the point. "We have a problem, Henry."

She got no further before he said, "Let me guess; his name is Amherst Kenyon."

"You know?"

"Let's just say I suspected." He gave her a long look, then added, "I would have thought you'd have come to me sooner."

She stared at him, not certain what to think. "I thought I could handle him myself, that he could be talked out of it. But now he's threatening to start rumors that will tarnish my and Janet's reputations, unless we bring him in and sell him false notes." She paused to eye Emerston with a speculative look. "I've told him nothing. Nothing at all. But I can't imagine it would be good for your own business to have rampant rumors of a counterfeiting ring start to take hold here. Or for George Loomis either, now that I think of it."

Henry Emerston nodded pleasantly. "Yes, you're quite right about that. And it's a shame, really, for we can always use another passer, especially now that you and Janet have departed our ranks." He raised his eyebrows in mock disapproval. "But Amherst Kenyon is much too loose a cannon to trust with information of any sort. We'll have to think of a way to quiet him that will protect all our good names."

"You do still hold a lien on his mill, do you not?"

"Oh yes, most certainly. You think I should threaten to call it in if he's not quiet?"

"Well, something along those lines. I hadn't thought it through."

Emerston's eyes crinkled as he smiled. "That's rather crass, my dear. I prefer something more subtle. Let me give it more thought and I'm certain I'll come up with something that will make us all happy, even the good Mr. Kenyon. I have a feeling that throwing him a bone will do wonders for his mood."

Lucille regarded him with a level look. "I have every confidence that you'll think of something clever, Henry. You always do."

"Thank you, my dear. I do my best, for what it's worth."

Lucille began to rise, but Henry Emerston motioned her back down. "Stay just one more minute, won't you? I have another small matter to discuss with you. It's about your niece and her design for the flax engine."

Lucille cocked her head to signal him to continue. He said, "I fear there was quite a bit of ill feeling around how that unfolded, and their sudden departure. Some time has passed by now and as tempers, including my own, have cooled, I hope to relay that I do not wish these hard feelings to remain in place indefinitely. Not given the close history between the families." He paused to see her reaction. "I understand her motivations for acting as she did, given what she suspected me of trying to do. I hope, given the opportunity, that you'll make clear to her I regret allowing it to appear that I was in any way acting for my own advance." He paused again. "I would be grateful if you'd be kind enough to tell Miss Kenyon that the matter did not stand as it appeared. That I would never in any way interfere with her rightful ability to patent the machine."

"To what do you refer?" Lucille asked, thinking it prudent to remain neutral.

"You don't know?" he replied, incredulous. Then, after a moment, he continued, "Upon breaking into my strongbox, she found papers that must have suggested I was attempting to patent the machine in my own name, rather than hers. What she couldn't have known, not having asked me, was that those were merely drafts in which I was working out the language of the application and didn't bother to fill in the names properly. If she'd taken the time to look at them more closely, she'd have seen they were hardly completed application documents."

Lucille considered his words. At last she said, "It seems a shame, does it not, that both you and she have acted so hastily? Where you might have assisted one another, now you are at odds. I wouldn't count on easy forgiveness from that girl, for she's as stubborn as they come. Yet, despite that, I will keep it in mind to forward your explanation if ever the opportunity arises. I would prefer to see harmony between the families, given all that has passed to date."

"Thank you, Lucille. I know that's the best you can do."

UPON REACHING HOME she found her feet taking her past her own house, down the path that led to Pete's lodge. She stood in the clearing, staring at the cold lodge. *Just a little hint of smoke from the top, that's all I ask. Is it too much that he should be here when I need to speak to him? Do I have no claim at all on his time?* She shook her head at her own silliness and turned back to her own house.

Funny, she thought yet again, her twisted life—how she had turned down Emerston and her other beaus to hold out for love, and then, in the end, married someone she didn't love. While all along loving someone she could never marry. With an ache she thought again of how long it might be until Pete returned. It was always like this when he was away, even after all these years. In some ways it was always a relief, that he wasn't nearby to tempt her to indiscretion. But mostly she just gritted her teeth to bear that he wasn't near. That she could not go take shelter in his arms. Those unlikely brown arms, so muscled, so thick. She shivered slightly despite the heat. It was always like this, with her and Pete.

She could no longer recall what it was like before she knew him, those brief few years of girlhood when she tried to adjust to life in this cold northern town, banished from the heat and pulsing life of the New Orleans she'd always known. She'd come north to be trapped in a frugal house with an aunt and uncle who were kind enough, but let her feel her obligation to them.

It had all felt so barren, with so little hope of change. Then had come the summer of her sixteenth year, when she'd finally been allowed to ride out alone on her uncle's black mare. She'd ridden all day, letting the horse have her head as they explored the hills together. Until at last her thirst brought her to the sparkling creek on the far side of a clearing. She was picking her way down to the creek, pulling her gown from the grip of brambles, when she managed to put the toe of her delicate boot into the loop of the snare, which she'd never have noticed if she hadn't tripped it. As the bent tree released, the snared yanked her foot straight into the air. She had only the briefest of moments to be shocked before her head smacked a stone and all went black.

When she woke it was full dark and she was hanging by her foot, which was bound so tightly by the snare that she could no longer feel it. A wave of pure panic washed over her. Her first instinct was to scream, to cry out for help. Then she remembered there was no one to hear her, except the bears and the wolves, and the savages, and it was best not to attract such attention. When she forced herself to calm down and think, she quickly realized that all she must do was release the laces of her boot so her foot might slip out.

In the dark she reached up and attempted to untie the laces, but she found her fingers refused to work properly after she'd been hanging upside down so long. She beat her hands together to attempt to restore feeling to them, took several deep breaths, and then went to work once more on the laces. She'd never imagined it could be so difficult to work a shoe-lace. When she at last managed to disengage the laces, her foot slipped out of the boot and she hit the ground with a sharp thud that once more rendered her senseless.

She woke at the faint light of earliest dawn because she had the sense of an animal approaching. The spark of fear immedi-ately brought her alert. When she'd focused her eyes she saw it was not an animal crawling toward her, but rather a man. An Indian man. He had been approaching on hands and knees and he saw her at the same time she saw him. He stopped and stared, first at her and then at the loop of the snare hanging above her head, in which yet dangled her black boot, the laces swaying loose.

Her body tensed in fear. She looked around for her mare and tried to gauge whether she had a hope of making a dash from the savage, perhaps catching him by surprise. She had climbed a tree once and perhaps she could do it again, especially if it were the only means to escape this fierce-looking man. He wore feathers in his hair and had some type of paint smeared across his broad chest, which looked to be twice as wide as that of most men. His arms rippled with thick muscles and she knew she would stand no chance once he had a hold of her. She readied herself to make a dash.

Just then the Indian pointed up at her dangling boot. He said, "Don't leave without shoe." Then he stood upright and looked down at her, and his face split into the widest grin she'd ever seen. He threw his head back and gave a great soundless laugh.

Her immediate reaction was relief. If he was laughing he wasn't about to murder her. Or kidnap her. Or worse. Following close behind relief was a heated fury. How dare he laugh at her? After all she'd been through, and seeing as he must have been the one to set the snare that did this to her. What right had he? The anger coursed through her and she reached her hand to find a stone, which, when she found one, she threw at his chest with all her force.

It bounced off his chest and he looked down in surprise, noting the small red welt it had left. Then he looked at her and laughed even harder, apparently because she had thought to attack him. She had already grabbed another stone and was prepared to throw it at the same spot when he said, "No, miss. No need throw at me. I do not hurt you."

"I'm not concerned that you'll hurt me. I'm concerned that you're laughing at me. What right do you have, when you've put me through this...this nightmare? By setting snares where you shouldn't?"

His laughter stilled and he looked at her steadily, though there was yet a twinkle of amusement in his eyes. "Where I shouldn't?" he repeated. His eyes took on a glint of challenge.

"Yes, what right have you to set snares here? Does this land belong to you?"

He stared at her a long time. "I hunt these lands since I small boy. My father he hunt before me. His father before him. When you come here?"

She began to defy him, to challenge him, to argue with him, but then she had the grace to become ashamed. Her face colored and she said, "I am new here."

Instead of looking smug or otherwise pleased, the Indian said, "Then welcome. We must live here in peace." He paused and then added, "I am Tewagtahkotte, known as Standing Bridge. Americans, you call me Pete."

He looked at her expectantly and she obliged by saying, "I am Lucille Dubreuil. I live with my aunt and uncle in Deborahville. Down there." She pointed into the valley.

"Yes, I know town." He nodded and then reached up to free her boot from the snare. She sat and laced her boot while he re-set the snare. When he was done he turned to her and said, "I think you fat rabbit. Food for many days."

"Sorry to be a disappointment to you."

"Not disappointment," he said with a twinkle. "Next time let rabbit walk in snare. Not you."

She began to sputter and then realized he teased. Before she could say anything else, he said, "You have horse. We find. Come." He made off into the woods across the clearing and she had to run to catch up to him. She then had to continue running, for despite moving silently he moved at such a rapid pace that she could only get an occasional glimpse of him ahead. She had no idea how he followed the horse, for she could see no prints of any kind on the dry bed of the forest. She ran to keep up and every time she thought she had lost him altogether, he'd be waiting for her just ahead. After a time she realized he must be listening for her behind him, and that he could do so because she was making so much noise.

At last she came upon him waiting at the edge of a small upland meadow. In the center of the meadow was the black mare, grazing. She raised her head as Lucille approached and Lucille ran to her, running her hands up and down the black legs to check for wounds. When at last she remembered to thank the Indian for finding her horse, she looked up at where he'd been and he was gone. She called to him but there was no answer.

It was nearly a whole year before she saw him again. So much happened in that year she turned seventeen that she nearly forgot all about him. Her aunt and uncle had died abruptly that winter, when they'd caught a pox within a few days of one another. She'd inherited their house and their land, which wasn't any great holding, but she had little idea how to manage it. She had even less idea how to manage the flock of young men who'd begun to surround her after church, vying for her attention. She was flattered and pleased by this new game, but secretly felt herself an imposter in the role.

Her only anchor in all that time was Catherine, her closest friend. In fact her only friend. Catherine lived just across the woods with her pa the captain and her brother John, and she was the only person in town with whom Lucille could speak her mind. Despite their many differences, Catherine put her at ease as no one else could.

The next time she saw Pete she was strolling down Main Street with Catherine on a summer afternoon, pretending not to notice the young men who stopped to watch her. She had a parasol tipped in front of her face, such that she couldn't see much of the street in front of her. It was only when Catherine nudged her in the ribs of her corset that she'd lifted the parasol to look at the Indian standing against the hitching post, his arms up on the railing behind him, watching them approach. He wore little more than a breechcloth and a set of beaded arm bands. His hair was shorn close on the sides and sported several feathers. But what caught her gaze and held it was his chest, a broad expanse of glossy reddish brown skin.

She didn't notice she was staring until she looked up a few inches into the face of the man and saw he was laughing at her with his eyes. It was then she recognized him as the same Indian she'd met in the woods the year before. The one she'd chastised for laughing at her. The way he looked at her now was somehow intimate, as if they shared a secret. She flushed a deep scarlet. In confusion she turned to Catherine, who gazed at her and then eyed the man. "Do you know that Indian?"

"No," she lied. "I have no idea why he's staring at me."

After that she was never able to forget him again. She told herself to do just that, but she continued to disobey herself. She would find herself thinking of him at odd moments in the day. It would have been left at that, except that Catherine hurried into her kitchen one day saying, "I know who that Indian is. He came to deliver a message to my pa at the house. It seems he was an aide to my pa when they fought in the war against the British. My pa said he's Oneida. They call him Standing Bridge, or sometimes—"

"Pete" Lucille interjected.

Catherine, startled, had said, "How do you know that?"

So Lucille told her the story of the snare and the black mare. When she was done, Catherine said, "I think you'd best be cautious, Lucille. He's a right devil, that one. You can bet he has his pick of the Indian ladies, and I wouldn't be surprised if he's known some white girls as well. There's something about him that says he's used to having his way."

Lucille nodded and once more determined to put him out of her mind. She succeeded, mostly, at least until the day he'd appeared at her back door. She opened it to discover him standing there, holding a brace of pheasants. He'd smiled at her, a broad white smile that made her catch her breath as he handed her the game. Then he was gone in a flash of black and red.

After that he haunted her thoughts. It wasn't that he was a handsome man. His features were rugged, certainly commanding, but not handsome. No, it was something in the contrast between his hard face and his laughing eyes that was so arresting. That made her eager to know more of what he thought, how he saw things. That somehow gave her the sense that he *saw* her, more clearly than anyone else in this remote place could see her. And it was so intriguing that he'd suddenly brought her a gift. What might he be thinking?

He'd brought her gifts twice more, leaving quickly each time. Only at the fourth visit had he ventured to ask if she'd care to take a walk with a handsome stranger. She'd started to retort on his presumption, when she realized he was teasing again. She smiled and said she'd get her cloak, despite her apprehension that they'd be seen together. It could never have happened if her aunt and uncle had been alive. But she was alone now; there was no one to stop her.

They'd walked across the fields and into the woods. Down old trails and paths she hadn't known existed, but that he seemed to know well. At first they made awkward talk, leading nowhere. But then he made one of his boastful jokes that caused her to laugh out loud, until she was wiping tears from her eyes. After that they spoke more easily. He told her amusing stories of his travels. She struggled to find anything nearly as interesting to tell him and finally settled on telling what she could remember of New Orleans, a place he'd yet to see.

All the while as they walked, she was aware that her skin prickled. That she itched to move closer to him, to feel how warm he might be. To feel his skin. Once she caught him looking at her with eyes that weren't laughing for once. That wanted something. She held his look for a moment, was unable to break away from it, but then felt the danger and said something to restore the light tone they'd held to all afternoon.

She'd resisted that day. As well as the next day, and for many days after. But she couldn't resist seeing him altogether They walked miles on miles together, telling one another increasingly intimate stories of their lives, the things they'd never told before. With him she felt herself, as she did with no one else. Herself and fully safe. It was a potent brew.

At last there came a day when they could resist no longer and were wedded. At least in body, for Lucille wouldn't hear of a legal wedding. It made no sense to her. A white woman couldn't live with an Indian man as husband and wife. Not here in Deborahville, at least. Not without being shunned. No, she needed the protection of a white husband and she yet held out hope she'd find one she could regard half as well as she did Pete. That this dangerous love for Pete would fade.

But it never had, as much as she'd hoped for it. If anything it burned only more hot and bright over the years, bringing them as much misery as joy, but never letting them out of its fierce grasp.

He'd traveled for much of the time, because he would grow restless with the restrictions of his life in Deborahville. Certainly there must have been other women, though he never said and she never asked. But then, somehow, he would always come back, to light the fire in his lodge and welcome her when she went out to see him.

MANY MILES SOUTH in northern Pennsylvania, a boy and a man rode away from a small Indian village amid the muted shades of early winter. A silver sky and dark grey branches stretched above them, a snarl of blowing leaves circled on the frosted brown dirt below. Neither the horse beneath him nor the man behind him could see the frown carved into the boy's face, but both could feel it. With every muscle Jimson expressed his opposition to leaving the village. To leaving his adopted brothers. His place among the Seneca.

Pete had known the likelihood the boy would flee and hide when he heard Pete wished to leave before winter. The boy would call on all his nascent skill to cover his tracks. Pete had also known he could and would find the boy, and in the end he'd force him to leave. He'd considered this possibility, and then he'd done something to avoid it. He'd done the one thing that would test the true depth of the boy's learning: he went to the boy and quietly told him it was time to leave.

As his elder, his guardian, he spoke with a simple authority that no other boy in the village would consider opposing. Jimson knew this. His eyes flashed with rapid resistance, but then, after a moment, he dropped his chin to signal submission, just as a well-raised Seneca boy should. Pete put an approving hand on his shoulder.

It wasn't until they were mounted to ride away that the boy's control began to slip. That he could no longer keep himself from resisting the parting, from the urge to slip off the horse and run straight back to the village. To his credit he said nothing with his mouth; only the way he held his body revealed the struggle within. Pete's face remained impassive. He guided the horse back onto the roads that led north, back to Deborahville and the white faces they'd left months earlier. For the first time in a long time, he allowed himself to think of Lucille.

FIFTEEN

IN THE PINES, they had every intention of taking Mr. Sooy's advice, but it was beyond their control that the winds shifted and brought the fire northeast by mid-afternoon. They smelled the smoke long before they saw the first ashy clouds over the tops of the trees. When they came to the next intersection of sand roads, they took the one farthest to their left, leading farthest northwest, away from the fire—despite that it was no longer the most direct road to Martha Furnace.

Ella knew they should probably stay in place and wait to see which way the fire would turn, but it was so much easier to keep moving, so difficult to sit and wait. The road began to curve, once to the east, another time west. The sun became obscured by both smoke and clouds, such that it gave them little direction. The sand roads began to blur one with another as they hurried to reach the next intersection.

When they arrived at an intersection that looked just like all the others before it, the smoke was now at their backs. They had no idea which road to take, so they took the one that seemed to head away from the smoke. They did the same at the next, and the next, until finally, when they came to yet another intersection that looked just like the last, they no longer had any idea which direction they were heading. Jenny slid off the horse she shared with Ella and put her hand around the rein. "I would swear we've traveled in a dead circle. We're lost—let's admit it."

"That's a fool thing to say," Ella said sharply. "You're never lost if you can go back the way you came. We can always do that."

"Oh you think so?" Jenny said, her eyes sharpening on Ella. "I don't think so. I think we've been traveling in circles on these roads that all look the same, and the sand holds almost no print."

Ella shrugged. "That's because you don't know much of tracking. There's always sign to follow. We can always go back."

"Then let's do it," Jenny challenged her.

"What do you two think?" Ella asked Zeke and Molly. Zeke shrugged, apparently disinclined to take a side.

Molly, who had begun to show the wear of last night's late card game, said, "I just want to get off this bloody horse. My backside's likin' to fall off any time now. 'Tisn't possible we'll make Martha tonight in any case. I say we pull off and make camp and use the sun to find the way in the morning, when the smoke has cleared some."

Jenny nodded at this suggestion. Ella gazed from face to face. She'd been so looking forward to reaching Martha today that the thought of not getting there hurt like a stab wound.

"It's just one more night," Zeke told her, as if reading her thoughts. "We've been traveling for months; what difference will one more night make?"

There was no arguing with this logic. It would be dark soon enough and this was as good a place as any to wait until they could navigate again. Wearily they put together what was left of their dried meat for a meager supper. Then they rolled out their blankets and fell asleep under a hazy sky.

THEY HAD ASSUMED the fire to be well out by the time they bedded down for the night, for Nicholas Sooy had told them all the men from all the towns around had rushed to help fight it. This assumption showed how little they knew of fire in the Pines. Sometime in the early hours of the morning Ella and Zeke were startled awake at the same moment by the acrid smell of smoke.

"It's close," Zeke said, immediately awake.

"Wake the others," Ella told him. "I'll saddle the horses. We need to get moving and quickly."

Molly and Jenny were already awake, aroused by the combination of voices and smoke. They were both groggy for several minutes, staggering around as they attempted to roll up their blankets and collect their belongings. When they were all four finally mounted, Molly was awake enough to say, "We need to get to burned ground. This fire's too close to run from."

"What?" Ella demanded. "What are you saying? That we need to *cross* the fire?"

"Aye, that's exactly what I'm saying. We need to cross the fire and get to burned ground if we've got any chance. Ye have no bloody idea how fast these things can move. I heard of a man burned alive when he was caught between fires, just last year. And if this one's a smaller offshoot of the main fire—carried on the wind as they do—crossing it will be possible if'n we can find a thin spot."

"How the hell do you do that?" Ella had never heard of such a thing. There were a lot of things about the Pines that were different from anywhere she'd ever been. Molly knew them better than she did, but to purposely cross a fire? That seemed madness.

"Ye look for a spot where you can see black behind the fire. Leastways that's what my brother told me when he schooled me on it. He said if the fire's close enough to make ye hold your nose, ye must look for a place where ye can see black behind the flames and make a run for it."

"Shouldn't you get your clothing wet first?" Zeke asked.

"He didn't say. But that seems right smart to me."

"Me too," Ella and Jenny said in unison. Then Ella said, "There was a creek just a few hundred yards back down that trail, let's head that way." She clucked Dapper Dan into a gallop, and in fright at the fire he was happy to make speed. At the creek they rode the horses in, then slid off and doused themselves and the horses as thoroughly as possible. Then, taking a deep breath, they looked at one another and headed toward the flames that were just now visible through the trees.

When they reached the front of the flames, the horses reared and refused to move forward any farther. It was all they could do to keep their seats. The one stroke of good fortune was that this did appear to be a smaller offshoot of the main fire, as they could see to either end of it and could also see black behind it. In places it looked to be no more than ten or fifteen feet wide.

They slid off their horses and took hold of the reins to lead the horses into the ground fire in front of them. They'd walked just a few steps when Molly tripped on a branch and fell, losing her grip on the reins. Her horse quickly reared and backed away, and in a moment was streaking off in the opposite direction. When they saw her go, Dapper Dan and Philippa rolled back their eyes and reared, twisting free so they too could streak away from the advancing blaze.

They watched the horses go and then turned to one another. "I hope they're fast enough to outrun the fire," Zeke said.

"They are, at least without us on their backs," Ella said with a greater confidence than she felt. They turned back to the wall of flame and then, holding hands, they counted to three, held their breath, and raced across the blaze, not slowing until they were a full fifty feet or more into the blackened ground behind the fire.

They exchanged a look again, their faces streaked with soot and grime. The ground beneath their feet was hot, but not hot enough to burn them. They gazed around at the blackness surrounding them. They were safe. On foot now, but safe. Their teeth blazed white in their grimy faces as they exchanged tired grins, grateful to be alive.

It wasn't until they'd walked a little ways and begun to relax did they realize they'd not only had no breakfast, but what little was left of their food was in the packs on the horses, together with all their other belongings. Their intended one-day journey from Glassboro was now into its third day.

"We'll just have to make Martha today," Jenny said. "It shouldn't be much farther, should it?" she asked Molly with a plaintive note to her voice.

Molly looked at her and shrugged, clearly not sure of the answer. Then she smoothed back her vivid copper hair with one grimy hand and said with a forced cheerfulness, "We're bound to find it afore too long, aren't we?"

"Yes we are," Ella agreed, unwilling to let Jenny be so worried. She looked up at the smoke-dense sky and said, "It should start clearing soon, and then all we must do is head east toward the sun. We're bound to come out somewhere close to Martha. I think I can even make out the sun faintly—over that way." She pointed above the trees. "Let's head into it."

They tried to ignore their rumbling stomachs as they walked toward what they thought might be the sun, though it was hard to say for certain. They picked their way through a patchwork of burned and unburned ground, a black and green quilt with a pattern that made little apparent sense. The burned sections were easier to walk through, for they'd been cleared of underbrush, but they trudged straight on east without veering one way or the other. In the unburned sections they stopped to look for something edible, but there was nothing to be found. Zeke tried chewing an oak leaf and spit it out quickly. "It's like chewing leather."

There were a few other plants that looked potentially edible, but nothing Jenny recognized. She'd seen enough accidental poisonings back in Deborahville that she wouldn't let them taste anything to test it. Ella kept her knife handy and an eye out for game, but everything big and little had fled the fire. The few animals they came across were burned beyond recognition. Ella sniffed one pile of burned fur. "Skunk."

They had walked for nearly four hours before at long last they came to one of the sand roads. It was fully burned over, but they had never seen anything as beautiful as this road, for it must somehow lead out of the woods. But, according to what little they could see of the sun, the road didn't lead east toward the ocean, toward Martha, but instead ran nearly due north and south. They knew from their ramblings on these same-looking roads that it could take a sharp turn at any point, but there was no way to know when that might happen.

After some discussion they could not agree what to do. Ella held forth for ignoring the road and continuing due east, for at last they could see the sun well enough to navigate by it. Jenny and Molly sided together for sticking with the road and heading north. Zeke thought maybe south, but could see the logic in all the options. They briefly considered splitting up their party, but quickly saw the ill wisdom of that.

So it came to drawing straws. Molly gathered up twigs, broke them to size, and started to hold them out for others to choose. But Ella put her hand on Molly's arm and said, "Here, let me do that." She took the twigs, examined them, and held up two short straws. She raised a sharp eyebrow at Molly, who twitched a corner of her mouth. "'Twas worth a try, weren't it?"

Ella replaced the second short straw with a full-length one and held them out to draw. Jenny got the short one that allowed her to choose and quickly made her choice to stay north on the road.

"Are you certain?" Ella asked.

"Yes, I'm certain. I don't want to leave the road again."

"Fine. Then let's be off."

The road stayed north for about two miles before at last making a sharp turn, but the turn took it due west, away from Martha Furnace. At least as far as they thought, for they had no real idea where they might be in relation to their destination. They'd left the area of the fire soon after they'd made their choice to head north, but as yet they'd met no one nor seen a single live animal. They'd eaten nothing all day and little the day before. They slumped down in exhaustion and frustration.

Jenny's eyes brimmed with tears. "I'm so sorry. This is all my fault. I shouldn't have chosen to head north, as the road hasn't brought us any closer to Martha. I was just afraid to leave it again. I should have listened to you, Ella."

"Stop that," Ella said to her sharply. "I didn't know anything more than you did. This road could just have easily led us straight into the heart of Martha Furnace. Stop making this your fault—it's not."

Jenny gazed around at them all, and then, taking a breath, stepped off the sand road and led them due east into the trees again. The going was slow from the thick tangles of underbrush, becoming faster only in the deeper shade of thick-growing trees, where there was only a carpet of leaves below. It took them nearly two hours to cover another mere two miles, and as yet they'd seen nothing different from what they've been looking at all day. They kept walking as the light began to fade, but they started to trip and stumble in the deepening dark of a moonless night and realized they had no choice but to make camp again, especially as Zeke had twisted an ankle and was limping.

The temperature was dropping as they wrapped their arms around themselves and tried to sleep, dearly missing the blankets that had been on the horses. During the night the temperature continued to drop, such that they stirred uneasily in their half sleep, unable to escape the cold.

In the granite grey light of dawn they woke to a drizzling rain and yet another drop in temperature. Zeke's ankle had begun to swell and they stayed where they were for a while, pressed together for warmth and too exhausted to face getting up and trying to find their way once more. The rain increased to a steady downpour, until at last they arose, shivering, and collected wood to make a fire to warm their stiff limbs and brittle fingers. But the wood all around was wet, such that even Ella, normally an expert with a flint, could not get it to light. It didn't help that her head was pounding and her hands had begun to shake from the cold, and from the relentless gnawing in her stomach. She sat heavily on a rock and put her head in her hands.

For a long moment she sat there, wishing herself someplace else. Anywhere else. Then she forced herself to look up. She peered into the three faces circling the spot where the fire should be, at their crusty, swollen eyes and pinched blue lips. Zeke had his eyes closed with the pain in his ankle and he looked unnaturally pale. She realized they weren't as accustomed to the woods and could die of cold if she didn't find a way to get them dry and warm. Hard walking would do it, but when she looked up at the sky she saw it remained grey as stone. They might walk all they like, but there was no way to know which way to go. Until the sun returned once more, they were just as likely to walk in the opposite direction. Which meant that as much as she wished to curl up in a ball to stop the pounding in her head, or let the cold take over until she could feel nothing more, she needed to buck herself up and get a fire going. There was no one else to do it so she might as well get on with it. *At least I have my flint*, she thought. *It could as easily have been in the saddlebags instead of my pocket.*

She stood, wiped her flint on the inside of her tunic, where it was warm from her body and at least relatively dry, strode toward the pile of twigs and bark she'd assembled, and with two sharp strikes made a spark that grabbed quickly at the bark but then, after a few moments, went out. She tried it once more, but again it failed to take hold. She tried five more times. Ten. Then she took a deep breath, willed herself to remain calm, and struck with a measured intensity. This time the tiny spark caught a piece of bark and by some miracle, it held. She cradled the tiny smoldering pile of shredded bark strips until the puff of smoke kindled into a small flame. Then she blew it lightly and it spread and caught the twigs. She watched it for a few moments, thinking she'd never seen anything more beautiful.

She shivered in her wet clothes and reached inside her tunic to make sure her oilskin packet was still safe and whole. At least her papers and the gold watch had stayed dry. When she had the fire going well, she stood and found the single water sack remaining to them and made for the sound of a stream a little way into the woods.

She filled the sack and returned to the fire to make tea with the few crumbs of tea leaves she had found in her pocket. They'd carried a small pot on their saddlebags, but it too was now gone; she'd have to find another way to heat water. She thought it over and then, after a time, took a deep breath and sought the patience to do as she must. It took her over an hour to scratch out a shallow depression in a block of wood with her carving knife. Then she filled it with water and hot rocks. As she waited for the water to heat, she thought of how close they might be to her grandfather, and how absurd it would be if they died of exposure having come this far.

When she finally served tea to Molly, Zeke, and Jenny, huddled together by the smoky fire and shivering fiercely, it was a soupy black mess of ash and faintly tea-colored water, but they drank it eagerly, for it was hot and gave blessed relief to their chill-wracked bodies. As they sank back down, feeling the warm liquid inside them begin to take the edge off the cold, Ella went back to the stream to fill the water sack again. This time she came back also bearing a handful of leaves. "Isn't this a leaf you used to make tea back at the Seneca village?"

Jenny stared at the handful of leaves, her eyes having difficulty focusing on them. Then, all at once, recognition sparked in her eyes and she said, "Yes, of course. I've even heard it called 'New Jersey Tea.' How did you recognize it?"

Ella shrugged. "No idea. Just thought it looked familiar." She returned to the stream, trotting to stay warm, and returned with an armful of leaves that she used to fill the bowl she'd made. This time when she poured in water, it turned an even darker shade of blackish brown as the leaves steeped, but it had a good, earthy taste and went down much more smoothly.

The rain kept up steadily and Ella kept making bowls of tea, mostly for something to do after they'd drunk as much as they could hold. Eventually, late in the day, the rain finally waned to a mist, though the temperature didn't rise. They considered getting up and trying to make a little travel toward Martha, now that the sun has just begun to be barely visible, but it was already so late in the day that they were hesitant to leave their fire, for fear they'd be unable to make another.

Thus, as darkness settled back around them, they huddled where they were, clinging to one another as the rain picked up again, soaking them more thoroughly than ever. For lack of any better options, they each, in their turn, eventually dozed, a welcome relief from the shivering cold.

Ella was first to wake the next morning and the first thing she noticed in the pre-dawn haze of near-darkness was that the rain had finally ceased. In the strange quiet of the woods not drumming with raindrops, she realized she could hear something she couldn't hear the day before; she could hear the faint, distant sound of a hammer—the rhythmic thumping of a forge hammer, or possibly a stamping mill. Could that be

Martha? For all she knew, it could be some other iron town altogether. Supposedly these Pines were full of iron towns, but for all she'd seen, these woods were full of only one thing, and that was trees.

She nudged the others awake and pointed off toward the faint thumping of the hammer. Their eyes brightened at the sound of it and they rose on stiff legs to begin walking once more. Ella's empty stomach emitted stabbing pains. She filled her mouth with a handful of tough New Jersey Tea leaves in a futile attempt to appease it.

It became harder to hear the hammers as they walked, mostly because the rain had given way to a rising wind which created as much noise or more in the susurrus of blowing leaves overhead. They were all weak with lack of food and began to stumble on the rough ground. Zeke's ankle was barely supporting him and he gritted his teeth with the effort of walking on it. He took up a walking stick to use as a crutch of sorts.

In a lull in the wind they stopped to listen for the hammers and were rewarded with a distinct ringing sound. Jenny smiled and stepped forward just as a powerful wind gusted once more and the top of a dead cedar tree broke off and began to fall. Jenny looked up at the sound, but was rooted to the spot and didn't move. Ella pushed past Molly, also staring upward, and shoved Jenny out of the way of the falling tree with all her might. Jenny was thrown clear, but Ella didn't have quite enough momentum to make it past herself. The heavy broken trunk landed on her legs, pinning her down and burying her in an avalanche of branches.

Jenny screamed her name. Zeke dropped his crutch and rushed over, pushing through branches to get closer to her. The branches were thick and impenetrable, and the most he could see was the top of her head and a section of one arm. "Ella, Ella, oh lord, Ella, can you hear me? Talk, goddammit. Say something."

He moved around to the other side of the tangle where he could get slightly closer to what could be seen of her. The trunk of the cedar was crushing her legs and a thick branch pinned down her shoulders. It seemed impossible she could be alive underneath, that a branch hadn't speared through her innards. Her eyes were closed and her face had gone white beneath the film of soot.

He called to her again and when there was no response, struggled out of the tangled upper branches and made his way to the butt of the broken trunk. He got both hands underneath the thick trunk, well over a foot across, and strained to lift it, but it weighed many times his own weight and didn't budge. Jenny and Molly came to help and they tried over and over again in vain, Zeke ignoring the pain in his own leg as he strained it.

At last Jenny and Molly sank to the ground in exhaustion while Zeke once more crawled into the tangle of branches to reach Ella. He took her hand where it lay limp on the ground. He moved her hand gently, but it remained lifeless, and he called to her, begging her to wake. There was nothing. He wrung her hand harder, refusing to let it be still. When there was no response he at last let both their hands fall together to the ground and stared at them with eyes blurred with tears. After what seemed a very long time, her hand gave the slightest twinge, the smallest touch of a pressure from her hand to his. He squeezed her hand and said, "We'll think of something to get you out of this. Just don't quit on me, all right?"

She got one eye open and gave him a look of such utter disgust that he had to smile. Such that when he wriggled out from under the branches and stood, the smile lingered on his face while the tears continued to make swirling rivulets down the soot on his cheeks. Jenny and Molly glanced at one another with quizzical expressions, and then each closed her eyes, too beaten to say or do anything more.

THEY WERE STILL SITTING in the same places hours later when, in the waning light of afternoon, there was a rustling in the undergrowth and the sound of someone or something approaching. From underneath the tree, Ella's eyes sprang open at the sound and she peered up at Zeke, who had sprung to his feet and was looking down at her through the branches, his face still streaked with tears. She had no time to think about the tears.

"Do you have your knife?" she whispered. He nodded and moved away, taking up a position behind a tree, facing the oncoming sound.

Ella, in her trapped state, felt as helpless as she'd ever felt in her life. She ignored the pain in her leg and tried to focus on what they would do if there were more than one outlaw approaching. Or if Zeke could not disarm him quickly. She squirmed, trying to get a hand in her waistband to reach her knife, but the searing pains that shot down her leg stopped her cold and she felt the blackness washing over her once again. She struggled to stay conscious as the sounds came closer and then paused. She turned her head to try to see, and then, beyond the web of branches surrounding her, from between the trunks of two trees several yards away, a face appeared. Not just any face, but a black face, a negro face, staring at them as if they were an apparition.

All they could do was stare back at him. They remained in this impasse for several minutes before another set of footsteps could be heard approaching, Another face appeared next to the first. Two negro outlaws. What would they want?

Then Ella peered more closely at the second man and realized he looked familiar, that he was the same man they'd met on the road above Trenton, the one who'd first told them of the Pines. She saw Zeke relax his grip on his knife and realized he too must have recognized him.

The two men stared at them for a long moment, then recognition dawned on the second one's face. He said, "You folk again?" Then he noticed Ella, nearly invisible beneath the branches of the limb that pinned her. He said, "Oh my, that there's some trouble."

Zeke said, "We can't lift it off. But perhaps we might...if you were to help...together?"

The two men nodded and the three of them took up positions around the limb. They managed to lift it just enough to allow Molly and Jenny to drag Ella out from underneath. She nearly lost consciousness again with the pain of being jostled. As if from a great distance she heard Jenny, looking up from feeling her leg, say, "It's broken in two places. Perhaps three. She won't be able to walk." Jenny looked up at the man they'd met near Trenton and said, "Can you tell us how to get to Martha Furnace, Mr...?"

"Perry," he said, "Nate Perry. It's not far, miss. What you be hearin' is the forge down at Wading River—that's a way south a here. Martha is just up over that small hill there. Don't you worry now, Quintus here and me'll help you carry her there. We can make her up a stretcher."

SIXTEEN

OVER THE HILL, in the town of Martha Furnace, two older workers made their way to the cookhouse. One of them shuffled, his back bent nearly at right angles to his legs, his gait stiff and painfully slow. In one hand he held a walking stick, while his other arm was supported at the elbow by his companion, who walked slowly and patiently beside him. His companion's hair was snow white but his eyes twinkled a bright blue and he walked with the light, springy step of a much younger man.

A young boy backing up to catch a flying stick bumped into them, causing the bent-over man to totter and nearly fall, and requiring his friend to work hard to keep him upright. The bent-over man exploded. "What's the matter with you, boy? What kind of a devil-spawn behaves so stupidly? Running around with no thought for who you might flatten as you run. Where's your mother? I've got a right mind to cane you flat myself." He brandished his walking stick at the boy, who was already backing away quickly, his eyes wide with fear.

The white-haired man interjected to say, "Go on now, boy—
it was an accident. Just be more careful where you're playing,
won't you?"

"Careful? How can a child that stupid learn to be careful? What
kind of idiocy is that to tell a child to be careful. Children are born
careless and stupid. They should all be deemed criminals from the
start and locked up somewhere until they're grown."

His companion laughed. "You take original sin to a whole
new level, don't you, Tunnicliff?"

They entered the cookhouse and found seats. Then the
white-haired man with the springy step left his companion to
go collect plates of food for them both. When he returned, two
other smiths from the forge had seated themselves nearby and
his companion sat frowning as he listened to them.

"How's the back, Tunnicliff?" one of them was asking.

Captain Tunnicliff scowled more deeply and didn't answer.
The smith who asked turned a questioning look to Maurice
Simons, who answered for his friend. "The pain is terrible, I
think. He should stay in bed but he's stubborn and insists on
getting up to come take a meal. Thinks it will heal better to
use it more."

"'Tis a right shame, that is," the other smith said, "him getting injured in that accident when he weren't even supposed
to be on shift that night." He paused and then said to Captain Tunnicliff, "You look a right sight better than Cross does,
though. Him being six feet under and all."

After the meal, the two companions made their way back to the
men's bunkhouse, where the captain rolled gratefully back into
his bunk and his companion prepared for his shift at the smith.

"You'll be all right then, Tunnicliff?" Maurice Simons asked.

"Yes, yes, stop asking me that." Tunnicliff rolled over to
face the wall, turning his back on Simons. After a moment he
turned back and said in his gravelly voice, "You'll go by the
stable and give my horse his bucket, won't you?"

"I wouldn't forget old Edgar—you know that."

"No, no, of course not. You wouldn't forget him."

"Well then," Simons said, "I'll see you after my shift. See if you can't get some rest."

Tunnicliff grunted, pulled up his blanket, and turned back to the wall, dismissing his friend.

Simons shook his head, finished lacing his boots and went out the door, crossing his arms over his chest to protect himself from the biting wind that whipped through the town, swirling dry oak leaves and nipping at ears.

AN HOUR LATER, a bedraggled party of soot-blackened strangers straggled into Martha, carrying a wounded girl on a stretcher.

"They're asking for Tunnicliff," was the word that went around. Maurice Simons heard it at the smith and got leave from the foreman to go tell his friend.

He found Tunnicliff curled into himself on his bunk, clearly battling the pain in his body. "Tell them I'm not here," Asa Tunnicliff told him through clenched teeth. "I don't care who they are."

"They say they're kin to you."

Tunnicliff glared at his friend and then closed his ragged eyes. "What if they are. Tell them I'm not here."

Maurice Simons went to greet the party of sooty travelers at the company store, where they'd been taken to get them out of the cold wind. He found them seated around the iron stove in the store, with their hands wrapped around cups of thick, hot coffee. The iron stove was stamped "Martha" on the front, as were the shovel and poker hanging on the wall nearby.

The injured girl lay on a pallet of blankets next to the stove. Her face had been wiped clean but there was still considerable ash and soot in her black hair and clothes. Simons joined the remnants of the crowd who'd been interrogating the strangers about the fire and where it had been, for fire was always major news in the pines. When the last stragglers had moved away, he took a seat with them and said, "I hear you're asking after Asa Tunnicliff."

The brown-haired girl, who looked younger than the other girls, said, "Yes, do you know him? We hear there was an accident of some sort, but no one will answer any of our questions about him. We know he was here earlier this year."

Simons looked down at his feet, then brought his blue eyes up to meet Jenny's. "I'm afraid it's true he was caught in the explosion at the smith."

Jenny's brown eyes grew wide. "No," she said in a small voice. "Please don't tell me he was killed in that. He wasn't, was he?"

"No, he wasn't killed, but he was injured in the accident, and I'm afraid he's not doing very well. He's in considerable pain, and he's also very angry. He seems to think the explosion was someone's fault and he's determined to find out who it was—so he can force some kind of retribution." He paused to look at them. "I'm afraid there's no truth to this notion it was anything but an accident, but there's no telling Captain Tunnicliff this. He seems to have come a bit loose in his senses. Perhaps from the pain?"

Jenny frowned with concern and said, "You must take me to him. I can try to ease his pain."

The boy with black hair, who hadn't yet spoken, said softly, "Jenny, we should see to Ella first. She needs a doctor to set that leg."

Jenny's frown deepened and Maurice Simons said, "There's no doctor here, but Mistress Reeves, wife of the furnace manager, she can doctor just about anything. I'll go tell her."

"Might she look at Zeke's ankle as well?" Jenny asked, pointing at the boy's leg, which was propped up on an iron doorstop. Maurice nodded and went out.

When he'd gone, Jenny said to Zeke, "We never even introduced ourselves to that man. What's his name, I wonder."

"That's Simons, Maurice Simons," Molly said, looking up from the floor to speak nearly her first words since before Ella's accident. "He's a nice man."

"Why didn't you greet him?" Jenny asked.

Molly, for the first time since they'd known her, flushed beneath the soot on her face and said, "Nay, the last time I saw him, he pulled me out of the way when the husband of one of my brother's women was chasing us with a stick raised." She looked up at them, her face rueful. "It's not much to boast on, is it, being the sister to Billy McGilligan?"

MISTRESS REEVES APPEARED in the doorway a short time later and took matters into her own capable hands. She examined Ella's leg and said in her quiet voice, "She'll need a plaster after I set it. I'll have the men bring her over to my house." Zeke's ankle she pronounced unbroken but in need of rest. After overseeing Ella's transport out the door, she turned and said, "Thee three mainly need a bath. Let me see...Yes, I think Mrs. Gaskill will be happy of thy company, now that her husband's gone to Batsto and her youngest son's joined the army. I'll have a boy bring you over." She looked them over once more and settled her gaze on Molly. "Thee are William McGilligan's sister, are thee not? I recall when thee were here before."

Molly nodded, her face still flushed. Then she said, "Aye, that's me. And my uncle is Michael Mick. He may have a place for me—do ye know where I might find him?"

Mistress Reeves nodded. "I'll have the boy take thee there."

PHEBE REEVES PROVED A CAPABLE stand-in for a doctor. In her kitchen she administered a hefty dose of laudanum and then went about setting and plastering Ella's leg. Before Ella woke from the laudanum, Mistress Reeves had her back on the stretcher and on her way to Emily Gaskill's cabin to join her companions.

The cabin was a ramshackle affair in a cluster of cabins on the edge of the town. Mrs. Gaskill, who cheerfully confessed to being terribly lonely since her husband and sons were gone, was a small, round woman who did all she could to welcome them. She'd already sent Jenny and Zeke in and out of her bathing tub, and now she installed Ella in one of the beds in what had been her sons' room. While Ella slept she quickly stripped her down and sponged off what she could of the grime from the woods.

She assigned Jenny to another bed nearby, assembled extra bedding to make a pallet on the floor for Zeke, and then told them they must waste no time in getting rest or they'd all be ill. She brooked no argument and they were soon wrapped in quilts, sound asleep.

They slept for sixteen hours and woke to the smell of frying meat. Mrs. Gaskill didn't stop talking all the while they ate a breakfast of fried ham and oatcakes. She rambled on and along about various matters of the town, speaking of people they'd never met so that finally they gave up trying to follow her talk, only nodding occasionally when it seemed the appropriate moment. She fed them well, including Ella with a tray, and then, when their heads began to nod over their plates, ushered Jenny and Zeke back to join Ella in their sleeping room, talking all the while.

They slept another six hours.

LATE THE FOLLOWING AFTERNOON, Jenny and Zeke, limping only very slightly, set off to find her grandfather. The day was overcast but a bit warmer and less windy than the last few had been, and Jenny was glad of the change. On the way to the bunkhouse where they'd been told they'd find Grandfather, they ran into Molly McGilligan coming from the store.

"Mornin' to yeh," Molly said, "How's Ella, then?"

"She's well, or better at least," Jenny said. "Her leg is plastered and she's already restless, though the mistress said she must stay off it for at least a month."

"Aye, glad to hear she's had some doctoring, though. Where are ye staying?"

Jenny told her how to find Mrs. Gaskill's cabin and then asked of Molly's brother and uncle.

"Me uncle he's well enough. He said tell you, Zeke, to come to him if you're wanting work on the furnace. Me brother, well...It weren't Mrs. Anderson's cabin he was at after all, as I found out when I'd already asked after him and she'd near taken to my head with her iron skillet. I ran from there and asked around at the bunkhouse until I finally found him with Hannah McEntire, whose husband is off in the drink."

"Sounds like a dangerous business," Zeke said. "Looking for your brother, I mean."

"Aye. 'Tis. I should carry a weapon for defense of meself." Molly grinned, but then, suddenly, the grin faded as her eye was caught by the sight of a young woman walking toward them.

The young woman had glossy light brown hair covered by only the merest wisp of a hat. While there was nothing specifically unconventional in her dress, she carried herself with a distinctive air that arrested attention, almost as if she expected all eyes to follow her. As she drew closer, Jenny could begin to see her features and they were of unusual beauty. She had light brown eyes, nearly the exact color of her hair, and a pale peach skin, with high cheekbones and lush red lips. Jenny could not help but stare at her, for she seemed greatly out of place in a hardscrabble furnace town such as this one; she looked as if she'd been born in a mansion somewhere, or at least a grand city. Jenny glanced at Molly, who stared hard as the girl drew near. She was about to ask the girl's name, when Molly abruptly turned on her heel and disappeared between two buildings, with the merest flash of red hair.

Jenny shook her head at Molly's odd behavior and Zeke shrugged. Then they moved off to find the bunkhouse. As they approached it, Jenny said, "You best stay outside here at first, seeing as we've heard he wishes no visitors."

"Probably best," Zeke agreed, and stepped aside to lean against the building. Jenny climbed the two steps to enter the bunkhouse and stopped to let her eyes adjust to the gloom. There were one or two smoke-blackened lamps along the wall, and the oilcloth windows allowed only the promise of light. The smell of unwashed clothes and dirty beards hit her like a hammer, and she had to turn her head back to the air outside. When she recovered, she steeled herself to ignore the smell and made her way in. It was warm inside, or at least much warmer than outside, with a small potbelly stove radiating heat from the center of the long room. When her eyes finally adjusted to the gloom, she could see the bunks on one end of the room were full of sleeping men, presumably the furnace night shift. Toward the center of the room, closer to the stove, a man was tossing in his rumpled bed, as if uncomfortable. Jenny glided toward him and peered down.

"Grandfather?" she asked quietly, mindful of the men sleeping nearby.

He turned over to look at her and she had to keep her face impassive so as not to register the shock of seeing the change in him; he appeared shrunken, shriveled almost, with his hair a dirty grey and his face unshaven.

He peered at her through bloodshot eyes, looking as if he hadn't slept in days. "What do you want?" he asked roughly.

"Grandfather, it's me. Jenny. Don't you know me?"

He squinted at her and his eyes showed a fleck of recognition, maybe even the faintest hue of pleasure, but then they clouded over and he rolled over to face away. "Leave me alone," he said in a voice muffled by bedclothes.

She tried again and was similarly rebuffed. After a time, she reached down to stroke his back with the softest of strokes, and said, "I'll come back tomorrow, Grandfather. Soon I'll find medicines to help you grow strong once more."

With Jenny still frowning at what she'd just seen, they went to see Molly's uncle Michael Mick, the chief founder, as he'd offered Zeke work and it appeared they'd be here at least until Ella could walk again.

"Aye, then, you're just in time, lad." Michael Mick clapped him on the shoulder. "Seeing as Jimmy McEntire and Jacob Emons are off in the drink somewheres, I'm in need of a bankman on the night shift. Are yeh strong enough for such work?"

"Yes, sir. Absolutely, sir. I'm plenty strong enough."

Michael Mick squeezed Zeke's upper arm. "We'll make a man of you yet. Soon ye'll be drinking us all under the table at Bodine's.

"That part I can already do, sir," Zeke said with a playful smile. "I'm a hero at drinking beer."

"Oh is that so? I dare say ye've got yeself a wager then, son. But never mind the beer. We start with whiskey. Good Irish whiskey."

Zeke looked at Mr. Mick's thick barrel chest and swallowed hard. "Yes, sir," he said in a smaller voice.

Jenny laughed.

ELLA SAID NOTHING when Jenny told her of visiting their grandfather. In truth she was struck dumb, unable to believe her grandfather would behave in such a way. After all these years of missing him so hard. And then all these months of striving to find him, thinking that the pleasure of seeing him once again would make it all worthwhile. At last she said, "Are you quite certain it's him? How can you be certain?"

Even after Jenny assured her she remained skeptical, finding it nearly impossible to make sense of his actions. She cursed her own bedridden state, certain that if she were able to visit herself, talk to him herself, her grandfather couldn't fail to come around.

The next day, as Jenny prepared to visit once again, Ella gave her a list of things to say to him, to try to prod him into reacting. But Jenny's efforts were futile once more, and Ella scowled when she heard of it.

She had plenty more to frown on in the following days, trapped in her bed under Mistress Reeves's strict instructions not to get up or she risked never walking again. The pain of the break was bad enough, but then came the itching under the plaster that made her wish to just cut the whole leg off and be done with it.

Mrs. Gaskill was a cheerful nurse and seemed glad of an audience to tell of her life and of her three absent sons. Ella heard many tales of the youngest son who had left to join the army—so as not to miss a day of the impending new war with Britain—but en route to enlist had been taken up by a British press gang and impressed into serving three months on a Royal Navy warship. Mrs. Gaskill learned of his escapade only after he was rescued by a fortuitous encounter with an American merchant ship, but she was now of the mind that the Royal Navy were no better than pirates and the Americans must call a new war to show the British what's what.

Of the elder two sons Mrs. Gaskill said less, for they had left to seek their fortunes in the new territory in Ohio several years previous and she'd heard so little from them that it made her tearful to wonder whether they might even be alive. Ella enjoyed Mrs. Gaskill's tales for the first and even second rendition, but by the third she grew restless and subsequently began to feel an all-too-literally captive audience.

After a week Zeke moved into the men's bunkhouse to accommodate his work on the night shift and Ella's days grew ever more tedious. Jenny kept her company most mornings, but then left to accompany Mistress Reeves on her calls, for Jenny's skill with healing had been quickly apparent when the older lady encountered her at Asa Tunnicliff's bedside and the good Mistress had wasted no time in enlisting her aid with other patients.

When she wasn't attending sickbeds, Jenny, spurred by their new proximity to a post office at the company store, spent much of her time writing letters back to Deborahville. She often encouraged Ella to take up her own pen as a means to occupy her time, but Ella couldn't see that struggling to craft words was likely to *reduce* the dullness of her hours. Instead she did her best to entertain herself by building a scale model of the flax engine, thinking it might be a useful tool in engaging her grandfather's interest.

In mid-November, on a day when Jenny was off to bring a new salve to their grandfather, who hadn't softened much at all to her ministrations, Ella was shaping a piece of wood with a file when there was a commotion in the front room and she heard Mrs. Gaskill exclaim, "Moses! Can that be you?"

Ella leaned as far over as she dared to spy out the doorway of her room and saw a young man with a child in his arms being wrapped in Mrs. Gaskill's embrace. Then Mrs. Gaskill stepped back to peer at the blanket-wrapped child and said, "And who have we here? Oh, isn't she sweet? Is she ... my ... ?"

The young man nodded, his face solemn. In a voice that was nearly a whisper he said, "Yes, Mother, she's mine. Her mother ... she died, just a fortnight ago. I had no one to care for the child so I made my way back home."

"Your brother?" Mrs. Gaskill asked, her voice croaking as if strangled.

Her son said quickly, "He's well, I believe. It's only that he left last spring to move on west and I don't know where he's gotten to. But I believe he's well." He paused and then said, "I should have written more, I know."

Ella saw Mrs. Gaskill nod and then almost visibly collect herself and cluck, "Oh dear me," as she pulled her son to the table and pushed him into a seat. When she reached out for the child, though, the young man said, "Wait. You must be careful." He unwrapped the blanket and showed his mother something of the child's legs. Mrs. Gaskill gasped, and then, more gently, slipped her hand underneath the blanket and lifted the child to her bosom.

Ella, watching from the bedroom, waited impatiently for Mrs. Gaskill to come show her the child. She didn't typically find children of particular interest, but she had grown so desperate for activity that anything new was a welcome distraction. After she coughed to attract attention, Mrs. Gaskill came in with the child in her arms, her face a pure mask of conflicted emotion. She leaned down to show Ella that one of the child's legs was twisted and shriveled.

Ella looked up from the leg to the child's face and saw that she was perhaps four years of age, with big round brown eyes that reminded her of Catherine's. Her face was sweet but anxious, waiting to see what Ella would make of her leg. She was so quiet and still and there was something piteous in her look, but also hopeful. Something that made her more interesting than the usual boisterous lot of busy children. Ella smiled at the girl and said, "That's a rotten bother, isn't it? Makes it hard to get around. Just like me," and she pointed to her own plastered leg. The child's eyes grew wider and Ella added, "I'm glad you've come to play with me. I'm in need of another player for cards. And see here," she gestured to the miniature pieces of her flax machine, "I'd be very grateful for another set of hands to hold the pieces of this model while I tap them together. Could you do that?"

The little girl nodded, but yet looked nervous. Ella considered her, then said, "Look here, I'll make you a deal. You help me with holding the pieces of my model and I'll put on for you the best ever juggle you've ever seen. It's guaranteed to make you smile or I'll refund the price of admission thrice-fold."

The girl, clearly not certain what to make of this, looked over at her father, who'd come to the door of the room. He said, "I do believe she's teasing you, Emily."

"Emily?" Mrs. Gaskill cried. "You named her after me myself?" When her son nodded, she burst into tears and made her way from the room, saying, "Oh I never thought to see the day."

The little girl looked scared and Ella rushed to say, "I think she's not weeping because she's angry, but because she's happy. Isn't that so?" She looked up at Moses Gaskill in the doorway with an unspoken entreaty that he say something to reassure the girl. He merely nodded. "See, your pa agrees. Old people like your grandma cry when they're happy and do all sorts of other things that make no sense." In a raised voice she added, "Isn't that so, Mrs. Gaskill?"

Mrs. Gaskill, who Ella well knew to have the ears of a hawk, said in a sob-muffled voice, "Yes, that's so." Then she shuffled back into the room and wrapped little Emily in her arms.

SEVENTEEN

"**M**R. KENYON. PLEASE, sit down. What might I do for you?" Henry Emerston gestured from behind his big walnut desk as Amherst Kenyon was shown into his office, but he didn't rise.

Amherst Kenyon circled to one side of the room, studied a framed portrait on the wall, then walked to the other side and inspected a wall sconce, before restlessly aiming for the chair across from the desk and lowering himself into it with something like reluctance.

"I come to see you about something important," he said after a considerable pause. His voice was thick, rough with tobacco and rum.

"Yes?" Emerston waved an impatient hand when he said nothing further. "Come to the point, man. There's business to be tended to." He glanced at the stack of papers on his desk. "This isn't about your loan payment, is it?"

Kenyon puffed out his chest. "See here, I have information I'm looking to sell. I believe you'll find it quite interesting. Interesting enough perhaps to, say...tell that steward of yours to cancel a payment." He eyed Emerston expectantly, apparently believing he'd said something momentous.

Emerston said, "I'm sorry, Kenyon. I do not conduct business in such a way. If you have something to tell me, then say it. If not, please take your leave. I'm not going to *buy* information from you. And if I were, I wouldn't do it by canceling a loan payment, as that would leave a written record of the matter."

He looked levelly at Kenyon, who narrowed his eyes and stared back. Finally Emerston said, "The best thing you can do is go back to your mill and get to work so you can earn the money to make your payment. And cease spending all your evenings at the tavern, where the little you earn goes quickly. If you were to agree to do that, I would agree to reduce your interest payment so you could get ahead." He paused and then added, "It's a good offer, Amherst. You know it is. Why don't you take it?"

Kenyon continued to glower at him. Then he said slowly, "As I said, I have information you'll be wanting. You'd do well to take the advice to buy it from me, one way or t'other."

Emerston sighed and drummed his fingers on the stack of papers on his desk. "All right, Kenyon. Why don't you go ahead and tell me your information, and if it's indeed as useful to me as you say, I'll give you something for it."

Kenyon grimaced, clearly not pleased by this offer, but seeming to realize it was the best he was going to get. "You'll be wanting to call the U.S. Marshal when you hear this news," he said at last. "It's to the ill of all of us in business here in Deborahville that someone in this town is dealing in bad notes. Bad notes written on good banks, if you see my meaning."

Emerston arched an eyebrow at him. "Oh? And who is that?"

"I'll tell you that when you hand me a note yourself. Or silver would be acceptable," he replied with an oily smugness.

Emerston got to his feet with his finger pointing toward the door. Then, appearing to think better of it, he lowered his arm and sat once more. "Please excuse me. This is a bad business and I don't care for it. I won't pay you much for this information, especially as I cannot verify that it's even true. I'll give you a coin for your trouble if you'll tell me who you suspect and then be done with it. I'll look into it and then decide if there's any reason to summon the marshal."

Kenyon snorted in disgust, but clambered to his feet to take the silver coin that Emerston had fished from his desk. As he turned toward the door, he said, "Have the marshal search Mrs. Tunnicliff's house. He'll find plenty there to warrant his trip."

RATHER THAN RETURN TO HIS MILL, Kenyon made a straight line for the tavern and eased himself into his customary seat. He was still in the same seat later that evening, as the silver coin had served to buy more drink than he'd been able to afford in quite a while. He drank until he'd forgotten why he started drinking, forgotten the gall of the man who'd looked at him from across that massive desk and told him how to conduct himself, how to live his own life.

But rather than blissful ignorance, the more he drank the more bitterly angry he became. The tavern keeper, long skilled at managing him, saw the rage in his eyes and said, "You look like you could use a good night's rest, Kenyon. I'd say it's a good time to be getting home to bed, don't you think?"

Amherst Kenyon jerked his chin toward the man and started to protest, but then something stopped him, perhaps the knowledge that the tavern keeper was the one man in town he could not afford to offend. He was about to acquiesce when suddenly it rose up again, the interview he was drinking to forget. The fact that he hadn't succeeded in besting that woman, that again she'd slipped from under his grasp. She'd

225

done that every time, hadn't she, ever since they were young? Well, except that once. That one time he could remember with satisfaction.

Then suddenly it was there, the forbidden knowledge he'd kept buried deep down, had never let pass his lips, even in drink. Now, suddenly, he saw it differently. He saw it for the one weapon he had left, the one means of letting everyone else know what he knew, what she'd always managed to keep hidden.

"That Tunnicliff woman, she's no good you know," he said, apropos of nothing. He looked around to make sure they were all listening. "She's a tart, she is, a full-blown tart. She goes off to Boston saying some long-lost aunt is ill, then she turns up at my door with the baby. She gives it to me and my wife because she says it's more ours than hers. Then later she marries that miserable little John Tunnicliff just to cover up her sins, because no one else would have had her then." He looked around the room, daring someone to take the bait he'd dangled.

A brave soul from a nearby table ventured to say, "What are you saying, Kenyon? That one of your children is actually Lucille Tunnicliff's?"

Another man pulled together his addled wits enough to say, "It'd have to be his eldest, wouldn't it? As the Tunnicliff boy married not long after Kenyon did—what was the year? '89 was it? Or '90?

The first man said, "Are you saying that your eldest girl isn't actually yours, then, Kenyon?"

Kenyon scowled. "I didn't say that. I said her ma was the Tunnicliff woman. That's all I said." His scowl deepened and they didn't dare question him any further, as it was clear he'd said all he had to say, and then some.

A LITTLE LATER THE TAVERN KEEPER led him to the door and saw him shuffle down the road toward home. The keeper turned back to the men still in the tavern and said, "That was a close one. He'll be all right, though."

"What was that he was saying, then? That his eldest isn't really their kin?"

"No, you sot. That's not what he said. He said his eldest was born of Mrs. Tunnicliff. He didn't say she wasn't his own, only not his wife's."

"Ahhh. That's different. I see what you mean. She's his, then, just not his wife's." Then, after another moment of absorbing the implications of Kenyon's pronouncement added, "Well, that's some news, is it not? Why, I could stay out all night and not hear a word of it from my old gal if I came home with news as precious as that."

Someone with a few more wits left to him said, "How would folks not have known that Mrs. Tunnicliff was with child?"

This question befuddled them and there was much head shaking. The drinker with the remaining wits thought it over further and said, "I can't explain it. But the one thing I feel certain about is that my wife will believe it, and will have a dandy time working out the dates to make it plausible. She's never liked Lucille Tunnicliff."

"She's just jealous is all," a slurred voice commented.

"Hear, hear," another concurred. "Who wouldn't like to get the feel of that woman? She's soft on the eyes, that one—always has been, and always will be."

WALKING HOME FROM THE TAVERN, Amherst Kenyon's shuffling walk gave way to a longer stride as a strange energy began to course through him. His arms began to swing in rhythm with his legs. Soon he was punching at the air, practicing the jabs and swings he'd mastered in his youth. He thought of Henry Emerston, sitting behind his big desk with a smug look on his face. *I'll show you what happens when you tell me how to live my own life. When you look down your nose and across your big desk. When you tell me my information's worthless and useless until* you *prove it's true. I'll show you.* He took a sharp right jab at the air and followed it with a left hook.

He strode down the rode to his farm, reached the gate, and kicked it open. He strutted past the gardens and across the barnyard, and then flung open the front door and strode manfully into his own house. It took only two or three steps to cross the sitting room. Manfully he pulled his wife up from her chair where she sat knitting and gave her that same right jab, followed by that same left hook. Ah, that felt good. He took her arm and picked her up from the floor with one hand, holding her in the air while he practiced his left hook some more. It was looking good now, that left hook. Right away he could see what kind of damage it could do. *You wouldn't be telling me to go back to my mill and stay away from the tavern if you could see my left hook, now would you? You'd be running for your life if you could see me in action, isn't that so, you little desk rat?*

His wife began to struggle to get away and it became too hard to hold up her up at the same time he swung at her. She was saying something but he couldn't hear, and didn't really care. When he threw her down to the floor, she began to try to move away, so he gave her a good kick to the side of the head to make her stay in place. Then he gave her a few more, just for good measure. He looked down at her a moment, just a tangled heap on the floor, and then he crossed to the door and made his way back outside. Tonight, for some reason, he was still full of spirit.

He looked around outside and considered the barn, but then his thoughts turned to *her.* The one he'd finally told about.

The one who'd dared him to go tell, who said she had no fear of him. *She may have gotten that damn Indian to put locks on her door, but that Indian wasn't around any more, was he? He'd show her what a fool she'd been, what a fool she still was. What a fool she'd always been. Why had he let himself be stopped by locked doors? He'd been a fool himself. He could put his hand through any window, probably put his foot through any wall if he cared to. He could do anything. Who was going to stop him?*

He ran nearly all the way down the path between their houses. He hadn't felt so good in years. He reached the house and slowed, peering to see if any candles were lit. It was late, but he knew she sometimes kept late hours. He thought he may have seen a flicker behind the kitchen window, but then he thought he must have imagined it, for the room remained pure black.

Light as a cat he glided toward the back door of the house. He paused for a moment, then, taking a deep breath, he thrust his fist through the expensive glass window, making an impressive crashing noise. He thought at first he'd cut himself on the broken glass when he felt a stinging in his hand as he reached for the bolt on the inside of the door. But then he felt the pain again and realized something was jabbing at his hand. He looked through the window and saw she was stabbing at him with a kitchen knife, a look of fierce determination on her face. He supposed it should hurt more than it did, but it felt more like a bee sting. *Stupid woman. Thinking she can stop me with a kitchen knife.*

He wrenched open the bolt, pulled his hand back through the window, and then, without a pause, kicked open the back door. She came at him with the knife again, fierce as a she-bear with cubs, but she had no real skill with it. It was a simple matter to grab her arm and twist it behind her back until she dropped the knife and cried out.

Ah, that's good. Hearing her cry out like that. It's been much too long. Using his grip on her twisted arm, he steered her farther into the room. Then he pulled her back against his body and wrapped his other arm around her front to grope at her breasts. He'd done this once before, when they were both young. He'd had cause to regret that act, but he'd never forgotten it and always secretly hoped to repeat it. He taunted her. "You're not sweet like you used to be, are you? You're sour now. But not sour enough to defend yourself, eh? You should have taken lessons from your daughter, you know. She learned how to defend herself. You should have had her teach you. You just let that stinking Indian do all your defending. You should have learned to do it yourself. You're useless, you know. Good for nothing. Or rather, good for only one thing, now that your warrior isn't here to protect you."

She tried to bite at his hand and kick at his shins, but her efforts were futile. He turned them both to the table and pushed her forward onto it, holding her down with one hand behind her head as he began to unbutton his trousers. He said, "I told them, you know. I told the whole town what a whore you are. And I told Emerston about the fake notes. You've got no more secrets now. All your pretty little airs are for nothing. Everyone knows what you are."

Beneath him, she wrenched her free arm out and felt around for a weapon. Not finding one, she reached back and scratched at him, trying to do damage but failing. He merely laughed at her, enjoying her helplessness. He grabbed her free arm and pinned it to the other one, crushing her body underneath his own. Then he slowed down and began to take his time, pulling up her skirt and rubbing at her leg with slow, measured strokes. "We might as well enjoy ourselves, eh?"

He'd waited too long. For just when he first heard a sound, it was too late. He'd barely looked up toward the door when the knife was already in the air. He saw it flash and then it hit him square in the chest. He was dead before his body could slump all the way to the floor.

THERE WAS A LONG SILENCE before Pete strode across the room and looked down at Amherst Kenyon's body. He extended a hand to Lucille and gently pulled her up and toward him. "Too good a death for him," Pete said matter-of-factly. Then he added, "Should have done this years ago."

Lucille looked down at the bleeding man, and then she turned and vomited all over her floor. She retched, and retched again, unable to stop trying to purge herself of all that had just happened. She stopped only when she looked up to see the face of a very brown boy appear in the doorway, looking apprehensive.

"Jimson, oh goodness. Is that you?" She held a handkerchief to her mouth. Then she flung herself across the room and embraced him, squeezing him so hard that he finally yelped.

"Aunt Lucille, please, I can't breathe."

She made herself let go. Then she looked at Pete and said, "Thank you. But where the hell have you been?"

Pete shrugged. "Just now return. We travel all day. Not want to wake you so we go to lodge. When we hear glass break we run." He looked at Jimson. "I tell boy wait outside. Not know what I find."

Lucille looked around and remembered Amherst on the floor. She pushed Jimson out the door. "You shouldn't see this." Over his protests she said, "Pete, please get a blanket and wrap him up. We must take him out of here. I can't bear to have him here."

Pete carried Amherst's swathed body outside. Jimson was trembling and suddenly very pale, but he fetched shovels from the shed behind Lucille's house and brought them to where Pete had lowered the body to the ground in a clearing several hundred yards into the woods. Together Pete and Jimson dug a grave while Lucille sat on a log and watched them. The moon, just past full, gave plenty of light for the task.

It was only when they were nearly finished that Lucille said, "Oh no, we haven't told Catherine. She would want to be here, stinking dog that he is. Or, rather...was." She heard the note of bitter triumph in her own voice. Then her face clouded and she said, "Good Lord...Catherine. I'll bet he came from there, and he was so drunk. Pete, I'm afraid of what...We should all go," she said firmly.

The three of them walked in silence along the well-worn trail between the houses. Jimson, looking more like a Seneca boy than a white boy, walked silently behind Pete. Lucille followed, trying to keep her own steps quiet, but knew she was making a racket to their ears. *Oh well, I've never claimed to be an Indian. It's good to have them back, though,* she thought, *Indians or not, they're family.* A spark of happiness flared briefly inside her, but sputtered out quickly when she thought of Catherine. She felt a shiver of fear for her friend.

The house when they reached it was full silent. There wasn't even the glow of a lamp in the window. Lucille dared to hope that Catherine had already been in bed and he hadn't bothered to wake her. That he'd just bypassed the house and come straight across the trail to her own. But just in case, she had Jimson stay back from the house.

Her hopes were dashed as soon as she saw the front door, which hung open and looked much as her own door at home. She drew herself up straight and fought the urge to hide behind Pete. With dread clawing at her racing heart, she stepped as firmly as she could through the door and looked into the sitting room. It was much darker inside than out, even with the moon coming through the windows. She took a moment to let her eyes adjust, and then the pieces of broken and scattered furniture began to take shape.

They couldn't see Catherine at first, but then a soft sound, a broken croak of sorts, came from somewhere in the center of the sitting room. They made their way toward it, and when they reached Catherine's broken and crumpled body, Lucille put her hand over her mouth and swallowed hard to keep from retching again. She wouldn't have been able to recognize her friend except for the familiar well-worn skirt and apron. The blouse above the skirt was fully spattered in blood. The face above that was a pulp.

Now she couldn't help herself, she felt the retching begin again. Pete looked at her and said, "Go outside. I put her in bed. Make her comfortable. Then you come back."

Pete very gently lifted Catherine and began to carry her upstairs. Lucille, watching from the doorway, heard her moan once, softly, and he said, "Do not worry. All will be well. Rest now."

Lucille tried to keep Jimson out of the house but he was insistent that he wanted to see his mother. He'd grown in the few months he'd been away, become more forceful. He wrested from her grip and went into the house. She followed him, despite that she'd rather have stayed outside. Pete was just settling Catherine into the bed. Jimson went to her side and looked down at her. He said nothing, but after a moment he whirled and dashed out of the room and out of the house. Lucille watched out the window as he ran across the back fields to the woods.

THREE DAYS LATER, Catherine continued to breathe in ragged, shallow breaths, but had yet to wake. Her face had swollen to nearly twice its size, and one of her cheekbones had been pushed back toward her ear. Her chest seemed broken too, with an indentation that could not help but press at her lungs, as the labored breathing suggested.

Lucille hadn't left her side in these days. Wishing for her friend's skill in such matters, she'd bandaged what she could and put salve on what she couldn't. She'd spooned broth into Catherine's slack mouth and made every medicine tea she could think to try.

She called for the local doctor of sorts, who, after shaking his head in dismay, told her there was little to do but pray. In desperation she then called for Mrs. Dunkin, the other local healer, who had never been a friend to Catherine but was good enough in her trade. Mrs. Dunkin had run her hands over Catherine, feeling the broken bones. Then, with a grimace, she reached for Lucille's hand to place it on Catherine's side, where Lucille could feel a lump, large as an orange. Lucille had pulled her hand back as if bitten and Mrs. Dunkin said, "This beating only hastens matters. It may even be a blessing of a sort. You're doing all that's to be done. Try to keep her comfortable."

Jimson stayed away for a day and a half and then returned to sit in silence by Catherine's bedside for an hour or two at a time. Lucille attempted to draw him out, but he only gave her a blank look and refused to speak. He seemed to be in shock.

In the long quiet hours Lucille fretted over what to tell people of Amherst's disappearance. So far she'd said nothing and no one had asked, but sooner or later the men from his mill would come out to look for him. He hadn't run the mill as he should, but he did appear there most days. At least she supposed he must have.

She wished she might go see Emerston again. He'd know what to do. But this was more than she could confess to him. Especially not now, not since Mrs. Dunkin intimated the town was buzzing with the news Amherst had dropped before he died, the news that she was Ella's mother. What had Emerston made of that? What was everyone else saying? She could hardly bear to think of it. It made her grateful for the excuse to remain cloistered for the moment.

Instead she focused on the present dilemma of what to do about Amherst. She feared the fresh-dug grave would be found and searched if people suspected a foul deed. She considered launching the rumor he'd fled town to escape his debts. That would at least delay the search for him. But after many hours in silent debate she saw there was only one safe course of action: they couldn't hide his death but must instead uncover the body and move it to where it could be found by others and the death be made to appear an accident. Pete would be good at that. And everyone had seen how much Amherst had drunk that night. No one would care to look too deeply for the truth.

Her mind swirled in these thoughts for the long hours she sat by Catherine's side. One part of her felt idle and fretful, wishing to go out and take action. Another part of her, the larger part, knew her only place was here by Catherine's side. That she was all Catherine had left now and her friend deserved her undivided care. Catherine who herself had cared for so many people over so many years.

Lucille stayed in place and did all she could. But on the fifth day she woke from a brief nap in her chair to feel something was different. She took Catherine's hand and it was cool to her touch. She put her hand on Catherine's chest and it felt still; the labored breathing had ceased. Catherine had ceased.

EIGHTEEN

THE TOWN OF MARTHA was oddly quiet. With the river and mill pond too frozen to work the bellows, the furnace had been out of blast for a week now. No ringing slag hammers, only the occasional ting of a smith at work on repairing a tool, and the far-off pounding of the forge four miles away at Wading River. The furnace crews had mostly turned to working on the new schoolhouse, with even the furnace manager, Mr. Reeves, cutting wood to make the schoolmaster a desk. Only the ore men were hauling ore and the colliers making charcoal, stockpiling for when the furnace would come back in blast.

Ella limped a bit as she made her way to the shed where she had begun erecting a full-size version of the flax engine. Her leg had healed to where she only needed a crutch on occasion, but it yet ached and couldn't be trusted. As soon as she could walk at all she'd gone to see her grandfather and done her best to interest him in the engine. They'd come to bitter words when he refused to take an interest and she'd pressed him, unable to understand. Until at last he'd said, "Asa Tunnicliff died that night. All you see now is the ghost of that man.

I can't help you," after which he turned away in his bed. She'd left without a word of farewell and hadn't gone back.

Work on rebuilding the engine felt slow, with her leg paining her when she stood too long. She hated the lack of her own tools, and, not least, her sense of hopelessness about trying to solve the puzzle of the design without a new idea. Zeke offered encouragement when he came to help, which wasn't often as he was working days on a carpentering crew and spending most of his evenings playing cards at Bodine's Tavern.

Today the skies overhead were beech bark grey and there was a sharp wind blowing shards of snow here and there. Ella felt the wind in her fingers and toes and wondered why she bothered to drag herself out to work on this machine. What was the point?

Zeke appeared in the door of the shed as she was getting out her makeshift tools. When she looked up she could see her own low spirits cause him to frown. He said, "What are you doing out here today? It's too miserable to work in this weather. Come to Bodine's and let's get you a hot cider and a game of cards. You haven't had a game in ages."

She was tempted. A hot drink and a crowded room would be lovely. But then she remembered why she couldn't go. Why she'd been keeping her distance. She remembered that the card table at Bodine's was presided over by Molly McGilligan and the rumors swirling so thoroughly that even *she* had heard them said that Molly and Zeke were courting. That they were rarely apart these days. Zeke hadn't said a word of it to her, but then he wouldn't, would he? It wasn't his way.

She shook her head and his frown deepened. "Why not? What's the trouble with it? You can't get any work done out here in this wind. Why won't you come to Bodine's?"

She gestured to the machine, as if it were the reason she couldn't go. He shrugged and said, "Suit yourself, but come along if you change your mind."

She began to imagine him walking into Bodines, striding over to receive Molly's warm smile of welcome, her copper hair glinting in the light of the torches...and forced herself to stop. What was the point of such thoughts? She thought instead of the day last autumn, soon after they'd arrived here, that Jenny had sat down on her bed at Mrs. Gaskill's and leaned in to whisper of what had transpired that day in the woods, when the tree had fell on her. Jenny had asked, "What do you think it means? That he wept like that?"

She'd said, "It means nothing, I'm sure. Only that he was half out of his mind with all that happened in those woods."

Jenny had looked skeptical, but then shrugged and said, "Whatever you like."

Ella had meant what she'd said at the time, but later she'd begun to wonder at it. Had he really been out of his mind? Could it have meant something else? Something more? And despite herself, a little bright light of something had kindled in her, and resisted her wish to quench it back to black. That is, until the rumors of Molly and Zeke came to her ears and shame washed over her, for being such a pure idiot and fool.

Well, it wouldn't be the first time, she thought, as she limped her way back to the cabin later that afternoon, *Lucas Emerston made a perfect fool of me*. At recollecting his name his golden face appeared unbidden in her mind and, despite herself, she had a moment of catching her breath at the sight of him. Before she remembered his perfidy. Remembered how she'd last seen him, standing with his damned book after she'd torn out the sketch of her machine.

A FORTNIGHT LATER, when her leg was feeling better but not much else had improved, Ella arrived back at the cabin to find

Jenny sitting at the table near the cookstove. Jenny looked up from the letter she was reading and her face was streaming with tears. Little Emily was sitting nearby in the little chair with wheels that Ella had built for her, and she too looked about to cry, apparently from watching Jenny.

Ella pulled out a chair and sat to face them, tense with apprehension. "Jenny? What's happened?"

Jenny tried to speak but a sob got in her way. She swallowed once, twice, and then, with a deep breath, choked out the words. "They're dead. Mother and Father are both dead. Aunt Lucille writes that she'll tell us more when she sees us, but she had to let us know what had happened."

"But what? How?"

"She doesn't say any more. Only that Mother lingered for five days and then passed, and she was asleep and didn't suffer in all that time. Of Father, nothing—she doesn't say anything."

"I'll bet he did it," Ella said flatly.

Jenny nodded, understanding what she meant, but the tears came too hard for her to speak. Ella turned to look at little Emily, whose wide eyes were round with fear and who yet reminded her of Catherine. Her voice was softer as she said, "It's not for you to worry, Emily. It's nothing to do with you."

But then she looked around the room and suddenly it was stifling to her. She got up and walked into the sleeping room, where she had spent so many days trapped in bed. She looked around and it all felt tight and small. She could not stand to spend another minute here. She grabbed her satchel, threw in a few belongings, including a blanket, and walked to the door of the cabin. On the way out she said to Jenny, "I need some outside air. I think I'll stay in the woods for a day or so. Don't worry after me, I'll be back."

On the way out of town she stopped at the shed that housed her machine. She ran her hands over the frame and then the rollers and the wheels. She closed her eyes and tried to let her mind sink into the machine, to see how she could make the pieces fit together differently. Nothing came to her. She squeezed the back of her neck and looked at the roof of the shed. It was leaky and old. *Becoming useless. Just like me.*

She let go of her neck and squatted to the ground, her head bent and her arms resting on her knees, her hands dangling in front of her. She glanced at her hand and saw the scars on the back, from various injuries. It looked like the hand of a much older person. She stood and rummaged in the corner of the shed for an old oilcloth. She shook it out and pulled it over the machine. It had holes in places and wouldn't be a perfect cover, but it was all there was.

She hefted her satchel and made her way out of town heading north, on the road that went by Bodine's Tavern. She kept her head down as she passed the tavern, willing no one she knew to come out at that moment. No one did and she kept walking north, where she knew there were no towns, only occasional cabins, bogs, and charcoal pits, and the sand roads that ran between them.

He is dead. Mother is dead. He is dead. Mother is dead. The words repeated in her mind, but their meaning failed to penetrate. There were twinges, a slight pleasure at the thought of Deborahville without her father, then a wresting twist of pain at the thought of her mother's chair without her in it. It all blurred together. The one thing she knew was she wasn't going to make herself try to feel grief for Amherst. Whatever love she'd ever had for him was killed years ago. Why pretend it was any other way?

SHE SPENT THE FIRST FEW DAYS feeling cold in the chill wet of February, wearing the blanket around her shoulders like a robe. But after a time she didn't feel it any longer. She walked when she cared to, sat and rested her leg when she needed to. Without a rampaging wildfire to scare them off, she discovered there was plenty of small game in the woods. She set snares every night and in the morning there was usually something for breakfast.

She had no destination, but it felt so good to walk that she just kept walking, at least as long as her leg held up. The walking warmed her, but mostly it gave her things to look at that helped keep her mind off the things she didn't wish to think about. She didn't care to think of the machine. Or her parents. Or her grandfather. Or Zeke. Or, really, anything. She only cared to think about the woods. And the more she walked, the more she saw of them.

After a week of this, she realized suddenly that she *was* seeing more of the woods. What had all looked similar when they'd first come to the Pines didn't look that way any more. Each small corner of the pine woods now looked different, unique somehow. She could tell when she crossed a sand road she'd crossed before. There were subtle differences in the color of the sand between here and over there. There were more oaks here, more cedars there. This brook ran to that bog, and that bog ran all the way back to where those brooks cross. A map of the woods began to take shape in her mind.

The days blended together. There was a little bit of snow on the ground, but in places she could still find cranberries in the bogs. She had no rifle, as she'd lost hers when the horses bolted. She thought about making a bow and arrows, but she'd never liked the feel of the bow as well as that of her knives— and hunting by knife was more satisfying, for the challenge of having to stalk that much closer to use it. As Pete was fond of saying, "If my brother the big cat take a rabbit with his teeth, why I cannot with my knife?"

She was beginning to tire of small game when she came upon the track of a young buck with an injured leg, all too apparent in his track. Keeping upwind, she was able to get close enough to where he lay resting to take him with a well-aimed blade to just behind the eye. She roasted the meat on skewers and ate it together with cranberries for a fine meal. She did her best to dry the skin and the remainder of the meat in the smoke of her fire. She hadn't thought to bring any salt, but she'd done without it before, at least for a while.

While she was scraping the skin, she had a sharp vision of the last time she'd done this, back at the Seneca camp. It had been warm then, and she'd been with Zeke. The sense of him next to her, working quietly, came back sharply, almost like a pain. She pushed it away.

Too much thinking, time to pack up and walk again. Walking helped. The days slid together and she realized she hadn't even kept track of how many there had been. At night she watched the stars, rubbing the gold watch she kept in her pocket.

One morning she woke with the sense that she was very warm but it was becoming difficult to breathe. She shook herself awake and realized she'd been buried in snow while she slept. She'd have to dig her way out or smother. She clawed with her fingers and then pulled a knife from beneath her to help dig her way upward. It was an eerie sensation, to be underneath a blanket of snow, where there was so little light. When she finally punched through to the air above, it was just dawn and the snow was still falling thickly. Snow was so silent. Unlike rain, which was always loud, wherever it fell. And snow, when it fell on you, made you warm, while rain almost always made you cold. Yet snow required cold and with warmer days came rain. It was all backward. She puzzled on this a while longer, and then longer after that, realizing at last that she must have come closer to smothering than she'd realized—as she was yet half mad.

She sat in the snow. The complex thoughts of rain and snow were replaced by a picture of her own farm in Deborahville blanketed in snow. How beautiful it looked when the snow gentled the edges of the farm, covering the ill-mended fences and unfinished projects. She thought of how sweet it was to walk up the lane on a winter afternoon to find her mother stirring a soup, or mixing a tonic, always with a pot of tea brewing. But now it was empty, wasn't it, the farmhouse? She tried to imagine it. To stand in that house without the threat of Amherst hovering in every room. It was what she'd always wished for, wasn't it? But now there was no Catherine either. No Jenny. No Jimson. No fire in the stove, no tea brewing. Just a shell. Then, in her mind, she saw the barn. She walked inside it, and inside was the flax gin. It gleamed with polished wood; it was in perfect working order. She walked toward it and stroked it. She lifted the hinged flap that covered the gears and peered inside. The pieces of iron shone with oil, especially the round ball that caught the light with its curve.

Then, in her mind, she looked around at the empty barn and felt the emptiness of the house beyond. It was so *quiet* here. She couldn't stay here, even in her mind; it was too quiet.

She shook herself back to the present, and the woods where she sat in the snow were ringing with sound. A chickadee sang his bright morning song and squirrels chased one another in branches over her head. She felt grateful to be here and not back there, in that mausoleum. She dug out the rest of her belongings and got walking again. But the walking became too difficult in the deep snow. Her bad leg ached and she wasted too much energy in taking each step. She'd have to make snowshoes. It was well she had the skin from the deer she'd killed, for she could cut it into strips to make the webbing. She looked up at what she could see of the sun and realized she was heading west, back toward Martha. For the first time in many days, she let herself think of Martha, and of Jenny. Jenny was still there, alone except for her grandfather and Zeke, neither of whom was much company at the moment. What was she thinking, to have left Jenny there like that?

She hurried to finish the snowshoes and made a hasty job of it. They were crooked in various ways—she'd be ashamed to show them to Pete—but they'd keep her up on the snow at least enough to walk without struggle. She'd been in no hurry at all for so many days and she didn't want to hurry now, but the thought of Jenny sitting alone in their room kept goading at her, prodding her along. Further nagging at her thoughts was the vision she'd had of the flax machine—of a round curve of a ball inside it. At the time, in her dream of sorts, it seemed to belong there. But there had never been any kind of ball in that design.

Finding her way back to Martha was no trouble now, for she knew the woods in a wholly different way than she had when they first came here. It was slower travel on snowshoes, but she developed a rhythm and began to make better time. She rested a few hours when it grew dark, but was up and moving again before first light. When she reached Bodine's Tavern by midmorning, the snow had given way to rain and the road into Martha was a slushy soup. She could hear the stamping mill in the distance—she was almost back.

NINETEEN

SHE WALKED INTO TOWN with some trepidation, afraid suddenly of what she might find. What if something had happened to Jenny? She made her way toward Mrs. Gaskill's cabin, trying to ignore the people staring at her. She realized she must look rather frightening; her hair was tangled with sap and twigs, and she imagined her face must be as dirty as her clothes.

When she reached the cabin she was greeted by a surprising sound—music. There was singing inside. She opened the door as quietly as she could and saw the backs of many heads, all facing toward Mrs. Gaskill, who appeared to be conducting a rehearsal of hymns. She saw the back of Jenny's head in the front row, softly bobbing with the song.

As no one had noticed her, Ella pulled her head back and shut the door. So much for arriving to save Jenny from loneliness. With no clear idea of where to go next, she headed toward the company store. On the way she thought to go check the flax gin, make sure it was still covered against this rain.

She found the machine fully stripped of its covering, but it wasn't from neglect. Rather, someone was standing beside it, reaching into it. He was tall and wore a heavy coat, and he had a cloth wrapped around his head in place of a hat. She began to open her mouth to complain of his trespass when he turned, and it was her grandfather.

She stared at him. He looked at her and then turned back to the machine. "There's some straw in the tack room of the stables over yonder. Fetch it and we'll run this little dandy."

"Excuse me," Ella said coldly. She looked at him a long moment and then added, "I fetched what you told me to fetch when I was a child, but that was quite a while ago now."

"As you like," her grandfather said with a slight shrug. He began to turn the crank on the machine. He turned it several times and then paused and peered at the gears. Then he turned it several more times forward and once back, to see what would happen. Then he stopped and looked inside again.

Ella stood immobile, watching him. She'd wished so hard for his interest in the machine to flare, but now that it had, after all that had happened, after all this time, she found she hardly cared.

At last she interrupted the silence to ask, "Why the sudden interest? I thought you were no longer an inventor named Asa Tunnicliff."

He glanced back at her, as if he'd forgotten she was there until she interrupted him. He said in a gravelly voice, "None of that impudence now. You're still my granddaughter." Then, after a pause, "I saw that girl in the chair with wheels and I knew right off it had to be your work. Who else would have thought of that brake she could operate with one hand, or the lock for the wheels? I got thinking on it, and soon enough it got me curious to see what you'd done with this thing here. I've come a few times now, but my back isn't so strong that I can stay long at it."

He went back to examining the machine. "It's my intention today to see the rollers work." He straightened and reached for his cane. "Seeing as you won't fetch straw, I suppose I must go fetch it myself."

Ella was out the door before he could take a step and he nodded in satisfaction as he turned back to the machine. She reappeared a few minutes later carrying an armful of oat straw that she dropped in a pile. She passed him a handful to feed into the machine as she turned the crank. It wasn't the same as flax straw—it didn't handle the same, and of course it didn't yield the long fibers that were spun to fabric—but it was enough to see how it worked, how it *might* work.

"So what's the trouble with it?" her grandfather grumbled at last. "It seems to work well enough."

Well, she thought, *that's high praise indeed*. "It's this, here." She pointed to the linkage assembly that had given so much trouble—the one that tied the shaft of the crank to the gears that turned the teeth of the fiber combs. "The pieces grate against one another and wear down much too quickly. It works well for a few weeks and then they need to be replaced. Something in the design isn't right there, but as much as I've rearranged the pieces, they continue to wear and then slip out of alignment."

Her grandfather leaned closer to see the assembly. As he looked, she said, "While I was away I had a thought. It just came to me—I have no idea if it's any good. I didn't spend much time thinking it through."

"So? Spit it out."

She found she was reluctant to speak of it, afraid it might be a stupid idea and he'd waste no time saying as much. She hesitated, then took a hard breath and said, "I had the thought that we might use round bearings of a fashion— let them rotate in grease to keep the pieces from grinding at one another. I don't think it's new—I suppose I read of it somewhere—but I don't quite know how to employ them. They'll need a casing of some sort. I thought of something round…perhaps."

Her grandfather gave her an appraising look, and there was a hint of admiration in his eyes. He pursed his mouth as he considered the notion and then said, "It's not a bad idea. I've seen them used before, bearings of this sort, but not very often. I think you'd have a solid circle encased within two interlocking concave half-circles, as you say, with the bearings inside in a layer of grease between them."

"So you'd recast either side of the linkage with a concave edge the size of the ball plus the bearings, and then cast a large ball for the center and a set of small balls for the bearings?"

Captain Tunnicliff nodded. "That sounds about right. It's worth a try, I suppose." He stopped and considered a moment, then reached into the machine and tugged at the crank shaft. "I think you'll also need to move this linkage arm, so they join at less of an angle. The ball won't roll as easily if the angle is too acute."

Ella looked at where he indicated. "You mean..." she reached in and pointed. "Attach it... here?"

"Possibly. Or here," he pointed at another location on the other side of the frame.

"But...how? Oh, I see, you'd move the gears as well."

"Yes. That should do it. You could try it either way. You'll have some time while I'm casting the ball joint."

Ella looked up from the machine. "How difficult will that be?"

"The balls are easy to cast," he said. "It's the concave pieces that will be tricky."

"Can you do it?"

His face took on a look of annoyance. "That's the stupidest thing you've said yet. I may be a near invalid, but that doesn't mean I don't remember how to cast iron."

She grinned at him. "It's good to have you back, Grandfather."

"Oh be quiet, would you."

THE PIECES FROM THE first two castings didn't fit together at all. The pieces from the third casting fit together but refused to turn. Her grandfather didn't make a word of complaint, only took another set of careful measurements and went back to the sand molds and began to reshape them.

The fourth set of concave covers slipped neatly into place around the central ball and the layer of bearings around it. They clamped them in place on the linkage arm that Ella had reconfigured to attach to the gears with less of an angle, and then they turned the crank of the gin. After a few minor adjustments, it operated as smoothly as it had before. They fed straw through and it appeared to run as well as it had, at least with oat straw. They had no flax straw on hand.

"Where's the closest place they grow flax?" Ella asked her grandfather as they made their way to the company store for a cup of coffee.

"Don't know. Perhaps down near Hammonton. We don't need it, though. This new joint will hold up—there's no reason it won't."

"Maybe not, but I'd feel better if we had a chance to prove it out. I didn't know the first joint wouldn't last either."

"You should have. That joint was full of friction from the first moment. That's a primary rule of good engineering, reduce friction. It's fully spelled out in Oliver Evans's book—*The Abortion of the Young Steam Engineer's Guide*. You should have seen it straight off."

"Thank you, Grandfather. Next time just say it straight, won't you? Don't dance around the point like that."

He gave her a baleful look. "Don't be all sensitive like a poet. If you're going to stand up for yourself in a man's world, you have to hear things you don't like without flinching. That's how men talk to one another. I'm doing you the favor of treating you like one."

She raised a skeptical brow. "Thank you. I think." She puzzled over this a moment and then shook her head and returned to the topic of the flax straw. "I suppose I might go haul a load of flax from Hammonton, but it's awful far. We came through there on our way up here. It took us ages from there—what with the fire and all."

"How come you came that way?" he asked. "That's south of here."

"We came from Glassboro. We were looking for you."

"Ah yes." He nodded. "Looking for me. After all this time. Looking for me where I didn't want to be found."

"Why not?"

He gave her a sharp look but didn't answer at first. After a time he said, "You came all this way from Deborahville just to find me? That's an awful long way to come."

"We didn't come from Deborahville just to find you. We had already left Deborahville when Zeke caught up to us and told us you were probably still alive. We'd thought you were dead all that time."

"Yes, you did, didn't you. They staged a funeral and all."

"Apparently."

"So why *did* you leave Deborahville?" he asked. "You were close to completing this machine, with or without me. You could have set it up there as well as anywhere."

Ella gave a heavy sigh. "That's a very long story, I'm afraid. All to do with the patenting of the thing."

"Ah yes, the patent. I'm glad to hear you're mindful of the importance of it."

"Unfortunately I'm not the only one." They'd reached the store by now and she helped him up the steps, his frailness still terrible to her. She settled him in a chair by the stove and helped him out of his coat and scarf and head wrap. When they were seated with cups of coffee, she leaned forward and quietly began to tell him of what had happened in Deborahville. Of how she'd almost had the patent stolen out from under her by Emerston, of how she smashed the machine and left with the drawings. At the end she said, "So you see, good intentions or none, he couldn't keep himself from trying to grab it."

The old man snorted in derision. "I'll eat my hat if he ever intended to let you have that patent. His father always worried on that boy, saying he wasn't right somehow, in knowing what was right to do and what wasn't. Missing a moral cue, his father used to say. I wouldn't be surprised if he crafted up a means to convince you to trust him."

Ella looked at him in disbelief. She'd hated Emerston good and long, all these past months, but she'd never believed him to have been corrupt from the start; she'd thought only that he'd been swayed by temptation. "How can that be?" she challenged. "How can everyone in town think he's honest? Won't bad dealings of that sort come out in time?"

Her grandfather nodded. "It should come out. Someday it will. But he's smart is what it is. Too smart to even let on to how smart he really is. He was always like that, even as a boy. His father would rarely catch him at anything, only suspect him. We'd speak of it sometimes, when the worry grew too strong. I'd worry on your mother and you children, on what a monster she had married. He'd worry on his oldest son, on what a monster he might prove to be. But that Emerston boy was always three times as smart as the one your mother married—that fine father of yours. No, the Emerston boy seemed to know how to hide himself from the very start. I suspect he's only gotten smarter in time. In fact I know it to be true, for I had occasion to find it out for myself."

She looked at him in interest, but he said he no more. She considered what he'd told her, turning it over and over in her mind, pondering the implications. At last she said, "I wonder, would that affidavit that attested to my status as inventor have secured anything, after all? It seemed a good idea at the time, but now I see that someone as wily as he might easily write another that attests to the same status for himself."

Grandfather Tunnicliff chuckled. "I see you're coming to understand more of how that man's mind works. He uses the law like a weapon. It wouldn't surprise me, in fact, if he invented the whole business of using an affidavit to secure inventor status. What's to say it's real other than his own word on it?"

Ella frowned. "I see the danger of knowing nothing of the law. It begins to seem as if navigating the patent is of greater difficulty than the engineering of the machine." She paused, then reached into her tunic and removed the papers she'd been carrying all these months. They'd remained dry within her oil-skin packet, but were ragged and grey with travel. The creases of the folds had taken the most wear, such that when she unfolded them there were tears and long holes along the folds.

"Those should impress the Superintendent of Patents," her grandfather said drily.

"Obviously I'll need a fresh set of papers. One difficulty is that I have no means to replicate the nature of the application papers Emerston wrote. See here..." She pointed to the paper that bore Emerston's printed letterhead above his letter of application. "This looks so...official. I can't simply take any old paper and do the same." She read down the page. "His wording all sounds proper and oh so formal, but he doesn't have all the facts correct, for he doesn't understand the engineering. I'd like to write this better. Can you assist me with it?"

Her grandfather took the paper from her and read it over. When he was finished he sighed and said, "It's not me you want, but Oliver Evans in Philadelphia. He's the man to be of aid to you, for he knows the patenting process as well as any man." He paused, and then added, "I had always intended to go to him directly when I was ready to make my application."

"Just like that?" Ella asked. "You thought to go to him and he'd assist you, just like that?"

"Don't be a simpleton, girl. Of course not. I've met the man. And he owes me a debt."

When he didn't elaborate further, Ella said, "You're not the only one who knows Oliver Evans, you know. Aunt Lucille has a merchant friend who knows his wife, and she met Mr. and Mrs. Evans when she was in Philadelphia. She wrote to them for me, to warn that I might visit to ask his opinion on the merits of my patent application."

"Bah. That'll get you nowhere with Evans," her grandfather snarled. "A letter from a friend of his wife's? Bah."

"You know him better than that?" Ella asked, thinking herself rather clever.

"Course I do. I've known him for twenty-five year or more. Or rather, I knew him twenty-five years ago. But he won't have forgotten me. Not for a minute. You'll remind him of the day he met a young smith still in his soldiering clothes, traveling through Delaware after the war with the British, looking for work to help make his way home. You'll remind him how the smith knocked on his door to ask if he needed a millwright and found him at work on his paper models of a milling operation. How the smith was the one who made the suggestion that if you made the hopper arm long enough, the flour at the outer edge of the circle would be driest, and could be sent down a hole in the floor. Then you'll remind him of what he said that day. He said, 'I owe you a debt, Captain Tunnicliff. Someday you'll collect it.' I never have, but now you'll collect it for me."

"You think he'll remember those words, all these years later?"

"He'd better." But then, a few minutes later, he added, "I'll write him a letter with a few more details in it, to prod his memory. Just in case."

"Excellent. In the meantime I'll ask Jenny to begin on a new set of drawings that captures the ball joint, and I'll see about finding a cart to go for a load of flax straw. Despite what you say, I want to see for myself that the joint will hold."

"Bah. Suit yourself. Seems a waste of time to me."

THREE DAYS LATER, a pair of horses stumbled into town. When Mr. Simons stopped by the shed to mention that a pair of strange horses had been stabled behind the ironmaster's house, Ella asked him to describe them. She nodded and put down her tools, then loped up the hill to the ironmaster's house, which overlooked all that went on in the town. The only other time she'd been there was her first day in Martha, when the iron-master's wife had set her leg.

She made her way directly to the stable, not stopping to ask permission of any sort, and there, munching oats from a bucket in borrowed stalls, were Dapper Dan and Philippa. They didn't look well. Both were exceedingly thin, their ribs showing in sharp relief under their skin. Their coats were dirty and their manes and tails heavily threaded with needles and small twigs. Philippa seemed to be listing slightly to the right, favoring her front left leg as if she'd injured it.

Whatever they'd been through didn't seem to have dulled their senses, as they immediately recognized Ella and gave wel-coming whinnies. Dapper Dan began raising his head up and down in his way of demanding that Ella come rub his neck. It took her two strides across the stable to reach him, and her nuzzle into his neck was grateful and long.

"Ah, I see you've found each other." Zeke said as he came into the stable, "I heard two horses had appeared and thought it might be these two rogues." He walked over to Philippa and gave her neck a similar nuzzle.

Behind them, an amused voice said, "I see we needn't advertise much further as to whom these horses might belong. They clearly know thee."

They squinted at the backlit figure in the doorway and recognized Mr. Solomon Reeves, furnace manager and ironmaster. He came across the stable to join them. "Not to disparage the mare, she's a fine horse, but that gelding is rather a remarkable one, is he not? I've rarely seen one as fine."

"I see you know horses," Ella said. "Yes, he's quite valuable. Though I'm afraid he's not looking his best at present."

Mr. Reeves gave her a sharp look. "I see thou has a gift for understatement."

"You might say that." Ella turned to stroke Dapper Dan once more. "Might we borrow grooming equipment for them?"

"Certainly, use whatever thee like." Mr. Reeves gestured toward the tack room at the end of the rows of stalls. It was quite a fine stable, very clean, with a wide central alley, good windows, and a spacious tack room. "They might stay here as long as is necessary to nurse them to health."

"Thank you, that's quite kind," Ella said.

When he'd gone, they collected grooming equipment and tackled the knots and tangles. They worked in companionable silence for a while, but then the silence began to stretch and Ella realized she could think of nothing to say. She'd kept her distance from Zeke all these weeks, and now, suddenly, there was nothing to say that didn't feel awkward.

At length he broke the silence by saying, "I wonder what became of Molly's mare, Nell?"

"She was with these two when we sent them off—do you imagine she died in the fire?"

"Don't know," Zeke said. "She certainly wasn't as fast as these two, but she was a smart beast. If she survived she might have made her way back to Glassboro somehow. Perhaps Molly knows of someone who's been there recently. I'll ask her."

Ella's face grew cold and she curried with increased fervor. Zeke said, "Come now, Ella. This is absurd. You've been avoiding me for ages now. Why won't you just tell me what angers you?"

She shook her head. He stopped currying and said, "Stop it, won't you. This is childish."

"Fine. If you must be told, you daft idiot, it's that I just cannot...watch."

"Watch what?" He sounded truly puzzled.

She enunciated each word. "Watch...you...and...her."

"Her? Who?"

"You know who."

He thought. "You mean...Molly?"

She nodded.

"Oh, Ella," he said with an amused shake of his head, "you're a complete blathering idiot. You've actually *believed* all that talk? Why didn't you ask me?"

She gave him an icy look that wiped the amusement from his face. "All right, fine. I'll tell you now, once and for good. Molly has no interest in me as a suitor. I think she likes all that talk about us courting because it's better that way. I wouldn't be surprised if she began the rumor herself, in fact."

He stopped and Ella's head snapped up. "Why?"

"I can't say. And I don't even know for sure. It's just from what I've noticed. I think there's someone she can never be with and she doesn't want anyone to know."

"You're saying she's taken with a married man?"

"No," Zeke said sharply. "That's not it." When Ella continued to pin him an icy stare, he at length grew uncomfortable and said, "Fine, I'll tell you what I think but you won't believe it any better." He took a deep breath and rapidly, while exhaling, said, "I believe she loves Samantha O'Grady, that girl you've seen walking around town as if she owns it." When Ella's fierce look only deepened, he added, "They came over on the boat from Ireland together. Something Molly said ages ago first gave me the idea, and then I watched whenever they were nearby one another and it's true, she acts like a jilted lover. Samantha pretends not to notice, but I can see there's much unsaid between them. It's all very strange. In any case Samantha is engaged to be married this summer and that will be the end of it."

"But... what? That's not possible..."

"I know. I wouldn't have thought it either, but then I recalled Miss Whitmarsh, the pastor's sister back in Deborahville, and Miss Lefevre, who lives at the parsonage as well. I heard someone in the store once say there was something unnatural between them and I asked my mother of it. She told me it wasn't anybody else's business what people did in their own homes and I should mind my own business—as should everyone else. That's all I ever knew but I wondered about it for years."

Ella dropped her eyes and tried to absorb what she'd just heard. It made no sense. Two girls? As thoughts raced across her mind a vision suddenly locked into place and stayed. It was Pete and Lucille, when she'd strode unannounced into Pete's lodge and found them sitting elbow to elbow, sipping tea, their faces alive with a quiet joy that made each appear startlingly beautiful. In her mind their unguarded faces continued to smile at her as she stood awkwardly in the doorway, watching something she didn't understand. Her grandfather had always said they loved each other as well as any married people did. That it was no different despite that they couldn't have a regular life together. But still... this was even more different. She looked up at Zeke and said, "It makes little sense but I believe you—that you aren't courting Molly."

"Nice of you." Abruptly Zeke's blue eyes looked angrier than she could remember.

"It's just that I thought…"

"What? That some one else had claimed me? That you couldn't take me for granted as your own any longer?"

Ella was startled and then stung. "No, it's not that. It's more…Well, Jenny told me of what happened in the woods, when that limb fell on me and you feared it killed me. How you wept, and, well…I thought— "

"Thought what? That it was proof I belonged to you? It's not even as if you care for me that way, is it? You have eyes only for that Adonis back home. Isn't that so?"

She looked up sharply. How could he say such a thing, and in such a way? She saw the look in his eyes as he turned them to the floor; he was regretting what he'd said. She almost wished she could say something to forgive him, to relieve the pain in his eyes, but she was stung too deeply. Slowly she put down the curry brush, patted Dapper Dan, and walked from the stable.

TWENTY

THE NEW SET OF DRAWINGS of the flax engine were nearly complete when the first child developed a rash and fever. Ella had to restrain herself from restraining Jenny when her sister announced she'd go see the child right away. They could not be certain it was scarlet fever until two other children developed the same bright red rash on their faces and necks. Soon it had spread to five others and Jenny and Mistress Reeves were hard at it to keep up with the nursing demands. Three of the children died amidst the rage of fever, while the others appeared to be toughing through it.

When the contagion seemed at last to have abated, Mistress Reeves looked at Jenny, wringing out dirty linen. "Thou look flushed. Are thee feeling well?"

"I'm fine, Mistress. Just tired is all." But later, when the rash erupted together with a fiery fever, she could argue no further and allowed herself to be pushed into bed.

"It's odd, is it not?" Ella asked Mistress Reeves. "For one as old as she. I thought only children contracted this illness."

"Ah no, 'tis a pity but I've seen it before. And she's not that much beyond a child, is she, despite that she seems as one so much older."

"I suppose. But what do you know of this disease for someone of her age? Is it more or less severe?"

Mistress Reeves shook her head. "I cannot promise either way. It depends on the person."

Something in her face alarmed Ella. "Why? What have you seen in the past?"

Mistress Reeves shook her head once more, then she looked at Ella directly. "I can see thee wish the truth. I have yet to see but two cases at this age. One young lady... she passed on, and the other, a young man, he recovered. Yet his hearing was impaired and never, to my knowledge, restored."

"You mean he was deaf afterwards?"

"Yes, or nearly so, I'm afraid."

IN THE DAYS THAT JENNY'S FEVER RAGED, a vicious March wind took up outside and drifted snow three and four feet high in places, stranding the ore carts and making travel near impossible. Much of the work in Martha slowed to a standstill as it grew difficult to walk even a few feet outside. Ella noticed none of it, for she refused to leave Jenny's bedside. The poised young lady her sister had become had given way to the small frightened girl of their earlier childhood. Mistress Reeves and Mrs. Gaskill, both competent nurses, attempted to shoo Ella away, encouraged her to take rest, but she ignored them with nothing but a baleful look.

In her repugnance for illness she'd learned little of nursing and now could do little for Jenny, except wipe her face. This she did with a near-religious fervor. Somehow, in defiance of logic, she felt it her own fault that Jenny was lying here, reduced to looking so small, and so terribly fragile. If not for her, Jenny would yet be home in Deborahville, not in this ragged iron town that wished to break them all with ill health—in one manner or another.

Jenny slept most of each day, opening her eyes for a few moments here and there, with little apparent recognition for anyone. She couldn't swallow even water, for her throat was swollen and raw as a wound. As Mistress Reeves noted signs of water loss and began to look concerned, Ella became desperate to force liquid into Jenny. She took to dribbling it into her mouth as she slept. Mistress Reeves warned her to be wary of choking the poor girl, but she persisted in her mission, albeit slowing her ministrations to a few drops every few minutes. Late at night she would at last sag to sleep over Jenny's body. When Jenny stirred, Ella would wake to take up her tasks of wiping and dribbling.

"Thee will make thyself ill," Mistress Reeves cautioned. "What good will that do thy sister?" Ella gave her the same baleful look and asked again for a different medicine to try. Something, anything else. She dutifully dribbled in one herb tincture after another, until she'd exhausted Mrs. Reeves' supply and received a shake of the head when she asked for more. So she returned to dribbling water a few drops at a time, hour after hour.

Near midnight on the fifth night, the fever rose beyond where it had been and Ella sat in mute terror, wiping and wiping, trying to cool her sister's blazing body as Jenny writhed on the wet sheets. Ella refused to let herself think of what the fever might be doing to delicate ears, or eyes. Instead, as she'd done at times all along, she chanted to herself. "I won't let you die. I won't let you die. I won't let you die."

At some point in the early hours of morning, she lapsed into sleep with her rag in hand and her head on Jenny's middle, and woke in a puddle of her own drool. She looked up at Jenny's face and saw she'd grown still and quiet. "No!" she shrieked, but it came out more as a croak.

She ran her hands over Jenny's face, where the skin was peeling from the rash, and felt how cool she grown. What did it mean? She found the place in the neck where she'd seen Mistress Reeves press her fingers and pressed her own fingers into it. Beneath her fingertips, a steady pulsing beat emerged. She was alive. But why was she so cold now?

Mrs. Gaskill came into the room and put her hand on Jenny's forehead. "Ah, the fever has broken," she said. "This is good."

"She'll live then?" Ella asked, her eyes drooping with exhaustion.

"She could yet take another bad turn," Mrs. Gaskill cautioned, "but she's at least got a respite from the fever."

Indeed the fever made a brief reappearance that evening, and again Ella wiped and wiped until she dropped into sleep. But again Jenny was cool in the morning, and even opened her eyes later that day and smiled at Ella.

In a cracking voice she said, "I dreamt I was being held down by a giant cat and licked all over with her tongue."

"That was me," Ella said. "I was the cat."

"You've been licking me?"

Ella held up her rag. "My tongue wasn't up to the task, so I employed this. Well, maybe thirty of these. Mrs. Gaskill keeps taking them away to wash them."

Jenny smiled and began to fade back to sleep. Before she could do so, Ella said, "Wait—Jenny! You heard me—that I was the cat. That means you can hear?"

Jenny flicked open her eyes once more but could not stay awake to appreciate whatever it was that had her sister weeping happy tears all over the blankets.

Mrs. Gaskill came in. "Here now, I've just washed those blankets and here you are slopping all over them. Have you not a handkerchief for that?"

JENNY SLEPT FOR THE BETTER PART of another full week, but little by little Ella's worry abated. She continued to have trouble leaving the bedside, afraid that a turn for the worse would come if she ceased to stand guard, but she made brief forays, including a visit with her grandfather over coffee at the company store.

He nodded as she told him of Jenny's improvement. "Ah, that's good. I'm grateful to hear it, for I've been a mite worried over her. I haven't wanted to…intrude at the bedside, or anything."

"That's rot," Ella said flatly. "You're as terrified of illness as I ever was. In fact I probably took it from you, as much time as I spent in your shop all those years."

"Yes, probably so," he agreed with a wry smirk. He stirred his coffee. "So what of you? Now that Jenny seems to be on the mend, you'll make your way to Philadelphia as soon as the roads are clear, won't you? The drawings she's done will suffice—they're near enough to completion."

Ella gave him a startled look. She hadn't expected this question, not so soon. Jenny still needed her. "I don't know yet. I'll have to think on it."

"I wouldn't tarry too long. That Emerston is a wily one. Now that he's seen the machine and smelled the opportunity, I'll be surprised if he hasn't already applied for the patent ahead of you. But you'd best go find out."

"But how can he? He has no drawings, and even if he did, the new ball joint and new arrangement of crank arm and gears make it a different machine."

"Do they? That's up to the office of patents to decide. If the superintendent thinks the two designs are too similar, he'll award only the first of them. The second is out of luck."

"How can that be? If the second is clearly superior, isn't it in the interest of patents to award them both?"

"Perhaps, but he might not see it that way. From his view, having ten people apply for essentially the same machine with small adjustments is nothing more than a nuisance."

Ella nodded. "I suppose I see the logic in that. But I've taken all this time now, looking for you and working on the machine. It seems absurd to be in a mad rush all of a sudden."

"Yes, that's so, but how will you feel if you get to the office of patents only to find that the patent was awarded just last week? My point is only that it's foolish to dally."

Ella left him at the store, still sipping his coffee, and took a longer route through the woods back to Mrs. Gaskill's, to give herself more time to think. The harsh winds had ceased, replaced by warmer breezes that were melting the snow and making a wet mess of everything. Spring had come.

Skirting puddles on the road, she considered her grandfather's advice as she walked. She saw the wisdom in making haste, but something in her rebelled at the thought of leaving Jenny, who wouldn't be strong enough to travel for some more weeks. Not now. Not after just getting her back from the brink of, well… She could recall the time when she'd wished so hard for the chance to leave alone, to go off with no encumbrances. But now, when she thought of it, she knew she'd do nothing but fret over Jenny if she left her behind. But then again, the machine, it was so important. So much bigger than them, in their own small lives. It would live on so many years beyond them. And would provide for her family if she could make success of it. Shouldn't those considerations matter more?

Her thoughts got as muddy as the puddles around her while she tried to find her way clear to a decision. When her path took her back into town, her thoughts were interrupted by a familiar whistling as Zeke came into view walking toward her. He had been several times to see Jenny in her illness, but his visits had been short and Ella had usually made an excuse to leave the room. She'd yet to find a way to think about the things they said that day in the stable, and she wasn't anxious to revisit that talk.

Today, though, he broke into a wide grin at the sight of her and held up a fiddle. "Look what I've got. I traded a peddler for it." The fiddle was dripping broken strings, had a number of deep scratches, and was lacking varnish in several places. "I know it looks rough," he added, "but I can fix it up in a trice and it's got quite a nice sound." He plucked on the remaining strings to show her.

She could not help grinning back at him, for he looked so pleased. And he'd looked pleased so little lately. Without thinking she said, "You might come play it for Jenny, to cheer her up. I know she'd like that."

He grinned again, the bright colors of his face vivid against his dark hair. "I'll get her fixed up—at least the strings—and come over later today."

When she nodded, he waved a farewell and sprinted off. Left alone again with her indecisive thoughts, Ella made her way toward the shed that housed the flax engine. She hadn't been here since Jenny took sick and it seemed much longer than that. She removed the cover and stared at the machine, willing it to tell her something to help her know what to do.

While she was standing there, a bright voice behind her said, "I've come to say good-bye, then." She turned to see Molly McGilligan, standing in the opening of the shed, her copper hair gleaming in the spring sunlight. She'd avoided the girl all winter, but when they'd come face to face in town, Molly had been invariably cheerful, solicitous of her own and Jenny's health. She'd been one of the first to visit Jenny when she first took ill, and had sent small gifts of food every few days. Ella swallowed her immediate impulse to be curt and instead attempted to be gracious.

"Are you returning to Glassboro, then?" Ella asked.

"Aye, by means of Batsto. I told the widow I'd be back."

"As I recall, you promised to be back before winter fell." Ella twisted her mouth into a teasing smirk.

"Oh aye, but the widow'll take me back one way or another. If I know that old drunk, she's likely not to have noticed how long I've been gone." Molly smirked back. "Ye'll be wishing me to give her your sincere regards, I imagine?"

Ella snorted and then laughed. She looked at Molly with a frank stare and said, "Why did you do it, Molly? Take up with Zeke and let the whole town think you were courting, when you were just playing games?"

Molly looked startled but then she collected herself. "Tah, 'twas nothing, that. Just a bit o' fun, 'twas all. I was...needing company." She paused, and then gave Ella a shrewd look and said, "What's your great concern in the matter? It's not as if you wish him for yourself."

A wave of anger surged over Ella at this presumptuous statement. A sharp retort came to her tongue but she bit it back just in time. "Perhaps not," she said, "but I don't care to see him toyed with, either. Just for sport, or for covering your..." She cut herself off before she could say any more.

Molly looked at her, clearly knowing what she'd been about to say. More serious than Ella could recall, she said, "Nay, Ella. Don't wish me more ill. I suffer enough already, and I wouldn't wish it on anyone else." Ella's regret for her own words must have shown in her face, for Molly said in a soft voice, "I'd give anything for someone to love me as that boy loves you. I wouldn't toss it off like rubbish, of that you can be certain."

Ella swallowed hard as Molly's words entered her mind like a familiar-looking stranger. *Did she truly say that?* There was no obvious response to this startling statement; she could only nod.

At last Ella said in a cracking voice, "Will you tell me, then, seeing as you're leaving, how you always win at cards? You do cheat, don't you?"

Molly laughed, her bright humor restored. "Nay, of course not. 'Tis only the luck of the Irish. We're a sight lucky people."

THAT EVENING ZEKE ARRIVED at Mrs. Gaskill's cabin with his new fiddle in hand. It looked much better with the strings restored and some preliminary polishing of the wood.

After an exchange of greetings, he sat near Jenny's bed and took his time tuning, his long fingers gliding over the strings. He played a sample tune and then asked Mrs. Gaskill, standing in the doorway, if she had a favorite tune he might play for her. She was quick to oblige, and after this he played one for Jenny, and then for little Emily parked in her wheeled chair, as so often now, in a corner of Jenny's sick room, from where she missed little. He improvised as necessary for the tunes he didn't know. Mrs. Gaskill seemed entranced by the music and before long she'd pulled Emily out of her chair and was dancing her around the room in her arms. Emily was laughing as she rarely did, and Jenny and Ella smiled to see it.

He played for nearly two hours, until Jenny's eyes were well closed and Emily and Mrs. Gaskill were both drooping. He ceased playing and had begun to pack his fiddle into his make-shift case when Mrs. Gaskill said, "Might I ask you a grand favor, my dear boy? It's a lovely night, would you play a few more minutes outside my window as Emily and I fall asleep?

My father used to do that on spring and summer nights, and it would be such a treat to me."

"Of course, Mrs. Gaskill, it would be a pleasure."

He went out with his fiddle and when everyone else had left as well, Ella readied herself and slipped into bed. Outside, behind the cabin, she could hear the first notes of Zeke's fiddle as he began to play once more. This time, with no requests to meet, he played Mrs. Gaskill's favorite tune and then let the fiddle take him where it wished to go. At first the tune became haunting and sad. Then it picked up a bit of speed and became melodic, a ballad of sorts. Ella, listening from her bed, rubbed the gold watch and tried to sleep, but found the music was keeping her awake. The beauty of it nearly hurt, as if the notes pierced her skin. At last she slipped from her bed and pulled on her boots once more. She wrapped her coat around herself and made her way to sit beside Zeke on the log where he was perched. She was perfectly silent, not wishing to mar the music.

It was a warm night for late March, with a bright moon and alternating gusts of warm and cool breeze. The air held spring in the musky scent of rotting leaves emerging from beneath soggy old snow.

If Zeke noticed her presence he didn't show it. His eyes were closed as he listened to the voice of the fiddle, and Ella, sitting beside him, felt as if she too could hear that voice. As never before she could hear every nuance of every note, and knew by some instinct what the notes mean to say, as if they were words. Zeke's words. He told her of his sadness, and also his joy. Of his love of the beauty in the notes, and in the lovely evening, and in her company.

She thought of him. His gentle good humor, his constant kindness. She thought of how little he put himself forward, how he was content to stay a step behind her. To push her forward rather than step forward himself. What would it be like to be that way? To be content to remain in the shadow? She envied him and she admired him, all at once. Was it the music, was that what made it possible? Did the music give him whatever she herself got from stepping forward, from taking charge, making things happen? She needed that and he didn't. Whatever he needed, he got it elsewhere.

She watched his fingers as they moved over the strings. His fingers were long and perfectly formed, not delicate but very supple. They seemed to know exactly where to be with no apparent effort. Her eyes moved to the planes of his face, the long jaw, the pointed nose, the shadows of stubble under his cheekbones. With his eyes closed, she noticed the long lashes lying across the tops of his cheeks. As much time as she'd spent with him, she'd never watched him like this. She looked from the lashes down his face to his lips, which, even in the cool moonlight, were very red and, she noticed, curved in the slightest hint of a smile. Suddenly she felt her own face grow hot.

She tore her eyes from his lips, but her face remained flushed, and her breath began to catch in her throat. As if he could sense it, Zeke's eyes opened and he looked at her. She didn't know where to put her own eyes and she knew she must look confused. The heat grew in her face and she felt the instinct to stand and run. Before she could do so, the music faltered and stopped. She snuck a peek at him and saw that he was gazing at her as if puzzled by something. With care, he placed the fiddle into its case at his feet. Then he turned to her and he put out his hand.

Her own hand, as if of its own accord, reached out to his. His fingers felt cool and dry. She grasped his hand more tightly, as if it were a floating log and she was being sucked under by current. They held on, squeezing one another's hand, not looking at one another. They stayed this way for several minutes, their hands speaking for them.

Then Zeke moved. He twisted around and down until he was on his knees, kneeling in front of her where she sat on the log. He looked up at her and his eyes said all that needed to be said. His eyes held all he'd said with the notes of his fiddle, all that she'd already heard. They stared at each other for a long moment, tentative at first, and then more boldly. Ella felt her breath grow rapid, and then become ragged, and she could hear that his sounded the same. She didn't know what to do.

Then she leaned forward, just a little, and it was as if she'd struck a flint. Their lips found one another's. Melted into one another's. In her stomach were suddenly those same great leaping somersaults that she'd felt all those months ago, with that other boy. The sensation was so familiar, and yet so odd, here, now, with this boy. This other boy. This boy she knew so well, who was so familiar. But not like this. Never like this.

She felt more of herself begin to heat and melt and she knew it wouldn't be long before she had no more say in the matter. She wrested her lips from his and turned, her breath coming in sharp, ragged gasps. She was about to say something, to stop it, but when she looked at him something in his eyes changed her mind. He needed her, needed this; she could not refuse him. And she didn't want to.

But then, hours later, when they woke in one another's arms, something about the imminent approach of dawn struck a chord of alarm in her, such that when he turned to her and began to kiss her once again, she fought down the melting feeling. "No, don't...I can't."

She turned away from him to catch her breath and collect her thoughts, and then, steeling herself, turned back to speak to him. Before she could say anything more, she looked in his eyes and saw something she'd never seen there before, in all the years she'd known him; she saw naked raw hurt. Then he intervened to erase it, forcing himself to give a rueful smile and say, "Not a good idea, huh?"

She gave him a grateful look. "We'd likely regret it. Don't you think?"

"Don't know," he said with another pained grin. "Right this minute I don't know that I'm thinking straight. Are you?"

"Don't know." She smiled back at him. Then she sat up. "Don't know that the different parts of me all agree with one another."

He blushed at this. Then he said, "Uh, mine do."

She took his hand. "Let's not make this too terrible. It just happened. It was a beautiful night—the moon, the music. We don't have to let it ruin everything, do we?"

"Don't be daft. We won't make it terrible."

But as she lay on her pallet trying to sleep after creeping back into the cabin, she knew it wasn't the same. As much as they might pretend it was just their bodies, reacting to the night and the music, she knew it was a lie. She'd seen it in his eyes, heard it in his music. It was all so confusing. Confusing and dangerous. Whether or not it was a lie, she determined to make it be the same. She wouldn't let anything be different between them. Yet her body felt strange and she couldn't help thinking about him. How he'd touched her with those long fingers. She was like a maple tree in spring, in which the sap had begun to flow after a long winter and now wouldn't cease.

He joked with her when she saw him the next day and, with some effort, she joked back. There was one time they held each other's eyes a little too long and she had to restrain herself from saying something she shouldn't. But it passed. He seemed as grateful as she to put the awkwardness and anger of the winter behind them.

It was the same for a few more days, but then, one morning, she woke to find Mrs. Gaskill reading a note she'd found on the table.

Dear friends,

My apologies for not giving more notice, but I'm leaving to go home to Deborahville today. I had a dream in the night that my parents were both ill and in need of my aid. It got me thinking I've been away too long.

Mrs. Gaskill, thank you for your hospitality. Ella and Jenny, here's all the money I can spare. I'm taking Philippa.

Zeke

TWENTY-ONE

JENNY CRIED when Ella showed her the note and Ella had to choke down her own tears as well. How could Zeke just up and leave them like this? For so much of this past winter she'd hardly spoken to him, but she'd always known he was nearby. Was with them. Watching out for them, even.

For the first day after his leaving she walked around in a daze of sorts, trying to understand. Had he really dreamt of his parents and left for that? As much as she'd like to believe this, she couldn't make herself. No, he was saving face, for all of them. So did this mean...if it was really too hard for him to be near her now, could they never be friends again?

Then, on the second day, as if the smoke parted for a moment, she saw that Zeke's leaving had one advantage; it made her own decision about leaving sooner rather than later all too clear. She could not leave Jenny alone here in Martha, without even Zeke to rely on. No, damn the machine. She refused to have that on her conscience.

She talked of it with Jenny, who said, "But Ella, if there's a chance you risk the machine, you should go. I'm fine here. Mrs.

Gaskill and I will take care of one another. I'll be well soon enough and I'll join you."

"No. I see all the reasons, but no. I can't do it. I've risked your well-being enough, and no machine is worth it. I don't care about the machine."

"Yes, you do. It's stupid to say you don't." Ella's head snapped up at this, seeing as Jenny rarely spoke with such force. Jenny went on. "I don't want it on my conscience either. What if you were to miss the patent by a week and it was because you sat here too long? How would I feel then?" She stared at her sister a moment. "I think we've exhausted our respective abilities to out-sacrifice the other. Let's come up with a reasonable plan that doesn't leave either of us cause for regret. If we give it just a few more days, not more than a week, I'm certain I can travel at least by carriage. If we can arrange transfers that require little walking, we can ride all the way to the port, and then, from there, it's a ferry crossing the Delaware into Philadelphia. I can manage that."

Ella gave her a skeptical look. "That seems rather soon. I don't want you taken over by fever again."

"No one gets scarlet fever twice. It doesn't work that way. The worst that will happen is I'll get fatigued and require a rest somewhere. That's not so terrible." Jenny looked at Ella with her wide brown eyes.

"I'll ask Mistress Reeves about it," Ella said, still skeptical.

"You don't believe me? You think I'm lying so that . . . what? I can die of fever on a ferry somewhere? Or on a street corner?"

"Now you're being dramatic."

"And you're being stubborn. I'm being reasonable."

"And I'm not? Well, that's a fine how d'you do for the sister who's nursed you all this time."

"Yes, but you're in danger of turning from a nurse to a nanny." Jenny's eyes snapped and Ella, looking at her, could see she was losing this argument.

After conferring with Mistress Reeves when she visited later in the day, the decision was made that they'd leave in a week's time. Ella went to tell Grandfather Tunnicliff, who, with the warmer weather, was back at work at the smith, replacing the men who were preparing to put the furnace back in blast.

She found him at the smith twisting thin rods of iron to make coat hooks for the new schoolhouse, which was nearly complete. "It's about time," he said gruffly, when she told him she'd be leaving for Philadelphia in a week. "He could have written four different patents in all this time."

"Grandfather," she said slowly, "I'm putting the patent in both our names."

"No you're not," he said at once. "I left it behind me long ago, and left it unfinished. I haven't been thinking on it in these years, or at least not much. If it's ready to patent now, it's because you solved it and built it. I don't want credit for something I didn't do."

"That's absurd. I'd never even have *thought* of building a flax machine if you hadn't been working on it my whole childhood. You built the greater portion of it and I only put in the last pieces. It rightly belongs to both of us and both our names should go on the patent. Don't argue with me any further."

"Hmmph," he said, which she considered ceding the point.

"You'll take some money with you," he said. "You'll need it in the big cities."

"You mean you want to give me money? I won't take it."

"Yes, you will. I've got some saved and I'll probably die before I use it all. You'll need it if you're to travel to Philadelphia and then to the capital. You can't pitch camp and hunt game in the center of Philadelphia."

"Pity, that's how I intended to account for lodging and dining."

"Don't be smart, young lady. I can still whup you if I have to."

Ella didn't answer because her attention was drawn to the treadle behind where her grandfather worked. She looked at the horse working the treadle, then shook her head and turned away. Then she looked back once more and slowly walked over to the treadle. The horse was an old gelding, swaybacked and fully grey at the muzzle. "Grandfather, this can't be Edgar, can it?"

"It can, and it is," he said in his rough voice.

Gently she reached out a hand to touch his mane. "Edgar? Do you remember me?" When he turned to her with a milky white eye, she knew he recognized her voice. She wrapped her arms around his neck and, after inhaling his scent and stroking him a long while, turned back to her grandfather. "But how is it he's still working? He must be over thirty years old by now. He was ancient when you had him back in Deborahville."

Captain Tunnicliff shrugged. "He's thirty-three, I believe. But he doesn't mind working the treadle. It's easy enough work for him, and he might as well earn his keep."

Ella stared at the old horse, who looked as grizzled as her grandfather. At last she asked, "I knew he'd been at the Seneca village, but then, after that, you *rode* him all the way here? But why, with all the beautiful horses in your stable, why take this one?"

Tunnicliff shrugged once again. "He was the one who wouldn't be missed. He wasn't on the inventory."

She stared at Edgar and then nodded in slow appreciation of this logic. She watched the horse work, thinking that every step forward took him exactly nowhere. He wasn't even heading toward the promise of oats and a pile of hay. He had no ambition to go anywhere at all. But when she studied him, she saw he didn't look unhappy. In fact he looked content.

"He's good company, isn't he?" she asked her grandfather. "Edgar, I mean."

To her surprise, her grandfather's lined face softened and spread into the ghost of a smile. It was a look she hadn't seen on his face since, well, she couldn't remember when. "Yes," he said, "he's the best company there is. Don't know what I'd do without him." He turned away from her to tend to his forge and she had the suspicion he was hiding his eyes.

She had another spurt of intuition and said, "You had him saddled up to go the night you left, didn't you? How did you know the horse thieves would come that night? How did you know to make me swear to finish your work?"

"I didn't," he said. "Or rather, I did know, but I don't know how. Sometimes you just know things and you don't know how you know them. I felt it coming, like a storm. Maybe my horses told me. Maybe Edgar here told me."

She nodded, for she understood him perfectly. She'd had the same sense of knowing things without knowing how she knew them. She gazed at her grandfather and then, up from her gut, the question she'd been trying to keep down rose up and swelled out of her mouth. "Why did you leave, Grandfather? How could you leave me there?"

He looked at her and then stared down, and in his eyes she saw something she'd almost never seen there; it was shame. She thought a moment and then asked, "Did you think Loomis would come for you?"

"Bah, that's just the half of it." He spit into the forge, where the spittle hissed and jumped on the coals before it was gone. He glanced around at the other smiths in the forge, as if reluctant to talk in front of them, despite the persistent din of the hammers that made it hard to hear anything at all. He said, "Come for me when the shift is done. We'll talk then."

SHE WAITED FOR HIM by the door of the smith, and when he was done they stepped out into the damp spring night with the light fading around them. They walked a ways without speaking, heading south toward Wading River. Her grandfather's pace was slower than it had once been and she found herself having to walk more slowly than was comfortable. She was about to ask him her question again, when he said abruptly, "I don't know that it's a kindness to you, but I've thought on it and I think you deserve to know why I left. Otherwise you'll wonder on it and keep wondering on it, and there's no one else to tell you."

They went another few feet and then he took a deep breath and said in his gruffest voice, "I knew Loomis was coming for the horses. I'd seen his lackeys lurking about, taking stock of the place. He'd been thieving horses up and down the valley all winter, and it was only a matter of time before he came for mine. Like I said, I didn't actually know the day he'd come, but I had a sense it was close, and the horses being nervous that night told me it might be on us. I never expected it to get bloody as it did. I saw you kill that boy, the one who was about to shoot Pete. I was across the yard, lying there trying to catch my breath from where the other one had stabbed me. I saw the whole thing. It was quite a fine throw, by the way."

"Thank you," she said quietly.

"So, as I say, I saw it, and then I heard the other two argue about taking the horses or not, and then saw them carry the boy off. I lay there thinking, and it came to me that since they hadn't seen you throw the knife and thought it might have been me, and they knew I was wounded, I could make it seem that I'd thrown it and then later I'd died of the wounds. It could be neat and clean" He looked at her and then looked away again. "And I might as well admit that an urge to get away hadn't been far from my thoughts all that winter. It had grown too hard to sit back and watch as your father grew worse—and to be helpless to do anything. You'll recall that you'd already begun to lie to keep me out of it. But all the time I worried and I hated that more than anything. I wanted to be away."

She said nothing and they took a few more slow steps before he said, "Back to that night, I saw you leave to get help and then I dragged myself up and went to see young Emerston. I wasn't hurt all that bad, but I had a bloody shirt to leave with him as evidence and I figured he'd help me stage the death for the sake of my friendship with his father. Also because it was in his interest to avoid Loomis coming down to stage a hunt for me." Her grandfather paused. "Loomis is not someone you want to cross. You might do well to remember that."

Ella nodded but again stayed quiet.

"Also I knew, or suspected with near certainty, that Emerston already did business with Loomis. I'd seen Loomis visit his office and I'd seen his weaselly-looking men ride into town several times. Probably counterfeit money, although I don't know for certain. It's one of Loomis' specialties though, and more likely to be of interest to Emerston than horse thieving. In any case, I was certain Emerston could get the message to him that I was dead. I didn't want Loomis sending men to look around, to harass Pete or you or anyone else."

Captain Tunnicliff's voice remained steady, but his steps slowed even further, until Ella looked around for a place to sit. She spotted a stump beside the road and led her grandfather over. He sank onto the seat without comment. Ella made herself comfortable enough in a pile of brush nearby. A light, misting rain had begun to fall.

Her grandfather wiped the sweat from his brow with a hand-kerchief and took several deep breaths to regain his strength. "Emerston and I took several hours to work out the details of the plan. How he'd pay the doctor to sign the paper saying I had died. How he'd write up my will and date it from a year earlier, and then put on a funeral. He had a trusted man to help with the tricky parts and we agreed I'd spend a few days recovering and then make off on Edgar as soon as all the fuss died down. Then, in the deepest part of that same night, he sent his man back to the smith to collect up Edgar and hide him in the stable up at the mansion house. I couldn't take any other of my possessions, as that might raise suspicion, but I knew Edgar wouldn't be missed. Loomis wouldn't have had an old nag like that on his tally of my horses to steal—he'd hardly have noticed him at all. I was certain no one would much notice his absence. It was only ever me who noticed him." There was an odd, sad note to his tone.

Ella gazed at him, her face impassive, waiting until he was ready to go on. "Now I come to the part I don't want to tell," he said at last, his rough voice low and somber. "You see, if I'd had the courage I should have had, I would have gone ahead and killed myself instead of staging that elaborate ruse to make everyone think I was dead. As it was, I was too much a coward, so that when young Emerston presented me with the paper he wished me to sign at the final hour before I was to leave, I could see no other choice. He as good as said that if I refused to sign he'd give you up to Loomis, that if I wished his complicity I'd sign and be on my way." He took a deep breath and then said in a rush, "To my everlasting shame I took the cowardly path and signed the paper."

Ella did her best to keep her voice steady as she quietly asked, "What did the paper say?"

Her grandfather dropped his face in his hands and then lifted it to look her in the eye. "The paper gave him the rights to the flax machine. What I had of it so far and any future improvements you might make to it." He took out a handkerchief and blew his nose. "I don't know enough of the law to know if it would suffice in court, but by God, I signed it. I signed you over."

"To save me from Loomis," Ella said more gently.

"Yes, but to save myself as well."

"The paper would be no good to him, anyhow," Ella said.

"How do you know?"

"Because I think..." She reached into her tunic and removed the grubby oilskin packet she always carried. From amidst the stack of folded papers, she produced one that she held out to her grandfather. It had the same tears and stains as all the others in the stack. "I looked at this when I first found it and then put it at the bottom of the pile and refused to read it again. I didn't want to believe it said what I first thought it might."

"That I'd betrayed you."

"No, I had no idea it had anything to do with me. I thought only that he'd paid you for a share of the rights. It's dated close to the same time as the will you left."

"Yes, he was clever enough to back-date it with the will."

Ella gave him a long, thoughtful look as he unfolded the paper. "You didn't really have any choice, Grandfather. And if you had killed yourself instead of signing it, you wouldn't have been here to help me now."

"Perhaps," he said gruffly, ripping the paper into tiny pieces and letting them fall to the wet ground. "But in any case I left you there with that monster of a father and little protection. I can't even bear to ask what that was like."

She shook her head. "It wasn't good, but it wasn't as bad as it might have been. As you saw, I could throw a knife by the time you left. That provided a measure of protection."

Her grandfather peered into her face with piercing eyes, as if trying to determine whether she lied or not. He seemed to find the reassurance he sought. "Good. I'm grateful to hear as much." He looked away but not fast enough that she failed to see his eyes fill. His voice trembled as he said, "Don't tell me any more, though. Not a single day has passed that I haven't regretted letting your mother marry that man. And then for me to leave you all there...to make away from it all....I thought I could forget, could start over in a new place. But you see what I made of that idea. Whatever I may suffer now, it's much less than I deserve."

ELLA SAID LITTLE as they made their way back to Captain
Tunnicliff's lodging. When they said farewell he hesitated a
moment and she had the sense he wished something of her, for
her to say something. But she didn't know what it was.

Walking back to the cabin, she realized he must have been
hoping for a word of dispensation. Of consolation. But was that
really hers to give? Should she have tried to console him? And
with what? With her confused brew of sympathy and rage? He *had*
abandoned them, after all. It might have been to spare her from
Loomis, but he'd left her to face Amherst alone. Was that any better? She'd already done what she could to reassure him it wasn't
all he'd feared. But it was worse than he knew in other ways. And
he'd signed the paper that betrayed her, at least as much as he
knew at the time. No, she had no easy absolution for him.

Returning to the cabin, she told Jenny nothing of what she'd
heard from their grandfather. For all the ways their mother had
protected them, and her grandfather had done as well, in his
way, it was the least she could do to protect Jenny and Jimson
from what they didn't need to know.

IN THE MIDDLE OF THE WEEK, two of the owners of the Martha Furnace Co., Samuel Richards and his cousin Joseph Ball,
came to take an inventory of the property. They arrived with
an entourage of servants and baggage, and, strangely enough,
had picked up a sodden saddlebag that appeared at the edge of
the road once the snow had melted. They deposited the bag
at the store and it wasn't long before it came to Ella's attention that the bag was hers, dropped by Dapper Dan the past
autumn, all those months ago.

Returning to the cabin with the sodden leather satchel, she emptied out her coagulated belongings and tried to dry them as best she could. Most everything was ruined, but she was able to salvage two knives that she could repair by replacing the handles and polishing the metal. The yellow gown her mother had packed all those months ago appeared at the very bottom of the bag, nearly unrecognizable in its thick coating of mildew and smelling like something you'd run from in the woods. She would have tossed it in the fire immediately, but Mrs. Gaskill spotted it and, with many a tsk, tsk, had it soaking in a strong solution of lye and who knows what else in a matter of moments.

Even her magic touch with laundry could not return the gown to its former yellow color, but she was determined to salvage what she could and thus dyed the gown a deep green that covered the remaining mildew stains. She then rinsed and wrung it mercilessly. When she was done it smelled only faintly of smoke and bear grease, though strongly of lye, which Ella thought nearly as bad.

Mrs. Gaskill stitched the rents and holes with careful small stitches, pressed it flat with a hot iron, and then wrapped it in a clean cloth for travel. "There," she said at last, "now you'll have a gown that will at least look halfway respectable among the city folk. We can't have them thinking you came from Martha Furnace looking like a wild savage. What would they think of us here?"

"That you live in an out-of-the-way place in the forest?" Ella asked.

"That might be so, but we can still be respectable even out here in the forest." Mrs. Gaskill drew herself up to her full height of just under five feet, including her mop cap, and put her hands on her hips.

"I'm certain they'll be comforted to know that," Ella said mildly. "They've likely been wondering on it."

AT JENNY'S URGING they asked their grandfather if he'd like to accompany them, seeing as his name would be on the patent application. Ella could see from the light that sparked in his eyes that he was tempted, but then he shook his head. "Ah no, I'd greatly like to. But it'd be too much of a trip for old Edgar here, to go into the big city like that, and I couldn't leave him. And I'd slow you down too much myself—I'm not fit for traveling anymore."

"Jenny here is hardly fit for it either," Ella said, and Jenny rolled her eyes at her. Then they looked at one another for a moment, asking a question with their eyes.

When they'd silently agreed, Jenny turned back to her grandfather and said, "Grandpa, would you like us to return for you before we go back to Deborahville? We'd very much like you to come back with us and it's not much out of the way. Perhaps we could find a ship to come up river to Martha from Tuckerton, so it wouldn't be much overland traveling for you."

He raised one shoulder and said, "Well now, that's nice of you to offer. But as I said, I'm not fit for traveling anymore. If you'd like to come back and collect up Dapper Dan before you head north, I'd be pleased to see you again. Certainly it'd be good to hear of all that happens down in the big cities. But I don't expect I'll be going very far myself."

Jenny hugged him hard. "We'll do that Grandpa, I promise."

JENNY PUT THE FINISHING TOUCHES on the drawings of the machine and then Ella carefully rolled the full set of sketches and tied them with a string. As they were packing their last belongings, Captain Tunnicliff appeared and, with no fanfare, handed Ella something he'd made for her. It was a tube made of stitched oilcloth over a frame of thin iron rods, into which the drawings and other papers might slide, with an oilcloth flap that covered the top and wrapped around to keep it firmly shut. Sewn to either end of the tube was a leather strap that went over her shoulder, so she could wear the tube like an arrow quiver.

"Keep you from losing them, or letting them get wet," he said roughly.

She hugged him. Then she slipped the rolled papers into the sleeve, tied the flap, and pulled the strap over her shoulder. She climbed onto the cart that would take them to Batsto, where they'd meet the stagecoach to Camden. From Camden they'd ferry across the river to Philadelphia to seek advice from Oliver Evans in writing the new patent application.

They saluted Captain Tunnicliff and waved to the other friends who'd assembled to wish them well. Then the cart rumbled off onto the sand road.

PART TWO

April 1811

TWENTY-TWO

LUCILLE TUNNICLIFF broke the seal and opened the letter with fingers that fumbled in profound relief at seeing Jenny's handwriting. It wasn't like Jenny to have ceased writing as she'd done, when she'd written faithfully for so many months of their journey. The long silence had caused Lucille a depth of worry she hadn't felt for many years, not since her baby was taken so long ago.

Thus, reading the letter with shaking hands, she wasn't surprised to read of Jenny's illness. She was more surprised to read Jenny's account of Ella as devoted nurse—despite that Jenny couldn't convince her to write letters. *Merde alors*, Lucille thought, putting down the letter to absorb the news. Then, in the kind of thought she'd never allowed herself until recently, she added, *Who would imagine a child of mine as a nurse?*

She picked up the letter to continue reading, but soon put it down again with a sharp rap of her knuckles on the table as Jimson came into the room. "What's wrong, Aunt Lucille?" Then he saw the letter. "Is that from Jenny?"

"Yes, they're fine," she said quickly, seeing the pang of worry cross his face. He'd mostly stayed with Pete since their return, with occasional overnight stays at her house, but he had yet to return to being the lively boy he'd once been. After his forced separation from the Seneca, and then what he'd seen of Amherst's and Catherine's deaths, he'd become more cautious. Fearful of another sudden death or other painful twist of events. Lucille had done her best not to let him see her worry when Jenny's letters stopped coming, but she knew he'd noticed, for he missed very little.

"Jenny came down with scarlet fever but she's recovered and is fine now," Lucille told him. "They're preparing to leave for Philadelphia, and..." she paused, because Jenny had cautioned secrecy, but then thought the boy needed to hear good news, "...and it seems Ella and your grandfather have at last solved the difficulty in the design of the flax engine. But you must keep this news to yourself. Or at least discuss it with no one else. Save Pete, of course," she added as an afterthought.

"Can I go tell him?" Jimson asked, with a sudden spark of joy in his face that gave Lucille an echoing delight.

She reached out and rubbed her hand down his cheek, which yet retained a curve of baby fat. She let her hand rest under his chin, smiling at him. "Yes, of course." She gave his cheek a last pat before swiftly reaching down to poke his side, trying to tickle a smile from him.

He bent forward and quickly wrested away. "None of that, Aunt. You know I hate being tickled."

She smiled sadly as she watched him lope across the back field, making his way to Pete's lodge. He used to love to be tickled, to giggle and squirm and beg her to do more. How could he have grown old so fast? She sighed and went over to her writing table. Taking up her quill, she wrote a long letter to her friend Ann Lincorn, who owned a shop in the heart of Philadelphia that sold nothing but beautiful fabrics. Earlier she'd warned Mrs. Lincorn that her niece might visit, and now she related the impending arrival of not one, but two nieces, hoping the letter might take a fast packet to get there before they did. She then wrote to Jenny, expressing her relief that Jenny had recovered and telling her once more of how to find Mrs. Lincorn in Philadelphia. Fortunately she'd told them once before and hoped they might have those instructions if her newest letter failed to reach them in time.

THE NEXT DAY SHE RECEIVED a second unexpected epistle in the form of a request to pay a visit to the offices of Mr. Henry Emerston. She was never displeased to meet with Emerston, but it was unusual for him to summon her.

She made her way to his offices that very afternoon and was soon seated in one of the soft velvet chairs across from his big walnut desk. "You asked that I come see you?" Her smile bore a rakish hint, for she could not help but be charming for him, as she'd done ever since they were young.

"Ah yes, thank you, my dear Lucille. Very kind of you to come on such short notice." He smiled back at her. "I asked you down because I've received a correspondence from our friend up in Sangerfield that he has a shipment of notes he'd like to deliver to us. I know we've been on an extended…hiatus of sorts. However, now that Amherst Kenyon has passed on…" He let his sentence remain unfinished.

"You'd like me to make a trip to Albany?" Lucille said, arching her brow.

She considered his offer. She'd been missing the excitement of passing the money, not to mention the fabrics she purchased with the profits. And with Amherst gone, there was less risk in resuming her activities. She let another moment pass, then nodded. "It would be my pleasure."

"I was hoping you'd say that."

"It's always a pleasure doing business with you," Lucille said with that same rakish slant to her smile.

Before she could rise from her seat, Emerston said, "I hear through the usual routes of gossip that you received a letter from your niece. I trust she's in good health?"

"Yes. Well, that is, she's in better health now. She's recovering from scarlet fever."

"Oh my, that's unfortunate," he said, making appropriate noises of sympathy. "Please tender my regards when next you write to her. And how is her sister's health? I trust she didn't contract the same contagion?"

"Oh no, not her. She is well enough. It appears she took up nursing to care for her sister. Who would ever imagine it?"

He gave an appreciative chuckle, and it occurred to her that he might have easily asked after Ella as her daughter, rather than her niece, now that her secret had come to light all over town. But he was nothing if not tactful and she was grateful for his discretion. Many, if not most, had not been nearly as discreet. Wherever she went around town, conversations tended to break off as she drew near.

Emerston gave her an appraising look. Then he straightened some already-straight papers on his desk. "As I said when we met some months ago, I do hope you'll convey to Ella my apologies for the confusion over the patent application papers she found and misunderstood. I am at her service in any way I might be of assistance, and I greatly desire that she know this. You will tell her this?"

"Of course, Henry. Though I prefer to tell her in person, as you may well imagine."

"Oh? Is that so? I'd thought you might write to her of it, seeing as she's likely to require assistance sooner rather than later. Especially now that she's succeeded in perfecting the design."

Lucille flashed a hard look at him. "Where did you hear that?"

"Oh my—was that not something I was meant to hear? I do apologize, my dear. News of that stature does tend to travel, you know."

She searched his face. "It must be a false rumor of some sort. I haven't heard it myself, and I would prefer that you not pass it any further."

Emerston made a motion of contrition. "Of course not. I had no idea it was untrue or I would never have mentioned it at all."

Lucille arranged her wrap and prepared to leave. Emerston said, "I'll send my boy with a package when the delivery arrives. I would think you might plan to leave for Albany in a fortnight or so."

"Thank you," she said, "I'll make my arrangements."

Later that night, with Jimson tucked into bed in her guest room, Lucille walked out to see Pete at his lodge. Yesterday she'd read him the letter from Jenny and seen the relief in his eyes, for he'd been as worried as she had, though neither had spoken of it. Tonight she went to tell him of her conversation with Emerston. They sat across from one another over the coals of the cook fire in the center of Pete's lodge, sipping tea from thick clay cups.

"Emerston wishes that I should apologize to Ella for him, for what he calls 'the confusion' over the application papers. What do you make of that?"

Pete examined the interior of his cup, the wide planes of his face lit by the glow of the fire. "It smell bad to me."

"But don't you think it's *possible* he might be telling the truth? That it was an actual misunderstanding?"

Pete shrugged. "Possible, yes. Nothing impossible. But it smell bad to me." He put down his drink and took up his carving knife. He made several draws with the knife as he considered the matter. At last he said, "He not go in autumn because he think she get there first. And he not have drawings. Now, after winter, I think he go there."

"So you believe he wishes to steal the patent?"

Pete gave her a measured look. "You think not?"

Lucille raised her shoulders in an uncharacteristic gesture of frustration. "I don't know what to think. Ella found those papers and was certain he planned to steal it. I've known him many years, I've had various business dealings with him, and I have difficulty believing he'd do something that underhanded. And he continues to insist that she misinterpreted what she found. That he regrets letting it appear as it did, but that it had never been his intention to take the patent." She paused. "Earlier, when I was speaking to him, I was persuaded that he was genuine in this. But then he mentioned he'd heard a rumor she perfected the design and I had to feign ignorance and caution him not to say anything more of such a rumor. I hadn't even been aware that he *knew* of the problems with the design."

Pete said, "Lucas know. Must have told his father. I hear from Ella."

"Oh," Lucille said with some surprise. "I hadn't realized that. In any case, something in what he said didn't sit right. I'm certain I wasn't fast enough to fool him—and it came to me afterward that he as good as tricked me into confessing she'd solved it."

Pete carved in silence as Lucille wrestled with the implications of what she'd just said. She looked up at him. "Even if it proves to be true, what chance does he have of stealing the patent when she's already so close to the capital and he's here? How could he get there before she does? And how would he account for the change in the design?"

Pete thought on this, then said slowly, "He know she must write new application. For this he know she go see man who make milling patent. She not hurry after big delay all winter. She think Emerston not come."

"Yes, you may be right. And if he does intend such a thing, it would be in his interest to keep us ignorant of it by professing a misunderstanding and offering to help her. I'm still not certain of it either way, but it cannot hurt to warn her there's a chance he might make for the patent, so she mustn't tarry. I will write to her again without delay."

Pete took several more draws with his knife. Still looking down at his carving, he said quietly, "You must also tell her of you. As her mother. Before she hears from him. Or someone else."

Her eyes snapped to his face. "What do you mean? That I should tell her in a letter?"

"How you like. Before she hear it another way. She will be angry."

Lucille stared down at her hands. After a long silence she said, "I tried to write to her. It kept coming out all wrong. Or I kept writing and not saying it. It was so easy to avoid. I think..." She paused and shook her head several times. "I think it would be better to tell her in person."

Pete gave her a skeptical look. "You think easy face to face? I think hard. I think you not have courage to say these words."

"What words? That I'm her true mother? Why wouldn't I have the courage to say them? I have the courage to continue living in this town, do I not? To face down all these people who know my shame. I only need to say the words the right way, at the right time."

Pete still looked skeptical but he didn't argue further. He carved a little longer, then he took up his cup and drained the dregs of tea. She was looking down into her own cup when he said, "Enough talking. Now come here."

Lucille felt a jolt and soon a heat rose up in her. She was suddenly awkward and shut her eyes. Then she stood and glided across the short space between them.

THE NEXT MORNING she slipped into her own house before first light and sank into a chair in the front room. Last night Pete made her forget her worries, but now they came flooding back. Most horrible was not knowing what to think, what to believe. She'd known Emerston for so many years. He'd handled all the details of her finances; he'd been her accomplice in the money exchange—and had always been perfectly fair and just in those matters, treating it like any other business arrangement—and now what? She was to believe him capable of the most vile kind of stealing, from a young woman who clearly had more need of the income from the patent than he did?

No, she could not bring herself to believe it. He'd always been so pleasant. She could not recall a time he wasn't, other than that one time, of course. When she'd refused to marry him after he'd already announced it to everyone. No, it was true—she'd been afraid of him that night. The night he'd walked her to the river and then knelt to make his proposal, and she, in all her youthful arrogance, had laughed at him. A look of such pure black fury had come onto his face. And the things he'd said . . . . But then he came back to himself and with good humor made light of the matter, as if it had been good fun all the time. He'd held onto his good humor even when he became the butt of town jokes for a season, up until he managed to take a Boston wife with a dowry and began building the big house on the hill. Then the jokes had stopped.

Pulling herself from her thoughts and her chair, Lucille rose and made a breakfast of oatcakes and honey. After a quick freshening up, she wrapped a herringbone shawl against the morning chill and walked the short way into town.

She stepped into the Winebottoms' shop and stopped dead in her tracks. She gaped in shock at the grinning young man, who was thinner and looked much older than the boy who'd left nine months earlier. His cheeks had hollowed and a fine black stubble coated the lower half of his face, which had been nearly smooth when he'd left. Yet his laughing blue eyes and red lips were the same, and his smile still etched thin half moons on either side of his mouth.

"Zeke! What are you doing here? I've just had a letter from Jenny and she made no mention that you intended to return home."

"She mightn't have known when she wrote it, for I didn't know myself until the night before I left. I had a hankering to see the folks here." He turned to Janet, who'd come up beside him. He draped an arm over and around her shoulders and planted a hearty kiss on her cheek. "I had a sense that me ma here might be missing me."

"Ta, what rot," Janet said, but her shining eyes made a liar of her.

They spoke a few more minutes, with Lucille asking Zeke of his journey home. Then he excused himself to go see what the town had gotten up to in his absence. When he'd gone, Lucille ushered Janet into the back room of the shop and whispered of her meeting with Emerston. That he wished them to come back into the trade.

Janet looked thoughtful for a moment but then shook her head. "Ah no, I can't see it. It's been hard enough getting out once. I fear that if I take it up again, I'll never see my way clear to get out. Not until the U.S. Marshal comes to take me away."

"Oh so dramatic." Lucille rolled her eyes.

"Why? You think it's not possible we'd be sent to prison for trading in false currency?"

Lucille shrugged. "It's possible, I know. But it's not us they'd want. We're just the small catch. They'd want Loomis, or even Emerston."

"But it's us they'll *catch*, silly woman. They'll never catch Loomis or Emerston or any of the others who hardly get their hands dirty. Then if we betray their names, they'll just deny any knowledge of it. It'll be our word against theirs. And what will become of us then, when we're on the wrong side of such men? No, you're a fool my dear friend, not to look at it clearly."

Lucille frowned at Janet, feeling as if she'd been slapped. The urge to strike back with a sharp retort came on her quickly, but then it waned, replaced by the knowledge that her friend was right. She'd been a fool. Yet again. Janet, watching her face, said softly, "What did you tell him?"

"I told him I'd go to Albany in a fortnight." Janet twisted her mouth in distaste. Lucille said, "There's more as well. When I met with him yesterday, he asked of Ella and her machine, and I believe I let on that she's solved the trouble with the design, despite that I tried to be quick in denying it. He claims he never intended to steal anything, that it was all a misunderstanding, and when he speaks it seems so plausible. But Pete doesn't trust it, and I don't know what to think. What of you? Do you think him capable of such willful fraud?"

Janet thought a moment, then nodded. "I do. I don't know why, but I do."

"Yes, all right. But it yet defies reason. How can he make for the patent with no drawings, no descriptions?"

Janet shrugged. "I don't know. All I know is young Lucas has purchased drawing paper, reams of it, all throughout this past winter. More than he's ever used before."

Lucille stared at Janet as she absorbed this news, willing herself to face what it meant and not shy from it. At last she said, "I must go to Philadelphia. Find them and help make certain Ella takes that patent. I cannot rely on a letter to reach her in time."

"And tell her the news of her birth that the whole town knows before she does, isn't that right?" Janet said with one eyebrow arched.

"Yes, of course. You sound just like Pete."

"Thank you. I think. And will you take him to escort you? You shouldn't travel alone."

Lucille considered the question. Take Pete to Philadelphia? To the city, with Mrs. Lincorn and the other well-heeled merchants. Where would he stay? How would she explain him? No, it wouldn't do. "I think not," she said. "I've traveled alone before and I can certainly do it again. Unless... well, no, I cannot ask it of you. He's just now returned home."

"You wish to have Zeke?" A look of dismay came over Janet's face.

"No, no, I couldn't ask it."

"Yes you could. And you just did." She pulled herself up straight and squared her rounded shoulders. Her mop cap hung crooked, yet she bore a look of dignified fortitude. "Let me discuss it with him. There's much at stake and much to consider."

THREE DAYS LATER, Lucille and Zeke stepped onto a schooner from Poughkeepsie to Philadelphia. Zeke was immediately taken with the ship and the many aspects of the nautical business, declaring after half a day that he might not mind trying out the sailing life.

"That's because you've seen naught but good weather," Lucille said tartly.

Zeke shrugged. "Perhaps."

"And wait until you get a closer look at the food," she added. "You've never seen a meal worm boiled to such perfection." She stepped back and eyed him from shoes to hairline. "You might appear rather striking in a royal navy uniform, though."

"How do you mean?"

"Only that the British have become shameless in boarding our ships and impressing our sailors into their navy. Merchants and politicians seem to speak of little else these days."

Zeke raised a brow with a certain skepticism. "Whatever the case I'm starving. What has my mother sent with us?" Fortunately Janet had packed them enough food for several weeks, despite that the journey was expected to take a mere few days by water. She'd also, at the last moment of parting, slipped Lucille a small packet carefully wrapped in oilskin.

"For an emergency," she'd said. "I expect you'll be getting yourself into trouble in no time."

Later, after an hour on deck in the evening, watching the many lanterns of the city of New York sparkle at them from shore, Lucille descended to the close cabin she shared with four other women. In the near-dark she undressed and settled onto her pallet. Then she unwrapped the package from Janet and found it full of brand-new bank notes.

TWENTY-THREE

ELLA AND JENNY stood on the deck of the ferry from Camden as it made its way across the river to Philadelphia. They'd thought Camden a busy place, but as Philadelphia came into view Ella was struck mute by the sight of it. The port they approached was packed with ships, many of them huge, and the wharf was teaming with an army of men moving sacks and crates of all shapes and sizes. Behind it, stretching uphill, were streets paved in stone. Yes, stone. She'd never seen such a sight, and could not fathom how much labor it must have entailed.

Along the stone-covered streets were rows and rows of houses, stretching back as far as she could see. Many were bigger and grander than the Emerstons' mansion in Deborahville. As they drew closer they could make out pairs of fashionable people, eye-catching in their colorful clothes. Ladies wore high-waisted white muslin gowns below brocaded silk jackets, their hair in elaborate curls strung with feathers and glittering beads. Men in shiny tall boots with tall black hats and long coattails cut elegant figures among the flowing gowns of the women. More numerous were the people in working clothes, variable more in the colors of their skin than their clothing. The men drove carts or carried wooden crates; the women, fewer in number, carried baskets or cloth sacks. Everyone appeared quite purposeful. Among them Ella caught flashes of movement by children in shapeless clothes, heads down as they navigated their way amidst cart wheels, horse hooves, and thick-soled boots.

They stepped off the ferry and joined the throngs of people milling around the wharf. Ella had memorized the instructions Lucille had given them for locating Mrs. Ann Lincorn at either her shop or her home. It being a day of business they sought the landmarks Aunt Lucille had described for finding her shop on Market Street. They wandered the streets, attempting to spot the church tower or the great tall clock. They might have asked any of the number of people walking by, but something made them shy—everyone seemed so busy. They realized they'd located Market Street at last when they spied the great covered market, stretching a full two blocks long. Market Street was twice as wide as the other streets and packed with shops and stalls of all description, though the covered market itself was barren of vendors and wares as today was not a market day. Mrs. Lincorn's shop was supposed to be among the many on this street, but they walked from one end to the other several times without seeing anything fitting Aunt Lucille's description.

Along the way they were jostled unmercifully by various pedestrians and nearly flattened by several different teams of horses. Ella found herself in a tussle with a street urchin who lurched into Jenny and began to paw at her pockets, but also at her person beneath the clothing. With a brief glance at Jenny's horrified face, Ella grabbed the dirty boy by the arm and bodily wrested him from her sister. "Leave her be," she said harshly.

The boy gave her an insolent stare. "What are you—the husband?" Then he opened his mouth and released a stream of obscenities such as neither of them had ever heard, at least not in consecutive use, and Ella used her greater size to hustle him farther off down the street so Jenny need listen no further. When she returned, Jenny's face was ghostly white and she looked stricken. Ella took a few deep breaths to calm herself, then gently took her sister's arm. "Never mind, Jenny. He didn't mean anything by it. He's just a poor motherless kid, I'm certain." Yet her own heart was thumping at an abnormally rapid pace and she began scouting the passersby with a new wariness. If a child could assault them, what might the rest of the populace be capable of?

After making yet another fruitless transit through the mob, they turned down a side street to seek comparative peace and safety. They intended to walk a mere few steps on what they later learned to be Fourth Street, but it was so peaceful and appealing that their feet took them farther than they'd intended. They stopped only when they reached a sign that announced they'd found the Quaker Meeting Home. The sign evoked the furnace master at Martha and his family, who had been unfailingly kind to them.

Five minutes later they were still standing awkwardly in front of the building, wondering whether to enter, when a man rounded the corner from Arch Street and barreled into them. His face immediately registered horror at his action— the first to do so of the many who had jostled them with similar result—and he said, "My sincere apologies to thee. I have no excuse but that I was intended to be at the meeting house a quarter hour ago." He stopped and peered at them with a greater intensity. "Thee look troubled. Are thee lost? Here, come inside the meeting house with me and we shall see to thy needs. Thee look exhausted, my poor dear," he said to Jenny, who had indeed begun to sway with fatigue in the aftermath of her convalescence.

He took Jenny's arm and led her down the walk to the door, nodding to Ella to indicate she should follow. As they reached the door he said, "Pardon me again, I have neglected to introduce myself. I am Friend Isaac Hopper. I am very pleased to meet thee."

When they were seated on a bench in the hall of the meeting house and had leaned back against the wall for a welcome dose of repose, Friend Hopper glided off down the hallway. Watching his retreating figure, Ella suddenly sat up straighter. "Hopper," she said quietly. Then she turned to Jenny. "Didn't the negro man from the Pines mention that name to us? Didn't he say there was a Quaker fellow in Philadelphia named Hopper who was known to help runaway slaves?"

Jenny twisted her mouth in the effort of recalling the name, but said at last, "I can't remember. I vaguely recall Mr. Perry saying he'd intended to stop in Philadelphia but then he'd slept through the stop altogether. Which isn't surprising, is it? Given what his back looked like when we first met him."

"No, I suppose not," Ella said distractedly, still thinking on the name. "I do think the name is the same. Something in the way he pronounced it, or that it reminded me of a cricket or a grasshopper, made it stick in my mind. I do believe I'll ask him."

"Ask him what?" Jenny said with uncharacteristic skepticism. "Mr. Hopper, do you help runaway slaves? That's a fine way to thank him for his kindness."

"Hush, he's coming back. Leave it to me."

Friend Hopper returned leading a small woman in plain dress, much the same as Mistress Phebe Reeves had worn at Martha.

"Young ladies, may I introduce thee to Mrs. Warner. She's prepared to assist thee in any way thou might require."

"Kind sir, Mrs." Ella began, looking into their two kind faces, "We thank you, but we require no assistance beyond directing us to the person we seek. We are grateful for the moment of rest you have offered us, but Mrs. Lincorn has been told to expect us and we need only to find her. I'm afraid we are new to the city and cannot seem to find our way."

"Is that all?" Friend Hopper said with evident dismay. "I had hoped to be of greater assistance to thee. It is my great pleasure to be of use to worthy people in need."

"Yes, we have heard that of you," Ella said. Then, after a pause to allow her meaning to percolate, she added, "That *is* you, is it not, sir?"

Friend Hopper looked doubtful for a moment, not certain what to make of this odd, outspoken girl. But then, after looking into her eyes and seeing the intent of the question she asked, he nodded. "Yes, I do believe thee have heard of my small attempts to be of use."

"They're not small to those in need," Ella said simply. Jenny nodded a vigorous agreement.

"Well, I thank thee. Now, then, a Mrs. Lincorn thee said? What type of shop does she operate?"

With Isaac Hopper as a guide, locating Mrs. Lincorn's shop proved embarrassingly simple. They'd passed it several times when they'd walked Market Street, but in the hubbub they'd failed to spot the sign. Ella felt her face flush with...what? Shame? She didn't know. She only knew she'd been too hasty, too cowed by the city. She should have shown more fortitude.

After thanking Friend Hopper and taking their leave of him, they looked at one another and then Ella opened the door of the shop with a firm hand. The woman behind the counter was in discussion with a well-dressed matron who apparently harbored keen feelings about the choice between a fustian and a velveret, both of a deep nut brown. As Mrs. Lincorn attempted to guide her customer toward a decision, Ella, while fingering various bolts of cloth, had the opportunity to observe her.

She was older than Aunt Lucille, perhaps fifty-five years or thereabouts, but she had a similar elegance to her demeanor and the cut of her high-waisted gown. She wore no cap, but rather a fashionable Turkish turban above a spray of silver curls across her forehead. She showed remarkable patience with her customer's indecision, which appeared to stem from the wish to prolong the pleasure of making her purchase.

When at length the matron chose her cloth and departed, Mrs. Lincorn turned to them and said, "May I be of assistance?"

They introduced themselves and brought out the letter of introduction, but she waved it away. "Of course. I received the letter from dear Lucille quite a while ago, but I hadn't forgotten you'd be coming. I'm so pleased to see you here at last." She smiled at them warmly, then said, "I only regret that I cannot offer you lodging at present, for I am a widow and my son and daughter-in-law have moved in with me, together with their children. I'm afraid we are already packed in like salt cod in a barrel." She laughed at this, then added, "You might consider yourself fortunate to escape the opportunity of sharing a residence with my grandchildren, much as I dote on them. They're not as well disciplined as they might be." She rolled her eyes slightly. "I shall be very happy to find you a respectable inn, though. I know just the place and I'll take you around as soon as I close the shop, which is less than an hour now."

They expressed their gratitude and agreed to return at closing, at which time Mrs. Lincorn guided them to a well-appointed inn on Spruce Street and negotiated a reasonable price for it. The inn had a number of guest rooms on the second floor and a great dining room and sitting room below, in which guests might congregate as they like. It was an exceedingly inviting place, and was kept by a Miss Susannah Griffith, who was of similar age to Mrs. Lincorn but never married. Miss Susannah, a high-busted woman in a flowered calico gown, bustled with energetic advice and they felt themselves taken into competent hands.

"I expect you to come round to supper with my brood as soon as you may. I'll send word in a few days," Mrs. Lincorn said as she prepared to take her leave of them, "and in the meantime, please give my fond regards to your aunt when you next correspond with her."

"Oh Mrs. Lincorn," Jenny said, putting a hand on her arm. "I'll write to her directly to tell her all you've done for us in finding such a lovely place to stay here. Truly, it is a great service and we are grateful for it. The city is so large and there are so many— "

"Oh posh, it's what anyone would do. Only tell your aunt to come visit me sooner rather than later—she's long overdue for a visit." She tied the hat strings on the great floppy hat she'd donned over her turban for going into the street. "Also give my regards to Sarah Evans if you go to see her. She's a saint, that one."

THAT NIGHT ELLA SANK with a wave of gratitude into the wide feather bed they shared in their room at the inn. Jenny had nearly fallen asleep over supper and had barely made it upstairs before she'd succumbed to a deep slumber. Ella herself was more exhausted than she'd been in a great while. But more than that, she was shaken by the experience of their first hours in the city. Of being lost and feeling so small and helpless in the midst of so much humanity, so much ingenuity. It was utterly humbling. She'd never felt quite like that, not even when they'd been lost in the Pines before they found Martha. That had been difficult, but not terrifying in the same way this had been. She'd known this city would be big, but she hadn't known it would dwarf her in this way, reduce her to perfect insignificance.

After tossing for more than an hour, she concluded at last that today had not been her finest day, but tomorrow would be better. If this city took no notice of her, then fine, she'd take what she needed from the city and be done with it. Tomorrow she'd go see Oliver Evans. Soon after she'd leave for Washington City and make her application. When she received the patent she'd have no need of either city, not for a good long while. If they did not care for her than she would return the disregard. She would care for herself. With that resolution she slept at last.

THE NEXT MORNING she unfolded the paper that protected the formerly yellow, now green dress and lay it on the bed to smooth out the creases. It still smelled of lye and very faintly of smoke, but despite that it looked a respectable gown. As she was eyeing it, the door to their room opened abruptly and Miss Susannah swept in. Spotting the gown, she hustled over to pick it up and her quick eye noted the repairs and the dye job. "Polly's ironing this morning. I'll have her go over this to take out the creases and she'll bring it back up while we're at breakfast. Come on down then, won't you?"

True to her word the green gown, looking remarkably fresh and bright, was back on the bed when they returned. Polly had even done something magical to the smell, such that the lye and smoke had been largely replaced by the scent of rose water.

"Oh Ella, it looks nice," Jenny said. "Put it on, won't you?"

Ella approached the gown with some trepidation, but then she squared her shoulders and picked it up. She wriggled into it with assistance from Jenny. Her sister examined her and said, "Here, let me do something with your hair."

Her nimble hands soon had Ella's unruly black locks hitched into a flattering approximation of a Psyche knot behind her head, with a tumble of loose curls around her face and forehead.

Together they held a small hand mirror and peered into it, their faces registering equal astonishment at the transformation. When they'd put down the mirror, Jenny said, "You'll need a hat."

Just then the door opened and Miss Susannah breezed in carrying a straw bonnet trimmed with a deep green ribbon that very nearly matched Ella's gown. "I *knew* I had this green ribbon, I just had to put my hands on it. It should do very well, don't you think? Don't you dare crush my hat, though," she warned with mock severity.

"Don't worry, I'll watch her," Jenny assured her.

After Miss Susannah settled the hat onto Ella's head, they held up the mirror again to examine themselves. The green of Ella's gown nicely set off the tawny cream of Jenny's, an old gown of Mrs. Gaskill's which Jenny had cleverly altered to a more modern fashion. Jenny's silken brown hair had less curl than Ella's black tresses, but the warmer color suited her fair complexion and matched her eyes. Over the past winter her face had lost the awkward curves of childhood, and her recent illness had further chiseled her cheekbones.

"You two are quite the handsome pair," Miss Susannah said with some satisfaction. "I suspected you might clean up well."

Ella and Jenny exchanged a quick amused glance. Then Ella asked, "I don't mean to sound ungrateful, but what makes you assist us as you have?"

Miss Susannah gave a tinkling sort of laugh. "Oh, it's not you I'm assisting, really. It's your Aunt Lucille. She's stayed with me several times and she's always been very good to me. She brings me ribbons and other trifles. In fact, I would bet a silver dollar this green ribbon on the hat was a gift from her some day long past."

ARMED WITH THE FULL SET of drawings, the stack of papers regarding the patent application, and the letter from her grandfather to Mr. Evans, Ella strode with a new confidence down Spruce Street. It came to her that she was suddenly in the midst of all she had planned and dreamed for so long; she was on her way to visit *the* Oliver Evans, the great man himself. And she had something to show him that she could be proud of—a machine that worked well and contained a number of clever contrivances—such that he could not help but see the utility of it.

She tried to walk slowly, but as these thoughts came to her one after another, she quickened her pace until she was walking a fast trot. She realized at last that Jenny was running to keep up with her and she slowed her pace. As Jenny came abreast, she looked at her wise little sister and gave her a great wide grin. Jenny had waited as long for this day as she had; they might as well enjoy it together.

Miss Susannah had given them explicit directions to both the Evans residence on Filbert Street and the Mars Works foundry, his place of business, at the corner of Ninth and Vine, just a block farther away. Being the noon hour by now, they thought to try the residence first.

As they strolled up the walk to the brick house Miss Susannah had described, they began to hear the babble of several young voices. Ella had heard the Evans family had a number of children, but somehow that hadn't entered into her daydream. *Never mind it*, she thought, *it won't matter once I show the drawings and tell him of the machine.*

They knocked at the door and, as instructed by Miss Susannah, handed the serving girl who answered the door a card on which they'd written their names. She gave them an odd sort of look and left them standing outside as she went to deliver the card.

Returning, she recited the words she'd obviously been coaching herself to remember: "Mr. Evans said he don't accept strangers at his home. Come to the works if you like."

Ella and Jenny glanced at one another. Then Ella said, "Please, will you give this letter to Mr. Evans for me?" She handed the girl the letter her grandfather had written to remind Evans of his unpaid debt.

The girl looked doubtful, but she dutifully took the letter and went back down the hallway toward what must be the dining room. This time they could hear Evans as plainly as if he was speaking to them, for he roared at the poor girl. "I have no intention of reading any letters. I am a very busy man. Tell these people to *leave my house—immediately*." From the doorway they could see the girl back out of the room as if she was afraid he would begin throwing things at her. And, in fact, he did throw one more afterthought. "Tell them if they're working for that banker fellow with the flax contraption, I'll be ringing for the constable next time they come round here!"

IT WASN'T DIFFICULT for Ella to work out what had happened once the shock had worn off. Emerston must have attempted to enlist Evans's aid with the patent, the same as she intended to do, and had botched the job. She supposed she might be grateful that he'd botched it, as it meant he didn't have the assistance he must dearly want from Evans. But on the other hand he'd made her own job that much more difficult. Also, it showed he was as yet in pursuit of the patent, while she'd dared to hope he might have forfeited the contest by now. *But what,* she wondered, *does he intend to use for a set of drawings?*

She stripped off the green gown as quickly as possible once she reached her room at Miss Susannah's. She then paced the room for nearly an hour, examining her options with a furious focus. Reaching a decision, she once more packed all her papers and, leaving Jenny behind at the inn for fear there would be more unpleasantness, strode once more onto the streets of the city. Back in her usual shapeless, comfortable clothing, she loped down the street in rapid time and located the Mars Works foundry at the corner of Ninth and Vine Streets.

Reaching the works, she stared at the imposing cluster of buildings and quickly discarded all her ideas of what she might say to gain an audience. She felt certain he would be interested once he saw the design, yet how would she *show* it to him? She was no good with selling anybody anything. She observed the works for several more minutes, then made her way around to the back of the main building and approached a window to peer inside. What she saw made it difficult to breathe. She'd heard that Evans had turned his attention to steam engines, but she hadn't realized that he'd put the engines into operation. Or that he'd developed clever ways to use the engines to power various aspects of the operation to *build the engines* themselves. She spied a steam engine that powered a lathe and another that powered a boring mill. They were building steam engines here. Actually *making* the engines themselves. *How many people will ever get to see this?*

She made her way to the back door and went in. The din of the machines was loud inside, though nothing to compare to the stamping mill at Martha. Scanning the massive room, she located the man who seemed to be in charge of the work. He was a tall man in a herringbone waistcoat and, moving toward him, she heard a worker call him Mr. Taylor. His accent revealed him to be an Englishman. She watched as Taylor and two of his chief assembly men began fitting a piston into the cylinder of a new engine. She saw them try the piston, take it out and polish it, then reinsert to try again. She moved closer and watched from a few feet away before Taylor suddenly noticed her.

"Can I help you, Miss?" he asked in a voice that said, "What are you doing here?"

"I have a question to ask of you," Ella said with a self-assurance she had to manufacture on the spot. Before he could protest that he was too busy for questions, she barged on. "How is it you're able to use such a small beam above the piston? Shouldn't it be much larger?"

Taylor had begun to say, "I have no time for—" when he interrupted himself to look at her more closely. "What did you just ask, Miss?"

"I asked how you're able to use such a light beam overhead. Shouldn't it be heavier—like the ones on the steamboat engines?"

He gave her a piercing look. "This here Columbian engine is a different kind of engine from that. It uses higher pressure steam and it has the piston and the crankshaft at the same end of the beam, which is why we can use a lighter beam. The beam works from these two pivot bars here." He pointed to bars attached to either end of the beam. "All together in a straight line. Folks are calling it the Evans straight-line linkage." He eyed her sharply. "Who are you, then? How do you know about engines and the like?"

Ella ignored his questions. "What of the pressure? Is it really a hundred and twenty-eight times as high when the temperature of the steam is doubled? I read this in Mr. Evans's book but I'm curious as to whether it's true in practice."

Charles Taylor's face played the spectrum of possible responses, from being insulted at her cheek to impressed by her perspicacity. He took a long moment to answer, but then he shrugged slightly and launched into a discussion of steam temperature versus pressure output. He went on for quite a while and Ella was just beginning to pose questions about the possible uses of the hot water that was exhausted from the waste end of the engine when they were interrupted.

"Taylor! What's going on here? I don't pay you to prattle on with females during work hours. What's this all about?"

Ella looked up sharply to see the man she knew must be Oliver Evans himself. He stood at the top of a thin staircase set against a wall on the far side of the room, from whence he could look down on the works all around. Ella supposed it must be his office at the top of the staircase. His thinning grey hair was standing up as if he'd been running his hands through it for quite a while, and his round face was dark red.

Mr. Taylor remained calm under this assault. "This young lady makes an interesting point, Mr. Evans. She wonders on the work that might be done by the hot water that exhausts from the engine. It could be used for heating a building or the like."

"Could it?" Evans asked, his anger fading as quickly as it had risen. "It would take some piping, I suppose." He hurried down the stairs to the floor of the works and joined the discussion. Then, after examining several angles on the matter, he suddenly remembered that Ella didn't belong there. "Who are you then, young lady? Why are you here?"

This time Ella knew she could not distract him. "I'm here because I need your assistance in crafting a patent application. I believe I have the right to ask because you once told my grandfather you owed him a debt, and he sent me here to collect it."

Evans looked at her with suspicion. "I have no debt that I recollect. How do I know you aren't another envoy from Stevens?"

Having read Evans's book on steam engineering, Ella knew of his long-standing feud with John Stevens of New Jersey, who'd challenged the soundness of his principles regarding high-pressure steam engines. In fact it would have been difficult to miss this aspect of the book, as Evans had dedicated over a third of the text to arguing his side of the feud.

"I've never met John Stevens," she said as mildly as possible. "I've read your book and I agree with your arguments. I have only admiration for your high-pressure engines."

When Evans continued to stare at her, apparently unconvinced, she said, "I have a letter that explains my claim to a debt. My grandfather is Captain Asa Tunnicliff, a smith and millwright by trade, who spent an afternoon with you many years ago, when you were working out the problems of the hopper boy for flour milling. He was able to be of some assistance to you and you told him you'd be pleased to return the good deed some day. He wrote you this letter to remind you of the exchange." She handed him the letter she'd extracted from her pouch.

Evans scanned the paper once, then went back to the top and read it more closely. At last he gave a small chuckle. "Oh, he was a cocky boy, was he not, thinking he could help me see the hopper boy better than I could see it myself? But he had a good grasp of the problem, I'll give him that." He looked at Ella again. "So what is it you want then, in repayment of this long-forgotten debt?"

"I'm afraid it's in respect to a machine that you've already heard about in an unfortunate manner, from a man who's trying to pirate the invention from me." She used the word "pirate" with intention, knowing Evans to be sensitive to the rights of the inventor. "The flax engine he told you of is my own invention. Or rather, mine and Captain Tunnicliff's, as my grandfather devised the premise and I added the rollers that make it fully functional. He and I together developed the ball joint that makes it operate without wearing down the teeth and slipping out of alignment, as well as a new arrangement for the linkage arm assembly that reduces the angle to accommodate the ball joint. These last pieces were worked out just this past winter, so you'll find them absent from any drawings Mr. Emerston might have shown you. My own drawings are complete."

"Let me see them," Evans said brusquely. Ella slipped the sketches from the oilcloth tube her grandfather had made and handed them to Evans. He looked at them a moment, then he said, "I'll look them over in my office. But I don't need you staring over my shoulder the whole while. Go look around the works and then come back. Say in a half of an hour."

Ella had an immediate qualm about leaving her drawings in the care of someone she didn't know, someone quite capable of stealing her ideas. Then she looked around at all he had developed of his own and remembered his exhaustive arguments against piracy of inventions. She knew she might be a fool, but her instinct was to trust the man, for he was a fellow inventor. Evans saw her hesitation and said, "If I had any interest in flax machines I'd have studied them long ago. You can see that I have more than enough to concern me here and have no need to pirate ideas from other people. Be on your way now, that's a good girl."

With a lingering trepidation she obeyed, slipping out the back door to make her way around the other buildings of the works. She visited the iron foundry, where they cast the many parts of the boilers and engines, as well as various gears and other pieces of all descriptions. She even saw the mold for a long barrel that she suspected might be that of a cannon. She realized her time at Martha Furnace had taught her much of what one might notice at an iron works.

It occurred to her to wonder why these works made so few pieces for flour milling, for she'd seen nothing related to gristmilling beyond a pair of millstones stacked in the weeds behind the buildings. She supposed it meant the great man had turned his attention from flour milling altogether. She hadn't thought people could do that. But now that she thought of it, it made good sense that when you'd solved one set of problems, you moved on to other, newly challenging ones.

When she'd finished peering in all the buildings, she went back to the main building and Charles Taylor pointed her to the set of stairs that presumably led up to the office. She made her way up and rapped softly on the door. To her surprise, her knock was answered with a pleasant, "Come in."

She found Evans seated at his desk, studying her sketches with a magnifying glass. With little preamble he began to tally the salient points of the design. Then he asked her point-blank from whence the idea for the rollers had come. She described the threshing machine from Scotland on which she'd first seen the use of them in a different configuration. He nodded at the logic of converting that usage to the one required for the flax engine.

This segued into a discussion of agricultural machinery and then his own milling inventions, which in turn led naturally to talk of patents. After a long diatribe on the minions who would wish to pirate one's inventions, Ella was eventually able to guide him into telling her what she wished to know of the components of a successful patent.

Finally Evans asked, "Your application differs only by the ball joint at the pivot point and the rearranged linkage arm. Is that correct?"

"Yes, that's so. Is it true what my grandfather tells me, that if the two designs are similar enough, they'll award only the first of them?"

"Yes, I'm afraid that's the case. If he patents the one you originally designed, you won't be able to use your improved one unless you pay him a license fee." Ella sank back in her chair, disappointed to hear her grandfather's warning confirmed. Evans watched her. "I can't do much if he succeeds before you get there, but in the chance that the applications are considered against one another, I'd be willing to write you a letter of support, for whatever that's worth—avowing you and Captain Tunnicliff as the true inventors. I wouldn't dally about it, though. If this banker fellow throws around money as he did with me, he may be able to secure a clerk who will see his application through more quickly."

Ella looked up at him. "Then I'd best get down to the capital straight away?"

"Not a bad idea, I'd say." He thought a moment and then gave her a shrewd look. "You came to me for assistance with the patent application. Do you have a draft for me to look at?"

Ella gave a slightly sheepish shrug. "I'm afraid I don't. I'm not good with writing and the only draft I've seen was the one that Emerston wrote. It was on his own printed stationary and employed only his name. I don't see how to replicate that and make it look, well, official enough."

"Leave that to me," Evans said. "I've more than enough experience with writing letters to the Office of Patents. I'll draft something and send it along with the letter of support. You can take a look and copy it over with whatever changes you like. What address might I use for correspondence with you?"

When Ella had finished writing the name of her inn, she began to thank him but he interrupted her quickly. "Do you know where you're going to find the new patent office in Washington City?"

She looked at him in mild surprise and confessed, "No idea,"

"Here, I'll draw you a map from the stagecoach landing." He made her a quick sketch. Then, standing, he said, "I'll write those papers for you and have a boy bring them over to Miss Susannah's as soon as I complete them." He gave her another sharp look. "I'd prefer to have those sketches in front of me for writing the description in the application. Would you be willing to leave them here?"

Ella gave him an appraising look. "Do you have a place to lock them up?"

He gave her an approving nod. "Come here and see this—you'll appreciate it." He drew her to a set of dark wooden bookshelves on the back wall of his office. He took the books off the shelf one up from the bottom and said, "Look here; what do you see?"

Ella peered at the back of the shelf. "I don't see anything. Just the back of the shelf."

"That's what you think." He pressed lightly on a spot about one-third of the way from the right side of the shelf. What had seemed a solid block of wood released a small panel that sprang forward about an inch on one side—the side he had pressed. He pulled the secret door open, revealing behind it a flat plate of metal with a keyhole on one end. He reached in his pocket and held up the key. "I had this lock built by a master locksmith who assured me no one can pick it. The lockbox reaches down into the wall. I will store your sketches with my own, and I think no one will disturb them here."

Ella handed him the long oilcloth tube in which to store the sketches and watched as he rolled the papers, put them in the sleeve, and locked it in the secret panel. Then she looked up at him and felt a gratitude surge in her. "Thank you, sir. You've been helpful in so many ways." She paused, then said in a rush, "Meeting you and seeing your works here has been, well… more than I ever thought to encounter."

Evans said, "Yes, I can well imagine. A young engineer takes inspiration from the inspiration of others. Hard work every day and inspiration every once in a great while, that's what makes an engineer. Remember that."

"I will."

"Though how a young lady might earn her keep as an engineer I have no idea. I've never heard of such a thing."

"It would take a brave man to hire me."

He was about to speak and then did a double-take as he absorbed the import of her words. "Ah yes, a brave man to hire you, it would. If you're ever in want of a job in Philadelphia, at least come ask me of it." He thought a moment, then added, "My son and I are planning for a new branch of the business in the western part of the state. We'll call it the Pittsburgh Steam Engine Company and my son will operate the works. I wonder if my son might be able to employ someone of your ability."

"It might be amusing to ask him," Ella suggested. Evans gave her a quizzical look. "Only in the sense of gauging his courage."

It was nearly evening by the time Ella left the works to return to Miss Susannah's. Walking through the quiet streets, she immediately began to think of the ways a steam engine like she'd just seen might eventually power her own flax machine. How simple it would be to hitch up a flywheel to run the rollers and power it with a steam-driven piston. She could run the boiler on whatever fuel she could get, whatever was most economical, and the wastewater would be useful as well. If nothing else than as a heating source. Or perhaps she might find a means to send the water back into the engine, reuse the heat and the . . . her thoughts were interrupted by an abrupt sense of unease.

She looked behind her and saw nothing—the street was quite devoid of people. Perhaps she sensed nothing more than an alley cat. She turned to gaze forward and saw, a block or so ahead, a man who stepped out of the alleyway between two buildings and leaned back against the wall, apparently waiting for someone or something. She wondered if she might call to him, but she hardly knew what she'd say.

She walked a little farther toward the man ahead of her. She heard nothing behind her, especially not over the sudden pounding of her heart, but the sense of someone following her caused prickles to rise on the back of her neck.

Just then the man leaning against the wall stepped out and turned to face her. He spread his feet, blocking her way. He was a big man with long sideburns reaching down either side of his face. Before she could try to sidestep him, or indeed take another step at all, the presence behind her slid close and pushed the tip of a knife against her side, grasping her arm firmly at the same time.

"Just stay quiet now," he growled. "No need to make a fuss."

Her body clenched, but then she took a deep breath, another, and relaxed herself into the man behind her. The tip of his knife nicked her skin just before she felt his body give way, losing his balance and taking a step back. She spun with a sudden twist and delivered a taut blow to his knife hand with her stiffened forearm. He dropped the knife and grunted, and, compared to Zeke or Pete, was so slow to react that it was all too easy to press one hip into his side while grabbing his arm to rob him of his footing, delivering him to the paving stones with a resounding thump.

She felt the sideburned man approaching quickly as she worked to pin down the man she had underneath her. As the shadow of Sideburns' raised club fell on her face, she rolled rapidly to one side, taking her captive with her. Then, grasping her man by his crossed wrists, she yanked him up with her and held him in front as she backed away from the wild swings of the club. She was about to shove her man forward to give herself a chance to run, when her fine plan went awry by virtue of the third man. He slipped from a shadow behind her and, with a crack, brought the butt of a heavy cudgel down on the back of her head. She slumped forward.

TWENTY-FOUR

JENNY STARTLED AWAKE in the early hours of the morning and immediately reached out a hand for Ella in the bed beside her. Ella's side lay flat. The pillow untouched.

Jenny stared into the darkness, wondering what to do. She'd gone to bed only slightly worried, for it wasn't unlike Ella to go on long rambles at all hours. Perhaps exploring the city. But she'd been certain her sister would be back by morning, especially as she would know Jenny would worry. She debated whether to awaken Miss Susannah and decided she better at least wait until first light, for it was hard to see what they might do at this hour. So she lit a candle and tried with little success to read, until at last the sky outside lightened and she could rise.

Miss Susannah's initial complacency gave way to mild alarm when, in the grey light of her chamber, amid the rumpled white bed linens and nightdresses, Jenny explained the cause of her distress. They agreed the Mars Works, being the last place Ella was known to visit, was the first place to look.

"But it's yet early for anyone to be there, my dear." Miss Susannah told Jenny. "Even for working men. I think you best take some breakfast first."

Jenny choked down what she could of food but was out the door before any other guests of the inn had arisen. She was waiting outside the Mars Works when the first man arrived, and in her need to find Ella she was able to swallow the embarrassment that would otherwise have strangled her in approaching a strange man in a foreign setting. She told the man what she sought and, as he had nothing to tell her, he brought her inside to await the arrival of the foreman Mr. Taylor.

She was seated to one side of the huge room, on the bench the men used for eating their mid-day meal, as the works came to life for the day. The first clank of iron made her flinch, but soon the hissing steam and ringing metal became background as she watched for Mr. Taylor, whom the workman had described to her. When she first caught sight of his unmistakable tall figure in a herringbone waistcoat, she jumped up to rush toward him. But as he was immediately engaged with a machine and delivering instructions to several men at once, she sat once more to await an opening in his attention.

Indeed she may have waited quite a while longer if he hadn't finally noticed her and barked from several yards away, "May I help you?"—his accent thickly British. But then, when he moved closer and saw her anxious eyes, he said, "Nothing to fear, young lady. What might I do for you?"

"I ...." she swallowed hard. "I'm looking for my sister. She's tall. With black hair."

The Englishman smiled slightly. "Oh yes. That's your sister, is it? You share little resemblance, do you? She was here yesterday afternoon. I won't be forgetting that visit for quite a while now, will I? She had us on our ears in no time with all the questions she asked."

"Yes, that would be Ella," Jenny said, relaxing. "You haven't seen her since then, have you? She never returned from her visit here."

The man raised his eyebrows. "I've naught seen her since she left yesterday. Later afternoon it was, perhaps nearly evening."

"Did she speak to anyone else here who might know more? Mr. Evans, perhaps?" Jenny asked with a slight tremor to her voice. She well recalled Evans' harsh words from the day before.

"Why yes, she did speak to Mr. Evans. But I don't know that he'd know anything further. You're welcome to ask him, though. He's upstairs." He looked at Jenny's face as she glanced at the stairway, remembering the yelling man from their visit to his home. "Would you like me to ask him for you, lass?" he offered with an amused glint in his eyes.

"Oh yes, please. Thank you very much."

He returned a few minutes later to tell her what she feared. That Mr. Evans believed Ella had been returning to her lodging and knew nothing further of her whereabouts. "He did add," Charles Taylor on, "that if she doesn't appear very soon you should visit the constable at the jail on Walnut Street and tell him Mr. Evans sent you."

Jenny nodded. "I'll do that. Thank you very much, Mr. Taylor."

"At your service any time, young lady." He patted her shoulder and said, "Best of luck in finding your sister. I do hope to hear of her safe return, so please stop in or send a note if you don't mind."

"Most certainly. It will be my pleasure."

ON THE WAY BACK it occurred to her that perhaps Mrs. Lincorn might know something and she turned her steps to go ask her. The good woman was behind the counter at her shop and pleased to see her, but she could only shake her head as to Ella's whereabouts.

Jenny returned to the inn and had hardly removed her bonnet before she was restless to be back out doing something to find her sister, for there was no sitting still with the many desperate fears that wracked her mind. Having no further ideas of where to look, she tracked down busy Miss Susannah to ask directions to the Walnut Street Jail, feeling she could wait no longer to enlist the aid of the constable.

It was a good distance to Walnut Street and the fatigue of her recent illness caused her feet to drag, but she found the prison with little trouble. It proved a massive grey stone building behind a twenty-foot-high wall. Along the top of the wall ran a sort of fragile wooden shed extending a few feet into the interior yard, apparently for the purpose of preventing escape. The two-storied central building was crowned by a pediment containing a semi-circular arched fan window. A one-story cupola rose above the full structure, sporting a copper weather vane in the shape of a gilded key.

It was an imposing building and she stopped to stare at it, wishing she could be elsewhere, but then reminding herself that she'd already succeeded in breaching the Mars Works and this could be no worse than that. Could it?

She followed a delivery cart through the gate and asked a cleaning woman inside the entrance hall where she might locate the constable. She was directed to the underkeeper's office, where Constable Facundus was usually found in company with Mr. Halloway the underkeeper.

She waited a moment for the constable and the underkeeper to look up from their game of dice. When they didn't, she cleared her throat and said, "If you please, which of you gentleman is the constable?" The older of the two, with a pox-pitted face and sandy hair going to grey, looked up just enough to raise a brow at her. She attempted to sound assured as she said, "Mr. Oliver Evans has directed me to request your assistance in locating my sister, who never returned to our lodging last night."

"That Evans is an ill-tempered old windbag and I wouldn't lift a cheek to fart in his direction," he said, sending a wad into his spittoon to punctuate the statement. He noted Jenny's appalled face and said, "Pardon my language, Miss. I didn't mean no disrespect. I just can't abide that man."

Jenny maintained a level voice. "I understand your feeling, sir, but it is yet your duty to search for a missing person, is it not? My sister has been missing for nearly a full day and I require your assistance to find her. Will you not do your duty?" She looked around the dirty office and then straight at the constable, forcing herself to hold her gaze steady until, at last, he slithered off his stool with a groan and reached for his hat.

"All right, miss. Tell me her name and where she was last seen and I'll see what I can do. You go home now. Where did you say were your lodgings?" When Jenny told him he said, "All right then, you go mind to your business and I'll have your sister back in no time."

SHE RETURNED TO FIND Miss Susannah's inn in an uproar. Apparently, in her absence two men strode in the front door and made themselves at home, looking for something. They'd searched the sitting room and the dining room and the other small common rooms, and then frightened the wits from the serving girl Margaret until she led them to Jenny and Ella's sleeping room. There they'd torn apart every bit of personal belongings and then the bedding, and even the bed itself. Jenny surveyed this scene of their room with wide eyes. It reminded her of the farmhouse in Deborahville on a morning after Amherst came home late and loud, ripping at whatever he could reach to dispel his terrible fury.

Suddenly she felt just as she used to feel back then, when her terror of his uncontrolled rage would rise up and threaten to choke her. It was a desperate urge to get away, to run and run until there was a safe place to hide and she would never come out. But there was never anywhere to go, then or now.

Instead she did as she'd had to do throughout her childhood; she blinked away the tears that pricked the back of her eyes and went about putting things back in their places. She gathered up the straw from the floor and restored the mattress, then refit the linens and smoothed them until there was nary a wrinkle. She carefully refolded her own and Ella's clothing, stowing the pieces neatly in the small set of drawers, along with their other few belongings.

When she was done she surveyed the neat room and felt the terror inside herself thin a bit. Then she did what she hadn't allowed herself so far: she thought directly about what had happened, and why. Why would someone search the inn, what in heaven could they be looking for? Except... well, yes, of course. They must seek the drawings, their only possession of any actual value. But Ella had had them with her when she'd gone to see Oliver Evans. So where were they now? Perhaps it meant Ella had escaped these would-be pursuers and was now running far and fast, toward somewhere. But where? No, Jenny wished for it but she could not believe it. An instinct she couldn't explain told her Ella was not far away.

She took another deep breath and forced herself to think of what she might do to be useful. She went downstairs to find Miss Susannah, who was likewise out at the time the men came, but had returned shortly before Jenny. Together they restored order in the sitting room and dining room, in which drawers were rifled and furniture shoved about, but no other harm done. For once Miss Susannah was quiet, with no advice or opinion to air. Jenny could see she was shaken.

As calmly as she might, Jenny said, "Miss Susannah, whoever has done this is likely to know something of Ella's disappearance. Do I have your leave to question Margaret about their appearances so I might describe them to the constable?"

Miss Susannah looked mildly astonished at Jenny's question, but nodded and gestured to the back of the house, where Jenny soon found Margaret cowering in the pantry. With soft words she drew the girl out and sat her at the scarred table on one side of the brick-floored kitchen, where she asked her what she could remember. As she listened, Jenny commenced to draw what she heard in her sketching book, occasionally showing her sketch to Margaret for approval or redirection. Within an hour she had a decent sketch of the taller man with the long sideburns and the shorter man with the crinkled sand-brown hair.

She showed them to Miss Susannah, who was impressed but insisted that Jenny eat some supper before venturing out again, for she'd hardly eaten a bite all day. To appease her, Jenny moved her food around the plate for a bit, but as soon as she could she reached for her shawl and made her way back to the jailhouse to show her sketches to the constable.

She found him sitting on his stool, spitting into his spittoon and talking to the underkeeper. She asked him of his searches and soon realized, through his excuses, that he had done nothing, had perhaps not even left the jailhouse. She attempted to show him the sketches, but he gave them only the briefest of glances before turning back to his dice game.

She stared at the side of his head a moment, at the longish greasy hair and dirty collar, and then, as molten lava erupting, all the worry inside her exploded. "Sir, you will listen to me or I will have you placed in irons yourself. I will go to the Governor before I will give up on that promise. You have failed in each and every aspect of your duty from the largest to the smallest. The taxes of this city pay your wages and you are bound not only by duty but by law to perform the offices of this station, which includes finding people when they cannot be accounted for. Your failure to search for my sister breaches every tenet of propriety and I simply will not stand for it. You will do your duty you...you...you filthy dog—or I will make certain you pay the price for your utter disregard for this office. I shall not stand for it. I *will* not! Is that...perfectly...clear...sir?"

As she spoke she drew closer to the man to whom she directed her angry tirade and he sank in his seat, veritably cowering under the torrent she'd unleashed. By the time she was done she was towering over him. When she waited but he still failed to meet her eye, she used the sketchbook to take several swats at his shoulder. He winced and shrank down farther as the edge of her book bit into his flesh.

Suddenly she was horrified. Had she truly lost her temper so recklessly as to hurt someone? Was she no better than her father? With her fury spent she burst into tears and turned to stumble out the door. She raced through the hallways of the jail, bumping into walls, and emerged onto the street gasping for air. She turned toward Miss Susannah's, but was forced to stop every few minutes to wipe her eyes and blow her nose, for she could not staunch the flow of tears now they'd begun at last. She'd soaked two handkerchiefs and was rooting in her pocket for a third when she felt a presence in front of her and found herself looking up at someone quite tall and light-haired. When her eyes focused at last, it was Lucas Emerston.

"Mister Emerston," she stammered, staring as if at a spectre. "What are you doing here?"

He looked just as surprised to see her. "I..." he seemed unsure what to say. "I'm here on business with my father. To assist him in his...business," he finished lamely. He studied her a moment. "You're distressed, Miss Kenyon. May I help you with something? You're not lost, are you?"

Jenny stared at him as dozens of thoughts whirled through her mind. What did it mean that he was here? That his father was here? Could this really be coincidence? In her state of agitation she could not think what to say—and was only afraid to say too much. "Excuse me, won't you please." She ran past him down the street, back to the comparative safety of the inn.

WHEN SHE GOT THERE she could not find her key and lifted her hand to knock, but as she did so the door opened with a brisk movement and Aunt Lucille stood before her.

"Jenny Kenyon. Oh my goodness. Get in here this minute." Jenny was pulled into a tight embrace that smelled of lavender water, and then just as quickly released so Lucille could hold her back and study her face.

"You look like you've been weeping for days. What's happened? Where's your sister?"

Jenny just shook her head. She didn't trust herself to speak. Miss Susannah swept in the door behind Jenny and said, "Lucille? When did you arrive?"

"Just now. And someone must tell me what's happening. I found no one here except a lady with a little dog who knew nothing of anything, and now Jenny has just returned in tears and won't speak. Susannah, what is all this about? Has something happened?"

"Now, now, give me a minute to remove my hat, will you not?" Miss Susannah began removing her hat pins as she said, "Ella left yesterday afternoon to visit Mr. Evans at the foundry and we haven't seen her since. Jenny has been to see Oliver Evans—the last one to see her—and then to see the constable to set him looking for her." She stopped and looked at Jenny's face. "I take it that didn't go well, dear?" When Jenny shook her head she said, "And then two horrible men came here when we weren't home and threw everything about, apparently looking for something."

The front door opened again and Zeke blew inside carrying several cases. "Is this the right place?" he asked. Then, seeing Lucille, he said, "Oh yes, there she is. Found it."

Jenny stared at him, her cheeks blotchy red and her eyes redder still. He turned to her and his expression immediately shifted. "Jenny—what's the matter? What's happened?" He opened his arms as he stepped toward her and she fell into them as the sobs commenced. He held her tightly, and, when she continued to sob, looked up once more. "What's happened?"

Jenny sobbed harder as Lucille recounted the details. Miss Susannah nodded and said, "She's been so brave and then, just tonight, she went to see the constable again. Wait—you didn't learn anything, did you?" She peered into Jenny's face where it was pressed against Zeke's coat. "You didn't hear ill news, did you?"

Jenny shook her head. Then she pulled back from Zeke and wiped her face with her hands. She began to root for a handkerchief and Miss Susannah was quick to supply one from the depths of her bosom. When Jenny had blown her nose and composed herself as best she could, she told them in a halting voice of the worthlessness of the constable—though not her own tirade—and then her encounter with Lucas Emerston outside the jail.

"All right then," Miss Susannah said when Jenny was done recounting her tale, "Come into the sitting room and we'll devise a plan to do some searching of our own. There are enough of us now that we can accomplish something. I myself will see to it that the city does its duty of putting at least one man on the job."

TWENTY-FIVE

ELLA WOKE IN DARKNESS. She'd lost track of hours; she could only sense night versus day by means of the weak light that came through the small barred window set high on the wall of her stone-walled room. She was in some kind of a cellar in a building that appeared to be empty save for herself.

They never came during the day. They only came at night. They carried a smoking lantern and wore heavy nailed boots that clattered along the alley outside her window and down the stairs from the alley door, then toward her down the hallway of the cellar. No one else came in the building, at least not since she'd been here. It had an odd smell, though. One she could not quite place. It was a sickly sweet smell of rot, but rotting what? At night she could hear the rats scurrying around, but so far they'd left her alone; presumably they were more interested in whatever caused the smell.

She tried to sleep again. Sleep at least passed the time, was better than just waiting. The best she could do was doze on and off, at least until she first caught sound of those boots in the alley. Tonight she heard the steps grow closer, then the keys jingled and the door to the building clanked open. For the thousandth time she wished she still had one of her knives. With having changed into that damnable green dress and then back again, she'd neglected to replace the two extra small knives she normally kept hidden on her person—and they'd found and taken the one she'd worn on her belt.

Tonight they were laughing. A bottle gave a loud clink and one of them said, "Watch it there, don't want to be spillin' none o' that." It was the younger one, the one with the light hair who made the decisions. He was the one she'd never seen before. The older of the two was taller and dark-haired, with the oddly high nasal voice and long curved sideburns she remembered so well from that night six or seven years ago. And then again, more recently, through a window at a farmhouse in northern Pennsylvania. Dennison seemed content to let young Bixby run the show, but where Bixby was merely doing a job, DeWitt Dennison was enjoying himself.

He hadn't enjoyed himself as much that long ago night when he'd been forced to fight Pete and she'd thrown the knife that killed his companion. That night he'd had to fight for his life and he hadn't like that. No, he liked this much better, where he fought only a wounded and disarmed girl. This was more his kind of fight. At least he hadn't seen her either of the times she'd seen him before. She had the advantage in this, in knowing more of him than he knew of her. She knew he worked for Loomis; she knew how quickly he went down when he fought Pete; and she knew how quickly his loyalty to Loomis had waned when his own life was at stake.

The one minor relief was that Bixby was a different sort from Dennison. She wondered if Bixby had been drawn into the business because he happened to be in Philadelphia when Loomis needed men, but that his usual work ran more to keeping books or exchanging money. He appeared to have little practice at the thuggery that Dennison so relished. In fact she sensed Bixby found the whole business somewhat distasteful. She'd tried to talk to him, to reason with him, but Dennison always cut her off quickly.

Tonight she could tell from their footsteps they were already drunk. She drew her knees up to her chest and steeled herself for their entrance to her room. "Evenin'," Bixby said as they opened the door. "We've got a present for you." He held up a bottle of rum. "Brought a nip for you to share with us this fine night."

Ella gave him a level look devoid of expression. She'd found it effective to keep an eye on them but offer no response to their various entreaties. Eventually they grew bored and left. Tonight was different, though. They were already drunk and in no mood for preliminaries.

"All right, now, tonight you're going to tell us," Dennison began. "Where are those drawings?" When she said nothing, he said, "We searched that widow's inn yesterday. That sister of yours wasn't about at the time, but perhaps next time we'll have a go at her as well." He leered at her.

Ella drew in a breath, trying not to show her reaction. How slow and dull she'd been. Of course they'd search the inn—where else would they search? They'd taken her oilskin packet when they'd thrown her in here. She'd woken to find it gone, together with her knife. They'd plied her with questions about the drawings and the application papers as soon as she'd woken, and she'd told them how she'd mailed the drawings directly to the patent office. She'd made it sound as plausible as possible and they left as if they'd believed her.

But of course Emerston—she could only suppose he was behind this, though she hadn't seen him or heard his name—would have disavowed them of this idea. He would recognize it at once for an absurd bluff, that she'd never trust the drawings to the post. He wanted the sketches that showed the improvements she'd made and he wasn't going to settle for anything else. Whatever arrangement he had with Loomis, it included finding the drawings.

Dennison was waiting for a response to his taunt and she considered how she might convince him that she'd never leave the drawings at the inn, where there was no security of any type. She opened her mouth to say this, but tonight he had less patience than usual. Before she could get out of the way he'd crossed the tiny room and landed a heavy kick to the side of her thigh. It was nearly the same spot he'd kicked two nights before and the pain almost made her faint. It was the same leg that had barely healed from being broken in three places.

Bixby said, "Now, now, Dennison, no need for that tonight. Like I said, tonight we're going to do things different. Hold her down."

Dennison pushed her over roughly and pinned her shoulders to the floor. She pressed her lips tight together, but Dennison pinched her nose until she had to loosen her lips to breathe. When she did so, he jammed three fingers between her lips and pried her mouth open. As Dennison held her, Bixby poured the burning rum down her throat, pausing only when she began to cough and choke. When she'd caught her breath once more, Dennison pinned her back down and Bixby poured down the rest of the bottle. She felt the heat on her throat and then felt it deep in her guts, seeping into her stomach. Her eyes blurred and she shut them. She could only faintly hear Bixby and Dennison as they continued to ply her with questions about the drawings and where she'd hidden them. She didn't hear them clearly until she caught the words, "...little sister of yours will have to help us find them." Then she tried to speak, to tell them whatever they wanted to know. But the words wouldn't come out, and after a time she had no more thoughts. She had only a sensation of heavy strong bodies pinning her down.

She woke alone to see a weak, thin light coming through the small window. Rain fell on the street outside. She tried to roll over but her body would not obey. It was a throbbing mass, as much from the rum as from anything else. She could not remember and didn't wish to recall what else they'd done to her. She sent her mind out the window, down the street with the rain.

That night when they came back, she forced her body upright and made herself stand. She pressed her back against the wall next to the doorway. When they opened the door she sent an elbow into the mouth that entered the room first—it was Bixby—and then pushed him over and tried to dash past Dennison before he could react. But in her wounded state she was too slow. Dennison chased her down the hall and grabbed her with little difficulty just as she reached the stairs up to the street. He hauled her back to the room and flung her back in the corner, the corner she knew so well. Then he made certain she paid for her mistakes. With that which she valued most.

TWENTY-SIX

THE SEARCH PARTY AGREED to part ways to cover more of the city. Zeke made his way down to the port to mingle with the stevedores and sailors, who hear all kinds of odd news in the taverns. Miss Susannah marched to the office of a particular city magistrate of her acquaintance, with the hope of lighting a fire under the constabulary for conducting a proper search. Lucille reasoned she and Jenny might do best to seek out the Emerstons.

"But what if he's involved in her disappearance?" Jenny asked Lucille as they readied themselves to depart the inn.

"Oh no, that's not possible," Lucille said as she adjusted her hat. "I know the man. It's true that he might be capable of fraudulent dealings in money or property, but that doesn't mean he's capable of nefarious doings such as you suggest. I can't think but she must have had the ill luck to fall in with a band of thieves or some such. The city is full of evil men. Emerston will undoubtedly put aside these matters of money when he hears of the danger to have befallen Ella. And he's likely to have broad contacts in the city for assistance in finding her."

"If you say so, Aunt."

"I do. Now, let's make for exactly where you ran into Lucas. We'll begin with the taverns closest to that spot. He's likely to have been on his way to his lodgings at that time of night."

Despite the soundness of this logic, they'd made no progress in locating either Ella or the Emerstons by supper time. They made their way back to Miss Susannah's on weary feet, to find Zeke just coming downstairs from changing his clothes for supper. He too looked tired and low in spirits.

"Did you hear any news of her?" Lucille asked him.

"No, nothing I'm afraid. Only a great deal of talk about a British press gang stealing into a tavern late last night and hauling five Americans back to their ship. And still the usual hubbub over the slave revolt in New Orleans. They're still talking about that. Yet . . . there was one odd thing."

"Yes?" Jenny said quickly.

"Well, it's just that I caught a glimpse from a ways down Market Street of someone I believe I recognize from Deborahville. I don't recall his name, but he's come into the dry goods shop on one or two occasions."

"Might you describe him?" Lucille asked.

Zeke shrugged. "He's a regular kind of fellow. He has light-colored hair."

Lucille and Jenny exchanged a look. Lucille said, "All right, I'll ask you questions. First, how tall is he, how long is his hair, and does he wear a mustache or any such business?"

Once satisfied with the answers to these questions, she said, "Now then, describe his clothing. And leave nothing out."

Zeke gave her a skeptical look. "He wore, I don't know, trousers, a shirt and waistcoat. Is that what you mean?"

"Not exactly. Now think. Were the trousers long or short? Of what sort of fabric were they fashioned and what color? And the waistcoat, what was the cut? How high were his boots? What sort of hat?"

Zeke dredged his memory for the half-observed details on that in which he took little interest. When at last he managed to recall that the man wore a coat with a row of large greenish buttons on the front, Lucille said, "Wait. That reminds me of something. Jenny, might I see your sketches once more?" The sketchbook was procured and she studied the lighter-haired man. "Yes, it might be. I couldn't see it before, but now that you recall for me those odd buttons on his coat, I can see it might be him." She tapped the sketch. "I believe this could be Lorenzo Bixby. He's one of Loomis' men." Jenny drew in a sharp hissing breath that Lucille ignored. "Now where exactly did you see him?"

"He was just stepping off of Market Street onto a side road. I tried to make my way up to him, but you know how crowded the market always is—he'd disappeared by the time I reached the corner."

"What corner was that?"

Zeke thought a moment. "It was Fourth Street. He went south on Fourth Street."

"Susannah," Lucille called into the dining room, where Miss Susannah was completing the preparations for supper, "do you know of a tavern on Fourth Street, just below Market?"

"That's the Indian Queen, my dear," Miss Susannah called back. "Could be none other."

Zeke said, "Let me have a bit of supper and rest my feet and then I'll go visit the Indian Queen. See what I might learn."

"Thank you, Zeke," Lucille said. "Jenny and I will go first thing in the morning to speak to the desk clerk and see if we might gain an audience with whomever of our acquaintance is lodging there. I'll need my wits about me for that."

Once Zeke was gone, Jenny and Lucille took their coffee to the sitting room. Jenny, though, was unusually quiet. So quiet that Lucille finally asked the trouble and if she could relieve her mind in any way.

"Oh no trouble," Jenny said. "Well, not beyond the obvious trouble. I just have a thought to consider." She took another sip of her coffee. "I do believe I won't accompany you tomorrow, Aunt. I have a place I'd like to visit first."

Just as they were preparing to retire, Zeke returned with the announcement that he had, by means of devious observation and a tip for the porter, confirmed the presence of Emerstons, both father and son, at the Indian Queen on Fourth Street.

ON THE WAY TO SEE EMERSTON the next morning, Lucille Tunnicliff had a good ten blocks to think over all she knew of what had happened and try to make sense of it. She found her steps quickening, and realized that, despite herself, she was hurrying toward the sight of Henry Emerston. Despite her reservations, she couldn't keep herself from hoping he'd show her suspicions unfounded and chide her for thinking such things of him. That once again he'd be a savior—as he had so many times before.

Including that most terrible of nights seven years ago now, when Ella had appeared at her door and led her back to the yard of the smith, to find Pete writhing in pain on the ground. After getting him home and leaving him sleeping under Ella's watch, Lucille had returned to the smith to look for Asa Tunnicliff and followed the trail of blood that led to the Emerston mansion. She'd arrived in time to offer her assistance and hear Tunnicliff describe the men who'd attacked them.

Emerston had said, "That sounds like the brother, Willard Loomis, together with a pair of their gang members. Once George Loomis hears what happened, it will be only a matter of time before he's back here, looking to even the score."

It was then that Captain Tunnicliff had made the suggestion for faking his own death, so as to leave no one to blame when

Loomis came looking for more blood. Emerston had considered the matter carefully, asking more questions of Tunnicliff to determine exactly who had seen what and in what order the events had occurred. Then he'd acted decisively. He'd had Tunnicliff lay as still as possible while he'd had him examined by old Doctor Beemis, who was paid to sign the paper and ask no questions. Then he'd proceeded to arrange all the rest—the closed-casket wake, the funeral, all of it.

The strangest moment, Lucille recalled, had been when Captain Tunnicliff, grimacing with the pain of his wound, had suddenly turned to Emerston and asked, "What of the letters, you have them safe?" A look of surprise had crossed Emerston's face, followed by a frown of such deep displeasure that Lucille knew the Captain had touched on a subject of significance. She had immediately wished to ask more of the matter, but Emerston's expression brooked no inquiry and he'd quickly risen and left the room.

He'd regained his humor directly and in the following days, as they nursed Tunnicliff in secret while preparing for the public funeral, Emerston had prepared the will and pre-dated it by more than a year, so it wouldn't cause any whisperings. She recalled how impressed she'd been by him, how clever and competent he'd been, and how she'd again felt a wave of doubt as to whether she'd made the right choice in refusing him all those years before. Why had she been so blind to his qualities?

She'd been further impressed when George Loomis had indeed arrived in town, saying everything Emerston had predicted he'd say. What he hadn't predicted was that Loomis would be so charming. She'd been there to greet him, for it was agreed she'd play-act a role as witness to the events of the night the killings took place, thereby avoiding the necessity of Loomis interrogating Pete.

Emerston had her recount what she'd supposedly seen and she'd played her part with tasteful authenticity. Loomis seemed pleased to believe the events had unfolded as she described, for they relieved him of the need to act any further, just as Emerston had foreseen. Then she and Emerston and Loomis had had a fine long discussion on many matters and he'd left them laughing at his departure. When he'd returned a few weeks later they had a cheerful reunion. It was not long after they'd offered her to bring her in on the bank note business.

Arriving at the Indian Queen, she expected that Emerston would likely be immersed in business and require her to wait for an audience. He maintained extensive trading interests between Philadelphia and the West Indies and came to the city to meet with various business factors and ship captains to whom he entrusted his cargo. To her surprise, the serving man who took her card and disappeared with it returned to say that Mr. Emerston would be pleased to receive her. "Well, all right then," she said, slightly taken aback.

She found Emerston at the breakfast table, just rising with his coffee in hand. "Hello, my dear," he said without a trace of surprise. Then, after examining her a moment, he added, "Here, come with me into the parlor. I expected you yesterday."

Lucille felt a tingle of shock course through her. He'd been expecting her? That could only mean... he *knew* of Ella's disappearance? More than that, it was the tone of his voice that shocked her. His words were courteous enough, but his tone was cold as frosted glass. He'd never spoken to her in such a tone before. Not since... but that was many many years ago.

When they were seated in the parlor, he in the gentleman's high-back chair, she on a lady's stool, he said, "You'd like my assistance?"

Lucille drew herself up, her back as straight as she could make it, and forced herself to smile engagingly. "It seems you already know something of my troubles. I do always seem to come to you with them, do I not?" She laughed slightly. "It seems you have a gift for resolving my difficulties. I regret to ask yet another service, but I've come to seek your help in locating my niece... or, rather, my daughter Ella. She's been missing several days now."

"Yes, I know," he said, his voice colder than before.

She waited but he said no more, only looked at her, his eyes appraising. She resisted the impulse to squirm in her seat. Had she offended him?

"I'm quite worried about her," she said at last, her voice soft, skirting the edge of pleading. "It's not like her to be gone this long. What do you know of her whereabouts?"

"She's alive. There's nothing to worry about."

Lucille absorbed the import of his words, feeling her back stiffen into a rigid board and her mouth fill with dust. Can he really have said what she just heard? That he had a hand in Ella's disappearance? As the shock eased its grip, a tinny bell of warning began to sound deep in the back of her mind. She sensed she was about to hear that which she had no wish to hear. The urge to flee the room washed over her, but for Ella's sake she knew she must learn what she could.

"But where is she? Is she hurt?"

"I have no idea whether she's hurt. She's alive is all I know. She's not particularly cooperative, is she?"

Lucille stared at him. "You... you kidnapped her?"

"Don't be ridiculous. She's confined until she cooperates. Or until I say she's free to go."

"But... what? Why?"

"That's rather dull of you, my dear Lucille," Emerston said with a small smile that twisted into more of a sneer. "The patent of course, my darling. Did you think I'd give up so easily on something worth several times my own present fortune? As soon as I've secured it, she'll be free to go. I merely need some information from her first."

It felt hard to breathe, but then Lucille's eyes snapped and she said, "Can the patent truly be worth this to you? Worth the risk of kidnapping a girl? What if she were hurt? Or…worse. If she died you'd be culpable."

Emerston took a sip of his coffee. "No, my dear, I wouldn't."

"Why? You think Loomis would take all the penalty for you?"

"Loomis will do as he has to. He has plenty of expendable men."

"But I know what you've done. You've just told me. Do you think I'll stay quiet?"

Emerston smiled pleasantly. "You can say whatever you like, my dear. I'll make certain no one believes you." He considered her a moment, than shook his head in mock regret. "Oh that poor sad woman. It's such a shame she at last succumbed to the madness that runs in her family. That she's resorted to making ill-founded accusations against respected members of the community…" He paused. "And who would *you* believe? The respectable banker and solicitor who built much of the town, or the sad old widow who bore a bastard child and is rumored to have a hand in bad bank notes? Who makes visits to a cabin in the woods where she keeps an Indian lover?" His eyes grew flinty. "You think people don't talk about that? Don't laugh behind your back? You're nothing now, Lucille. I could grind you up and blow you away."

Lucille felt her throat tighten as a school of words swam mad circles in her mind. It grew ever more difficult to breathe with the pressure on her throat, but she forced herself to set her shoulders and swallow, forced her throat to open, to let the words croak out. "I may be nothing, but that means you were jilted by nothing. What does that make you?"

"It makes me the winner, madam. The winner. The day you shamed me in front of all the town, I knew I would find a means to ruin you, and I'd take my time with it. Make certain it was done well. And now, what could be better? I have the pleasure of not only that, but of thwarting your ill-begotten daughter at the same time. You imagined I'd let her make off with the patent? See her reap the profits and elevate you and the rest of that brood? No, I was never going to let that happen. And yes, I'll confide that in the end, my revenge is rather sweet. I'm savoring it. Though in truth I had little to do when it comes to you, my dear Lucille, as you've done a fine job ruining yourself."

Lucille stood, willing herself to keep her back straight and her face composed as she strode out of the room. She nearly collided with Lucas Emerston coming into the inn as she made her way out and he gave her a quizzical look. She made the slightest of nods and left before she could hear whatever he started to say.

It wasn't until she reached the street and had walked for more than two blocks that her mind began to have a single coherent thought. *What a fool I've been. What a fool I still am. Fool, fool, fool, fool, fool.*

SHE RETURNED TO THE INN still flustered, her mind racing. She found Jenny in the sitting room with a middle-aged man sitting decorously with his wide-brimmed Quaker hat on his knee. They were examining the sketchbook in which Jenny had captured the likenesses of Dennison and Bixby. He and Jenny both rose at Lucille's entrance.

Jenny said, "Aunt Lucille, are you all right? You look quite ill."

Lucille shook her head and forced herself to smile at Jenny and the guest. After an awkward pause, Jenny remembered her manners and said, "Mrs. Tunnicliff, may I introduce you to Friend Isaac Hopper?" Lucille tilted her head in greeting and Mr. Hopper made a small bow.

Jenny studied her aunt with concern before continuing in a quiet voice. "Mr. Hopper has offered to be of assistance to us and he has a wide network of friends among the free negroes of the city. In particular he knows a negro man by the name of Levin Smith who is eager to repay a debt to Mr. Hopper. Mr. Smith would be more than willing to assist in any way we deem useful and it occurred to us that if Mr. Smith were to follow Mr. Bixby, Loomis' man, it is quite likely he will lead the way to Ella. Yet..." Jenny paused and looked at Lucille, "it seems perhaps you learned something more in seeking Mr. Emerston...?"

Lucille shook her head but did not elaborate. With an effort she managed to smile at Hopper again. "You're very kind, Mr. Hopper. I greatly appreciate your assistance. I agree that following Mr. Bixby is likely to lead someplace useful and I would be more than happy to compensate Mr. Smith for his time in assisting us."

Isaac Hopper nodded. "I doubt that will be necessary, but I will ask Mr. Smith if he requires such." He turned to Jenny. "If thee do not mind, I will borrow these sketches to show Mr. Smith and, as thee suggest, the young Mr. Winebottom might join us on Fourth Street this evening to see if we might confirm the identity of Mr. Bixby. In the meantime, keep thy spirits strong and do not lose faith. There is always cause for hope. Good day, ladies."

TWENTY-SEVEN

ELLA SAT UP. It wasn't easy, but it wasn't as difficult as it had been a few days before. She'd begun
to heal and they'd left so quickly the night before
that she had no new injuries to nurse. They'd taken
a new tack in having Bixby try to reason her into revealing the
location of the drawings and she'd done her best to let them
believe they were making progress, that she was wavering in
her resolve. She also said slyly disparaging things about Jenny,
as if she didn't trust her and thought her light-minded, in the
hope of discouraging their visiting the inn again. But she knew
it couldn't last. If she didn't make an actual revelation soon,
they would again resort to the threats to her person they began
with, and that Dennison clearly wished to resume.

The urge to lie down and escape back into sleep washed
over her. It would be so much easier. She gritted her teeth
and forced herself to stand. She moved to the section of wall
where several stones were loose and pried away the front stone
to reveal a small cavity behind. Inside was nothing but more
stones. These she took out and carried to the low bench that
provided the only furnishing in the room, save for the thin,

damp pallet she slept on. She had begun to suspect the building that housed her had once been used for slaughtering animals, for she'd heard several suggestive remarks to that effect. Certainly it would fit with the smell of rot that continued to pervade the dank air.

Seated on the bench, she sighed and took up two stones to begin once more chipping away at one stone with another, attempting to shape an end into something approximating a sharp edge. She'd seen Pete fashion arrowheads of stone and knew they could be sharp, but this stone didn't flake the same way. As Pete had taught her, she set her mind to see what she needed and willed her hands to take her there, but the stone continued to defy her hands.

She worked for several hours, losing herself in the effort but making little progress. At last, when she was almost too disheartened to continue, she got a lucky angle that broke the stone in just the right way, leaving a thin, sharp wedge. She grunted with satisfaction and held it up to the light of the small window to inspect. The small success restored her spirits so she worked some more, attempting to fashion a second and then a third sharpened stone. Then, when she could do no more, she put away her work before idly picking up the handful of pebbles she'd taken to throwing in circles, juggling them around and around for her own amusement.

LATER THAT NIGHT, when it had grown dark once more and she heard Bixby and Dennison coming down the alley, she took up the stones once again. When they entered the room she was spinning five stones in overlapping triangles in front of her. They stood gaping and she made an effort to smile, as if she sought to entertain them. Through the pebbles she saw

Dennison lean back against the wall to enjoy the show. When he did this, she altered the rhythm to a simpler pattern. When the sharp stone came around to her right hand she grasped it. Letting the others clatter to the floor, she pulled her arm back and threw, aiming for Dennison's temple to render him senseless.

The sharpened stone, with none of the grace of a well-tempered knife, sank during flight and hit him instead in the shoulder. Seeing this, Ella knew she had only a moment before she lost the advantage of surprise. She took a second sharp stone from her pocket and stepped forward to throw it from a few paces closer. This time she hit him beside the eye with enough force to make him stagger sideways, but again the stone hadn't flown right and hadn't done the damage it might have done. She made for him, attempting to bludgeon his temple with her fist in place of the stone. Bixby reacted quickly to intervene. He grabbed her from behind and pulled, so that her first swing missed its mark by inches. As she twisted to free herself, Dennison reached out with his undamaged arm to take a hard hold of her upper arm, squeezing her flesh with his powerful hand as he yanked her from Bixby's grip and then pushed her across the room. He shouted at her as she flailed at his head with her free arm, calling her a string of vile names and continuing to twist her arm harder until at last he had her against the far wall. She could hardly move as the rough stone bit into her cheek and his shoulder pressed hard against her shoulder blade. Realizing she'd lost all advantage and her meager strength was nearly spent, she instinctively attempted to curl her body, to shield herself, knowing what was coming.

Just then someone began to yell in the alley outside the tiny barred window of her cell. "Liam aboo, my son. Liam aboo!" Over and over, the same words in a tinny high falsetto voice, "Liam aboo, my son. Liam aboo!" She had no idea what the words meant, but despite the falsetto she knew the voice as if it were her own. Zeke was here. He had found her. Dennison grabbed her hair and pulled her head back before thrusting it sharply against the wall, until everything went black.

SHE WOKE IN DAYLIGHT with a throbbing head and Zeke's voice outside her window once more. "Ella? Ella, it's me, Zeke. Come over here, won't you?"

She sat up wincing, not sure whether her head or her bruised arm ached more. She rose and stumbled to the window, looking up to see Zeke's face half-silhouetted behind the iron grate. Zeke's familiar face. She wished to say something but no words came to her tongue. She could only stare up into his face as he stared down at her, trying to keep his expression neutral and not succeeding very well.

Before she could say something to reassure him she was all right, he said, "We need to get you out of there and there's not much time. I don't know whether they recognized me when they chased me down the alley last night, but if they did they'll almost certainly wish to move you. We have to get you out before they can, but..." he gestured down the alley toward the door to the building, "I've tried every door and every window and it seems they've done their work well—they're all stoutly locked. I think there's nothing for it but to wait for them to return with their key. I'll have to take them down and use their key to open the building."

"No," she said quickly in a croaking voice. She cleared her throat. "No, not that way. I've had nothing but time to think of it and I wish to do it myself. I don't want to be rescued. I need only a knife." She heard the lack of assurance in her own voice and hated herself for it. Had it really taken only less than a week of being imprisoned for her to become the timid victim she'd always feared to become? Was her confidence in her own strength all a ridiculous illusion?

"I don't know where to buy a throwing knife in the city," Zeke said. "Except...yes, there are sailors who have them—and there's a fellow at the docks who deals in knives. He'll have one or know where to find one." He paused and then added, "I don't know that I care for this plan, Ella. If something goes wrong and you don't take them down, I want to be able to get you of there." After another pause, he went on, "I know a couple of sailor fellows who owe me a good turn. I'm going to bring them back with me tonight, just in case we need to come in after you."

Ella started to protest, sensing what it would cost her later to have been rescued like that, but then she saw the prudence in his suggestion and knew it would be idiotic to refuse. "But you won't come in otherwise, will you?"

Zeke grimaced in disgust. "God's blood, Ella. How can you be so damn bossy even when you're in as much of a fix as this?" Then his face relaxed into peevish amusement. "I suppose it's a good sign that you're all right if you're still trying to issue orders."

At these words Ella felt better than she'd felt in all these days. She felt like herself once more. At least for this moment. "I'll see you later," she said softly.

"Yes, I'll be as fast as I can."

She drifted off into sleep once more in the later afternoon, then woke soon after dark as she heard a scuffling at the window. By the time she scrambled up to the windowsill he was gone, but on the sill her hand found not one, but two thin-handled, straight-edged throwing knives, along with a small scrap of paper. She deftly pocketed the knives and then held up the paper to the silver moonlight.

Don't kill them. Z

Her mouth curved into a weak grin, grateful for his confidence in her. She took out the knives and studied them, then tossed them gently in her palm, one at a time. She took aim at a spot on the wall that held the door—the only wall made of wood—and threw. It was difficult to know if the knife was at fault when she didn't hit her mark, or only that she was out of practice and the feel of it was strange. In a little less than an hour she heard the nailed boots in the alley, for they were early tonight. She had hoped to have more time.

Their footsteps coming down the hallway were cautious, not brash, which surprised her. They'd beaten her so thoroughly the night before that she'd expected them to be exultant tonight. Had they, perhaps, become convinced she wasn't to be trusted? She grinned faintly once more, for she liked the thought of earning their respect. Even if she had little to show for it. Tonight might be her last chance, for once they saw the knives they would know she was discovered and they'd either kill her or move her somewhere even more subterranean and guarded. Unless Zeke and his sailor friends could move quickly enough to interfere, of which there was no certainty. If only she'd had more time to practice with the knives.

Sitting on the bench across from the door, she let her body sag slightly, as if it were difficult to hold herself up. It was best to let them think they'd done her as much damage as possible last night.

The door opened cautiously and she knew they were on their guard. Bixby came in first with Dennison behind him. Dennison began to say, "We'll not take any more of that foolishness—" when the knife struck him in the soft flesh above the collarbone with enough force to pin him against the wooden wall behind him. Bixby gaped at the hilt of the knife sticking out from the wall, then, with no warning, threw the lantern he was holding toward Ella. The lantern collided with the second knife in midair, raising a sharp clank that echoed in the room. Bixby saw the knife and the lantern on the floor and wasted no time in backing out of the room, pulling the door shut behind him to block any knives en route. Ella heard his steps racing away down the hallway.

Recovering from the shock of sudden pain, Dennison yanked out the first knife and staggered forward to lunge at her. She quickly reached down to grab the knife on the floor and then stepped back to throw again, but he was so close by now that she only had time to thrust the blade back into the same collarbone and then step out of his path. He growled as he stumbled to the floor, still clutching the first knife in his other hand as he began to crawl toward her. The second knife clattered onto the floor from his collarbone but he ignored it as he dragged himself with a look of fierce determination. Apparently his hatred for her had overcome his innate cowardice, for she wouldn't have expected him to keep coming at her. Or perhaps he knew that his only chance was to reach her before she killed him, for she had every reason to savor the opportunity.

She stepped around him and picked up the second knife once more, watching him all the while. Zeke's only words to her had been to warn her not to kill them. Did he know how desperately she wished to do just that? She willed herself to remain impassive and think clearly. Why had Zeke taken the trouble to warn her? She'd thought at first that he did it mostly to bolster her confidence. Now she wondered if he didn't know her well enough to know she needed an actual reminder. That she would yearn so hard to make this man pay, to make him hurt as he'd done to her, that she'd forget how a murder would continue to shadow her. That it wasn't worth the cost.

Dennison had reached the wall and used his good hand, still clutching the knife, to steady himself as he rose to his feet. He turned his head to look at her and she saw in his eyes a bitter wish to bring her down, to make her his weakened victim again. The urge to kill him washed over her with a fierce energy. Before he could turn, she stepped behind him and slid the knife through the fabric of his trousers, slitting his leg behind the right knee. She used enough force to cut right down to the bone. He slid down the wall to the floor again, groaning, and then beginning to yowl as he felt what she'd done.

She wiped the knife with care as she examined him, making fully certain he would not be chasing anyone any time soon. In fact not ever again. She took both knives, along with the lantern, and without glancing back at the man on the floor, closed the door of the cell behind her. She made her way slowly down the hallway to the building door, resisting the urge to run, making herself remember there was no need to hurry now. Behind her Dennison began cursing her between howls of pain and fury.

She scanned the sky when she stepped outside the door, then she peered down the alley. She could discern the faint outline of several people standing in front of the window of the room she'd just left, listening to Dennison curse her. As she drew closer, she saw a man in sailor's garb holding Bixby as another man used his face for punching practice. *He won't be nearly as pretty now,* she thought. *We'll have that in common.* A third man stepped away from them and came toward her.

She shuffled toward Zeke, doing her best to walk in a normal manner, to make this a normal greeting. But it was no use, for the look in his eyes as he inspected her told her how she must appear.

He paused briefly and then stepped forward and wrapped his arms around her, holding her gently for a long minute. Finally she released herself and moved back. With an effort she looked up to meet his eyes.

"Don't look so pissing worried," she snapped at him. "I'm all right. I've been worse. I just need to clean up a bit."

His eyes filled with water before he turned away. He took the lantern from her. "It took you long enough to get out of there. You're getting slow now that you've turned twenty-two."

"That's enough of you," she replied.

TWENTY-EIGHT

STEPPING INTO THE INN, Ella felt as if she were returning from a far distant land, rather than a few blocks away. The neat decorum of the sitting room, the frilled curtains and lace table covers, they all seemed to belong to another place and time—somewhere she knew about but hadn't believed to be real. She didn't want to touch anything; it was all too clean.

Jenny stifled a gasp when she saw her. Then her eyes filled with tears just as Zeke's had done and she clapped a hand over her mouth. Lucille, in contrast, gave her a long appraising look. "I see you've been up to trouble again. Here, come with me, we'll heat a kettle in the kitchen and get you cleaned up. You'll want plenty of hot water."

As Lucille helped her into a bath, Ella winced at the heat of the water on her soreness. Lucille, to her surprise, was watching her with a concern she'd never seen on her face before. Her aunt turned away. "Never mind, now," Lucille said. "Everything will be all right."

She took up a brush and began to scrub Ella's back and shoulders with determined strokes, as if currying a horse.

Then, when she reached the bruises of various hues and intensity over much of her arms and legs, she took up a soft cloth and began to rub more gently. When nothing was left but the more private places, she handed the cloth to Ella. "You'll want to wash those well. But not to worry, you can wash it all away, if only you set your mind to it."

Ella peered up at Lucille and was again startled by her expression. She had the sharp sense that Lucille knew exactly what had been done to her and what it felt like. That she'd known the same herself and was purposeful in telling her it wouldn't last. That she wouldn't always feel so small, and so impossibly dirty.

They changed the water and repeated the bath once more, until at last Ella was dried and dressed in clean clothes.

Before they left the kitchen, Lucille said, "Miss Susannah has brought in several men to guard the house for as long as we require it. Shall we go to the magistrates and have the men who did this arrested?"

Ella considered the question. The thought of bringing in the authority of the city hadn't occurred to her, for men like Loomis seemed to operate outside of the law. At last she said, "No, it's not worth the effort. They were Loomis' men and they'll either be hidden or gone by the time any constable goes looking for them."

"I didn't mean them," Lucille said. "Or not them alone. I meant Emerston. He was the one who started it all."

"What evidence is there of that?"

"He told me as much," Lucille said angrily. She considered and then said more softly, "It would just be my word against his, though. Perhaps that's not of much use."

"No, I'm afraid it's not." Ella's shoulders sagged. "Might we discuss this tomorrow?"

"Oh yes, of course. You poor thing. I'm sorry to go on at you. Let's get you to bed now."

Despite her fatigue, Ella couldn't sleep for much of the night. As soon as she would doze she would feel herself back in that dank room and wake abruptly. She fell at last into a fitful rest in the early hours of the morning, disturbed by dreams that she could hear the nailed boots approaching. She woke again with a start, her fist clenched tight around the knife under her pillow. A massive rage surged through her and she didn't know what to do with it. She'd never before wished to kill, to murder, with such ferocity. She regretted that she hadn't made that beast suffer more, that she'd left him with his life. It would be better if he were gone. Altogether removed. She pulled the bedclothes tight around her head, wishing only to lie there on and on, not talk to anyone, not answer any questions. *How long could I stay hidden in this bed?*

When her mind lit on the question of the patent, which she had avoided thinking about for all the days of her captivity, it brought a surge of anxiety but also a relief from the thoughts of the cell. *What had happened in all these days? Had Emerston given up on the drawings and gone down to get the patent however he might? Or did she still have a chance? And if she did have a chance, could she summon up the strength to do what it would require?*

A deep yearning to be free of the worry over patents and inventions came over her. She wished only to remain here in this soft bed and never leave it. Or to wander out and away from this city of horrors and never look back. *Could I get far enough away to ever feel clean again?* She pulled her knees up and lay a long time before finally drifting back to sleep. When she awoke many hours later, there was nothing for it but to rise and dress with heavy arms before making her way downstairs to see what could be done about the patent.

Jenny was several steps ahead of her. Ella found her in the small study next to the sitting room. She ceased writing to look up and say, "I've been to see Mr. Evans this morning and he gave me his letter of support and the draft of the application letter. I'm just making a copy of the application letter now."

Ella stared at her sister. "How did you know to get those papers from Evans?"

"I went to see him, of course," Jenny said with obvious puzzlement. "Why is that odd?"

"You went there? Weren't you afraid, seeing how he yelled at us as he did?"

"I was, but I went to see him when you first went missing and I met that nice Mr. Taylor. After that it was much easier to go back. This morning Mr. Evans himself agreed to see me— after he'd heard what happened to you. I asked if he could be of assistance with the application and he said he could, and that, in fact, he already had. He gave me the papers to bring to you. He was really quite pleasant about it all."

Ella shook her head in wonder. "The Mars Works frightened even me when I went there— and you're so nervous of loud places like that. I can't believe you managed all that on your own."

"Don't be so impressed," Jenny said sharply. "You're not the only one who can take things into her own hands. And what choice did I have? You went missing and I had no idea Aunt Lucille and Zeke were on their way. And the Mars Works were nothing compared to the jailhouse, where I went to enlist the constable—that useless man. He was horrible to me, until I finally cursed at him. And hit him with my sketchbook."

"No!" Ella protested. "You didn't. I can't believe it."

"Why not?" Jenny said in a voice harder than Ella had ever heard it. "We all do what we have to do, when we have no other choice. I also went to find Mr. Hopper again. I showed him the sketches I'd made from the serving girl's description of the men who searched the inn and it was his free negro man Levin Smith who helped us to find you. He and Zeke followed them."

Ella stared at Jenny, still hardly able to believe what she'd heard. "But Jenny... It's all too much. I kept thinking that at least I kept you safe by—"

"By what? By protecting me from the truth? As you did all those years we lived with Father? Did you really imagine I didn't know how he was? That I was able to pretend it all away? Well I did, for a time. But after a while it was for you, and for Mother, that I kept pretending. That you needed to believe I was untouched by it all. So I kept it up. But it's made me soft, and I don't want to be soft any longer. I want to be able to take care of myself."

"Don't we all?" Ella asked harshly. Then, before she could stop them, the tears rose and began to flow. After resisting at first, she let Jenny rub her back, until at last, when they were spent, she gave a final hiccup and blew her nose in Jenny's handkerchief.

Her head still pounding from the weeping, she looked over at the writing table and reached for the papers on it. "Did Evans do a good business with the letters?"

Jenny nodded. "Oh, yes. He's remarkable. He says just what we meant to say when we talked of it. How does he see it so clearly?"

"You already said it—he's remarkable. I don't know that I've met anyone who thinks as clearly on such complex matters as he does."

"I have. It's you."

"Don't be daft. I couldn't see how to say all that."

"No, perhaps not to say it in letters, but you think just as clearly. And you have several *other* talents, which I'm guessing Mr. Evans could not begin to imagine."

Ella took a moment to absorb the import of Jenny's words. "At least you *hope* not."

"At least I *hope* not," Jenny agreed with a faint grin. She reached for the letter of application to continue her scribing.

Ella asked, "Where's Aunt Lucille?"

Just then the front door to the inn opened and they heard Lucille's voice in the entranceway.

"Never mind," Ella said. "I think I can figure it out.'

"You're clever that way," Jenny said without pausing in her work.

Lucille soon found them in the study and seated herself at the table. "I've been to see Emerston to find out what I could of his plans for the patent, and I'm afraid he's gone. The innkeeper said he left at first light."

They looked at one another. Then Ella said what was obvious. "He's gone to apply for the patent."

"Without the drawings?" Jenny asked.

Ella shrugged. "He must figure his best chance now is to obtain the patent for the original version and hope it's too similar to allow me to patent the improved version. It's not his first choice, but it's better than the risk I might get there first."

"How soon might you be able to leave for Washington City?" Lucille asked Ella.

Ella raised a brow to Jenny, who said, "I'll have this copy done in no time. Give me an hour."

"But he's had a half day's head start," Ella said to Lucille. "What's the point of trying to overtake him? Especially when he has his own horse and we'll need to take the coach?"

"We thought of that several days ago," Lucille said with an arch to her voice. "Jenny and I, that is. We thought it would be well that his horse fail to take him on any long journeys."

"You lamed his horse?" Ella asked, incredulous.

"No, of course not. Not lamed. Only inconvenienced by means of a piece of briar under the saddle cloth. And I didn't do it myself, of course. Jenny convinced the groom to assist us."

"Jenny... convinced?"

"Well, charmed is perhaps a more appropriate word. I followed it up with a payment, of course. Just to be certain."

Ella stared at Lucille. "So where does that leave us? He'll change horses and be on his way."

"Yes, but today is Thursday and it's a two-day journey at best, usually longer with the roads still slowed by spring mud. Assuming he doesn't ride his horse to death by riding all through the night, which I doubt he'll see reason to do, with the delay of trading his horse he'll have no chance to reach the city by the close of business on Friday. I have us ticketed for the two o'clock coach that runs through most of tonight. It arrives into the capital by Saturday, and no one will be securing any patents before the opening of business on Monday morning."

Ella nodded. "I see you've thought it all through. One more thing, however. You say you have 'us' booked on the coach, but this isn't a business that any others of you should be involved with. Emerston has shown how dangerous he can be."

"I'm quite aware of that," Lucille said with a tart twist of her mouth. "I wouldn't let any others accompany you, but I myself have paid for the coach, will pay for any further lodging or expenses, and that means I'm coming with you. I don't care to argue about it any further."

Ella organized her next argument, but then she saw the stubborn glint in Lucille's eyes and recognized that she might as well save her breath. "What of Zeke and Jenny?"

"It's best that Zeke stay here with Jenny. Susannah has already hired guards for the inn and she's planning to have them stay on." Lucille peered out the door of the study and added, "In truth she's baked so many sweets for them I'm not sure she could beat them off with a stick."

"Well then, I'd best go retrieve my drawings from Mr. Evans," Ella said with a note of resignation.

"Oh no, I've already done that," Jenny told her.

"What? He gave them to *you?*"

"Oh yes, after he quizzed me quite thoroughly to be certain I was who I professed to be. Then he said he'd best save you the time of coming after them, as you might be pressed for time if you were after the patent office straight away."

Jenny started to say something further when the great brass knocker on the front door rapped sharply several times. Lucille rose to investigate and Jenny and Ella heard a brief commotion ensue. Miss Susannah bustled into the study and said to Ella, "There's a Mr. Emerston in the hallway. Says he'd like to speak to you. Shall I show him into the sitting room?"

Ella swallowed and tried not to gag. She and Jenny exchanged a glance. *He's supposed to have left at first light, what is he doing here?* Ella thought. *What might he possibly want now?*

"Yes," she said with an odd squeak in her voice. Then, more normally, she added, "Tell him I'll be right there."

"Shall I come with you?" Jenny asked.

"Yes. Please do."

They made their way to the sitting room. The man across the room, however, was tall and young, with bright yellow hair. It was Lucas. Jenny gave Ella a questioning look. Ella whispered, "You needn't stay." Jenny nodded, inclined her head to Lucas Emerston, then backed out of the room.

There was a long, awkward silence as Ella remained near the door while Lucas loitered by the fire grate across the room. He turned and paced in front of the hearth a few times, and Ella could not help but watch his lithe, liquid movements. She hadn't seen him since last summer, nearly a year ago now, and she was disgusted with herself as her heart began hammering. He was all gold and cream and radiated that sense of being invincible, something more than a mere person. He stopped walking and, gesturing to the furniture in the center of the room, said, "Might we sit down?"

Ella nodded and moved to perch on a green chintz chair. Lucas sank onto the pink silk sofa. Then he stood. Then he sat again. Finally he said, "I've come to apologize. For my part in this whole business. Which was small, but nevertheless, I... I never wished any harm to come to anyone." He turned to look at Ella directly, his eyes registering distress as he appraised her red eyes and telltale bruises. He swallowed hard. "I even incurred my father's wrath by drawing the plans more poorly than I could have. I wanted no part in his scheme."

Ella turned away from the sculpted planes of his face, the glittering light in his hair, the tawny hazel eyes. She said, "Have you never heard the word 'No'? I hear it's a common word about these parts."

"Ella, look at me, please."

She heard the note of pleading in his voice, but she couldn't look at him. It wouldn't be safe. "Ella, you have to believe me. I had no part in any of this. I had no idea they were keeping you captive, and when I learned of it, quite by accident, I did everything I could to stop him. You don't know him, though. Behind all the airs and manners, he's much like your own father. There's nothing he won't do." He paused, and then, standing, paced a few feet. "That night in the hayloft, when we were children and you told me of your father, of all he did, I had no words to say it then, but all I could think was 'He's no different than my own father. They're all horrible.'"

"It would have helped me if you'd said it," Ella said softly.

He sat once more. "Ella, you must believe it. I've tried every way I can think of to dissuade him, but he only laughs at me. I can't move him. He's obsessed with the machine and the patent for it, and that fellow George Loomis is just as bad. They have some arrangement to share the profits of the venture. You must see I've done what I can."

"Duly noted. You say you've kept your hands clean. Is there anything else?"

He was quiet a minute. Then he reached out a hand to her. She could see it from the corner of her eye, a large, perfectly formed male hand, with gold hairs glinting on the back of it and long, tapered fingers. She felt her stomach betray her, take a leap upward, as if it wanted to reach out for that hand. How many times had she thought of that day back in Deborahville, after the race, when she walked beside him, feeling as if she floated, and how he'd taken her hand in his own. How she'd twisted out of his grip to look at the sketchbook, and what might have been different if she hadn't done that, had just kept on walking hand in hand. And now, here it was, his hand once again, and she could no more take it than she could, well . . . take his father's hand. They were the same to her. Everything that had been fresh and lovely that day was now sacked and sullied. Especially her. His father had seen to that. A swell of nausea displaced the fluttering in her middle.

She stood and said, "Goodbye, Lucas." Then she turned away toward the hearth.

She heard him rise and cross the room behind her. She didn't turn as he left, and he didn't say goodbye.

TWENTY-NINE

ELLA WRIGGLED IN HER SEAT as she waited impatiently for the coach to be off. She was wearing one of Lucille's altered gowns with a jacket over it and Lucille had wound up her hair into something resembling a respectable style and tied a hat on top that matched the jacket. *This is a fine disguise*, Ella thought as she squirmed in the close-fitting grey silk jacket. The interior of the coach already felt close and hot, with too many bodies in too little space. She could smell the horses through the front window, but only as a faint scent beneath the heavy cloy of perfume wafting from the other passengers.

The coach would take them through the night to Wilmington, after which they'd stop to trade horses and refresh themselves. They'd reach Baltimore by the next evening, where they'd sojourn at a tavern overnight before riding into the new capital on Saturday morning. Ella fought down her impatience at the long journey and at having to wait until Monday to learn whether Emerston would have somehow achieved his object ahead of her, despite Lucille's confidence in her horse-delaying tactics.

She forced herself to turn her mind from these pointless worries and focus instead on what she'd say to Dr. Thornton, the Superintendent of Patents, in arguing her case for owner-ship. She knew she'd have only one chance to make her case and it would require that she speak as clearly and persuasively as possible. But she wasn't any good with words. Not anything like Emerston, that master of persuasion, who always seemed to say just the right thing in just the right tone. She feared she'd botch this last important piece and he'd walk away with the prize. That in the end it would come down to a war of words, having little or nothing to do with the truth of the mat-ter, the invention itself, or the many years spent working on the design.

Lucille, sitting beside her on the seat of the coach, watched as she fretted. At last she asked, "Perhaps I might be of assis-tance with your troubles?"

Ella turned to Lucille, annoyed that her own face had so clearly revealed her state of mind. But she saw in Lucille's expression the same genuine concern she'd seen since the night she'd escaped from captivity. She considered the matter. Was Lucille any better with words than she was? She didn't think of Lucille as an orator, but then again, Lucille was as sharp as anyone she knew and had knowledge of worldly matters well beyond her own experience. She decided she had little to lose by confiding in her.

She took a deep breath and in a quiet voice told Lucille of her worries. When she had finished, Lucille was quiet for a time and then said, "You're quite right to be planning for the worst, for I'm afraid there's more to this matter than pure business. I went to speak to Emerston while you were imprisoned and I was shocked by the things he told me. It seems he's determined not only to win the contest, but also to diminish his opponents in the process—and he sees us both as his opponents. For, as odd as it sounds, it appears he has a rather remarkable capacity for vengeance. He's been harboring the intention to avenge what he sees as the wrong I did him many years ago, when I rejected his suit for marriage. He appears to have been planning my demise ever since."

Ella's eyes snapped to Lucille's face. Lucille waved a gloved hand, as if to dismiss the matter, but her attempt at appearing blasé was undermined by the tight twist of her lips. "All the while," she added, "posing as my lawyer and friend."

Ella digested this startling news. "That's rather a long time to hold such a grudge, and to hide it. Are you certain that's the root of his actions, Aunt?"

Lucille gave her a sharp look. "Don't be as much of a fool as I've been, Ella. I've suspected Emerston at times of not being what he seems, but always it's been convenient to ignore or deny my suspicions. When I went to see him about your disappearance, he at last dropped all his pretense and said exactly what he'd intended to say for all these years—that he intends to ruin me, and that you are among his means to accomplish that. He chose not to hide anything because he knew whatever he said would be his word against mine and he intends to make certain my word is worth nothing. Or less than nothing."

Ella studied the woman beside her. "I don't think I understand, Aunt. What does this patent business have to do with you? How would it ruin you if I were to fail to get the patent?"

It was Lucille's turn to take a deep breath. Ella could see she wrestled with what she wished to say. Nearby two women were discussing the difficulty of finding honest servants and two men across the seat were speaking loudly of whether President Madison would ever lift the current trade embargo. Ella's attention was drawn to their conversation when her aunt remained silent over several minutes, until suddenly Lucille began to speak in a slow, purposeful manner.

"Yes, it has to do with me because, well… I have an investment in your affairs beyond what you know. You are…well…"

She paused and the said in a hurried whisper. "Because you are my daughter. Or rather, I'm your mother." She stole a look around the coach to see if anyone had heard what she'd said, but no one appeared to take any notice.

Not until Ella said loudly, "You're my *what?*" Then everyone paused mid-sentence and stared at them. Lucille stared back, a deep flush creeping over her face. "Go about your business, please," she said at last. "Nothing here that concerns you." She continued glaring until they'd resumed their conversations.

Ella whispered, "Did you just say what I thought you said?"

"That I'm your mother? Yes, I did. And yes, I am. I gave you to Catherine to raise, but you were born to me."

Ella raised her brows to say, "Go on," but Lucille shook her head.

"There's much more to it, of course, but this is not the place to discuss all that. Let's sort out the patent business first. I told you of being your mother because it explains why Emerston is so determined not to lose. If you were to win, then I as your mother would also win. For him to destroy us is a coup that puts each of us in our proper place, while also establishing him as an important man throughout the country and making piles of money at the same time. It's everything he could ever want."

Ella nodded slowly, scowling. "How does Emerston even know of this business of my birth? Who else knows?"

Lucille also frowned. "I'm afraid most everyone knows, as of this past spring when, out of nowhere, Amherst announced it at the tavern." Lucille sighed. "I suppose it wasn't utterly out of nowhere, as he'd been growing steadily more angry at me. It was his way of smearing my reputation."

Ella gazed steadily at Lucille. "I suppose he too was harboring a twenty-year grudge at your failure to marry him?"

"No, don't be ridiculous. Amherst could hardly remember a thing that happened twenty years ago. In fact I was surprised he remembered you weren't Catherine's child, given how drink had addled his mind."

"So what angered him?"

Lucille looked down at her hands, seeming to struggle with how to answer. At last she whispered, "I might as well tell you, he was angry at me because he wanted a share of profits from what he perceived to be a lucrative counterfeit bank-note arrangement. But of course he understood very little of the business."

"And was it?" Ella asked, arching one brow. "Lucrative, I mean."

"Not the way Amherst thought it might be." Lucille waved a dismissive hand once more. The tall feathers on her turban bobbed and brushed the top of the coach. "In truth I have been only a very small player in what is a much bigger business that I know little about."

Ella stared at Lucille yet again, attempting to sort out what she'd just heard. *Who is this woman?* She thought, *She's been nearby all my life, but clearly she has a penchant for harboring secrets. What does she really want? Why are these men so angry with her?* A further swirl of questions flooded her mind, but only one statement that seemed worth uttering. "So everyone knows, then, of my...birth, except me. Is that correct?"

Lucille looked her in the eye. "Yes, everyone who was in Deborahville at the time Amherst announced it. Only you and Jenny and Zeke weren't there to hear, and I didn't want you to hear from Emerston or anyone else. That's why I rushed down here. This is the first opportunity I've had to...well, say it."

Ella turned away to the window of the coach. Her mind refused to absorb all the implications of what she'd just heard. All she could think was, *They all know.* At last another thought pierced her mind: that it would be to Emerston's benefit for her to grow distracted by this news and fail to focus on the patent. Her mind raced with all the questions she burned to ask, but she forced them down and instead turned back to Lucille to say, "Let's talk about what I need to say at the patent office."

Lucille started at the abrupt tone but then gave a curt nod. "Good. Let's look at the points you'll want to make about it."

BY THE TIME THEY GOT OFF THE COACH to stretch their legs somewhere in Delaware, Ella had a list of points they'd rewritten several times and that she'd committed to memory in the process. They still had more work to do, but she was lightened of her burden, for she began to feel prepared for whatever arguments she'd need to make. Lucille had told her what Janet had reported, of Lucas buying drawing paper all winter. Which meant the set of drawings Emerston had in hand was done from memory, by a less accomplished draughtsman, and one who recently confessed to doing an intentionally poor job. Those sketches could not begin to match up to the set she clutched to her side in the oilcloth tube Oliver Evans had protected for her.

They spent an uncomfortable night at the tavern in Baltimore and then crowded back into the coach in the morning for the last few hours of the journey. Along the way they continued to hone their arguments, attempting to speculate on whatever Emerston might use in rebuttal. At last they alit at the stage landing in Washington City, where Lucille wasted no time procuring fresh directions to the Office of Patents and a tavern nearby to it.

Leaving the landing, they were startled by the stark contrast to Philadelphia. Where Philadelphia was thickly settled and prosperous, sporting paved streets, lush trees, and wrought-iron lantern posts, this city appeared raw and new. In fact it still seemed part of the countryside. Plain dirt tracks served for streets, more like those of a frontier town than a city. Along the muddy tracks new brick mansions intermingled with half-completed wooden houses, all of them with barren dirt yards. Where the government buildings were sited, wide expanses of bright green grass stretched between the structures, dwarfing the ornate edifices into toys on a lawn.

Soon they came into sight of the new Capitol building. Sitting alone amidst green fields, the new Capitol was a white, flat-topped building in the Greek style, with sweeping arches over tall windows. The gracious lines were marred only by the staging and workmen on the unfinished sections.

They had little difficulty finding the tavern they sought, where Lucille requested a room and paid for it in crisp new notes. When they stepped back onto the street after stowing their luggage, Ella gave Lucille an appraising glance. "If you're my mother, as you say, I think you'd best tell me more of the money."

Lucille sighed. "I'm afraid it's also part of the way Emerston means to ruin me. Despite that I let Janet convince me to get out of the business."

Ella cocked a brow. "What was her reasoning?"

"Oh, the usual—that it's best to get out before getting caught. The same reasoning I might have used myself if I wasn't such a perfect fool." She gestured to make light of what she'd just said, but Ella saw the truth in her light words. Lucille was shaken by recent events. After walking a little farther, Lucille said, "Despite her humble appearance, Janet's as shrewd a businesswoman as I know. In fact, these notes I'm using are not my own, but hers. She saved them back for an emergency and gave them to me to ease this journey."

"I thought you were out of the business."

"We are, but well, it's prudent to keep a nest egg. I'm afraid Janet did a better job of it than I did. I was cocky and thought I'd stay in the business longer. But now I've got the worst of it. I no longer have the income and Emerston is likely to expose me to the town. Given what they already know of your birth, and what they suspect of Pete, what wouldn't they believe of me?"

Ella appraised her again. "You've got yourself in a right pickle, haven't you? But it's no matter, except that you care so much for being respectable. If you'd leave it off, you'd be much the better for it."

Lucille grimaced, conceding that Ella might be right but she could hardly follow the advice. After a time she said, "Perhaps we'll sort it out after we've sorted this patent business."

THEY SPENT A QUIET SUNDAY exploring the city, at least until it grew too hot to be on the streets. They retreated to the shade of the tavern courtyard, where they went over their arguments until Ella had them perfect in her mind. She could not help feeling anxious about what they'd find when they got to the Office of Patents, but there was little to be done for it in the meantime.

Lucille's abrupt revelation of motherhood still sat intrusively between them, but neither seemed willing to broach the topic. Every time a question would jump to her tongue, Ella would abruptly bite it back. It felt dangerous to speak of all those years of lies and half-truths. The years when Lucille had been cold and disapproving, had made her feel useless and inadequate. No, best to leave it alone when she sorely needed Lucille as an ally. Instead she asked of Jimson, Pete, and other news of Deborahville.

That evening they had a light supper and went to bed early. They rose with first light on Monday morning and after a quick meal they strode up the dusty dirt road to the new patent office a full hour before it was to open at eight o'clock.

Sited on a small hill at the edge of the city, the new three-story building, surrounded by trees was, like most of the other buildings, still under construction. It was missing ornament at the peak of the pediment and along the tops of the six decorative stone pillars.

Ella clutched the sleeve with her drawings and papers tight to her side as they stood in front of the building, assuring themselves they would be first to greet Dr. Thornton, the Superintendent of Patents. At seven-thirty three laborers arrived and began to prepare the staging used to reach the exterior heights of the building. The workmen nodded cordially but seemed unsurprised at their appearance.

"I imagine they have people like us waiting here all the time," Ella said. "Inventors toting models and papers." Lucille nodded agreement.

Eight o'clock came and went and no one appeared to open the door of the building.

At 8:30 a young clerk hurried up carrying an untidy sheaf of papers and, without looking at them, pulled out a key and prepared to unlock the door.

Lucille said, "Pardon me, young man, but can you tell us of the Superintendent? Wasn't he expected here at eight o'clock?"

The clerk turned to her with a look of pure exasperation. "Dr. Thornton has been called away to consult on a point of architecture with respect to the new Capitol building. He'll be here whenever they've finished with him."

"Bu how can that be?" Lucille asked haughtily. "Is he not the Superintendent of Patents?"

The clerk stowed the key back in his pocket and ran a harried hand through his hair. "I only know that when Mr. Latrobe sends for him, he leaves right away. President Madison would be displeased if he did not."

"But what does the Superintendent of Patents have to do with the Capitol building?" Lucille pressed.

The clerk eyed her with profound disapproval. "He *designed* the Capitol building, Mistress. His model was chosen by Presidents Washington and Jefferson, despite that he was never an architect by profession. Now if you don't mind, ladies…" He pushed his way through the door and shut it firmly behind him.

Lucille and Ella looked at one another. "That's an odd business," Lucille said thoughtfully. "They must have rather a shortage of architects in this city if they have to use the Superintendent of Patents to design the Capitol."

"I don't know," Ella said. "Couldn't it be that he's a man of many talents? Perhaps his vision was the more elegant for not being hampered by long practice?"

"That seems rather a fanciful notion."

"Why should it? If anything, it's more true of designing buildings than designing machines. The point is that an original idea is of more value than all the experience in the world, since knowing how to build what's already been built only makes you more likely to design one much the same. A fresh set of eyes may be the best means to get a fresh idea."

"That may be," Lucille conceded, "but a fresh idea with no experience of things may be utterly impractical, impossible to build, or destined to be of poor quality."

"Yes, that's so, but this is where the marriage of an inventor and an engineer come into play. The inventor has the vision, the engineer makes the pieces fit together in the proper order to be of sound structure." Ella's eyes sparkled as she warmed to the topic.

"What are you, then?" Lucille asked. "An inventor or engineer?"

The spark drained from Ella's eyes. She shrugged. "I used to think I was some of both. But now… I don't know."

Lucille studied Ella's face as Ella kept her eyes downcast and her expression blank. At last Lucille said, "You've already proven you have much of both. No need for modesty now."

After a moment Ella said, "It might be too late in any case. If by some chance Emerston made superb time getting here, or was able to bribe or talk to this Dr. Thornton outside of business hours, it might all be for naught. He might have convinced this Thornton to issue the patent immediately—possibly even paying him for it. It might all be sealed already."

"Or it might not. Why look at the worst possibility? There's no way to know until we ask about it ourselves, so we might as well wait here until this Dr. Thornton sees fit to come open the office. We can only hope he's an honest man and will see reason."

"Reason...as in who has the greater claim to it?"

"Yes. That's what I meant. What else would I mean?"

When Ella didn't answer, Lucille said, "I see. You were wondering if I meant 'see reason' as a euphemism for 'allow us to pay him more for it.' That's rather insulting, my dear."

"I'm afraid I'm not as knowledgeable as I should be about the ethics among counterfeiters."

Lucille looked stung. She took a deep breath. "I suppose I deserve that."

"No, you don't. I'm sorry. It was horrible of me." Ella studied Lucille, then said, "I realize I don't know you as well as I once thought I did. I think I'm asking you to tell me what you would and wouldn't do, because it seems I should know, and I don't."

Lucille opened her mouth to say something, then closed it quickly. Ella could see she was fighting down the impulse to make a sharp retort, to sting as she'd been stung. At last Lucille said, "I can see how it must look to you. I've always been selfish, I suppose. I'm learning what that costs."

"No, you haven't always been selfish. You were always good to my mother. I mean...to Catherine. And to Jimson and Jenny."

Lucille shrugged. "Possibly. I had my reasons. They weren't always pure. In any case it's all different now."

Ella gazed at her. "I can't seem to make sense of all the pieces. You're a sharp businesswoman, with or without your criminal tendencies, but yet you let Emerston make a puppet of you." She watched Lucille's face and saw the statement bring pain to her eyes. Again she saw her swallow the retort that sprang to her lips.

Instead Lucille said, "I make no pretense of it; I am a vain and stupid woman. I trust where I shouldn't because I hear what I wish to hear."

"But yet Pete loves and trusts you. And I myself have benefited from the many loyal friends you seem to have cultivated. It's a puzzle of sorts."

"Perhaps. Or perhaps we're all a viscous brew of cross-purpose traits. All inventors and engineers, patent officers and architects."

"Work-horses and thoroughbreds," Ella said with a mild grin.

"All at once."

"Yes, all at once."

They waited another fifteen minutes outside the locked door of the office and then moved farther into the shade around the corner of the building to escape the brutal sun. Even at this early hour the city was already beginning to bake. "I had no idea it was so warm down here," Ella said.

"This is what New Orleans was like. When I was a girl we used to—" Lucille was prevented from saying more by Ella's hand on her arm.

"Shhh. Look."

They peered around the corner of the building as two men appeared as small figures in the distance, still several hundred yards away but walking with purpose toward the Office of Patents. "That's Emerston," Lucille whispered. "Who's the other one—? Oh. Oh no..."

"Yes, it's Loomis," Ella whispered back.

"What's *he* doing here?"

"I have no idea."

They watched another moment. Then Ella felt Lucille give a jolt of sorts beside her. "Let's go before they see us," Lucille said, pulling Ella backward by the elbow.

"Stop that." Ella pulled her arm out of Lucille's grip. "We're not going anywhere."

Ella sounded confident, but inside her nerves began an arrhythmic jangle. Was Loomis here to exact retribution for what she'd done to Dennison? And did he yet hold a grudge from when she'd stolen back Dapper Dan all those months ago in that little town? She watched them growing closer. She'd expected to face Emerston, but she'd expected to do it in the Patent Office, under the eye of the Superintendent. What will it mean to face him outside here, with George Loomis as his ally, before anything was resolved?

She willed herself to take a deep breath and tamp down her nerves so she could think clearly. What would he want from her? How would he try to gain it? The only thing of which she could be certain was that Emerston would try to use his wiles before anything else, which meant she had a chance to beat him at his game. After a moment, she pulled farther back into the shadow of the building and drew the strap of the oilcloth tube off her shoulder. "I need to fix something," she told Lucille. "Keep watching and tell me if you can see anything more."

After a few minutes, Lucille said in a shaky whisper, "They're nearly here,"

In another moment Ella settled the tube back on her shoulder and moved to take Lucille's elbow. "Let's say hello, then. But you'll let me speak, won't you?" Lucille nodded. They looked at one another and each took a deep breath. Then they stepped out to greet the two men.

Both men smiled as they recognized them. Bright, warm smiles with no hesitation at all.

"Good morning, Miss Kenyon, Mrs. Tunnicliff," Emerston said. "What a pleasant surprise this is, finding you here in this strange land."

Ella's smile was more of a smirk, but she replied, "Yes, quite a pleasant surprise. I trust you are both in good health?"

They exchanged small pleasantries for several more minutes. Then Emerston surprised her by saying, "You know, Miss Kenyon, I've had an idea that is being rather a nuisance, for it refuses to go away." He paused to meet her eye. "I'm not at all certain it's a good idea, but it seems to wish to be heard."

"Do go on," she said.

"Here, let us have a seat of sorts." He gestured across the yard toward a makeshift bench of paving stones that someone had erected beneath a tree. They walked to the tree and he gestured Ella to take a seat beside him, while Lucille perched on the other side of her. George Loomis lounged against the tree behind them, still smiling as if he were greatly enjoying himself. Ella noticed they were now out of sight of the laborers at the front of the building and she considered suggesting they return to the doorway.

Before she could do so, Emerston fixed her with a measured look and said, "It would be best, would it not, to speak frankly? I feel certain you must be growing as weary as I am of all this... this warring over the patent. The thought that keeps returning is that we might each benefit in putting both our names on the application and then sharing both the work and the rewards of the business. I dislike to share rewards of course, but the businessman in me sees that you have skills I lack and, with all due respect, I believe the reverse to be true as well."

Ella cocked her head to indicate he should continue.

"I would manage the business end, of course. That is, the issuing of licenses and the investigation of infringement. You, my dear, would be spared all that and might instead spend your time assisting licensees to build and operate their new machines. You might also build and sell your own machines, or simply operate one or two in a milling business. You'd have numerous options, all of which would be profitable and none of which would entail an excess of the correspondence you dislike."

Ella studied him, her mind reeling with the simple elegance of the plan he'd suggested. In a certain sense it was the perfect solution to their dispute, applying their varying skills and then sharing the license fees. Might she have proposed something like this early on and avoided the full dispute? But then she thought, *No, you idiot! It's a ruse. What kind of fool would I be to trust him again? And how could I partner with him, who has attempted to steal the whole patent, who took part in imprisoning me to extract the better drawings?*

She managed to keep her face unreadable and Emerston's expression similarly didn't change as he watched her consider the matter. At last she said, "You present an attractive proposition, one I feel certain would be of mutual benefit. My only modification to the proposal would be that the patent application be made in my name as the sole inventor. The division of labor and reward would be just as you outlined, with the reward divided equally between us. I'll sign a legal agreement saying as much at any time you draw it up. Right now, if you like."

Emerston considered her offer with his eyes on her face. Then with a wry expression he said, "Nicely done. I applaud you. But even if you had any intention of signing such an agreement—which I doubt—no legal document could enforce such a bargain, as federal law assigns license fees to the patent holder and no one else." He paused. "Did you have any intention of *trying* the arrangement?"

Ella gave a hint of a chuckle. "With the man who had me kidnapped and beaten? No. I hardly think so. And neither did you. You told Lucille you intended to destroy us both; I have no doubt you will do your best to attain that goal."

"She told you that?" Emerston sounded surprised. "And you believed her?" He looked between them both. "Really, my dear," he said to Ella, "you must be more careful what you believe of what Mrs. Tunnicliff says. She'll say nearly anything to garner your sympathy, or whatever else she might be after at the moment. She's quite persuasive."

Ella turned to Lucille, whose eyes had grown hard. Lucille shook her head in denial but kept an impressive lock on her tongue. Ella turned back and considered Emerston. "I suppose it was Lucille who wrote those documents I found in your desk? The application papers with your name alone. Or did she merely *persuade* you to write them?"

Emerston shook his head. "No, my dear. I wrote those papers, but they were never what you thought they were. As I told Mrs. Tunnicliff, what you found were merely drafts in which I was working out the language of the application and didn't bother to fill in the names properly. If you'd taken the time to look at them more closely, you'd have seen that they were hardly completed application documents."

Ella entertained a flash of doubt. Could it be remotely possible she *had* made a mistake about the papers? But no, her grandfather and Lucille and Lucas had all confirmed his ill intentions—there was no room for doubt. But his skill was truly remarkable, for something in his manner and words made you *wish* to believe him.

"And locking me up in that vile hole, with that . . . that beast of man? I suppose that was all a misunderstanding as well?"

Emerston looked at Loomis, who gave a rueful shake of his head. Loomis said, "I'm afraid that's my own mistake, miss. I told the boys to find you a safe place to stay for a few days, until we could work out the details of the business with Emerston here. I didn't give them more instruction than that and the boys took it on themselves to handle it as they did. Bixby told me of it after. I suppose I should have given better orders, but you done lamed Dennison full and good for the rest of his life. As I see it, you got your own back for whatever he done to you in there."

Ella felt a surge of nausea press against her ribs. He spoke so carelessly about that which haunted her dreams at night. That which had damaged her. Stolen something of herself she once had held precious. Something long gone and never to return. She forced down the nausea and gave Loomis a cool stare. "No, Mr. Loomis, I did not. By all rights I should have killed him. And I should have done it good and slow. It was a kindness that I let him live."

Loomis shrugged. "Dennison might have had it coming to him, but I don't see it as you do. All you needs know right now is that Emerston here had nothing to do with all that."

"Yes he did," Lucille hissed in Ella's ear, just barely loud enough for Ella to hear.

Emerston shook his head as if he'd heard the whispered words as well. "I'd be careful, my dear," he said to Ella. "Mrs. Tunnicliff is a wily one. She sees the profits to be made with this patent as well as any of us, and she'll do or say anything to have her share in it. I suppose you've heard the story she's been spreading that she's your actual mother?" Ella gave him a sharp look. He continued, "Don't you find it... *suggestive* that this bit of news came to light only when you were poised to file a valuable patent? And when the only person to refute her claim with certainty—Catherine Kenyon—died soon thereafter?" He paused, then went on. "Furthermore have you considered the role our Mrs. Tunnicliff might have played in your father's death? If I were to elaborate on the facts of the matter, you would conclude that Mrs. Tunnicliff most certainly had a hand in it."

Ella's thoughts swirled into confusion. What was to be believed? Could it be Lucille who was really out to ruin Emerston, not the other way around? And what did he imply about

Amherst's death? She thought of all the years Lucille would hardly speak to her. How could a mother treat a child that way? What had it meant? Then she thought of the way Lucille's manner had changed toward her once she'd solved the puzzle of the invention. Had that been about trying to get a piece of impending success? And then again, Lucille and Emerston had been in league over counterfeit notes all these years. Who was to say they weren't still in league? Perhaps they'd even staged all this today so together they could share the profits of the patent. Were they playing her as a fool?

Her mind spun and she could do nothing to rein it in, to make her thoughts take shape. She closed her eyes and shook her head to clear it. When she opened them she saw Emerston staring at her, waiting to see what she'd do. She stared back into his dark brown eyes, seeking for the warmth that might make truth of his words. When she didn't say anything, Emerston exchanged a glance with Loomis, after which Loomis moved quick as a snake and grabbed Lucille from the end of the bench and stood her in front of him, the tip of his knife peeking up from the fist he held to her throat. Ella and Emerston both sprang to their feet and stepped away from the bench.

Could this be part of their game? Ella wondered furiously. *Staging an attack on Lucille to make me believe they aren't all in league together?* Perhaps she should just walk away. Go stand with the workmen until the Superintendent arrived. Then she could make her application and be done. Let them kill Lucille if they liked. Not that they were likely to do so if they were all play-acting at this.

Then she looked at Lucille, looked into her eyes, and saw something that surprised her: Lucille's eyes showed a genuine terror. She wasn't playing a game but was truly afraid. Then she remembered Pete's words, telling her that Lucille saw her as family and would help her if she could. She had a flash of

Lucille bathing her in Miss Susannah's kitchen, scrubbing her skin with a brush and stroking the soap out of her hair. Could Lucille have done all that if she were out to trick her, steal from her? No, it was only Emerston again, employing his golden tongue to twist everything around so the light would shine favorably upon him.

She turned to Emerston. "I suppose you're going to tell me I'm misunderstanding this as well? That really the nice Mr. Loomis here is, perhaps...protecting poor Aunt Lucille there? Is that what I'm to believe?"

Emerston laughed, a cold, hard chuckle. "If you're willing to believe that, I'll let you, my dear. But really, I grow weary of all this. Kindly give me your drawings. When you've done so, nice Mr. Loomis here will *cease* protecting poor Aunt Lucille. I'll go make the application and we can all go home and get on with things."

Ella looked at him, then at Loomis and Lucille, and then she slid the strap of the oilcloth tube off her shoulder. She didn't let it show in her eyes that far down the road, behind Emerston, she'd spotted someone heading up the hill toward the patent office who could well be the Superintendent.

She pretended to fumble in nervous fear as she opened the top of the tube that held her papers. Then, in one fluid flash, she let the knife slip into her palm, twisted to face Loomis, and threw it hard and fast into the fist that held a knife to Lucille's throat. Loomis and Lucille both shouted, for the knife in his hand grazed Lucille's skin as he was hit, but Lucille was able to slip from his grasp as his hand became useless for holding her. He stared at the knife hilt sprouting from the back of his hand, the bloom of nearly black blood seeping from around the blade, and then, with a grunt, yanked it out. He turned a murderous look toward Ella and it was plain he intended to throw it right back. But she was holding another of her own by now and she said, "I have much the better aim, so I suggest we call a truce. Your hand will heal perfectly well, as I didn't intend to maim you."

She pulled Lucille close to her and they all four eyed one another, breathing heavily. Ella said, "I do believe I see the Superintendent coming to open the office at last. We'll be going, then. Gentlemen . . . " She took a step toward the Office of Patents.

"Not so fast," Emerston said sharply. "I had hoped not to resort to any of this, but as you should have learned by now, I always have an alternative plan. In this case it's rather a drastic one, but I'm certain you'll appreciate the effective simplicity of it." He arched an eyebrow at Ella, who was letting her disgust show plainly on her face. Emerston said quietly, "I have left instructions with Lorenzo Bixby and Loomis' brother Willard that if we do not return with the patent by the evening after next, they are to waste no time in making certain your sister Jenny will *not* be there to greet you upon your return. And no more nicety nice. She'll greet the bottom of the river and no one else. And if I manage to return in time to assist, I'll make certain she's fully awake when we tie the stones to her boots."

He spoke in a pleasant tone, but there was no yield to his voice; it was pure flint. Ella knew with a chill that he was capable of doing just as he said. The guards they'd left at the inn would be no match for this kind of determined assault. She'd grown wary enough of his wiles to realize he may or may not have left such instructions behind him, but that if he himself returned to Philadelphia without the patent, he might see the threat carried through, out of pure vengeance for having been bested.

Rapidly she considered her options. If she made the patent application, she could then try to buy a horse and race him back to Philadelphia. Could she get there in time? How much head start would he have? At least several hours if she had to make the application and then buy a horse. And of course she could be delayed by all manner of things. Could she get a message there faster, telling Zeke to whisk them away to safety? Was there a post that fast? No. If she didn't give him the drawings, he could mount and ride back immediately. There was no post that would get there anywhere near as fast.

But she was *so close*. Here she was, standing a few mere yards from the door of the office, holding everything she needed to secure the patent for herself and her grandfather. For the whole family. The family. She remembered the night in the Pines, when she'd been buried by snow as she slept and had dreamt of the empty farmhouse. How terrifying all that emptiness had seemed. How she had looked and looked for Jenny and Jimson and not found them anywhere. Then she thought of Jenny now, sitting in Miss Susannah's sitting room, undoubtedly worrying every minute over what might be happening down here. She'd never think for a moment to be cautious for herself.

What would it be like to ride the coach back with the patent in her hand, wondering every minute what she'd find when she got there? Whether Jenny would be sitting safely in the sitting room or whether the house would be in an uproar. Or, even worse, completely empty.

She thought of the hours she'd spent by Jenny's sickbed in Martha, willing her to heal. To be whole. What would the rest of her own life be like if something were done to Jenny and she were the cause of it? If they were to pull Jenny's body from the river? What would the patent mean then? And if he didn't do it now, would she ever stop looking over her shoulder, wondering when and how he might strike at her? Or her family?

No. There was no real choice here. He'd known she would yield. Knew she was soft. He'd known all along he would win, one way or another. He might have preferred to win by wit than by threat, but either way he wouldn't lose. She slipped the oilcloth tube from her shoulder once more.

Lucille said, "No! You can't. Not now, not when we're so close."

"There's no choice," Ella said. Then she handed the entire tube of papers to Emerston. "Enjoy your victory. I hope it's as sweet as you think it will be."

"I have no doubt of that, my dear."

Loomis came toward her. He'd wrapped his hand in a strip of cloth from his shirt and was holding it close to his body. Remarkably, his face had regained much of its good humor. He said, "Pity things had to turn out this way. I had many a good laugh over you and that boy riding off that horse from underneath my seat—that was mighty good sport. Been thinking I may have to try it myself some time." He rubbed his silky black beard with his uninjured hand. Then he clapped it on Ella's shoulder. "If you ever find yourself up near Sangerfield and in need of some work, don't fail to come see me. I could always use someone fast with a knife like you." He chuckled, then added, "Though my wife Rhoda may not see it quite like that. And she's even tougher than you. Or meaner at least."

"You haven't seen me be mean yet," Ella said mildly. "I've been on my best behavior today."

THIRTY

"**P**ASS THE PITCHER, PLEASE," Jenny said softly.

Ella handed it to her sister in silence. They were alone at the breakfast table at Miss Susannah's. After they'd eaten a few minutes, Jenny said, "You've got to stop blaming yourself. It's pointless. You had no way to know whether he would carry out the threat or not. It doesn't mean you were weak."

Ella ate a few more bites before replying. "I try to remind myself of how bitter it's made Oliver Evans, all these years of defending his patent rights, and that the same fate might have awaited me. That it might await Emerston himself. That part makes me feel better." She took another bite then put down her fork. "It's not Emerston I mind— he'll never be satisfied with whatever he's got, and he doesn't have nearly as much as he thinks he should. No, it's Grandfather I feel most badly about. When I think of returning there and telling him what happened, my stomach clenches up in shame. He was so excited to think we would finally get that patent. I know he'll understand—he was the one who warned me Emerston was much worse than anyone knew—but still, he'll be so disappointed. And he has so little time now."

"You don't think he'll understand the choice you were forced to make? Between the machine and family?"

Ella closed her eyes a moment, then opened them. "You're right, of course. It was the same choice he made himself, in a way. Leaving the machine behind when he left."

"Are you going to tell me why he left?" Jenny asked softly after a pause.

"No," Ella said just as softly, "I'm not. I didn't want to hear it myself and it won't do you any good to hear it either."

"Perhaps some day you'll stop protecting me as you do."

"Perhaps." Ella winked at her sister. "But perhaps not."

ELLA WAS ALONE WITH A BOOK, hiding in a deep chair in the corner of the study when Lucille strode in and pulled a chair near to hers. Lucille peered into her face with her sharp blue eyes and asked, "What will you do now?"

Ella sighed and sat up straighter. "Come right to the point, why don't you? No need to tiptoe around what you mean." When Lucille just continued to stare at her, waiting, Ella sighed again and said, "I suppose I'll go back to Deborahville. Stop first in Martha to pick up Dapper Dan and see Grandfather. Then I suppose I must help settle the affairs of the farm and the mill, and then...I don't know."

"That's fine," Lucille said with a tight little nod, "you don't need to know. But regarding the journey home it seems sensible that we depart by ship and travel together as far as Atlantic City. From there you'll have a much shorter journey overland to Martha Furnace than you would if you ferry across the Delaware. You could even take a small riverboat up into the Pines and make better time by water. The rest of us will continue on to Albany and then go overland from there. Do you think Jenny will wish to accompany you?"

Ella nodded. "We haven't spoken of it yet, but she'll likely want to see Grandfather. He's not well, you know."

"Yes, I know." Lucille was quiet a moment. Then she settled farther back in her brocaded chair facing Ella. "I'd rather not speak of it either, but this seems as good a time as any to tell you the rest of the story of your... birth."

Ella composed her face into polite expectation. She was curious of course, but also dreading to hear what Lucille had to tell her, for it was likely to be an ugly, sordid tale. Couldn't they have let Catherine go on being her mother and Lucille her aunt, and leave it at that?

"I was unmarried and with child, and I needed a plan," Lucille began in a flat voice. "I confided in Catherine that I'd been taken by force, intimating it was someone we knew, and then let her work out for herself that the most likely person was Amherst. This was key to convincing her to take you, for she seemed to think she should atone for Amherst's many sins."

Ella lost her polite look and frowned.

"She was with child herself by then and I had many lunatic ideas, including somehow slipping in my child as her own child's twin. But of course I didn't know for certain that I'd ask her to take you," Lucille went on in the same flat voice. "Not until you were born and I could see your color, that is. For I was afraid you'd come out red, or some shade I couldn't call white." She paused, not looking at Ella. "For you see, I *was* forced by Amherst. It wasn't a lie. Which meant I knew he'd have to take you if I convinced Catherine of it. The difficulty was that at the time he... forced me, I thought I might be already with child." She paused again, and then added, "With a red child." She waited for Ella to digest this and then glanced up for a brief gauge of the expression on Ella's face. "I wouldn't really know, you see. Who the father was, I mean. Not until you were born. And then, when you were born, I still wasn't certain. You were light enough, but you weren't pure white either. I'm dark enough myself that it could have been my own color you had. I just didn't know..." Her voice broke off.

She looked at Ella again. Ella, shocked by this candid revelation, had made her expression smooth and unreadable and she saw Lucille hesitate. Then, for the first time, Lucille's voice softened. "I was very young. I had no parents to guide me. And I was a plain stupid fool. That's the long and the short of it." She stared at the arm of her chair without seeing it and then, after a pause, continued in a more matter-of-fact tone. "When I began to get a few months along I pleaded a family illness and went for an extended visit to relatives in Massachusetts. I fabricated a husband I'd left behind in Deborahville and told my relatives he couldn't join me due to the demands of business, but that I preferred the superior medical care of the city. In truth I had no idea how I would return with a baby in tow. I had many more mad ideas, even the thought of killing off the fictitious husband by post so as to try for a husband to bring home with me. Then, in a stroke of desperate luck, Catherine wrote by rapid post that her own child had been stillborn. I caught the first coach and trudged back the last few miles in the dark of night to quietly slip you into her arms. And there you stayed, with no one the wiser. Except Amherst, of course, and the midwife, who fortunately moved away west soon after."

After a long silence Ella asked, "So which of them is my father?"

Lucille shook her head slowly, her eyes hooded. "I didn't know, not for a long time. I gave you to Amherst and Catherine because I thought you'd have a better life as their child than as my own bastard child—and I was certain I'd be discovered in time if I kept you, for there were always so many jealous tongues eager to discredit me. Even after I married poor John

Tunnicliff some months later. But I didn't know for certain either way whose child you were. Not until much later, until you'd grown and shown enough of yourself that I became more and more certain you had to be Pete's. You were so like him, you see. So *Indian*. I waited a long time and then at last I told him. Well, in truth, I didn't tell him. I didn't have the courage. I only agreed when he finally said he was certain you were his child. You'd done something that day—something while you were hunting or throwing knives or whatever you did together—that convinced him you had to be Indian, which meant you had to be his daughter. He'd had his suspicions all along, of course. He'd even asked me before, but I'd been able to put him off. That day, though, it was more than I could deny. I confessed at last."

"Then what? What did he say?"

"He said just what I always knew he'd say—that I should marry him and we should take you away from Amherst. He had always wanted to be your father."

"So? Why didn't you?"

"It's just not that simple, Ella. By that time you were grown to fifteen years. How could I up and announce to the world that I'd made a mistake and you were really my child because I'd had an Indian lover all those years, and now, at last, we wanted to be married? He made it sound simple, but it wasn't. We wouldn't have been able to continue living in Deborahville. We'd have had to go west somewhere, live with Indians probably. What white town would ever take us in? I couldn't face that. I'm not like you. How could I spend the rest of my days in a smoky lodge, cooking over an open fire? I wasn't born to that life and I've never wanted it. I couldn't help loving Pete—I had no control over that—but I've never wanted anything but a civilized life. He and I don't belong in the same world. The way we've arranged it is the best we could come up with."

Ella's eyes flashed. "That *you* could come up with, you mean. It doesn't sound like he had much say in it."

Lucille's eyes snapped back. "He could have left for good, couldn't he? Just gone off on one of his trips and never returned. There was nothing to hold him." Then, in a softer voice, she added, "It was what I always dreaded. And he was much of the reason I stayed in Deborahville, after all—to see him whenever he cared to return." She continued more loudly. "You should also know that the day he finally learned he was your father was the same day the horse thieves came to your grandfather's stable, and he's always blamed himself for what happened that night. He was upset over the argument we'd had, and distracted—not thinking clearly—and that was how he was knocked senseless before your grandfather killed that man. He thinks he should have prevented it."

"It was me," Ella said softly. Then, when Lucille gave her a quizzical look, she added, "It was me who threw the knife that killed that man, not my grandfather."

Lucille gave her a piercing look. "Did Pete know that? That you threw the knife?"

Ella thought back over the events of that night, how Pete had turned to see the man fall just before he'd fallen himself. Pete would have automatically registered the direction from which the knife had been thrown. He'd have known. "Yes," she said. "Maybe not at the exact moment, but later, he would have worked it out."

"Well he was determined to protect you then, for he's always maintained it was your grandfather who threw it."

"Is that surprising?"

"Yes," Lucille said with a trace of bitterness. "It is to me. It means he was protecting you even from me. I thought he would have told me the truth."

"Why would you think that?" Ella asked with a sudden harshness as the anger welled up in her. "When you were the one who gave away his child? Gave his child to the most brutal man in town and would let him do nothing to stop it."

Lucille looked at her, her eyes neither angry nor pleading. She said, "I gave you to Amherst and Catherine because I was certain you'd have a better life as a lawful white child than as a bastard half-blood. And I had no way to know at the time whether you were Pete's or Amherst's. Why is that wrong?"

Ella looked at Lucille, her gaze steady. She tried to collect the thoughts that were flapping around her mind. At last she said, "You knew what Amherst was. You should have known that even life as a bastard child would be better than that."

Lucille looked down at her feet. In a soft voice she said, "I did what I thought was best at the time—to protect you. And much that you'll never know. I had no way to know what you'd grow to be, what choice you would have made for yourself. I could only do what seemed the right choice at the time."

Ella struggled with herself. She wanted only to say, "It wasn't enough." But she heard Jenny's voice in her mind, knew Jenny would tell her to be kind. "It's done now," was what she said at last. It was the best she could do. She felt another question well up. "If it's as you say and you did what you thought best, why did you treat me so ill all those years I was young?"

Lucille turned away, her eyes scanning the room as she ran a hand along the brocade side of her chair. "I'm not proud of my behavior. I found it very difficult to behave as a loving aunt for I feared letting my guard down. It was easier to remain distant than try to strike a balance of being close but not too close. It had been easier when Baby Gabriel was with me, for I had him to love. When he was gone and you were all I had left of children, I feared I would melt if I let myself near you. But I did what I could to protect you." Lucille paused, taking a deep breath and looking away before continuing. "The gold watch I gave you was intended as a talisman of sorts. A means to remind Amherst you were under my eye, that I was watching him. To stay away from you." She paused again and, for the first time, her voice wavered when she spoke. "My own mother gave it to me when she sent me up north to live with relatives I'd never met. She gave it to me for protection, and I gave it to you. That was why I was always asking about it. I wanted to make sure you had it near you." She turned her eyes back and Ella could see in them the first hint of pleading, for Ella to understand and absolve.

"I didn't," Ella said flatly. "You were so intent on it that I was afraid of losing it. So I hid it someplace no one would find it: in the secret pocket of old Edgar's harness blanket. I never imagined that old mill horse would disappear as he did. It turns out Grandfather Tunnicliff rode away on him."

Lucille stared a long moment, then squinted her eyes in disbelief. "So you never had it after that night—all those years before?" When Ella shook her head, Lucille asked, "So did Captain Tunnicliff find it?"

"No, he never did. He traded the work harness and tack to the Seneca for a more comfortable riding blanket"

"So it's gone, then?"

"I didn't say that." Ella reached into her pocket and removed the watch. It bore many scratches and nicks that hadn't been there when Lucille had last laid eyes on it, but as Ella held it up and twirled it, the engraving of two V's, one upside down over the other, became visible. Lucille drew a sharp breath.

"I think you should take it back," Ella said, reaching it out to her. "You're likely to need protection now as much as I am."

"No, certainly not." Lucille shook her head emphatically and pushed Ella's hand back. "It's good to see it, but I gave it to you and I want you to have it. I like that you carry it with you."

They sat in an awkward silence for a minute. Ella rubbed the watch a few times and put it back in her pocket. Finally she said, "What made you take up with Emerston and Loomis over the bad bank notes?"

Lucille blanched at the abrupt change of topic. "I see I have much to answer for." She sat up straighter and laced her hands together in her lap, appearing more than ever like nobility. "Well, all right. I can't hope to make you understand, but I suppose I must try. And for that I'll have to go back a bit, and you'll have to be patient for a moment. You see, I spent my early years as a pampered child in New Orleans. I can't tell you much of my father, for he was rarely around, but my mother, well, she was the most beautiful creature I ever saw, and she doted on me. She taught me of true elegance, of how to appreciate the delicate things in life. We were happy, she and I, until she grew ill when I was in my thirteenth year. Before the year was out she'd arranged to send me north to live with my aunt and uncle in Deborahville because she had no one else to trust with my care. I tried to ask why my father couldn't care for me, but she put me off and I never did learn the reason. I expect it was a similar case of bastardy."

Lucille looked down at her hands and then back up at Ella. "It was most difficult to leave all the gentle ways I knew and move to a rough town on the frontier. But I eventually adjusted to it and was happy enough for a time. Then, when my aunt and uncle died, and then my husband, and then my baby was taken...well, it grew almost too difficult to bear. Not least of which was that I had no income to speak of. I scraped by for quite a while, but it was a miserable miserly life. I hated it, and in the dictates of my southern upbringing I couldn't speak of such vulgar matters to anyone else. Which was almost the worst of it."

Lucille paused and took a deep breath. "So then, when Loomis and Emerston proposed that I help them the one time, making an excursion to Albany to shop using new bank notes and return home with the change, well, I wish I could say I refused them immediately, but in truth I couldn't really see who it hurt. There are never enough notes and what difference does it make if they're printed by one bank or another or the koniakers up in Canada? Anyhow, that one time was so successful that it turned into another, and then another. That's all there is to it. We had a schedule and I did as I was told. I learned to make the secret sign but—"

"There's a secret sign?" Ella interrupted. "Can you show it to me?"

"Oh yes. There's a sign. Mostly for a means to recognize other members of the network when we exchange notes or messages in unfamiliar cities. I've never thought to divulge it, but now that George Loomis has held a knife to my throat I believe all obligations are voided. Here it is." In a quick flash she made the shape of an upside down "L" with her thumb and index finger and brushed them against her skirt. Ella pursed her lips in an appreciative expression and Lucille went on with her account. "I never wished to know any more than I was told and they were good to me. The income it brought allowed me to build up my stitching business such that I began to take in more than I had before, until at last the pinch eased from my life and I became comfortable once again, for which I am grateful to them both and I'm not ashamed to say it."

She gave Ella a steady look and Ella nodded, understanding as she hadn't before. Ella shifted in her seat. "You were grateful until Emerston announced he intended to ruin you, were you not?"

Lucille looked down at her hands once more, but not before Ella saw the ache wash over her face. Lucille said, "The signs were always there, but I refused to see them. It was my own foolish vanity that refused to believe he'd carry out the threats he made when I refused him marriage, all those years before. That somehow his care for me—or at least his pity—would make him forget all that. It just shows how little I ever knew him, or chose to know him."

"You think he'll be satisfied with gaining the patent, with stealing it from your daughter? Will that really slake his thirst?"

"Oh no," Lucille said with a wry expression. "At long last I've forced myself to think it over with a clear head and I'm quite certain he has more nasty surprises for me. I can't imagine I'll be able to remain in Deborahville, at least not for long. I can only hope his attacks on me won't reach the ears of every client I've ever had. That I'll be able to salvage my business somehow."

"They won't," Ella said quickly, her anger gone in a sudden flush of sympathy. "Or at least his attacks needn't go unanswered. If we put our heads together there will be a means to attack him in return, to give him reason to temper his fervor . You'll see—it won't be that hard. What more do we have left to lose?"

Lucille gave a tight smile. Then, after a moment, it widened into a more genuine one. Her eyes crinkled at the corners and her face grew brighter as she considered the possibilities. "Yes, of course you're right. It's he who has everything to lose now."

Ella chuckled. "Yes, that's the one advantage of losing the game; afterward you have considerably less to risk."

THIRTY-ONE

ZEKE HAD NO TROUBLE finding them berths on a merchant ship going to Albany. He'd become familiar with so many of the stevedores and shipmasters that he knew which ships were coming in and going out daily, and was even able to get them a bargain price on a schooner that didn't normally carry passengers. He himself would work for his passage as one of the crew. He spent the two days before departure helping to ready the ship for sail.

On departure day, Ella, Jenny, and Lucille made their way down the cobbled streets to the landing at dawn. The captain welcomed them aboard and the second mate showed them to the one cabin suitable for passengers, though it was exceedingly small.

The weather had turned mild and warm, such that they quickly dropped their belongings in the small cabin and made their way to the top deck. Zeke passed in his sailor garb and Ella said, "My, they even let you wear the clothes. You look quite authentic."

"He *is* authentic," Jenny said. "He's one of the crew."

"For this trip at least," Ella said. "Let's see if they still want him when they actually have to pay him."

Zeke smiled but otherwise ignored their banter. Ella, watching him pass, realized she'd hardly spoken to him since she'd returned from Washington City. She'd been absorbed with her own thoughts and he'd been down at the docks most of the time. Now that they were on their way home, she found herself hoping they'd be able to fall in together once more. She'd missed him.

On the first evening aboard, when the close quarters down below sent Ella once more back to the fresh air of the top deck, she leaned on the ship rail and breathed in the deep metal smell of the river water. Then, to her delight, a new scent overlaid the river water, one she'd never smelled before; it was of cod and brine. She took a long breath and attempted to sort the layers of the breeze, the tang of fishy salt amidst the iron spice of freshwater.

She'd thought herself alone, but then glanced to her right and noticed Zeke disappear behind a mast pole. Was he avoiding her?

She turned her body toward where he was concealed and watched as he emerged from behind the pole, assuming a look of exaggerated nonchalance that made them both laugh.

He joined her at the rail. She asked, "Why didn't you want me to see you?"

He shrugged. "I didn't wish to have to talk."

She studied him, understanding for the first time that, as much as they'd both played their parts, there was no returning to the past, to what they'd been like before that night behind the cabin in Martha. She thought to ask him why he'd left Martha so abruptly, without saying goodbye. But she realized she knew the answer already. And she also knew it was exactly what he didn't wish to speak about.

It occurred to her she should thank him for his part in getting her out of that locked room. And for doing his part so . . . so gracefully. So kindly. For not making her feel rescued.

She puzzled over how to say all this, but found no words to speak of it. In truth she couldn't bring herself to speak of anything to do with that room, or of that time. She could only put it behind her. At last she said the one other thing that hung in the air between them. "I'm half injun, you know. Now that Lucille tells me Pete is my father."

His blue eyes looked hard into her own grey ones. "It's what you always wanted, isn't it?"

She held his look for a moment and then needed to drop her eyes, before he saw anything more. "I suppose so," she said quietly. "I thought so, at least. Now that it's real, I don't know what to think."

"Why not? I think you're lucky, that's what I think. You're free to go live with the Seneca if you want, or wherever you and Pete might want to go. You don't owe anything more to Deborahville. You can leave and never come back if you like." Zeke's voice held a wistful note, but also a hint of challenge.

Ella considered his words. She hadn't thought of it that way. She'd always been tied by her obligations to her family. She'd never considered those might disappear, might be lifted this way. But then, without thinking more, the words rushed out of her. "I don't know what you mean. Jenny and Jimson are still my sister and brother. We were raised together and nothing has changed between us. I'm not about to abandon them."

Zeke tilted his head to one side and considered the rippling waves crossing the path of the ship, their tips twinkling in the moonlight. The breeze had picked up. "No one is telling you to do anything you don't want, Ella. I was just saying that things could change if you wanted them to. My parents would take in Jenny and Jimson, or Lucille would do the same. It's only an option."

Ella scowled. "It's not a good one."

Zeke shrugged. "Whatever you say. I'm off to my sleep now. Good night."

"Good night," she said softly. She didn't wish him to leave yet; she had wanted to talk to him longer.

ELLA SCOWLED THROUGH MUCH of the next morning, mulling over what Zeke had said the night before, wishing he hadn't said it that way. It didn't help to think of herself as unhitched now, free to go where she liked, do as she liked. But only at the price of leaving her siblings behind. Although...when she thought of it more, Jimson certainly wouldn't say no to a chance to go back to the Seneca village. He'd be celebrating before she got the words out. But Jenny? She'd been happy there as well. What would she think of moving there? Would she be willing to leave Deborahville? Once the idea took hold it was hard to keep it from her thoughts; it was too intriguing, too tempting. Also it helped to push back the other thought, the grim lurker in the deep caverns at the back of her mind: the thought that she should have had a monthly by now.

She was disturbed from her brooding when Jenny and Lucille approached her at the rail of ship in the half hour before dinner. They'd reached the ocean by now and had turned north to head up the coast of New Jersey, toward Atlantic City.

Jenny sagged against the rail next to Ella while Lucille grasped the rail on the other side of Jenny with gloved hands, turning her face into the breeze. Jenny said, "Oh Ella, I can't help feeling low. After all our hopes, to have to go to Grandfather and tell him of losing the patent, and then back to Deborahville and tell everyone there. And it will only reflect poorly on us if we tell the truth of all Mr. Emerston has done. Especially as no one—at least not in Deborahville—will believe it of him. And in truth I have trouble believing it myself. How could a man let vengeance warp his mind over so many years?"

Jenny too put her face to the breeze and closed her eyes, letting the wind lift the brim of her bonnet. Then she opened them and looked up at Ella. "Why are you not more low, Ella? You seem almost cheerful all of a sudden."

Ella glanced down at her sister and then at Lucille, who had turned to her. Then she gazed back out to the expanse of rippling waves in front of them, broken only by the sight of a large vessel appearing at the horizon. "I wouldn't exactly call it cheerful, but yes, I do find myself oddly amused just now. I suppose it's because I begin to imagine his face when he finally gets a full and thorough look at the machine he's patented."

"What can you mean? Did you not give him the drawings?"

"Oh yes, I did give him the drawings. But well, for whatever reason, I did Molly McGilligan proud in keeping an extra ace up my sleeve. Though it didn't necessarily help me win the game; it only helped me ensure no one else did either."

Lucille made a gesture of exasperation. "Ella, cease speaking in riddles and say what you mean. You didn't manage to give him the wrong drawings, did you?"

Ella smiled slightly. "Oh no, they were the real drawings. It's only that I kept a piece of them back: the sketches that explain the ball joint and the linkage arm." She reached into her tunic and removed her packet, out of which she drew several folded sheets. "I had no clear plan that day, when you and I waited in the shadows near the patent office and you watched them coming toward us. I only sensed that with Emerston approaching I should gain some insurance by stowing these key drawings closer to my chest—in case he made some desperate grab for the papers. So I slid them out and put them in my packet. And then, when I gave him the tube of papers, there was no reason to mention them."

She unfolded the papers and held the sketches up to show them. They all stared at Jenny's delicate ink strokes, at the perfectly rendered round ball that swiveled in place with no friction to speak of. "It's a beauty, this new design," Ella said with a hint of reverence. "Though it won't do me any good now—I can't apply with anything so similar to what he's already been granted. But it doesn't do him any good either. It's only a matter of time before word gets out that the machine doesn't work as well as he'll promise. After that he'll have a much harder time selling licenses."

They all stared a few more moments at the drawings. Then, in a swift, sudden motion, Ella ripped the papers in half, and then in half again and again. As Jenny and Lucille gaped at her, she reached out over the ship's rail and opened her fingers to let the breeze carry away the bits of paper. They all watched as the pieces feathered down onto the tips of the rippling waves in the ship's wake, the white paper blending with the white water of the curling wave tips. When they at last took their eyes from the waves, the ship in front of them had grown larger, though it was as yet too far off to make out the colors.

"Goodbye then," Ella said mildly. "This whole business has mostly caused misery—for me and Grandfather both. The invention part itself was quite entertaining, but trying to secure and hold the patent so I could be wealthy and whatever else it was supposed to mean, well, that was never any good. I never wanted any of it, not really. I only thought I *should* want it. It's a relief to let it go. And who knows—if he dies and voids the patent, or after it finally expires, I'll still know how to build it." She recalled her ideas about running the machine with the aid of high-pressure steam engines. "Perhaps I'll even improve it."

Jenny looked at her with troubled eyes. "But Ella, you just...you just killed it. I mean, letting him patent the unusable version. Would you really rather no one have it if you can't have it for yourself?"

"Oh, they'll have it in time. There's no doubt of that. Someone else will figure out the same thing we did—that it requires a different kind of joint. It will become self-evident in time.

But not for Emerston. At least not for a good long while—hopefully not before the patent expires in fourteen years."

Jenny considered her sister. "You're not too bad at vengeance yourself, are you?"

Ella shrugged. "I suppose not. Though I don't think I manage to enjoy it as fully as he does. I should work on that. Practice it more." She paused and her face grew more serious. "In truth I'm terribly relieved to be free of that machine. I regret I didn't succeed with it, but I did the best I could. I have no regrets on that score."

Jenny nodded firmly. "Yes, that's so." Then she tilted her head at her sister. "What will you work on, though, if you're done with the flax engine? I can't see you idle too long."

"Oh, I don't know—I could grow adept at being idle. I might simply hunt for my living. Or perhaps I might build something else, something of my choosing this time. The world is full of things worth building."

She looked out over the sparkling waves once more and saw they'd come considerably closer to the great ship in front of them. She squinted and saw it flew the colors of the Royal British Navy. As she watched, the ship of the line hove its sails to turn and present a broadside that bristled with a battery of many guns. From the starboard, a small boat was being lowered into the water, where it soon released its ropes and the men on board began to row toward them.

Behind them on their own ship, a great series of shouts suddenly erupted. "Man the guns! Raise the foresail!" Sailors began racing across the decks.

Still staring at the ship across the waters, Lucille said quietly, "That's a press gang."

~ END OF BOOK ONE ~

ACKNOWLEDGMENTS

NO BOOK IS THE WORK of only one person. The research phase could not have happened if not for Lisa Sammet of the Jeudevine Library, who cheerfully found me interlibrary loans of old texts from all over New England. Despite a painfully long first draft, I thank my tolerant early readers for their many useful suggestions: Beth Kent, Bryan Lew, Hedy Sussman, Jerry Sussman, Anne McPherson, Susan O'Connell, and Eric Remick. (And to Morgan O'Connell, for his willingness to point out each place the book could use a dragon.) To my editors Kelly McNees and Carol Gaskin, I am forever indebted for the wisdom and insight to see not only how to cut it down, but how to stitch it back together. And for finish editing I can only marvel at how my husband Michael has a gift for spotting the soft spots, the places where he knew I could do better work. And thank you to Kathleen Strattan and John Reinhardt for being so delightful to work with on the painstaking tasks of proofreading and interior design.

For many years of tolerance I am grateful to the good people of High Mowing Seeds, who have allowed me the flexibility to live a double life all this time. And to my immediate family, Solomon, Clara, Elijah, and Michael, I thank you both for putting up with me and making me laugh in the midst of being a mother trying to do too many things. And to Tucker the faithful dog, who has endured many an absentminded head pat.

ABOUT THE AUTHOR

JODI LEW-SMITH lives on a farm in northern Vermont with her patient husband, three wonderfully impatient children, a bevy of pets and farm animals, and 250 exceedingly patient apple trees which, if they could talk, would suggest that she stop writing and start pruning. Luckily they're pretty quiet.

With a doctorate in plant genetics, she also lives a double life as a vegetable breeder at High Mowing Seeds. She is grateful for the chance to do so many things in one lifetime, and only wishes she could do them all *better*. Maybe in the next life she'll be able to make up her mind.

For more about Jodi and about the lives and world of the characters in the novel, visit her at www.jodilewsmith.com